NOTHING DIES IN DARKNESS

NOTHING DIES IN DARKNESS

The first book in the 'Men of the Sword' series, a fantasy adventure set in the world of Karn.

JAY GRAHAM

Nae Danger Productions

CONTENTS

For my brother Fuzzy, who is as much a part of this book as any character inside it, in whichever dimension he may travel.

Thanks go to my wife and partner Dr Marieke Pingen for her unwavering support and endless hours of assistance and advice, such that she knew the book almost better than me before she had even read it. Also, thanks to Ciska and Elise, the first proofreaders to set fresh eyes on this world I've lived with all my adult life.

Kings End

They had ridden in silence for most of the day, now that the sun was starting to go down Urnath could hold his tongue no longer. "My liege, where are we headed?" his eyes burning into the back of the ancient King's head. The silence from the King was deafening, if he heard he showed no sign of it. The rhythmic crunch of the horses' hooves on the snow, and the howl of the freezing mountain winds were the only distractions from the silenced reverie. Urnath felt something from his King he hadn't felt in years, peace. If he hadn't known the High King of the tholan better, he would have claimed the ancient man was content. He watched as the old man who was fast approaching his three hundredth winter of life settled happily on his giant horse. It was known that tholan horses were bred for the cold, and adapted to it, like those who bred them they were giant, muscled, powerful, and resilient beasts. They excelled in the frozen, ice and snow-covered lands. Crothan's steed was an exceptional example of the species which he had named Hrasse. As was typical for Crothan, Hrasse was tholan for horse. The giant beast trotted along happily under seemingly little to no instruction from her rider. The old King, the great High King who had united the clans and disparate tribes over two hundred and fifty years ago, looked every inch of his three hundred winters, weathered and wizened his thin and sparse hair was white as the snow, and his tanned, weather marked skin was shrivelled and worn as the old man who looked a tiny, withered version of his youthful self. His strength and power remained though. He would never speak of his time away from the lands of Thol or where he got his mystical axe with its blade that seemed unnatural, terrifyingly sharp and made of a similar kind of black gleaming metal to the legendary 'Tilak blade' of the Unknown Swordsman. Whenever asked the old man would simply grin in that devious manner. He had always been known as a cunning and resourceful man and seemingly even after nearly three hundred years his wits and his cunning were still intact.

After a youth spent adventuring, travelling the world and fighting Witch-Queens and God-Kings the ageing warrior had returned home to find his people ravaged and practically enslaved by a powerful warlord turned King who it was said was half-giant. Kurst Bonelord of the Crollaran was huge even for a tholan, wielding an enchanted giant's thigh bone as a sharpened club come axe. He sat upon a throne carved from the bones of those he killed, having destroyed the carved wood and wicker throne of the ancient Crollaran Kings in what was seen as a defiling of Crollaran heritage. In facing Kurst, Crothan was so overwhelmed and beaten bloody by the Giant tholan King and his men that he retreated. He then hid amongst the other tribes, planned and built a resistance of friends and allies amongst the various and disparate tribes of the tholan people including Urnath's father, a great shaman and chief of the Rath'kalt clan. With his new allies, he laid a cunning trap for the part-giant warlord, luring them out ostensibly to finish the wily Crothan off and take his head as a lesson. Kurst took the bait, not knowing that the place of confrontation had been carefully chosen by Crothan and Urnath's father. The trap was quickly sprung and the warriors of the Rath'kalt descended with pikes, halberds and long spears, slaughtering the warlords men in what could only very loosely be described as a battle. The tradition of tholan Kings though would not have allowed Crothan to take the throne had he killed Kurst in such a battle, ritual one-on-one combat being required via a challenge which can only translate to kingsmeet in the common tongue to dethrone a King or choose a new one. Striding out amongst the carnage without a trace of fear or trepidation the wily Crothan strode into the field and demanded Kurst face him one-on-one for the crown of the Crollaran people. The giant warlord approached, leaned down and whispered in Crothan's ear. What he said was never revealed but it enraged Crothan so that he turned crimson with fury. The giant warlord stepped back and bellowed to the crowd that the kingsmeet was to begin, it was to the death and no man may intervene lest Great Thol himself strike that man down. The battle was said to be legendary but the rage, wits, resourcefulness and power of Crothan won out in the end and the giant warlord's head was removed from his shoulders with a mighty swipe. As it tumbled into the snow, without even pausing or looking back, the newly crowned King Crothan charged past the stunned crowds and into the King's hall where he took his axe and chopped the warlord's throne to pieces and spat on the remains before making his first proclamation as King, a new throne worthy of the Crolloran Kings of old.

Like the spring follows winter, unity, peace and a new way of life came for the Crolloran. This spread among the rest of the varied and myriad tribes and clans of the tholan people as King Crothan of the Crolloran became High King Crothan of All tholan Kingdoms. Slowly the various and disparate factions unified under the High King's banner. The Rath'kalt much more advanced and forward-thinking than most clans led the way under Crothan and a new era dawned for the people of the great glaciers. A new era, Urnath began to worry that was about to come crashing down before his peoples' very eyes.

Urnath didn't know why but he felt it in his gut, his friend, his King and the man he'd devoted his life to was very much coming out here to die. The old King craned round to look at him with mirth and that all too familiar look of grim humour in his eye, "Come on boy, we've still got a long way to go before we rest." Urnath smiled back at his King "I'm over a hundred you know old man, I'm the high wizard of the court of the High King, sage, diplomat and the closest thing you have left to a friend. I think I'm long past being called *boy,* if it so please your Highness." The old King scowled at that last word. After all this time, even after two hundred and fifty years as King the old man seemed still to wear his titles ill. "You know what Urnath, I've been King of the Crollaran for two hundred and fifty years give or take and High King of the tholan people for twice as long as you've been walking these snows. I've slain giants, dragons and men by the thousand. I've challenged Gods and I've walked into the hells and slain demons. I've wielded magic to make wizards more powerful than you cringe and used it to slay more than one of them. Do you know what I've learned Urnath?" The younger man shook his head solemnly with a slight smile "that you still love making speeches that no one asked for?" The old King bellowed with laughter from his gut, so deep, booming and loud that Urnath feared the old man might bring a mountain of snow and ice or a Frost Giant or dragon down upon them.

As suddenly as it had started though the old man's laughter subsided and he turned again at his friend, wizard and advisor, "No youngling, I never wanted titles, power or influence, the majority of my life and my duties as King were as much burden as they were needed. I know I've married many times, but I only loved once. Her name was Elina, she was a great warrior, better than me, we grew up together and she would have come with me when I left but her father died and as honour dictated, she took part in the kingsmeet. When I left Thol she was Queen of the Crollaran and they don't write about it in the stories, but the Warlord Kurst killed her, he tore out her spine and built it into his throne. That was what he whispered to me on that day so many years ago now. That's why I destroyed the throne, it wasn't some glorious act of symbolic tholan redemption or the statement of a great King; it was the fury of vengeance. I never wanted the throne I demanded they build to replace it, my arse itched for adventure every single day I sat in it. I've spent my life for other people, just like you Urnath, following about some old man listening to his rambling. I always meant to leave, just one more winter I would tell myself. I'm going to give you one last piece of advice old friend, here at the end. Don't spend your life living for someone else, not even your King. I have one more promise to keep before my time is up. You've stood at my side your entire adult life and I want you to promise me something? When we part ways at the end of our road here, don't go home. Don't go back and serve in the kingsmeet, serve the new King and waste your life living in service to someone who doesn't appreciate you Urnath, go and live! Find some man or woman or someone to love or go and find adventure or peace or whatever is in your heart." The silence was like the years between them, there was so much tiredness in the old Kings voice, so much regret that Urnath could barely bring himself to speak. He stuttered and spat in a broken voice to the old man "and you? My King, my dearest friend and my family more than blood could be. What would you do with ten more years? With one?" Crothan's withered and milky eyes grew hard and cold, Urnath had seen that look many times over the years "I have no need of more time. I've done what I stayed to do, I made my bargains and I have seen out my time. I want to see my Elina again, my friends of old and even some of my enemies. Thol calls me home to his bosom my friend, you know this. You're here to bear witness to the last days and the last steps of Crothan Thronebreaker and I'm grateful for your company." Urnath could swear he saw a tear in the old man's eye as the old King tuned briskly away and though he made no perceptible motion his horse resumed its steady, trudging journey through the endless blank white landscape.

Day and night they rode, never altering pace or course, the old King seemed to know instinctively (as it seems did his horse) where they were going. Occasionally the horses would stop and rest if a cliff edge or cavern offered some succour from the constant wind and snow, but the old King never left his saddle. If he slept or ate or even felt the cold, he never showed any of it. Even for a tholan the old man had always shown callous disregard for the cold. It was as if the old King could sneer the weather into submission, a feat Urnath believed the old man could accomplish by sheer force of will. Still, they travelled so hard and at such a slow but steady pace that Urnath believed his own horse might not make it to wherever their journey's end lay. After what felt like days if not weeks out of the clouds and intensifying snow, Urnath saw their obvious destination looming in the distance. Standing atop a giant glacier was a single path of dark, icy rock winding up the mountain towards a tower that reached so high its top seemed to disappear into the heavens in a way that made Urnath's eyes water when he tried to focus on it. "I thought it was a myth!" he intoned breathlessly at his King, "it is real? Is it really home to two of the Gods?" He realised he was gasping, not from the air or the wind but in a kind of panic, realising that monsters were real, and they were just at the top of this road. He composed himself, embarrassed to have shown such fear in the face of the greatest hero Thol had ever produced and what's more, a man who was like a surrogate father, older brother and closest love all in one to him. "I'm sorry my King, I am…" His words trailed off as he fought awe, fear and majesty within himself and as his eyes met the King's he added deep sorrow to that blend and he felt his heart plummet from his chest to the very pit of his stomach. He opened his mouth to protest but a weak and simple "no" was all he could muster lest his heart break in half, here as he struggled with all his strength to continue to look his great King in the eye. "Crothan." The word felt strange in his mouth so rarely had he used the King's name, "please, maybe I could come. Just up the hill, a little further my King." The King's soft smile and suddenly warm eyes sucked all the air out of the younger man, "I'm sorry my child, where I am going no mortal man may follow, what I am about to do is not for the living. Go back to the world my boy, tell them I am gone, tell them their King is dead and then hold to your promise and leave Thol, travel, see the world and get yourself some slice of life that is truly yours." The old man reached over his shoulder and unleashed his magical axe, it whistled almost musically as it swung from his shoulder down to his side as the old man gave it a few casual swings almost in goodbye. Looking down at the axe, fighting the feeling of guilt it was imparting to him, Crothan looked down at it and his smile turned to an amused grin. "No, my old friend, you must go too. You are too precious and too wonderful to leave this world with a foolish old man who's overstayed his welcome." The King looked up at Urnath and held out the axe, the wizard took it from his King, lurching slightly at first at the surprising weight of the thing before righting himself and looking back over at the old King. "I'll wait my King, at least until you're out of sight. Urnath didn't know if he could move in that moment even had his King commanded it, so overwhelmed and so heartbroken was the younger man. The old King smiled, turned his horse without seemingly moving and started up the impossibly long and winding path to the ice tower.

Crothan steeled himself, he felt his dear friend's eyes following him as far as they could. The old King had climbed this road before, and he knew long before he reached the top the younger man's sight of him would falter and he would lose sight of the King. He sighed and felt for where his axe should have been, making to pat its handle for comfort as he had done automatically so many times over the years before realising, he'd left it behind and smiling sadly to himself. He looked ahead at the impossibly massive doors realising that he was there, his journeys end. He slowly, gingerly slid off the giant horse, suddenly feeling every single hour and day of his nearly three hundred years. In that moment, strangely he thought back to when he was twenty-three, in some far away land fighting in some forsaken revolution to usurp some robber baron in the Swordlands. He was so young, so powerful. He had thrown himself into the air landing on the baron's horse, buried his sword up to its hilt in the baron's back and bodily lifted the man from his horse, throwing the body into the battlefield and taking the horse for his own. "I still miss it you know." He said to no one in particular, chuckling as he slowly pulled himself through the snow those last few feet to the tower door. He turned to the horse and nodded "Off you go, I won't be coming back with you." Seemingly understanding, the horse with no more ceremony or notice turned itself around and with the same measured pace clip clopped its way back down the mountain. Crothan watched the horse go as if it were the last vestiges of his life retreating into the white of the snow.

"Three hundred years? I must admit, I wasn't one hundred percent sure you would show." Intoned the thin tanned human with long wavy black hair, clad in long black wizard's robes clasped with a powerful looking girdle from which hung two massive Warhammers that he didn't look strong enough to lift, never mind wield.

Crothan turned and with clenched jaw stared coldly, "our bargain is done Ramlar and I held to my end, I stayed the years and I held to the hour and here I am for the freedom I was promised when we made our bargain." Ramlar nodded with a smile and with a wave of his hand a black near liquid smoke seeped slowly out of Crothan, pouring out through his eyes, nose, ears and mouth, crawling across the ground and under the black robes that brushed the ground beneath the God of chaos and war's slender avatar. "Our bargain is completed High King, Crothan Thronebreaker of the Crollaran, as I promised you are now free. Oh, and Crothan? Happy birthday." The God of Chaos, now suddenly both the slender wizard and also a gigantic shadow darker than night in the shape of a humungous dragon that spoke suddenly with a voice that seemed to echo inside Crothan's head as a whisper louder than an avalanche "He is all yours, promises made, and promises kept. Rest well King Crothan." Crothan turned to see what Ramlar was looking at and saw suddenly Thol in all his splendour, a tholan too large to even be a giant, skin made of black ice and armour of packed snow, a giant glittering ice axe over his shoulder the barbarian God held out a hand to his most honoured subject. "Come on Crothan, let's go home." Crothan said nothing, he could no longer see either of the wonderous beings before him. The High King was no longer there, Crothan had fulfilled his promise. He had met his journey's end and with a contented sigh there was no Crothan, no Ramlar and no Thol, just an empty path and the wind and snow.

CHAPTER 1

Arlo and Lucia

Old wood creaked under him as young Arlo rode the heavy wagon over the hill. He loved this journey; he loved the view on the road to the hamlet of Mar-thatch almost as much as he enjoyed the responsibility of getting the produce there himself. As he crested the hill he pulled and whistled to Marnie to stop, the old mare complained as they never usually stopped here but she did as she was bidden. Pulling up to his full height of nearly six and a half feet the young man stretched his arms to the sky and looked around. "I know Marnie, dad would never let us stop here but just look at it, what a landscape, what a view. We truly live in lands blessed by the Nine." Arlo shook out his mussy brownish blonde hair and stretched, popped and cracked his muscles hardened by long days in the fields as he stretched his large, calloused hands towards the sun. "You know Marnie, one day I'm going to the big city, I'm going to be an adventurer and see the world, so for now I just want to soak in this land while I can." Arlo stood there soaking it all in as the old mare nibbled at some dry grass by the side of the road, an odd shuffling noise like something digging beneath the hillside behind him. Arlo looked out over the shining green grass swaying lazily in the breeze while soaking up the morning sun, hills and valleys all around, silver blue streams and golden wheat fields, orchards and small woods interlaced with small villages and hamlets all around this idyllic countryside. "Okay, this stuff isn't going to sell itself, on to market day Marnie!" he intoned excitedly as he picked up the reins. Casting a glance at what he assumed to be a gopher burrowing beneath the hill and at the majestic green grass wavering in the morning sunshine, the rolling hills and trees and rivers beyond. With a sense of lightness and love in his heart at the breath-taking natural beauty of his home before urging the old horse slowly down the other side towards Mar-thatch.

As Arlo and his wagon rolled down the hillside towards the small market hamlet, the young man's whistling, as he amused himself with the journey faded from the hillside along with the rhythmic creak of his wagon's aged wheels. Leaving behind just the wind against the hill gently blowing the long grass like wavy green hair on the sun kissed hillside. The gentle rumbling grew louder as the sounds of persistent and steady digging increased before a single rotten skeletal hand pushed its way up through the hillside. What pulled itself through was some manner of undead, though not quite a skeleton as what hung from this thing was not flesh but a viscous, oily and bubbling shadow which held the appearance of liquid as it oozed, bubbling over the rotting core of this lumbering inhuman corpse. Though as droplets and globules of this oozing darkness dripped from the mass they would turn to shadowy wisps and blow away as if in a gentle breeze. Rotted leather, cloth and rusted metal adorned the figure with some manner of odd and ancient looking weapon hanging limply from its waist as others, no two dressed, armed or even rotting the same started to tear at this recently idyllic hillside with rotting, viscous, bubbling shadows clinging to them like some oozing and alien flesh. With terrible alacrity what had only recently been a picturesque scene of glorious hillside was covered in these dark, oozing shadow beings that all stood swaying gently in the hillside winds before the one in front, the first one to have risen shook itself off and with strange inhuman gait silently lurched down the hill causing the others to automatically and with only half a step delay follow and a mass of pustulant, dripping shadow soaked death made its way to the market hub that was the hamlet of Mar-thatch.

Mar-thatch had once been a roadside inn, a small two-story thatched roof and simple inn with a place for wagons and horses. It had been a stop on the journey to Valenstorm for merchants and farmers with produce and goods to take to the large city in its days before it had grown to become a city. Now most smaller merchants, farmers and artisans would stop here and trade to the larger merchants as well as the local villages and small hamlets who would come on market day to buy, sell and barter. As more and more stayed, the Inn grew and slowly a small hamlet grew up around it until it was as much a small community of its own as a marketplace and waystation for those heading to the ever-growing City of Valenstorm. Built on a crossroads just south of the city in a lightly wooded but green pasture it had a pleasant feel and temperate climate. Shielded by the trees and the surrounding hills from the worst of the weather it could trap the sunshine well, cooled by the wind as it blew down off the hills softened by their touch to be a cooling breeze in the warmest of summers. It was in days like today, in the heart of the month of Freldine the hottest of the summer months where this small hamlet was blessed as scorching summer heat would beat down upon the heartlands. That soft hillside breeze would bring cooling air into the large open market, where people would gather and meet and greet friends old and new to marvel at what could be bought, sold and bargained over. This day however the breeze felt oddly chilly for mid-Freldine summer, none of the gentle warmth was upon it and even as most were bare armed or even stripped to the waist in the heat a few found themselves reaching for clothing as that cold wind gently chilled the market area.

Arlo had found his usual spot; his father had been coming here for years and the same grooves where the wagon would stand as he unpacked and set up the fruits of the family labours. He never had as much or as glorious a haul as some of the larger farms and never any of the exotic items you would sometimes come across here but they did okay and such was the way of Mar-thatch that even if you couldn't empty your wagon at market, a merchant travelling on to Valenstorm would often take what was left from you for a reduced price. It wasn't a glorious life, but Arlo saw the sense in it and the comfort it brought to his father to know that the safety and prosperity offered by proximity to Valenstorm extended to their pocket. Arlo stood absently chatting to Tarna Dunsinore, an elven tavern owner from nearby, as her sons lifted heavy sacks of barley from his wagon while in his head Arlo daydreamed of excitement and adventure. He'd heard stories of the great and the dark, of distant lands and powerful magics, of dragons and monsters and of endless stories of adventurers heading off from Valenstorm to seek their fortunes. The city had grown up around a great hero, Tatral Valenstorm, a retired adventurer from the last great war. Arlo had seen adventurers passing on their way to somewhere exotic or dangerous and he imagined what it would be like to see these faraway places and seek forbidden knowledge or strange mystical power. He only half acknowledged Tarna Dunsinore and her sons as they wandered away from his cart into the market proper, Arlo's head was in an ancient tomb deep beneath the great scar hidden in a maze of caves uncovering some long-forgotten magic or ancient evil to be vanquished. He turned half casually and patted Marnie on the mare's long neck, sighing wistfully as only a teenage farm boy could at such grand imaginings and came face to face with what looked in the first glimpse to be a man, dead and rotting, but a man. His skin, hair and beard though seemed to be made of a kind of living shadow that moved and bubbled as he stared at Arlo with empty eye sockets, the holes running deep inside this rotting thing's skull into a deeper darkness that seemed to almost pull him in. Time seemed to slow as Arlo tried to shake off the frozen terror that had suddenly washed over him as a putrid, rotting smell like puss and vomit and rotting flesh seared its way up his nostrils. He opened his mouth to scream, but the same warped stench shot down his throat and instead of screaming he gagged. In gagging he lurched backwards, and this slight movement saved him from the thing's arcing clawed hand as it swung right where his face had been moments ago, burying itself into the flanked neck of old Marnie as the old horse whinnied in terror and pain. Arlo watched still transfixed with terror as the black shadowy bubbling matter weaved its way into the horses wound, dripping and seemingly caught between shadowy mist and liquid as it seeped inside the stricken horse whose sudden whinny of terror had become nothing more than a paralysed whimper. The shadow flesh coated thing turned to the old mare with a hoarse whispering noise that could have been a cackle of pleasure or some twisted glee. No sooner had it soaked in this single moment of torturous glee than its empty socketed head swivelled back to the still fear-struck Arlo who was gagging and staring at it wide eyed with no power to move or even blink, transfixed as he was on this putrid shadow creature before him.

Something grabbed the back of Arlo's shirt in a bunch and pulled. The teenager found his giant frame flailing through the air before skidding on his back in the mud, through the market and with a loud, painful crack his head crunched to a stop against what appeared to be a fruit stall. Before he could focus the thought popped into his head "the Tamway's fruit stall, I wonder if Lucia is here." He shook his head clear, felt with his hand at the blood coming from the back of his head and looked up. The screaming came from all around, cacophonic and mixing hysterically to a terrified crescendo, people were tripping over each other and trampling one another to flee but every corner another shadow creature hissed with an unsettling whisper at them and the screaming, the terror and the fleeing started again. The central marketplace started to overcrowd as the things herded more and more people to the heart of the market, surrounding them and slaughtering any who were too slow to flee into the growingly crowded throng of people. Incredulous Arlo lay there looking around, still trying to process what his own eyes were telling him, he saw Marnie, his old mare lying on the ground still, unblinking as blood poured out of the gaping wound her neck. The old horse seemed to still breathe shallowly whilst black shadows enveloped her from the inside. Tendrils of smoky liquid bubbled and wisped their way out of her eyes and appeared to be rotting the old mare from the inside out, her breathing slowing in the rhythm of whatever had infected her as it ate her slowly from the inside. Arlo was about to rise to go over to the dying horse when a hand shot out from under the broken wheel of the partially collapsed wagon next to him. "Arlo you fool! Get in here!" An angry whisper from the concealed Lucia, whose vice-like grip belied her slender form. "Hide! Before they see you!" Arlo obediently shuffled into the crawl space of the broken wagon and sidled up next to Lucia Tamway. He could smell apples in her hair and found himself flush red with embarrassment and blood in his ears as he realised how close he was to her, which was almost as dizzying as the fearful nightmare that was unfolding before them.

If Lucia had noticed Arlo's discomfort, she certainly hadn't mentioned it. A noise to his right made Arlo turn and at the other side of the wagon he saw the corpse of Marnie start to rise slowly, dispassionately to her feet, rot setting in and that same black bubbling shadowy substance dripping from the wound, her eye sockets and gaping mouth. With his head in that direction, he realised suddenly his face was partially buried in Lucia's hair as apples and cinnamon wafted up his nostrils taking the stench of disease and death from them for a second. Before he could stop himself, Arlo let out a wistful sigh, drawing a sharp angry breath from Lucia. "Arlo!" she whispered angry, frustrated and afraid. Arlo's head snapped back on a swivel at the steel in her voice as they watched how the shadowy undead had circled the survivors and trapped them in the centre of the market square, the dead who had fallen in the attack slowly starting to rise with the same shadowy undead substance and unliving style that Arlo's horse just had. An ice-cold shiver ran down his back as he stared at the elder Dunsinore boy, lifeless and lumbering along with the other dead, moving into place to trap his horrified mother and brother along with the other survivors as the market became an improvised holding pen. Arlo felt the familiar feeling of Lucia's iron grip as she slid her hand into his, their fingers interlaced, he looked down and then up at her wide dark brown eyes realising that his were rimmed with tears that threatened at any second to spill and open a flood. Arlo nodded, took a deep breath and whispered softly to her, "run?" They both nodded, unable or unwilling to speak lest the tears come and almost as one they slid back towards the barn behind them and with Lucia leading crept around the wooden edge of the barn, softly, slowly and almost not daring to breathe lest they be seen.

Lucia's sudden sharp intake of breath was the first hint Arlo had of trouble, just as he was about to slip quietly around the corner of the barn, the shadow of something pacing just beyond it flicked into view. Stopping suddenly and waiting for it to turn and retreat, pulling Lucia along, quietly he slipped past the barn and into a gap between the thorn bushes. He'd used it hundreds of times over the years to quickly get to the stream on the west of Mar-thatch. Sliding slowly down the muddy verge towards the river Arlo snapped to a stop, his hand on Lucia's chest to warn her as a sharp noise from above alerted him. They stared at each other in terror as the sound of arhythmic footsteps lurching closer till it was almost on top of them, looming over the very bush they were sliding under, down towards the stream. Arlo tensed, thinking in this moment that he would push Lucia down into the stream and then leap up to distract the thing while she escaped but just as he crouched preparing to leap the air was filled with a blood curdling scream of pain. The shadowy thing's arm had shot into another bush and plucked a young man out by his throat. Looking up, Arlo and beneath him Lucia stared on in terror as a shadow-soaked, clawed skeletal hand wrapped itself around the young man's throat, who they immediately recognised as Barsaw the stable boy from the Mar-thatch Inn. He screamed and clawed at the thing, thick strips of gooey shadow peeling from it with every swipe. As the strips of viscous shadow peeled off and fell from the young man's hands it fell as if it would land right on Arlo and Lucia, however as it fell it dissipated into mist and shadow and faded in the morning wind. A sick squishing, crunching noise followed as the bony claws tightened around Barsaw's throat, piercing flesh and cracking bone. Awful screeching, whimpering cries emanated from the young stable boy as his head started to pop and bend at an unnatural angle and the shuddering, twitching young man suddenly stopped and hung limply apart from a few posthumous twitches as he hung lifeless from the shadowy thing's clawed hand. Bloody and shadowy liquid dripped down the corpse's arms and plopped in droplets onto Arlo and Lucia, neither dared breathe never mind move as for what seemed like an age the shadowy eye-socketed, dark shadow-covered skeletal thing stared dispassionately, almost quizzically at the corpse of the young man. More of the black slimy shadow goo slithered inside the broken, burst neck of the dead stable hand. A sick sucking and slurping noise accompanied the slithering popping and bubbling near liquid as it slid inside the corpse and from this close range the smell of rotting flesh was accompanied with a burning smell that almost made them retch. Still holding the corpse by its neck, the shadow creature turned and walked away back in the direction of the marketplace. Still holding their breath, still barely holding themselves together they completed the slide down into the stream and slowly, under cover of the thorny overhang moved towards the outskirts. Pulling up the other side of the stream they slowly edged towards the small wood at the edge of the settlement. The further they moved from the centre the more abandoned and desolate the streets looked. Everything living and dead it appeared were in the marketplace.

As they turned to the edge of the hamlet Arlo saw the trees and beyond the valley leading to Lucia's family home, he looked at her smiling in what he hoped was a reassuring manner and squeezed her hand three times quickly. Lucia nodded at him, understanding the meaning in what up till now had been a way of saying things to one another without risking whispered secrets. She smiled and a couple of tears rolled down her cheek, Arlo felt his own cheeks dampen too. Sighing he let the tears come and while gripping her hand tightly as he could he started to run and with their hearts pounding in their mouths the two teens ran with everything they could deep into the wood and away from the carnage, wondering if they were the only ones to escape.

CHAPTER 2

The Edge

Valenstorm, the fastest-growing City in Vandarn, not too far south of the kingdom's capital of Vandarn City. Over two decades ago, after the last great war, the adventurer and hero Tatral Valenstorm, wearying of war and adventure built a home in a small village in the greenest fields of Vandarn he could find meant for his retirement. Such was the lure of his legendary luck that before long, more homes sprouted up around it and then it grew and grew until he was named the First Citizen of the ever-growing settlement, which was renamed by the locals in his honour, Valenstorm. Now a mere twenty-plus years after its inception Valenstorm has a wall around its namesake's house and another around the main City. Around that? Houses, shops, taverns and Inns as the economic and societal boom that has drawn people to this previously uninhabited farmland shows no signs of abating. Its First Citizen himself, Tatral Valenstorm had once been a great hero, explorer and adventurer. Once a member of a company known as the men of the sword, a band of rogues, rebels and rejects who had saved the world. At first, the lure of adventure kept the halfling hero on the road but every time he returned to Valenstorm he was hailed as such a hero that eventually his lust for comfort and adulation outweighed his love of excitement and the thrill of danger. Over time the adventures were rarer and rarer, the riches, risks and rewards of the open road harder to justify against the love of a growing settlement where he was looked on as a kind of saviour. Some of the stories were true, some wildly exaggerated, and some could never compare to the terror and the proximity to pure evil or the pain of wounds that would never truly heal. Tatral would tell tall tales and show off his skills and exceptional knowledge of the dark corners of Karn, he would even occasionally tell stories of the war. He would talk of his companions from Annia, Princess of Hven, the Priest of Necirate the Goddess of beauty and peace to her wayward husband the bard, Hanalan Harpsong, who the whole world knew, to the Unknown Swordsman whose name even he could not remember as if some great power had reached down and plucked his name, his appearance and his identity from the halfling's mind.

The invasion of Deathmount though? That large, raw final battle to end the Witch-Queen and her half-demon son? That the halfling would refuse to mention. As if afraid the Witch-Queen would rise out of the earth and strike him down should he so much as mention her name. Some dark and terrible secrets, the halfling would sometimes say, must shuffle quietly with us to our graves. And he would shudder and drink until the shaking in his weapon hand would subside. The burn scars and claw marks on the little halfling's right arm were terrible and he would normally keep them covered but occasionally after too many of his own vineyard's wines he would forget and let his glove slip or even take it off as the old wound would itch. As the halfling First Citizen aged, he was now well into his sixties, his drinks would become deeper, his sleep less and the things he'd seen over a life of adventure haunted him more and more. For as many of the trinkets and treasures the old halfling had gathered in his career, he'd given as many away. Sat most evenings in his usual seat in the public hall of his great house as a banquet of invited guests, regular visitors from the city and lucky adventurers who managed to bribe, cajole or convince the people around him that they needed an audience with the halfling legend. This was usually to uncover some hidden location or piece of archaic knowledge the halfling had uncovered in his years of adventure. Or chasing some artefact he owned or had once owned. Once, just last week, a young halfling warrior with eyes like cold blue steel who reminded Tatral of himself in his youth had asked if it was true. That it was he who had killed the Witch-Queen rather than the Unknown Swordsman? Before Valenstorm could wave him away, he had pressed on that he had heard the halfling had done it with a dagger whose blade was black as night, unnaturally so. Stabbed her in the back; pushed again and again, what had happened to the dagger? How had it felt to kill the most powerful mage that ever lived? Did he ever fear retribution from what remained of the scattered deathknights? Valenstorm had spluttered, panicked and thrown his goblet of wine up in the air using the distraction to run. The younger halfling hadn't followed the flight of the goblet like everyone else, his eyes had been scanning the older halfling, looking for something, anything in his reaction and coldly followed him as he fled the room. After that Valenstorm refused to see anyone for a full week claiming illness but such was the pressure from those who flocked to eat, drink and have an audience with him that he could not stay locked up for much longer than that.

At the Western edge of Valenstorm, where to the west and south there lies mountains, desert. Even further on the great scar, a giant tear in the land with a thousand openings to dark caverns said to link to the lands of the Drow and darker things still. In the frontier lands of Vandarn, countless adventurers flock to Valenstorm as a last stop before journeying on into these foreboding and dangerous lands. Here where there is no more room for the growing bustle to expand, lies a tavern and inn, unique at least in its premise if not its produce. They call it The Edge, run by a retired adventurer, much like Valenstorm himself, this sprawling rickety shack constantly in need of and undergoing a state of repairs, serves as the heart of this tavern by way of a campsite. A two-story ramshackle tavern with a taproom and tables to eat food indoors, to say nothing of the stocked warehouse of goods and supplies stored here. Often busy and so packed out that two lizardfolk bouncers manage access to the building itself. The main entrance lies at the north end of a sprawling gated field. At peak times filled with nearly a hundred campsites of adventurers, who almost as a tradition in Valenstorm, come to The Edge to spend their first night, camping under the light, behind the fence and in the safety of The Edge and of course Valenstorm itself. At various points throughout the day and night waitresses and barmaids can be seen wheeling food, drinks and last-minute supplies to and from campsites as adventurers talk of the sights they'll see and the legends they hope to become in the days and weeks ahead. Many who leave here don't come back, often little keepsakes, memories and signs can be found tied or nailed to the fence all around The Edge from would-be heroes who never returned or from loved ones wishing to honour, remember or reach out to the fallen and lost who passed this way.

Right at the southwestern corner of the campsite that made up the bulk of The Edge's land a small one-person tent, old and ragged though serviceable, sat next to a small, poorly maintained campfire. None of the supplies were from The Edge, they were used and worn and of a lower-than-average quality. A poor excuse for a hunk of unidentifiable meat hung on a tiny spit while a small figure covered in a black and shimmering midnight blue silk cloak and heavy cowl fussed around muttering to herself in a low voice. Stopping suddenly, hand in the air as if to silence someone who wasn't there. She shushed noisily and stared off to the southwest as if the sky had lit on fire. Thin lips pursed and then curled in a sallow smile, paler than they should be for a high elf they coupled with her lean and wan complexion to give an overtly angular and almost sneering demeanour to her lean and pale face. Aera Darkhorne whispered into the night air "Can you feel that? It's like a tear, a physical tear in the pit. Something is ripping souls out and using them as soldiers." Her cruel, mocking but oddly singsong voice was dripping with twisted glee. She spoke into the night as if she were teasing a tortured prisoner, though it would not look it to any who observed the small, frail-looking elven woman, she in fact was. The ghost of Larimus Marr, unseen to all but Aera herself, hovered disembodied just off the witch's left-hand side, his head cocked as if listening for some sign of this gaping wound between the afterlife and here. "That's impossible, don't be foolish Aera, not even Lazarus or Dracor themselves could tear open the pit of the lost and damned, much less control what oozed out if they did." His voice sounded hollow and far away as if it merely slipped in on the wind. The hatred and the mocking mingled into his voice was commonplace, it had been this way since Aera had murdered her arch-rival and childhood friend and enslaved his damned soul into service as her familiar, seneschal or however, she felt like referring to him that day. Her betrayal resonated like a reverberating bell through the former Larimus Marr's immortal soul like background noise, made of rage. "Pfft." She waved her hand at her incorporeal companion dismissively and stared ahead into the empty night, seeing something that physically at least, was not there. "You are as ignorant in death as you were in life Larimus, I feel the ebb and flow of the pit, I hear the cries and the moans of the damned in my dreams both waking and asleep. My power waxes and wanes with the flow of the pit and though it has been drained those souls are not free, my power grows as damned walk under control of some dark and intoxicating power." Swaying absent-mindedly as she spoke, her soft whispering voice like velvet sliding through fingers lending a haunting air to her words. Pulling back the flap of her tent, she slid inside and sat cross-legged in the dark. Reaching without looking into a thick leather satchel, which she deftly opened to reveal a several weeks old head, putrid and with missing eyes and thick trails of dried blood running down its face and out of its ears. Her own eyes closed and murmuring gently to herself, Aera whispered some dark prayers in a long-forgotten language that wasn't dissimilar to her native Takalan tongue. As she hummed and mumbled and cursed her way through her dark prayer, she slid fingers easily into the eye and ear cavities of the skull causing the putrid skin to pulse and writhe with sickening, undulating motion as a black viscous shadowy ooze filled the cavities. The vibration of the head changed and tuned in to the chanting and humming of the witch as she sat, eyes closed. With delicate care, like a mother soothing her babe, Aera gently leaned over and placed a soft almost tender kiss on the forehead of the oozing pustulating shadow-coated head.

The thing's mouth swung open and a voice, that of a young woman echoed out as if from far away in a damp cave by the sea. "Aera Darkhorne!" The trilling girlish voice called out from the head of this rotting middle-aged human man. "You seek the wisdom of the damned?" Her eyes still closed, her fingers gently caressing the inside of the skull's cavities they rested in almost affectionately. "Tell me spirit, why do the lost and the damned walk these lands? Why do they roam like nightmares given flesh?" Her voice had become flat, toneless, all her normal singsong whisper gone as if the mere connection to the pit of the damned had drained her of life and vitality. The echoing voice giggled nervously "Can't say, it won't let me!" the voice huffed petulantly. Aera took a firm grip of the head, squeezing her fingers hard in the holes "I compel you, answer!" The head in her hand started to shake, the vibrations echoing through the rotting skull and up through Aera's hands, arms and shoulders, a thin trail of black shadowy ooze trickled out of the elven witch's nose and down her face. She felt it seep between her lips iron and blood and despair and darkness all tingling horridly on her tongue, she found every nightmare and horror of her entire life replaying in her head along with a rumbling, bubbling voice like an earthquake under water given form "Aera Darkhorne, you peer into the darkness of the abyss, the lost and damned are not the only things hiding in the dark." Aera let out a blood-curdling scream as the skull shot out of her hands and bounced off the back of the tent, all the shadowy ooze disappeared from it though a small patch of the skull's skin and hair detached from the head and remained on the tent wall as the rotting skull plopped unceremoniously on the floor in front of the shocked Aera who merely wiped at her mouth seeing black, shadowy ooze rubbed onto her sleeve. She realized her breath was ragged and panting, something had reached out from the very bottom of the pit and touched her mind. Some ancient, evil and powerful damned soul had merely communicated with her, and it had nearly destroyed her mind. What lost and dead thing lurked in the deepest corners of the hell of lost souls? How powerful was it? Aera thought of her pact with the pit of lost souls, she had always seen it as her way to use and manipulate the souls within. Unlike some others who sought to free and save the damned and the lost Aera had only ever seen them as pawns and tools to be used and discarded this thing however, this ancient unliving thing that had reached out of the dark and touched her was something different, Some ancient evil with a power of a magnitude she'd never imagined never mind experienced, Aera thought as she cleaned her face with her sleeve.

What if she could harness this power, this evil and use it for her own? How much could she siphon from this thing for herself?

Ander Halfsword had been going over the day in his head, the last job had failed, the rest of the party dead and still no closer to finding the obsidian dagger he'd been sent here to find. "It's not quite obsidian though that's the closest thing to this you'll find. This dagger has a blade black as night and almost hypnotic to look at. Much like the legendary Tilak blade but in an otherwise small and unremarkable dagger." The old man had droned on and on. Halfsword was a killer for sure, cold dispassionate and as good with his swords as anyone had a right to be. Trained to the point of obsession with the sword his focus in training with his blade was as single-minded as his focus on completing a mission, the old priest had told him time and time again that the halfling Valenstorm was the last known owner of the dagger, but that old fool was half senile, half drunk and all idiot. Ander had realised early on that the priest had turned to him not because of his reputation as a killer, mercenary and professional but because he too was a halfling, thinking this would give him some edge with the sot, addle-minded old adventurer he'd been sent to rob. They'd lost three good men trying to ambush and burgle the First Citizen of Valenstorm and now he was hitting a dead end, stuck in the middle of a field with the one surviving member of their troupe the elf who quite frankly gave Ander the creeps even after all these years together. That whispering, sing-song voice and her obsession with taking little bits of eye, skull or liver from anything they killed almost as if she delighted in keeping gory and disgusting keepsakes from battle every time. Ander could understand trophies, though he'd no time for such weakness himself. Give him an honest sword or two and an excuse to test his mettle against others skilled with the blade and he was happy. "Keep to the job Halfsword" he grumbled at himself, staring into his small one-man fire trying desperately to find a positive in where things had landed.

Which is when an agonizing scream shook him from his day-dreaming. Aera, the witch had howled in agony from within her tent, various possible scenarios played out through Ander's mind, with a resigned sigh he grabbed his sword belt and leapt out of his tent, rushing towards the tiny one-person tent of the witch. Pulling up right outside the tent the halfling stood statue-like at the entrance straining to listen but silence greeted him, followed by the ragged breathing of the elf. Pulling the tent flap back with his sword tip, his second sword ready to meet any resistance as the flap opened instead Halfsword saw Aera sitting cross-legged looking for all intents like she had been assaulted, black blood oozing from her nose and the rotting skull of Martil the rogue pooling puss and rotten flesh at the other side of the tent, a line of rotting skin and blood sliding down the tent wall where the witch had apparently thrown it at the moment of her scream. Gingerly stepping in Halfsword prodded the rotting skull with one sword while casually nodding at Aera with the other "Are you okay Darkhorne? The rotting skull of our dead companion broke into your tent and attempted to headbutt you to death?" The dripping pointed sarcasm in the halfling's voice was reinforced by his sneer and the slow drag of his eyes from the open, gooey satchel to the skull resting on the end of his sword. Aera smiled sweetly at Halfsword causing him to repress a shiver from visibly running down his spine. "Well," she slithered in her whisper-ing sing-song voice. "He wasn't using it and I needed it for my spell. It's not Martil, it's just..." She paused, grasping for the word "Parts." Halfsword tilted his blade till the putrid head slid off with a slimy plop back onto the tent floor. "Fine," he shrugged, "just keep your foul rituals to yourself, the last thing we need is to be drawing more attention to ourselves if we're ever going to survive this job. Aera stared a hole through the halfling mercenary, "No." She stated flatly, "there is something coming, something more evil and more power-ful than the old Priest who sent us here. It's not going to be safe here for long."

CHAPTER 3

No One

"So, who was he then?" he cackled, a loose tooth wobbling as he licked and tested it while he laughed. His face flushed, framed by mottled skin and flaking scalp while he grinned, as they gathered by the bar, staring at the prone form slumped over the table. The others snickered emboldened by Leskat's cackle and the glint of his jewelled dagger. The story was, Leskat had taken it from a tholan barbarian he'd crushed to death with his bare hands. The truth was far less glamourous, Leskat had poisoned the giant barbarian's food and then waited for him to shit himself to death. It hadn't been pretty, but it had worked. Leskat had been in over his head as a thief, even worse as a gang boss. He'd fallen into this with bravado and by being more cunning than the rest of the filth. If they'd only known most of his success involved rooting through shit or slitting drunk throats in their sleep maybe the rabble wouldn't be so quick to follow the hunched braggart. He was part Orc; he'd kept that quiet, but it had lent him his strength. His grandfather on his mother's side, or something like that. He'd never been the sharpest knife, but he made up for that in cunning and willingness to do what it took to survive, the things others would retch or baulk at. It had given him a gang of over fifteen and an area of about six streets to call his own, Leskat's circle they called it. He was a King in this dirty, flea-bitten part of Kuvhne, the lawless cesspit of a city they sometimes called bandit home. If you lost it here, you wouldn't even be found, vultures and worse would feed on bits of you, if you were lucky enough to die quick. Steek nudged Leskat with a bony elbow and whispered "That sword looks expensive boss, feed us well that will, Murkin'd give us forty, maybe fifty for it. Slit 'is throat and let's be away wiv it before Krunicks mob comes around." Boster Kraen, overweight and bald with fewer teeth than even Leskat and a reputation for selling anything and anyone, leered at Leskat and the three ragged, foul spectres at his side. "Used ta be some big 'ero. Saved the world so they said. Killed whatsername, the Witch-Queen with that very blade. You'd sell that to Vas 'imself and live like a King for years. Worth a lot o' money to a boss like you Leskat." His hands were oily and greasy with a mix of pig fat, ale and his own sweat. The whole tavern smelled the same, still an improvement of the sewage and dampness that pervaded the streets of this dark little flea-infested corner of Kuvhne. All around hung an air like someone had bled out diarrhoea, wrapped it in wadded cloth and left to rot in the hot rain. A little pig fat and stale sweat was like perfume here.

Leskat had been about during the reign of the Witch-Queen, he remembered the man Boster meant but, the name escaped him. He had led a rebellion, he was said to be unmatchable with a sword, a charming roguish wanderer who seemed to step out of anonymity in the Swordlands with some kind of priest, wizard or bard by his side. Between them they rallied thieves, mercenaries, wizards and explorers. Rejects, idiots, clowns and rogues. A halfling with a knife, a wizard who'd gone mad and a one-handed mercenary. These misfits, drunks, villains and cowards had taken down the most powerful army Karn had ever seen. Leskat found it hard to believe that here, in the stale rot of Clemerance Lane sat the greatest hero the world had ever known, unconscious and face down on a table in a puddle of his own vomit. Besides the swordmaster would be no more than mid-fifties. This sop was at least sixty. Half grey and worn, pale and sagging, this was no hero, no lynchpin upon which the world moved. This was some caravans master whose wife had run off with a younger man. Or some glorified cutpurse who was running from the Knights of Vandarn or had crossed the circle wizards or maybe owed a debt of gold to the damned Dwarves. Maybe he was some servant of the mad God Dracor whose vanity had overcome his sense and led him here. Or maybe he was just some drunk nobody with a nice sword. Regardless, it was closing time, and his night was over. Leskat smiled with an outpouring of stale turnip stench and nodded to Steek. With an oddly damp clunk, Steek dropped a small pouch into Boster's sweaty grease-coated palm and something like a ferret crying escaped his thin blotching lips which could only have been a laugh. Leskat inclined his head towards the slumped vomit-stained body and the three darting little figures of his under-fed, leech-like henchmen spread out and cautiously, cowardly and with silent, capricious glee circled their slumped, gently gurgling victim. Leskat licked the sore on the left side of his top lip which always stung with a faint metallic taste to sharpen his senses, he wanted to enjoy this, the tingling feeling he felt before he killed, the excitement and glee he almost longed for. He'd killed so many times, he'd poisoned, he'd stabbed, and he'd even strangled someone once. A teenager no more than fourteen and he couldn't even say he had a reason beyond someone had sold him the thing as a servant and he'd never looked anyone in the face before as they died. He liked it, more than he admitted to his men. Guk or Gork or something like that the boy's name was. He thought of it now as his men surrounded this drunken sot. All the choices and he chose to strangle it and why? To prove to himself he wasn't a coward. Leskat had always known he was a coward, being afraid, being disgusting and doing anything to survive had always been who he was. Still, he'd killed that child, just so he could lie to himself that he deserved to be boss here. He looked as his three men slid snakelike in front and to either side of the unconscious body. Leskat moved slowly behind him and glanced around the dingy, empty bar. His famous jewelled dagger gripped fluidly in his hand. He put the past, his fears, worries and everything out of his mind. Soon there would be blood and the smell and taste of death. He could feel his darker tastes rising, he would hurt someone tonight and taste fear in their sweat, Leskat only felt alive when he killed someone whose first knowledge of it was the helpless realisation that they were dead, they were bested. He felt himself shiver with anticipation and leaned closer, forward into the rear of the warrior. The smell of ale and vomit and stale breath felt fresh and violent and dangerous on his tongue. Leskat leaned in, feeling his belly and crotch pressing against the chair and back of the slumped over, lightly breathing form. Inching his mouth to the ear he whispered, "It's time to wake up little man." It was then he noticed the breath, shallow, deliberate and slow. A tense and taught aura exuding through his touch Leskat knew, he couldn't quite tell how, but he knew. This human had been listening, half drunk and stupor bound he'd heard, somehow knew and focused by danger had waited in a pool of his own vomit for the moment to strike.

The greying black hair tousled as the drunk's head snapped back sharply connecting powerfully with Leskats nose. White blinding pain shot through his entire face and almost quicker than he could follow the human pushed his chair back throwing Leskat back with it. With a strength that belied the humans frame and drunken stupor the drunk leapt to his feet and in a flash his sword was out, swinging unsteadily but swiftly like an extension of the man's arm. As Leskat's three wiry henchmen rushed him the drunk spun like a dancer on one heel, the sword weaving through them one throat slit, another sliced impossibly across the stomach and the third run straight through the gut and like that, they were dead. The drunk stopped, swayed slightly and belched deeply and loudly, filling the air with the stink of fresh vomit. Almost as if he was only now waking up, he grinned at Leskat as he peered trying to focus. "That; was a mishake, mishtake... mistake." The drunk wandered forward, a vomit-stained braid on his forehead swinging back and forth in front of his face as he half lurched, half danced forward. Something in the small of Leskat's spine tightened, somehow in his bones he knew, this was no cutpurse or Caravan master, this man had seen death and had faced death and heard prayers to Dracor many times before watching the life go out of people's eyes. Leskat felt his panic and gourd start to rise, he tried to say something, but nothing would come out. The drunk's, swaying hand of death was almost upon him blade black as night still dripping with the blood of his friends. The Swordsman smiled though there was nothing, no humour, malice or feeling behind it. The drunk eyes were empty, bereft as if he were a jug that had been emptied not just of his stomach contents; but his heart and soul had been left on the table. Someone blurted out "MERCY!" Almost immediately Leskat realised it had been himself. The drunk Swordsman shrugged; "Shorry, none left." And finished crossing the room in the same hypnotic half swaying manner, like a drunk dancer gliding in more directions than he intended. Leskat held up his jewelled dagger "I've got money, magic and more I can give you anything!" The Swordsman looked at the jewelled dagger and seemed for a second to be lost in its glinting light before looking up and directly at Leskat, burning hole in his eyes with a hollow gaze. "There's nothing left I want." The Swordsman intoned, suddenly sounding sober, lost and defeated. "If it's any help, I kind of wish you had got me." He finished speaking and with a shrug the pointed tip of black, almost impossible to look at steel slid forward and through Leskat's eye as in another flash of blinding pain everything went dark.

A voice, insidious and dark like a tentacle slithering through his mind reverberated "What is this? What is a Leskat? It squirms and struggles, fresh and fearful. It doesn't even know it's dead yet. Look though. It has seen it; it has seen the blade. The key, our key. Prepare it to go back. Hunt that key." Leskat felt himself carried along like a tiny boat in a strong current, his very being felt like it was being dragged limply through a cave. Although he couldn't hear or see anything he was overwhelmed by the sensation of being grasped and writhed against like a barrel full of fish slithering back and forth in a too-small bucket. Leskat tried to remember how he got here, the memory of that blood-drenched impossibly black blade tip thrusting at his eye and then the flash of white. The more he pushed at the memory the harder it hurt. There was another flash of light and suddenly everything started to hurt. He could feel his eye, or more accurately where his eye, his face and his brain had been pierced and the agony where the gaping wound was. It filled with a black shadow he could feel from the inside and though he could not see from that eye he felt a presence in his body with him. "Open your eye." It commanded matter-of-factly, and without hesitation he did. He found himself unable to even think about a response, his one remaining eye opened on its own. He felt the black shadow ooze through his brain and his eye socket with the whispering of countless voices inside his head. Almost without realising he was doing it he slowly raised his rotting, black shadowy ooze-filled body to its feet. Leskat looked around to see he was in a shallow ditch just outside Kuhvne, his body partway rotted in the desert sun as he looked around to find others like himself, standing around oddly all staring at him. He realised without really knowing why, that what he was looking for was to the west, the lands of Dern near the Takal/

Vandarn border, he opened his mouth and a voice that was part him part shadow echoing and devoid of life poured out "west." And without any further delay he and a small group of walking, shadow-filled corpses started marching slowly but determinedly west with almost rhythmical, military precision. Leskat had no idea why, but he knew these other creatures were following him, somehow subservient to him. He also felt his free will was caged by the black oozing shadow substance within him that coursed through him like a crawling, slithering oozing parasite which not only gave him power and life but that caged his soul, his spirit and his actions to its will.

Leskat kept waiting to feel hungry or tired but it never came. Just the pain of his wounds and the burning like hot oil of the shadow ooze as it slithered around him like a living being pulsing from within and burning at his very essence. Occasionally on the march, he'd look around at the others and if they felt the same agonizing burning feelings, they didn't show it. Neither, he eventually realised, did he. Over time Leskat began to realise that the burning wasn't in his flesh and the pain wasn't in his skull, it was in his being, his body was no longer really his, it was a suit made of rotting meat carrying him; what was now him, to his objective. He watched part in horror and part in fascination as one of the others marched silently alongside him as it moved its arm, it lost a finger. So rotted was the body that the motion of swinging the arm had caused the finger to slide off the bone with a sickly squelching noise where it plopped on the ground just to be trod on by its dispassionate and seemingly unaware owner. As Leskat stared on a black, unnatural shadow slid down the inside of the hand and mostly covered the bone oozing and pulsing as it did. For what felt like the hundredth time since he had died, awful terror gripped what was left of Leskat's soul. He tried to speak, to cry out but though he could hear himself the noise echoed around his head. The low hissing, bubbling voice responded

"Calm yourself little being, you will be free when you prove your-self. Bring us the blade that slew you and we shall reward you with power and an afterlife that your living years could not match up to. We bring you opportunity and power beyond your tiny dreams Leskat of Kuvhne, you shall be an instrument with which we shall reshape the world."

At the far end of the bandit wastes stood the kingdom of Dern, a hard and militant kingdom ruled by a baleful lord who hangs like a menacing overlord. Flying under the Banner of their larger neighbour Vandarn, Dern and its lord often struggled to stay within the rules and laws of the larger kingdoms banner. Since the end of the war and the collapse of the Witch-Queen and her deathknight army, many deathknights flocked to the banner of Dern and now work within the walls of its cities. Those terrifying knights who had marched under the half-demon Deathskull distinctive for their skull-faced helmets and barbed blade swords to say nothing of the aura of fear and death that pervades them. No longer allied to the dark kingdom of Takal that even now is fractured, over the last dec-ades the deathknights gained more independence and even at times found their members working with other allegiances though their true allegiance was to war, combat and death. It was here in the small eastern town of Paran that a deathknight named Kanarr had risen to the captain of guards. A Takalan human with what looked like a little elven blood in him, standing just under six feet tall, he was short for someone with such a strong Takalan look but muscular and swarthy He had dark eyes and thick black hair and beard which was always wild under his bone white, skull helmet. His helmet and armour were traditional for a deathknight, black and burnished to shine like the mystical steel they are fashioned to impersonate. Like most experienced deathknights though, Kanarr's had been buffed, bashed and buffeted by time and combat and his armour and helm, like his raven black hair had felt the touch of the years upon it. His once proud raven mane streaked liberally with silver and grey in huge patches were the first showings of his age. It was known, that he was quite high up in the Witch-Queens army during the war, one of those unspoken things that no one would address. The fear the locals felt of Kanarr's past was sometimes useful in keeping the peace and maintaining the strict order required in Dern. So it was, that his past was never questioned. Kanarr's eyes would often appear black in the dark and his ears and features were slightly finer and angled than most humans, despite his bulky and muscular frame. Those who saw him with a blade were suitably wary, though he'd not often resorted to using it, when he did it was with a ruthless efficiency that terrified the less expert swordsmen who saw it and lived. There was no fancy acrobatics, no ounce of wasted effort, no threats or glib words, no words at all just the cold dispassionate glare of those dark eyes. When Kanarr unsheathed his barbed blade, it was ruthless, brutal, efficient and often terrifying. Rarely did he wound or disarm a foe preferring instead, to simply kill them with as little mercy or delay as others would open a door. A few short years ago a deathknight came to Paran, old enough to have been serving in the war, he had turned to adventuring after the collapse of the Witch-Queens army. He and his companions, on their way from one adventure to another were looking to rest up. He had reacted visibly when he saw Kanarr, calling him Sir and being very deferential. It would have gone unnoticed had the rest of the adventuring party not loudly enquired after the deathknight disappeared with all his gear in the middle of the night. It looked as if he'd hurriedly packed and fled without warning anyone. His companions had feared foul play although all evidence pointed to his having merely disappeared. Those close to Kanarr, especially those in town guard suspected the disappearance had something to do with who the captain had been in his previous life, but no one pushed that one too hard for fear of raising the ire of the brutal man.

He'd had a name once; he'd had an identity and friends and even been in love at one point. He'd wished for this; he'd wanted to run away and scrub the memories of years of war and pain and death from his mind. He'd wanted nothing more than to look down at his hands and not see the oceans of blood he'd spilled or that had been spilled in his name, or that he'd spilled by being too slow, too soft or too ill-trained. The Nine had been worried about the Witch-Queen, they'd seen this before when two Mortal wizards Ramlar and Dracor had risen to such power that they had challenged the Gods themselves. Two mortal wizards who now counted themselves amongst the Nine. It had been a change so shocking that the Nine ruled that no divine or infernal being should walk the lands of Karn ever again. A rule that stood for tens of thousands of years, until after the Witch-Queen died when suddenly, beings of divine and infernal blood started to appear in the heartlands. When he led the army to end the Witch-Queen's dominance of the heartlands of Karn, the Nine had granted him a boon, a wish 'without condition' they had said. He'd wished to be stricken from the history books, that no one should remember his name or quite what he looked like ever again. He had wanted, in the depths of his trauma to never be that person ever again. He should have remembered, there is no wish that comes without a price. He himself, forgot his name and so much of who he was. Even then every morning he would see himself in the water as he washed his face and the only thing that was gone was who he was, not one second or memory or burden of his past was erased. Nightmares still came and horrors still revisited him. He saw Harpsong after the boon and the bard had recognised him but struggled to remember his name "I know you." the bard had said though no sooner had he turned away than he'd forgotten that he'd even seen him.

He stirred from the pile of hay he'd been sleeping in, he vaguely remembered being ejected from the Inn and choosing an empty stable stall in his stupor. He half crawled on his hands and knees to the trough and dunked his head fully in it, "Hello no one." He said nodding to himself in ironic familiarity at his own face both familiar and strange. Once the most recognisable face on Karn now that face was one even, he himself felt a dissociative emptiness to look at. Staring at his face in the dirty water trough, what stared back was inscrutable and weary, devoid of hope and enveloped by bitterness and wrapped in ageing and poor living. This was not the greatest living Swordsman, this was no carefree rogue, no wartime hero or great general whose underground hit-and-run tactics had crushed an empire. All those men who had once lived in this face were gone along with the name that had held them to it. This was just a sad old drunk who was friendless and alone, waiting for the blade that had his name to find him and put him out of his misery. He sighed, softly, dejectedly "no one." It came out half a whisper, half spat. He felt the rage building in the sword, like a wave passing through him as his night black Tilak blade, a sword of legend that had been with him all this time. Its blade, black as night and seeming to shift and gleam when you looked at it, a black and gold wrapped handle and the pommel ending in a globe, the world of Karn with two tiny swords pierced right through it. Often it would reflect what he was feeling right back at him at times amplifying or nullifying what he felt depending, it seemed on the weapon's own whim; the building rage was like a warning though. A warning that he was not alone.

Still knelt over the trough he slowly turned his head to see the Inn-keeper that had ejected him last night, to his shame he couldn't even remember why. He knew he was somewhere in Dern; his last clear thought had been the fight back in Khuvne. A thought flashed across his mind that it had been a foolish idea to be anonymous in a land with no real laws. On the far side of the three men who faced him, across from the Innkeeper was what looked like a Dernian guardsman, a cheap sword which even by the way it hung on his belt he barely knew how to carry never mind use. In the middle though, nearly half a foot taller than the others, it looked like Dern guard captains' uniform but for the helmet. It was painted the dark green of the Dernian guards' uniform, but the skull faceplate gave it away as a deathknight's helm almost as much as the sword in his hand, the barbed steel of a deathknight's blade. The Helmeted deathknight turned guard spoke first, his deep voice and Takalan accent booming through the helm, "Who are you wanderer, you know it's a crime to trespass in Dern?" Something in the guard captain's voice stirred a memory of something familiar. Pulling himself to his feet he turned to face them full on, even from the other side of the stable he saw the almost imperceptible change in the grip on the barbed blade. "I know you, don't I?" The captain boomed through his helm before slowly lifting the faceplate up and back over the top of his helm to show his face. The Innkeeper turned to the large Takalan "Kanarr you know this sot?" The large guard captain glanced at the innkeeper in fury before turning his attention back to the drunk. He looked at the right hip of the man and saw the blade, he might not be able to recall the man, his brain might have squirmed to recall his face; but that sword? That sword would be burned into Kanarr's mind until he died. "On three occasions that blade nearly ended my life wanderer, I would know it anywhere. Hand it over and I may let you leave." The old drunk smiled, his clothes were shabby and unwashed as was his hair which was mottled black and grey though long and braided as it was in his youth. Though his features were haggard with drink and years hard lived they were familiar to the deathknight guard captain as were those piercing blue eyes which filled his mind with memories of pain and humiliation which swirled and fought desperately to be remembered, and then the man smiled. The smile was wolfish, humourless and a little cruel, the drunk knew what was coming and it appeared he was relishing it. His voice, though cracked and dry was oddly melodic and made Kanarr's brain itch to try and remember why as the drunk spoke "I remember you now, General Kanarr. The sword remembers you too." In almost blinding speed the Tilak blade was out of its scabbard, a whistling metallic tune as it swung back and forth easily in the drunk stranger's hand.

The Innkeeper stepped slowly back, his eyes widening. He knew nothing of swordplay but something in the drunks' step, his smile the sudden grin and the glint in his eye turned the very small of the innkeeper's spine to jelly. Slow enough not to be obvious he backed away, before fleeing back inside the Inn. Leaving the other three men alone in the early morning sun. The young guard took a step forward, his eye never leaving the drunk "Come on now sir, no need for that. Put the sword away, it's only a couple of silver fine or a couple of days in the cells for sleeping rough like this no need for spilt blood over it." The young man stepped forward his hand raised in a calming manner and suddenly with a noise he couldn't quite process, he saw the tip of his Captain's barbed blade protruding from his chest. He heard an awful sickening, sawing noise as it was removed again sawing at his flesh and bone, tearing at his insides as suddenly in shock the young man shook violently and collapsed on the ground. "He was right, you would have been fine. However, now you've gone and killed one of my men. I'm not sure who you are, but nothing can keep that blade from my mind's eye, I remember the wounds that blade inflicted on me. I will have my vengeance." Fury, incredulous and unyielding built on the deathknight's face as he slid the skull mask back down over his features and raised his sword as if in promise and salute. The Swordsman was well over fifty the deathknight surmised, and the years had not been kind to his obvious western Swordlands features, heavily beset by years of drinking and living rough Kanarr figured the older man would have lost a step, and certainly wouldn't be The Swordsman he may have been in his youth. Stepping slowly to the side around the corpse of his young guardsman, remembering as he did that the Innkeeper had heard the drunk call him general and to see to that later. Kanarr never once took his eyes from The Swordsman who appeared to be swaying ever so slightly if arrhythmically with the night-black blade whistling through the air so casually almost like it was an extension of his arm. Without warning Kanarr rushed, faster than he had any right to for a bulky large man wearing such heavy armour, his barbed blade thrusting out at waist height for The Swordsman's belly, finding air as The Swordsman landed with a thud on the floor. Almost pre-empting the blow and rolling into Kanarr toppling the deathknight who rolled and spun back to crouching with his sword ready for the swing which hadn't come. Looking down he saw The Swordsman flat on his back directly beneath him, having rolled back again and thrust his sword directly up. Kanarr saw with horror the black blade buried deep into his own gut and up into his ribcage. He tried to react but all he could feel was the Tilak blades' rage slowly sating itself as it sensed his coming death. Kanarr looked in horror trying to comprehend the speed, the movement and the actions of the drunk Swordsman. He opened his mouth to speak but the Tilak blade had punctured his lung and all that came out was a wheezing gasp and then blood. As he rocked on his heels and fell backwards. The Swordsman flipped onto his feet cat-like, releasing the grip on the Tilak blade still buried in the deathknight's body and then with a curious gentleness cradled the dying deathknight. Slowly lowering Kanarr to the ground, resting the deathknights head on his lap "I'm sorry general, I know the war is long over and you're not the man you once were. At least you'll go to your rest now in whatever afterlife awaits you." He gripped Kanarr's mailed hand tightly as the deathknight tried to speak his eyes wide with pain he struggled to spit out the words, "You're, him..." before all he could do was gasp. The Swordsman looked sad as he replied still grasping the dying man's hand "I wish I could offer you some comfort, some words of wisdom but to answer your first question, I'm not sure I'm the man you remember me as, he's gone. I'm not even a shadow of that man. I'm no one."

CHAPTER 4

The Retreat

She looked up from under heavy lids with stinging eyes at the hulking figure of her mentor. Arn was a virtual giant nearly seven foot tall and three hundred pounds of clear military muscle. He'd been a knight once she knew, someone of great importance in the Capital City of Vandarn. His hair tightly cropped and black as night had in recent years become peppered with grey. In these past years travelling together though she'd never seen it one hair out of place, nor an ounce of stubble on his massive jaw. His eyes were blue as crystal and stung with judgement as if they silently measured you with every glance no matter how brief. Everything about the old man was crisp, measured and level and he had a manner of stoic silence that sometimes, left people wondering if he felt at all or was some kind of simulacrum of a human being who merely did what it thought was right. His hard, cold steel exterior cased a heart purer than any she'd ever known though. He had been like a father to her through everything they'd suffered and everything they'd fought. He seemed to prefer the road, hardships seemed to invigorate him and she, molded by the road, had grown to appreciate the same feelings of success in the day-to-day grind.

She rose from her sleeping mat, the hunger in her belly roused by the crackling fire and the prospect of sizzling as meat hit the griddle. Wincing as she rose, her hand cradled the deep wound in her side. Arn had healed it mostly with some kind of magic the old man had occasionally used when needed but still the wound was raw and the scar fresh. She'd carry it a while before it was fully gone and even then, she'd never forget the wound that stung with failure, defeat and the possible ramifications not just for her but for everything they'd fought for. Her shoulders sagged at the reminder of how badly they'd failed, how badly they'd let down the people who had heaped their hopes upon her shoulders. The only hope now was to get back, report what they'd seen before the horrors they had discovered spread further, maybe even to Vandarn.

"Josyln? What bothers you child?" Arn's voice was gruff as old stone but had a softness like a layer of moss bringing gentle edge to the hardened base. "Nothing old man, just the wound, it still hurts." She looked up at him as she spoke and felt the lie hanging in the air, he raised a grizzled eyebrow at her and tilted his head. "Fine, we failed. We let everyone down and now Vandarn alone knows what might happen next. I wanted to change the world, to save it. To free everyone from this darkness, this pall of horror that has consumed the land. I wanted to make a difference." She sighed, lowering herself back to sit on her sleeping mat as she spoke, the wind coming out of her sails with the admission. Her spirit limped to its knees beside her, this was the moment she'd always feared where her fight started to seep insidiously away from her, and she saw no road out of the hole she was in.

With rare gentleness the giant Knight eased his stiff back and lowered himself onto the ground beside her. "Child, you do make a difference. Every day you strap on that sword, every time you pack up your things and continue down the road and travel out here in the wilderness, pursuing the darkness and chasing the hopes that we can make even the slightest difference in the fate of the future. We are scouts, we see and we report. Our duty is to get news of what we saw to home. You don't save the world with a sweeping slash of your sword or by wielding archaic mystical flame against the demons and monsters of the world. You save it with a thousand tiny acts of kindness, by holding true to your heart, by believing in yourself and others, by having faith in your companions and that the races of man and dwarf and elf and all of them will not yield to darkness that encroaches. You save it with Charity and with the occasional hand on a faltering shoulder." She felt the giant calloused hand fall gently on her shoulder as Arn gently pulled her near and gave a slight squeeze. "Now stop being foolish girl, we have to eat, travel, heal and report back what happened at the pass. I've followed Vandarn and prayed at his temples all my life, child. I've never believed in him like I believe in you. Never forget that." With that the old knight struggled to his feet and busied himself with breakfast.

Joselyn ground her teeth together and rose to her feet, instinctively she grabbed her sword from its sheath and walked off to the edge of camp. Staring back at the retreat they'd made over the last few days and at the road they'd travelled twice now, once with hope and the other in retreat. She promised herself she hadn't been down it for the last time, "no failure is forever." She said out loud at the road and gripped the steel in her hand ever tighter. "No." she said again, quieter and into her own breast nodding to herself as she steeled her spirit and her resolve. She had never felt any connection to Vandarn, no greater power to give her strength but the old man was right. It wasn't in her to let go or to give up. She'd fight the sky itself if she had to and she'd earn her own redemption. With that she dropped the sword onto her sleeping mat and turned to the fire, to breakfast and the journey ahead.

The old paladin smiled to himself as Josyln stood staring back over their retreated journey mournfully. He would allow her this indulgence, sometimes you need to mourn your failures to ensure you don't repeat them. He knelt by the fire and prepared more salted meat and hard tack bread for them both. Using some small magic subtly to make it more flavourful and satisfying. He'd rather she didn't see the extent of the old paladins magic, after all it isn't for vanity but for purpose and he was sure the girl could use a small comfort just now. He hadn't been lying when he said he'd never faced anything like those undead before, dripping in shadow which seemed to be the source of their undeath holding them together long beyond when even the most virulent zombie would have collapsed. Though they seemed as susceptible to the light of Vandarn if not more than most undead. The worry was the organisation, something that could raise these things and have them act in unison, coordinated like one entity or a well-trained army made them extra deadly. Arn tossed Joselyn's food onto a small plate and walked over with it. "We were sent to confirm that the half-demon is dead or at least no longer in charge. That much we accomplished." He stared along with her at the road they had just returned down as he continued. "Whatever that was, those things that were hunting us? We need to report back, we need to tell them exactly what we saw If those things, that shadow can take any corpse then some of the things lying at the bottom of the Quioty Swamp would be even more terrifying to behold than the things that chased us from the Southern edge of Takal." The old paladin felt the young warrior shudder at the thought of some of those things howling and chasing them. Whatever they had been in life, with large black leathery wings and razor-sharp teeth. in death and filled with a black, viscous shadow darkness they were terrifying. Like a curtain of darkness and evil they blotted out the sky before splitting to attack groups and attacking with uncanny precision; Joselyn shuddered again to think of them. She turned to Arn, "Have you ever seen anything like that before?" The old man's stare was as granite she almost imagined she could hear his teeth grinding, "No." His eyes never wavered from the horizon "There are things they could have been, devils, demons or some manner of thing from the hells. Infernal and divine things have been able to step foot on Karn for the last two decades, since the end of the war but never in those numbers and long enough ago to have died and been brought back? It doesn't make any sense." The old man stood motionless scanning the horizon. If he felt any fear Joselyn could pick up no trace of it, no surprise, shock or even curiosity. It was as if the old paladin simply saw the obstacle he had to overcome or a mystery he had to solve. It was easy to see she thought, why people felt him cold or unfeeling his focus was absolute. She decided to leave him to his reverie and cleaned up their camp, wincing occasionally from the healed wound as she did.

Arn stared back at the horizon, contemplating how empty the skies looked. An army of flying undead that seemed to move like an organised military unit? It made no sense and things that didn't make sense annoyed him. He glanced an eye over at Joselyn, the young soldier packing up their things to prepare to move out. He probably shouldn't have brought her on such a journey, but he knew she was tough and regardless of what horrors the Takalans had uncovered Arn had faith the young warrior could not only deal with it but thrive under the pressure. "There are always monsters." His brother Thirel had always said, "that's why we fight." Thinking now of his brother, his youth and the world he came from gave him pause. The life he would have lived if he'd not ended up (and decided to stay) on Karn. He wasn't often a man given to introspection, but he was getting on and the challenges just seemed to get more dangerous, more world threatening. For a moment, out here in the tundra, facing evil, unnatural things he thought of home, of the farm and those long summer afternoons. He'd like to see his brother one last time before he died, probably off saving some forest somewhere with that elf partner of his. Arn realised he was smiling, and he allowed himself it, a tiny moment of joy in the darkness of the day. "Yes, home." He said aloud as he turned to re-join Joselyn and finish packing for the road.

He smiled at his young student as he walked back to the camp, the sight of a smile on his face, especially at this dark hour reassured the young warrior, it occurred to her that if he wasn't worried, she should trust in that. She threw a couple of things into a pack and looked up with a smile on her face at the sight of the giant paladin blocking out the sun. The smile quickly faded when she saw behind him, something huge with a wingspan so large she struggled to fathom it. The humungous shape, blotting out of the rest of the sunlight and what was worse tendrils of shadow dripping from holes in its skin, flesh and even wings. This was no humanoid thing with horns, this was gigantic with a maw the size of a horse and it was bearing right down on Arn with malice in its gleaming black eyes. Seeing the terror in Joselyn's eyes Arn suddenly became aware of the huge leathery wings flapping behind him. Immediately he dropped and covered up, feeling huge claws ripping through his tabard and hearing it scraping off the black dragonhide armour he had hidden underneath. He waited till it had passed then rolled over, looking over to Joselyn he saw the young soldier had snapped right into her training. She lunged immediately for their weapons, she had grabbed her sword with one hand and Arn's giant blade in the other, launching the old paladins massive sword across the ground where it skidded towards him lifting dirt as it did. Pushing down and lurching he leapt forward yanking the giant blade out of the dirt, as he kept his eyes on the giant undead dragon, looping around in the near distance preparing to swoop back down. Leaping to his feet the giant sword in his hand he gave it a couple of preparatory swings, as much to get the feel as to prepare for the fight ahead. The large, impossibly sharp blade poised in his hand the old paladin bent his knees and waited for the wyrm like undead to swoop towards him. His mind and body suddenly calm and clear, he'd done this before against a thousand flying foes over the years, even a few times with dragons. He thought of the black dragon hide armour that rested under his tabard and how he came across it and set his jaw firmly as a familiar look took over the stoic man's face. The look of recognition in the undead dragon's eyes disconcerted Arn, almost as if it was calculating its next move like a conscious beast but then it flew straight at him without any of the subtlety he normally expected from a dragon. He noted its black shadow-soaked eyes pivoting as it tried to force its body to obey, his training and his experience fighting the giant beasts let him see the subtleties that others might miss, the shadowy tendrils that filled and dripped from the thing seemed to control it, guide it. At the last minute the shadows recoiled a little and a look of relief played on the undead creatures' face as it suddenly pitched to the left to swerve the large paladins blade. This would have given Arn food for thought had he time to consider the shift in tactics when the shadows recoiled inside the undead dragon. With an almost imperceptible shift in his weight Arn tensed, took a deep breath and then as he exhaled, he leapt, twisting as he did his gleaming razor-sharp blade moving in motion with his body as he flipped into the air. The giant sword plunging over three foot of blade into the undead dragons belly. Mid clash it turned its rear leg and made no howl of pain though it clearly felt the tear as its belly split pouring thick bubbling black shadowy ooze all over the old paladin. The undead dragons rear leg kicked at Arn as he passed a giant claw tearing right down the paladins front and ripping a deep gouge in the old man like the one, he had just inflicted on the it. As the black oozing shadows hit the old paladin they turned to simply mist and shadow, enveloping and filling him, covering his eyes with darkness. Arn heard screams, people and other things he'd sent to their Gods and to the darkness rung in his ear with cries of vengeance, forgiveness and fear in equal measure. For a second that seemed to last an eternity he floated lost in a deep, dark all-encompassing river of shadow and loss. He saw in his mind's eye the farm back home before one of the many portals in the land had brought him to Karn. His brother, who took to nature so much better than him trying to show him how to farm. Something Arn had never taken to, He saw the Chapter house and church where he trained as a paladin, he saw the lord he had served under as a youth ruling kindly and justly, and himself the paladin strong and true. His mind dragged him through the dark years of death and war and of battles where he was hip deep in blood and gore and where he felt like he would never wash the blood off. Through the darkness and the well of despair and the screams of the dead and damned a tiny, sliver of white/gold light shone through, and he heard a whisper soft deep voice he knew almost like his own "Varan Arfiran my old friend. Not yet, you have earned a place at my table a thousand times over brave knight, but that door is not yet open your own magic trinkets pull you back to the living even now. Vandarns most brave and most loyal will be rewarded but not yet." The voice of his God like a warm comforting embrace from an old friend warmed him and bathed him in light as he suddenly found his eyes blinking and his breath returning as he became aware of the agonizing pain of the tear in his chest. The undead dragon faltered Its body no longer able to physically support it the thing seemed to collapse mid-flight, falling in on itself and just plummeting to the ground, the black viscous shadowy ooze turning to black mist as it hit the ground leaving nothing but a dragon's corpse in its wake. Joselyn watched with horror, her sword at the ready as the black shadows recoiled from the dead beast and sunk into the ground and disappeared. leaving nothing but broken bones and skin, rotting flesh and skeletal claws. At the sight of one claw, soaked in human blood and worse she suddenly realised belonged to Arn, Joselyn's head snapped back in the other direction as she searched for the stricken paladin.

A trail of blood down the hillside led her to him, lying on his back with a giant rend from chest to navel which appeared somehow to be knitting itself back together. The ugly green gem he wore stitched into his dragon hide armour glowing gently as it seemed to be working on his wounds. Slowly, gingerly the old man felt the giant tear in his armour before looking up at Joselyn, a huge smile on his face which was somehow even more disturbing to her than the mortal wound that just closed and healed itself on his chest. Still laying there he began to laugh, booming and echoing around him as he howled with what felt like a mixture of relief and excitement. He glanced over at her puzzled and worried expression, "I was a lousy farmer!" He offered laughing between the words as he gasped for breath. "I didn't have patience for lessons, I put the entire chorus off if I sing and I dance like an angry mare in heat." As Joselyn looked more and more concerned and confused the old man started to sit up, reaching for his giant wickedly sharp blade as he did "but I can fight. Men, monsters or dragons, anything! I was always a great soldier. In Vandarn's name. I can certainly fight." As he dragged himself to his feet the old man's laughter continued "did you see that thing? Looked undead but just at the last minute it reacted like a real, live dragon! You can tell I'm getting old though eh! If not for this thing you'd be picking me up with a wheelbarrow!" Tapping the ugly green gem on his chest as his booming laughter echoed around the valley "Your armour? It's destroyed." Was all she could think to say to him in response as she stared incredulously at this sudden vibrancy, she'd not seen in him in her years as his student.

He looked down nonplussed and when he looked back up his joy had subsided as his breathing calmed, he nodded and looked over at the corpse "I don't suppose any of its hide is worth salvaging? I loved this armour, would be a shame not to be able to repair it." His emotions once again under control Arn's face turned serious and grim. "That thing won't be the last, I'd go so far as to say it was the tip of the spear and whatever is coming there's clearly more and possibly worse to come."

CHAPTER 5

King's man no more

The Dragon-sir River unofficially marks the borders between the frozen and uncivilized lands of Thol from the (some would say) equally uncivilized Swordlands. Running all the way from the mountains, where it is often frozen over in the colder months. It is a long and winding along the edge of the various kingdoms, baronies and assorted City-States that make up the Swordlands. This winding river once named the Southflow was renamed approximately twenty years ago for the peculiar bridge that spans it. The bridge is made almost entirely of the skeleton of dead giant dragon rumoured to have been killed here years ago by Tatral Valenstorm. Legend and the halfling himself tells of how he tricked the dragon and slew it with a simple sling and stone, though there are rumours he used a bladed dagger as black as night. Within days of news of the dragon's death and its corpse blocking the river the industrious people of the Swordlands had strip-mined its skin and flesh for food, clothing, trade and more. The skeleton already spanning the width of the considerable and dangerous river instead of being harvested was bolstered by supports and binding and turned into a bridge. A move which considerably helped trade and travel to and from the frozen north. Thus, the Dragon-sir River was born. At this time of year, the river was in full flow in the strong heat of the Freldine summer. The area around the dragon bridge would often feel heavy and dark even on the brightest day a strange shadowy pall fell over this entire area and travellers who cross at night often talk of a strange, dark presence haunting the bridge. Many point out that the bridge was in dangerous proximity to the ruins of Hven. A once dominant kingdom now reduced to rubble that has become home to monsters and unspeakable dark things. This could probably explain the uneasy feeling and strange experiences many feel crossing the bridge in the dark. Locals and traders will generally wait till daytime to approach and cross the bridge for fear of angering the spirits.

Urnath found himself lost in the weeks since his King bade him to leave the lands of Thol, not to attend the kingsmeet and to go truly live for himself for once. He had turned away and almost automatically went to head home until his King's words ringing in his ears forced him to turn his horse south. At one hundred and seventeen winters Urnath thought himself a little old for travelling the world, for adventuring or fortune seeking but his King had ordered him, and he was nothing if not dutiful. He promised himself he would seek out happiness, a life or whatever his King had ordered. Something had told him too, perhaps a feeling imparted to him by Crothan's magical empathic axe that he should not return home and that whoever the next High King or Queen of Thol is should not be wielding this axe when they did so. As he had retreated down the mountains of ice and snow, he had sent a simple sending spell back home to the waiting sages of the gathered tholan tribes, a simple message and straightforward like the great High King himself. "Crothan Thronebreaker of the Crollaran, High King of all Thol is dead at 300 winters. Call a kingsmeet." With that simple message he had shed himself of all responsibility, duty and fealty to the kingdom of Thol and the throne of the High King. For the first time in his life Urnath was free to go where he would and live how he wished. He had stood there just south of the mountain pass that led to the tholan mountains and beyond for what felt like an age. He found himself paralysed with indecision, just staring at the southland sprawling out beneath him like a loyal dog with no master, nowhere to go and no idea of how to be free. He felt lost and had no idea what to do, it was only in this moment he realised how shackled he had been by his choices in life. He'd spent half his life at the right hand of greatness, but his every waking moment had been in service of another and as he sat there staring at the open world beneath his feet. Not having anywhere to go, not having any orders to follow he felt giddy and guilty in equal measure as it occurred to him, he couldn't remember the last time he did something solely because he, Urnath felt like it. A life of service weighed on his conscience as he tried to process his next step, beneath him the horse tensed as if urging to move on. He wondered if it had been a mistake to sell his own horse and keep the old Kings seemingly unperturbable horse. He leaned over and absentmindedly patted the horse's rump, "he never named you, did he? The King. He was like that, hated having to remember names, I suppose that's what he kept me around for. He just called you Hrasse I know. It's ancient tholan for; well for horse I suppose. I guess we'll just stick with it. I'm not much better than the King it appears." Despite the large powerful beast not moving Urnath could almost swear he felt it shrug. He could feel the beast's impatience as it waited for him to pick a road. Urnath sighed, "well you choose then, you've probably travelled these roads more than me!" He laughed as he realised the old King would have loved this, his wise advisor lost in a world he didn't understand arguing with a horse and losing. Hrasse, started to trot slowly to the south and so without really knowing where, how or why, Urnath began the journey to his new life with a King's axe at his side and a King's horse guiding the way.

Urnath had heard all the stories of the dragon bridge. As the court wizard and closest advisor to the High King of all Thol most things came through him or stopped at him. Crothan didn't always have great patience for mundanities. In truth the kingdom had become more hierarchal in recent years and had almost got into a habit of running itself. Urnath hated to think what that would look like now that both he and Crothan were gone. He could almost hear the old King cackling away at the thought of his many friends, allies, children, grandchildren, enemies and strangers in-fighting over every position in the kingdom from High King to assistant stable hand. Of course, the old man would laugh at that. Most tholans only lived to be about two hundred years old give or take, the ride Crothan had taken up that impossible path had been how the old man had celebrated his three hundredth birthday. Nearly a century longer than any recorded tholan had ever lived. It had occurred to Urnath many times that Crothan felt like an ancient relic surrounded by children who squabbled over trivial nonsense and empty foolishness. When he'd asked Crothan about the dragon bridge the old man had laughed that deep belly laugh of his and crowed that he knew the halfling Valenstorm and with that little rogue anything was possible. Also, that he'd had *the* dagger, a dagger apparently made of the same strange black metal as Crothan's axe. Weapons forged of this steel he had said, were touched by the divine and more dangerous than any of us knew.

The old King's horse stopped, Urnath wasn't sure why until he looked, so lost in his reverie and his thoughts and memories of his dear departed friend that he hadn't realised the sun had gone down and here they were on the road that led right up to the dragon bridge. In the past Urnath had crossed the bridge as part of the High King's entourage for diplomatic trips but always during the high sun of midday. Standing here in the dark Hrasse stopped dead and looking quizzically and with trepidation at the bridge, Urnath saw why stories were abound about the place. Everbright torches hung periodically across the bridge. Rather than the lighting making it better though, it seemed to lend an air of ominous warning as giant shadows danced and flickered amongst the hollow dragon's rib cage and spine that formed the bridge's roof. The long path that wound through the ancient dragons' bone carcass, supported and bolstered by wood and iron reinforcements was coated in licking shadows that flitted back and forth across the bridge like demons dancing on a pin head. Urnath patted the giant mare on her nape and made a soft soothing sound. "Now girl, it's just a bridge." Hrasse snorted derisively and let out a low quiet whinny at the thought of moving forward. Gently Urnath urged the large horse forward and so slowly, Hrasse trotted forwards with such hesitance that Urnath found he was holding his breath. He imagined dark, shadowy terrors leaping out at him in every crevice of the dragon's torso. The soft rhythm of Hrasse's hooves turned to echoes as he started up the slight ramp that entered the giant dragons open maw and something low in the tiny part of Urnaths spine ran ice cold. Urnath realised, he was walking literally into a dragon's mouth, something that had never occurred to him so starkly in his daytime journeys over the bridge. With a palpable air of tension, the large horse slowly trotted through the giant dragon rib cage every hoofbeat echoing off the large bone cage they trod through.

A voice almost, seemingly from nowhere startled Urnath and even the large, usually implacable horse started a little, her ears flattening with her rising temper and nerves. "Urnath Spellbinder of the Rath'kalt, I believe? Crothan talked about you fondly and often.

I think as the end came upon him you were the last living thing the foul tempered old sot could stand." Urnath turned to see, leaning against a humungous rib bone, a slender, pale skinned human in long black wizards' robes. His frame was slight but muscled and his robe plain and unadorned, long black unkempt hair adorned his shoulders and head. At his hip, hanging from giant girdle made into the image of dragon wings with the dragon's head and body as its clasp were two oversize Warhammers that seemed too heavy for this slender human to lift. Even as a tholan, Urnath wasn't sure he'd be able to heft one of those hammers never mind two. Shining green eyes and a large grin that was almost predatory in nature looked up at him from a slightly too sharp nose. The look of recognition and expectation in the speakers' eyes had Urnath even more shook than the surprise appearance. Looking him up and down the still smiling man laughed, "come now Urnath! You don't recognise me? I know you've studied me extensively and surely your King must have spoken of me before? I'm almost insulted I thought Crothan and I were if not friends then certainly acquaintances, after everything I did for that curmudgeon. I almost wish I hadn't bothered saving his life." His smile reminded Urnath of a giant snow leopard, just before it consumed you whole, something about this slender human made Urnath uneasy, something he couldn't quite pin down. Urnath narrowed his eyes and tried to focus on what he was missing; the slow dawning of realisation on his face must have been obvious because the laughter started all over again. Jaw agape Urnath tried to compose himself, "R..Ramlar?" He spat out barely able to bring himself to move. Urnath realised that the flickering shadows across this whole section of the bridge swaying gently between the cleaned and supported rib bones of the dragon were the outline of a massive (even larger than the skeleton they stood in) dragon. The light from the torches cast distortedly up the river outlined a giant dragons head and wings as the shadow of this slender little human frame.

Here in front of him in this strange place in the dead of night was the God of Chaos, War and dragons. Urnath had indeed read many books about the mythical rise of Ramlar and Dracor from mortal wizards to two of the most powerful Gods not just in the pantheon but in the Nine itself. If the legends were true Ramlar had been a vicious and evil man as devious as he was cowardly. The story went that he had softened with age and had by the time he had ascended to demigodhood had become almost whimsical and carefree. All these layers were evident in the avatar before him now a playful smirk, an aura of terrifying power and with something cruel and unforgiving behind the eyes. "Godsblood." Ramlar said, his eyes staring at Crothan's axe strapped to the horse at Urnath's side, still grinning the avatar of Chaos continued "oh you mortals have many names for it, liquid ebony, living steel, and many more but really if we're being honest it's Godsblood. A hangover from my biggest crime, committing deicide. When I killed the God of War his blood seeped into the ground and of course when mortals found it, they made weapons of it. Other than the Witch-Queen of course. Barvara used it to fuel her magic, that's why she was so powerful, that and her other experiments with it. I'm sure I don't need to lecture you on the pit of the lost and damned Urnath. The poor lost souls and those of betrayers and the damned, doomed to eternity in that pit to suffer in torment at the hands of Lazarus, the God of betrayal and shadows. What most of the books and the priests and scholars won't tell you is that deep in the well of that pit, at its core are ancient, dark and evil things that have lain dead and dormant for thousands of years. Entities, alien creatures and Gods. Imagine all those souls, those things unleashed on the world to wreak their vengeance upon the living and even on the divine? I may love chaos Urnath but I'm no fool. I love this land and my role in it, I long to see it continue and not be torn asunder by the ancient rage of things long lost in the dark."

Urnath stared down at his King's axe and back at Ramlar, his head swimming with so many thoughts, so many questions. Before Urnath could speak Ramlar raised a hand and continued, "I'm here as a courtesy. Crothan closed a door that if opened could have destroyed the world. Little did I know, over two decades ago the Witch-Queen wedged that door open, she was killed before she could open it fully and we foolishly thought it slammed shut. It had not, and in the moment between Crothan dying and the portals energy passing from him to me that wedge became a crack and something ancient and evil that lurks in the dark realms squeezed a tendril of influence out into the world seeking that." His head nodded almost casually towards the axe, "seeking Godsblood weapons. That Axe, the Tilak blade even the dagger the halfling used to kill this very dragon, lying somewhere lost in the bottom of this river. Someone, or rather something has gone to great lengths to hide all this from the Nine but you Urnath, for a tholan you are quite sharp and even now you wish to serve your departed King. So, finish his work, find the portal he closed all those years ago and close that door before darkness is unleashed on the world and yes, rectify the mistake I made. It might sound like I'm asking but..." The unfinished sentence hung in the air, Urnath felt, like a threat as much as a command. He patted the axe and felt its worry as he touched it, looking back up he found himself staring at an empty bridge just shadows playing against the rib bone and off the torchlight as a chill wind ran through the wizard. Urnath nodded as a cold shiver slowly tingled the length of his spine causing him to clench his jaw as it reached his neck, "okay." Was all Urnath said and with that Hrasse slowly started her ponderous rhythmic trot over the bridge and towards the Swordlands border.

CHAPTER 6

Hven's Folly

Sitting cross-legged in the gutter, wrapped in layers of thick woven sack cloth with empty sacks of the same manufacture beneath her. An old mud caked beggar woman in her late fifties mumbled to herself between taking long draughts of a large foul-smelling bottle which was also wrapped in stench laden sack cloth. Her eyes darted about the street as if seeing invisible enemies everywhere. If anyone had looked closer, they would have seen bright, clear eyes that shone a light emerald, green colour and were picking up everything that happened on the street. When a plain unadorned door across the street from the rambling beggar woman slammed open, an overweight man with a waxed mustache and a dangerous looking sword lurched out. As he turned down the street he was angrily shouting at two younger similarly armed and armoured men who followed him out. Her eyes snapped towards them and her mumbling, if anyone was listening was clearer, "two with him. Has the keys, probably the gold on him. Let's be patient, we didn't go through all this to pounce too quickly now." If only maybe a wizard was watching, he might notice the faint magical aura of a sending spell focused on the earthen ware jug in the old beggar woman's left hand. Waiting for the three men to stalk off down the street the beggar woman slowly and with some difficulty rolled up to her feet and staggered off down the street, ducking into an alley out of sight.

Diaus Komarr had never been more furious. Three hundred of the finest slaves he'd whipped and trained into beautiful shape, and they offered less than ten thousand for them. Takalan gold fangs too, coins worth about eight tenths of the Vandarnian gold crowns he was used to trading in. Moving slaves through Vandarn had gotten too risky in recent years as King Branthar managed to bring the Church under control, causing a crackdown on things like slavers moving their goods through Vandarnian borders. So here he was in the walled city of Bal in the Takalan empire. A festering sewer of a city crammed wall to wall with disease and crime and merchants selling everything from dreams to darkness itself. The Goddess Ecaur herself couldn't have dreamed of a better place for greed and wealth. For all its squalor Bal probably had more wealth than any-where else in the heartlands. The only problem was, in a city full of dragons the few men who had all the gold fangs would sit upon their wealth gathering more and more. So much of the wealth that came into the city would disappear into those ever-growing piles of testament to greed. Diaus's mother had seen one of them, if the old thief was to be believed. She would tell him and his sisters the stories when they were little, of caverns under the city with mountains of gold, magic and gems larger than a dragon's hoard and one armful enough for a wise thief to retire on. She would tell them how she had conned her way in, filled her boots, her pockets, her pack and even her hood with gold and gems. Then snuck out of Bal, out of Takal and fled to the Swordlands to set up a small fiefdom with her ill-gotten gains. Married a nice soft, respectable lord and donned her new life like a new dress. Lady Komarr, she would tell them; was a fantasy made to hide her past glory. She had claimed to be one of the legendary men of the sword too, Diaus, snorted to think of that and looked down at the satchel clinking as it bounced off his thigh. "What would you think now mother? Your baby boy selling slaves for thousands. Maybe if you'd provided for me before you died, I'd have been a *man of the sword* too." Diaus spat the words out. He'd never in twenty years of slaving ever seen any trace of the legendary group of heroes who in the times before the war were rumoured to have hunted slavers, until that is they turned their eyes to the Witch-Queen as she invaded all the heartlands. Diaus, patted his gold and let a small snort of laughter escape. Realising he'd been laughing and mumbling to himself he turned to his lieutenants, "still enough to make it worth the trip eh lads?" He heard Nelis laugh that whiny, slithering little laugh of his. He looked around to Gorus and felt it odd the larger man's shadow wasn't looming over him like it usually did as they walked in formation. Stopping and spinning on his heel, Diaus drew his rapier and eyeballed Nelis, "where's Gorus?" The slender ratlike man behind him started to spin around with a mild panic shortsword already in hand, "he was here a second ago!" The whiny, wet reedy voice of Nelis screeched in sudden panic.

Diaus looked around at the quiet residential road they'd walked down. He'd prepared the route, he'd been careful to know every street they'd walk down. Average residential area, between four and seven people at this time in the afternoon, quiet but not too quiet. Only two streets over from the main road, to say nothing of the two skilled, crossbow wielding assassins he paid to follow them along the rooftops. His eyes quickly assessed the possible threats an old woman sweeping her porch, two children playing with a stick and ball, a man with a wagon full of old fruit trying to pull it out of a muddy rut in the road. As he turned back to the direction they were headed, there in middle of the road was an old woman. The same old beggar he had seen across the street from the merchant house where he'd been paid for his shipment of slaves. She must have been at least fifty, caked in mud and entirely covered in foul smelling sack cloth wraps. Here she was sat cross-legged in the middle of the road, smiling up at him. Diaus spun around and stalked carefully towards the old woman, his rapier pointed at the old beggar woman. She smiled at him, it was a warm and friendly smile but something in it tickled uncomfortably at the nape of his neck. He noticed almost absently as she smiled that her teeth gleamed, pearly white and not the teeth of beggars at all. She nodded at Diaus in a friendly manner "Diaus Komarr, are you lost? I never thought I'd bump into you, all alone in a strange city in Takal?" The blood drained from Diaus's face as the melodic voice washed over him and a sudden realisation hit him. He looked at her eyes, those shining bright green eyes boring holes into his soul. He stuttered as he tried to speak, "Princess? I don't, I mean I didn't... Surely you aren't?" His thoughts were all crammed into one as he stared at the foul-smelling old woman and his brain raced to catch up. He'd met Princess Annia of Hven several times, when his sister the baroness had thrown her famous balls. The Princess of Hven, a city that had now been ruins for decades, had usually been in a shining silver and blue dress. She would wander through these balls looking bored listening to people trying desperately to impress her, to get a story to tell back home. That they'd talked, danced or shared a story with the Princess of Hven, the heroine of the war who'd helped bring down the Witch-Queen. Royalty of a dead kingdom, who'd led an army of elven and dwarven allies against Deathmount's western flank. Splitting the Witch-Queens forces in that horrendous final battle and making the gap that her husband Hanalan Harpsong the famous bard had snuck his small strike force through to kill the Witch-Queen. Chosen of Necirate, Goddess of beauty and nature, one of the three founding members of the men of the sword. A chill like pure ice ran from Diaus's neck to the base of his spine as his brain caught up with his eyes, "men of the sword?" It came out like a question he hadn't meant to ask, "they're... you're... real?" He stuttered and spluttered the words. With a voice like flat iron the Princess responded mechanically, "yes. We are." In an oddly fluid movement, she unfolded as she stood with incredulous agility and waved her hand mumbling quietly to herself. The sack cloth fell away and fizzed out of existence and the dirt faded and, in its place, stood Annia Harpsong, chosen of Necirate, Princess of Hven, hero of the war, founder of the men of the sword and murderer of slavers. She must have been six feet tall, although in this moment, Diaus thought she looked taller. Clad in sky blue plate mail tinged with white and in several places' small symbols and icons of Necirate bloomed like flowers and a flanged mace clinked softly like a musical instrument against her armoured thigh. Her regal and elegant features were unmistakable; suddenly, angular, graceful and somehow given more gravitas and imperiousness with the framing lines of age. Her once raven black hair was liberally streaked with white and grey especially at her temples and sat like a monochrome waterfall mounted atop her head and bursting at the seams of a simple strand of gold like a thinly wound crown around her temple. The simple gold strand held back the cascading waterfall of her hair like a line of thread plucked straight from the weave of fate, attempting against the odds to hold back the tidal wave of history and inevitability and somehow managing to do so. Her eyes shone with the power of a personality that Diaus feared alone would burn him to a crisp.

This woman had commanded armies, been touched by Gods and had saved the world. Diaus wondered how many elves, men, orcs, dwarves and goblins he'd sold into slavery over the years, how many kobolds. Thousands? Tens of thousands? Had this woman, this hero, this glorious and terrible icon possibly killed more people than he'd sold? As the stories told Princess Annia had swept across the western front of the Takalan military machine like an avenging angel. That she had marshalled her forces with a subterfuge that belied their inferior numbers, hiding wizards, sorcerers, witches and warlocks in amongst the clerics and fighters, That she had invisible rogues, thieves and assassin's pour out of the lines and sew chaos in the enemy forces. It was said she destroyed the western front with a ruthlessness her husband, her fellow men of the sword founders couldn't match. They were boys playing hero, this was a woman who had been robbed of being Queen showing the world what a glorious and terrible Queen she would have been. Diaus found his rapier was suddenly so heavy, laden with the guilt of Annia's eyes on him it lowered with his arm, its tip practically in the mud as he squirmed to avoid the Princess's gaze. He looked at his sword tip, buried an inch in the mud and he realised suddenly he was on his knees. She had cowed him with her presence, with the weight of her history and her legend simply by standing before him. He dared look up, if for no other reason than to see what he was sure was the killing blow. Annia was looking down at him, her green eyes suddenly as soft as fresh green grass in the morning wind and suddenly she looked sad and tired, the grey in her hair more pronounced and her face soft and warm and peaceful. She smiled at him, and he found his stomach tightening, he longed to explain himself to her, explain his guilt and rage and fear. To somehow explain to this living legend how he had disappointed his mother, his sister and his poor father. He'd always hated his father, thought him weak and soft because he never fought, he never argued or raged or stood up and took charge. All he did was laugh and tell stories and urge his wife to tell tales of her adventuring days. He looked up again at Annia and saw her silently mouthing to him, "it's okay, Diaus let it out." To his own shame he realised his face was warm and wet, the soft warm salt of his tears touched his lips and decades of shame and regret washed over him. He blinked his eyes clear enough to see and looked up at the Princess, "I... I'm sorry." He saw her nod gently at his words and a voice at her ear angrily growled "he'll hang, I don't care how sorry he is." The Swordlands accent was thick and peasant and bristling with rage. The Princess sighed "yes, he probably will but that's why we need to show him kindness now. The price will be paid, of course it will but when a man is on his knees we have two paths, the sword or the open hand Kerwin. Steel is to change the situation; kindness is to change the world. You would do well to remember that, unless you plan on never making a mistake." Through tear blurred eyes Diaus saw Annia unfold as she rose from kneeling next to him to turn to the Ranger, clad in leaf motif leather with a glorious elven bow strapped his back and a look of barely contained rage on his face. The human ranger's rage, much like Diaus himself, wilted in the face of the Princess Annia, part mother, part Queen, part soldier, part healer and seemingly made of steel. She had cowed them both with nothing more than a look and a gentle touch. She called to a young dwarven warrior named Shana or Shuna to clear things up and as she turned away the job done. Diaus, still through blurry and emotionally overwhelmed eyes, could swear he saw this legendary hero sag. In that briefest of moment Annia's armour seemed not a glorious plate armour of glory but a suit of steel that sat heavy on her shoulders. Gone was the Queen, the soldier, the chosen of Necirate and the legend. For the briefest of seconds, she looked tired, a woman in her mid-fifties, greying, weary, putting everyone's needs before her own. Just a woman who missed her husband, her daughters and the life she had desired. Annia had looked over her shoulder and seeing the flash of pity in Diaus's face as the impossibly strong dwarven woman had pulled his shoulders painfully into restraints Annia had smiled a soft, empathic smile of camaraderie. It was as if she in that moment had understood his rage, shame, guilt and fear. As if she had spent months lying awake at night punishing herself for all the mistakes she had made. In that moment, in that brief, singular moment, Diaus felt a kinship with one of the greatest heroes he'd ever heard of. He knew her power, knew she could have turned him to dust and ash with a single spell. Instead, this hero who saved the world in her youth had treated him with kindness, softened her allies and given him dignity and patience that he himself didn't think he was worth. Diaus's mind cast quickly and briefly over the highlights and lowlights of his life, and he sunk into himself with a singular thought, "what have I done." If they had been listening, Kerwin and Shuna would have heard the small fat human sob, quietly to himself.

Annia, for as long as she could remember had longed for quiet, for peace, all she'd wanted was some kindness, some peace and maybe someone to tell her everything was going to be okay. Necirate had been her Goddess because of her belief in what growing up in the Swordlands seemed an impossible dream, peace. She'd prayed to Necirate for years to save her mother, her brothers and her sisters. She'd prayed for the power to change the world; she'd prayed for the strength to protect and save her sisters from her father. She hadn't, two of her sisters had died from the abuse by her father King Troom-Djerc of Hven, the scourge of the Swordlands. He was the man tipped to unite the Swordlands under one banner, a military genius with an incomparable army who had laid terror upon his daughters, his servants and his subjects. He was a ruthless and cowardly man who had been born to the largest kingdom in the Swordlands, inherited his father's endless resources and squandered them on his twisted and evil dreams. Troom-Djerc in reality, though it had taken Annia years to uncover the facts had killed, tortured and conscripted innumerable slaves to build his empire. He had lied and cheated his way to nearly conquering the Swordlands when Annia, in her youthful wishing that some young hero with blonde hair and a gleam in his eye would save her, had fallen in love with Han. Hanalan Harpsong, in his youth had been a callow, mildly foolish bard who found the right way by choosing every wrong way first.

Harpsong eventually learned over the years that wisdom is the result of a thousand wrong choices and learning along the way. She was eighteen, Harpsong was twenty, they'd have stolen moments here and there, the silly bard and his drunken Swordsman best friend had, as people in the Swordlands ended up in those days gravitated to Hven. The Swordsman was said to be unbeatable, most assumed due to the stories of his prowess. Beneath his flip nature Harpsong was a young man who was desperately lonely and lost and seeking an anchor, someone to be the flagpole to his flag. In those early days Annia had worried that he loved the story more than her. Hanalan Harpsong had been an idiot, but an honest one. He'd loved her doubts and fears and worries and her steel bound need to save her mother, her sisters and her kingdom from her father. She'd been smuggling people out of Hven long before it fell. Her father, his cronies and his press gangs had been riddled with her spies, agents and invisible soldiers long before two drunken adventurers had shown up determined to earn the King's approval or his daughter with acts of heroism. Of course, she loved Harpsong, he was beautiful, hilarious and his heart was as pure as fresh fallen snow. He was also a moment of opportunity and when Troom-Djerc had offered him the hand of his eldest daughter in exchange for tears from the Goddess of beauty. Annia knew, her love and her Goddess would not let her down. Necirate tested the young man's love for her and when it proved true, she shed him the tear, Harpsong returned with the tear and won her heart. This would have been the end of her plan. Her fathers plan though, almost ruined by the purity of Harpsongs love and the simplicity, of the God's understanding of human complexity. Her father, Troom-Djerc had accepted the tear, given the bard her hand in marriage and arranged a royal wedding. Harpsong, as clueless as he was, had gone along with it all not knowing the King had promised his future son in law to the necromancer Vidar of the Spiderwood who was as it happened the brother of

Barvara the future Witch-Queen. Vidar had access to the under-world and the dark pit of the lost and damned. This was the source of unlimited power and had made a bargain with Troom-Djerc to fuel his domination of the Swordlands in exchange for the blood of a family member. By marrying Annia, Harpsong had unwittingly volunteered to become Vidar's first Dasi-Widow. A spider made of black necromantic magic, cast with the material component of one living soul. This creature, able to birth hundreds of Dasi-Spiders the Dasi-Widow was proof of a sliver of the power that could be gleaned from the pit of the lost and damned if you could only open a portal. For now though, it was the damnation of a young bard whose only crime was falling in love. Doomed if not for The Swordsman's misdirected rage; Troom-Djerc had said The Swords-man would be taken to sign his papers allowing him safe passage in Hven, in truth he'd been taken to the slave pens. Realising at the last moment what was happening, The Swordsman spun around, slew three guards with one of their own swords. He'd slipped out, fought and disappeared into the city. Annia didn't know exactly what happened but as the legend went, The Swordsman marched straight to Daravan, the only Swordlands kingdom with a hope of standing against Hven and slew the King's personal bodyguards, demanding to lead his armies against Hven. Whatever happened in the months after he left Hven, The Swordsman returned at the head of an army of allies who razed Hven to the ground, The Swordsman came hunting Harpsong, determined to slay his former best friend for a betrayal he had imagined, in thinking Harpsong complicit with Troom Djerc's imprisoning of him. The Swordsman found Annia, her sisters and mother and his rage and vengeance melted in the face of the Princess, who led them out of the castle, with The Swords-man slaying several of his own army to do so. Upon hearing Harp-song's fate. The Swordsman and Annia immediately leapt upon a horse and rode straight to Vidar's Spiderwood to attempt to save

Harpsong. With the aid of Annia's powers granted her by Necirate they saved the bard. Hven was razed to the ground by the opposing armies. The trio fled and started an adventuring company smashing slave caravans across the Swordlands and so the folly of Hven created the men of the sword, a group dedicated to freedom for slaves, for everyone. A role Annia took very seriously, even now.

CHAPTER 7

In Death's Shadow

Strangled howling deep in the night startled Lucia awake. At first, she wondered why she was so cold, then slowly the last few days unravelled in her memory and the terror, the pain washed over her again. She had to admit, as startled as she was to realise it, she was also thrilled by the excitement, the danger and her response to it. Her mind pushed moment by moment, through everything that had happened from the screams of the dying to the tearing of Barsaw the stable hand's neck. She had struggled to sleep since then despite the running and hiding constantly, every time her eyes closed, she heard the cracking, popping noise his neck made when it snapped. She found though, the fear had been replaced with anger in seeing her friends and neighbours suffering so. Then the guilt, at surviving, at being so excited and proud of herself for holding her nerve in the face of such horror and for every time she had wished something would happen. She had wished for anything to take her away from Mar-thatch and the apple orchard that had been both her home and her prison for as far back as she could remember. Strong, but not as strong as her sister, all Lucia wanted was to forge her own path in life. She wasn't as clever or strong or studious or dutiful as her sister and her family had always let her know it. She would have given anything not to hear how she never measured up to her sister. She had promised herself after her sister left that she would run away to Valenstorm and then Vandarn beyond and maybe lose herself in the Swordlands as soon as she could, she just had to convince Arlo to come with her. She glanced over at him, exhausted, sleeping and pale. The guilt washed over her again she'd all but convinced him that soon they'd leave the valley together and start a new life and now what was left? If they survived this, it was unlikely there would be a valley and Arlo would no longer be torn between her and their community that she so desperately wanted to leave. Lucia watched almost envious of the serenity on Arlo's face to distract herself from the noises around them that made her think those things must still be hunting them. She had no idea what undead forces of darkness wanted with a couple of runaway teenagers with no more knowledge or influence in the world than a new-born lamb. As that thought crossed her mind, she heard the odd arrhythmic march of the dead shuffle and stop nearby. She held her breath and as slowly as she dared, moved over Arlo and placed her hand as gently as she could over his mouth to prevent him making a noise should he awake. There was a sudden clanging noise and another grouping of foot-steps as Arlo's eyes popped open wide, and he found himself staring into the face of Lucia. Inches from him with one of her hands over his mouth and her finger up to her pursed lips. Silently shushing him, her eyes glued on the ledge above them where something was clearly going on.

As marching footsteps led arrhythmically away Lucia mouthed silently to Arlo "they're leaving, they haven't detected us. Don't move I'm going to check." With that she scurried acrobatically up the embankment, remaining inside the bushes with her muddied face deep within the shadows of the brush. Lucia made not a sound, agile as a cat she lithely slipped between the branches and not so much as a footfall or a single leaf rustle from her. The half rotted, viscous, oozing, shadow-filled dead lumbered back and forth along the road. They seemed to have no interest in the river or the embankment that she hid within instead they appeared to be heading with purpose in the direction of Mar-Thatch. Returning she surmised from some mission to the west, maybe Lucia dared to think they weren't looking for her and Arlo at all. As silently and acrobatically as she had slipped up the hill, she returned to the brush-covered river's edge and almost silently whispered close enough to Arlo's ear that she could feel his pulse quicken as she closed. "They're leaving, they don't seem to be looking for us at all. If we just wait another bit, it should be safe to leave." She realised her heart was beating fast again, her breath heavy on Arlo's neck and ear. It occurred to her she could almost hear his heartbeat and just the sense of his eyes on her made her turn slowly around to look into those large blue eyes which were normally so full of hope and joy. Now they were wide with terror and rimmed with red from tears. Still, she felt the hair on her neck prickle and rise and a slow rising rush of blood course quickly through her. So quickly she felt almost dizzy as she fell forward and slid her mouth over his only to taste both of their tears mingling together. In that moment all their combined fears and trauma from the last few days washed away as they both clung desperately to feel something that wasn't pain or fear even just for a moment.

Arlo awoke as a small breeze blew past; Lucia still unconscious in his arms huddled under the embankment. He shivered when he realised it had gotten dark while they slept and even the thought that they had been asleep here for a few hours made him worry how close they may have come to discovery by those things. He looked around and saw nothing of note, heard no noise but the wind in the reeds. Carefully and as gently as he could he disentangled himself from Lucia and swallowed a breath when the moonlight hit her slender, powerful naked form as he disentangled himself from her. He pulled her clothes over her to keep her from the wind and slowly, as quietly as he could, lifted himself up to peek over the edge of the embankment at the road to Lucia's parents orchard and their house. There was nothing but gently blowing grass and trees in his entire line of vision. He turned back down only to see Lucia looking up him, having woken she had turned into a crouching position and was poised in case of danger. Arlo noted her naked body again her dress having slid off into the mud and tried hard not to stare. Lucia looked around at the empty, open plain and with a hoarse whisper said, "We should go, now while the road is clear." Arlo swallowed, louder than he had intended and replied "but, what if they, if those things are hiding out there?" He looked around furtively as he spoke as if by looking around quickly enough, he could shake the trees and empty them of hidden dangers. Before he could react, Lucia had leapt up onto the road, still crouching and in the shadows of the bushes they had been hiding beneath, In a fluid movement she slipped her now damp and mud-stained dress overhead and lifted a small, sharpened stick in a defensive posture. Arlo had not seen her sharpen it, but the stick looked as though she had spent some time preparing it. Lucia saw him looking at her hastily crafted shiv, blushed slightly and shrugged, she'd spent a large part of the last few hours sharpening it on a rock while Arlo slept. She nodded towards a large heavy branch nearby and Arlo dutifully picked it up. It may just be a hunk of wood but swung with those corded farm boy arms Lucia bet it'd hurt even one of those shadow zombie creatures that had been hunting them.

Lucia and Arlo kept to the shadows, with their jury-rigged weapons close to hand and proceeded low and inconspicuous. The silence not just around them but between them was awkwardness mixed with trepidation. Arlo's head was on a swivel as his eyes darted from shadow to shadow, expecting horrifying death to leap from every dark corner. Almost the opposite and uncharacteristically, Lucia had nothing to say, and slinked along silently, sullen and in the depths of a struggle that appeared to have her distracted more than was healthy. Arlo stopped at the edge of the trees only for the distracted Lucia to crash into his back, he spun alert, fearing danger behind them and found only Lucia, her face dark with worry. He looked down suddenly full of concern as a miasma of worries, fears and doubts flashed through his mind like a cacophony of terror both real and imagined, "what is it Luce? What's wrong?" His voice trembled as multiple fears floated to the surface, was it him? Was it the imminent fear of death? He felt foolish to be worried about petty romantic concerns when death was literally stalking them from every angle and his blood rushed to his cheeks as he thought of it. Lucia lifted her eyes and stared straight at Arlo. "Everything. Everything is wrong Arlo, I wanted to leave the valley but not like this, I wanted adventure and excitement, but I didn't think of the cost. I wanted you to leave the valley with me and see the world though I never thought you would! And now? I feel almost like I brought this on, like this is my fault and now we must run, even just to survive and the weight of it all, it's just too much." She shook her head as if to shake the negative thoughts out and stared up at Arlo as he smiled and said "it's okay Luce, we're together and we're alive. Let's get to your home and hopefully find your parents and some horses." He squeezed her hand three times in that familiar way he did, as much to reassure himself as her and pulled her along as they breached the treeline and ran for her parents' barn. A quiet whinny from within reassured them that the horses were still okay and that perhaps the creatures hadn't made it this far out. Even Arlo, normally like a lumbering Ox, maintained a level of quiet as the two approached the main house that even a mouse wouldn't be disturbed by their passing. Lucia took the lead, eager to see her parents were okay, she slipped up under the window and popped her brow over the sill. The windows steamed up she could make out her parents sitting at the dining table, her heart soared to them sitting up and moving with no sign of intruders anywhere. Her eyes widening in excitement, Lucia seemed to momentarily forget herself, the situation and the inherent danger around them.

She leapt to her feet and like a puma bolted past Arlo who had barely moved his arm to stop her before she thundered through the door loudly exclaiming "thank Vandarn you're safe!" suddenly pulling up, her face transformed from delight to utter horror as Arlo looked on. Both the heads of her parents turned slowly and methodically towards her, as Arlo peered through the doorway he could see the semi-detached jaw of Lucia's father, filled with more of that oozing shadow as it hung in a terrifying grin spilling oozing shadow onto the table as the head turned. Noticing Lucia was frozen in terror a myriad of emotions fighting for dominance on her face Arlo rushed in to throw himself between her and the advancing thing that was once her father. His tree branch made an almighty cracking noise as it connected with the skull. Arlo it seemed did not in fact know his own strength as the semi rotted head of Lucia's recently dead father flew from the neck, exploding shadowy ooze all over. Ooze that turned to shadowy mist and dissipated the second it left the body. The shadow, still attached to the neck, tried to form around the head for the briefest of moments before it realised there was no head to attach to and as if the sudden realisation had reached the rest of it the body simply collapsed. The shadowy ooze slithering out and turning to mist as it left the corpse. The gasp from Lucia was almost as startling as the way her father's skull had snapped off his corpse and flown across the room. The disembodied skull kept blinking repeatedly in disbelief as the light slowly faded from its eyes. Arlo turned to face Lucia as in the moment the realisation that despite the circumstances he'd just hit the rotting, undead form of her father in the head so hard it had come off. Lucia screamed. Arlo thought at first it was at him until he felt the lunging of Lucia's mother at his back and was barrelled over by the unseeming strength of her. He felt her bony hands and elbows pressing down on top of him, clawing at his shoulders and back as a dark inhuman noise rattled out of her rotting jaw. He felt the hot foul breath on his neck as she tried to bite him though her rotted hanging jaw would not clamp on his neck. He felt the weight of her being lifted from him as Lucia tried to pry the undead corpse of her mother off Arlo's back. Straining against her slight frame, she provided enough leverage for Arlo to roll over to his back and push his legs up under the things midriff. Arlo pushed hard and felt the overly rotted corpse ripping at the pressure of his knee. Panic began to set in as the near bisected writhing body of Lucia's mother started to split, giving the top half the room to lunge at him. Dropping his branch, he lashed out with his hands grasping at her wrists to stop them lunging at him.

He caught the first arm in his right hand and clutched at it hard, his left hand shot out and missed; Arlo opened his mouth to scream but a hot burning sensation in the soft flesh of his throat stopped his breath from coming. Instead he heard a soft, wet ripping and gurgling noise. His scream was etched silently all over his face as the undead, bony, clawed hand tore deep into his throat while Lucia stared in frozen horror, watching as the spark disappeared from his eyes. The entire situation was like a bad dream, Lucia stood there frozen trying to lift the thing that was once her mother off Arlo. Watching in terror as it had ripped out Arlo's throat so casually and suddenly it slowly started to turn its head almost impossibly towards her. Lucia recoiled from it, dropping it onto the now prone body of Arlo, slowly it turned and began a rhythmic, steady crawl towards her, its body torn into bits it still came relentlessly crawling, dragging its legs and smashed pelvis behind it. Its rotted head lolling absently in some grim death mask of her mother's face it narrowed the gap between them. Still stepping back Lucia took up a knife from the table and prepared to defend herself, just then the dark shadow in its eyes seemed to pool and it looked at her with recognition. For a second that seemed like an age it stared at her and tilted its head in that way her mother would when she was thinking until suddenly with a shake it roared with inhuman rage and resumed its slow charge towards her. Lucia knelt on one knee as it closed on her tears falling from her face as she reached out and whispered, "I'm sorry mother." The knife wasn't sharp, but Lucia knew more than she should how to use it. Plunging it into the skull of what once was her mother right through the temple, burying the blade halfway into its skull. Like blowing out a candle the thing simply went limp, the black oozing shadow pouring out of it and turning to mist until all that was left was the rotted corpse of her mother. The decapitated head of her father rotted on the floor and the still fresh corpse of Arlo lying in a pool of his own blood with a look of horror frozen on his pallid and cooling face. Lucia fell back onto her rump, pulled her knees up to her chin and hugged them tight and silently let the tears come.

CHAPTER 8

Even in dreams

He had been lost for so long that the last few months or years had been a blur. There was a time once before, long ago when he had been lost and he had found himself drawn to Kuvhne. Affectionately known as the Bandit Home, a sprawling walled city of lawlessness run by the gangs that inhabited it. The biggest amongst them being Basner Vas, a thief, bandit and mastermind who had turned this cesspool into a political force. Before the war, the Witch-Queen and everything else that had happened, as a young man The Swordsman had intended to lose himself in hedonistic abandon. His younger self had thought everything of value lost and gone there to drink and fight and die, to lose himself in the stink of lawlessness and violence, so drained of hope had he been. Harpsong had come to find him, the bard Hanalan Harpsong that had once been his best friend and constant companion. The bard and his wife Annia had found him, deep in a drunken stupor and working as an attraction *'the drunken blade'* they'd called him. They'd charge people two silver to try and slay him and when they came at him, even in his inebriated state as they would lunge at him, he would almost instinctively lash out with his sword. Sometimes he'd wound people, sometimes worse and yet they'd keep paying their silver and barely aware he'd swing his sword in finely honed instinct. To this day he had no idea how many he'd slain in the weeks or months that he was there, how many he'd maimed or injured during this time. It wasn't the only time he'd fought without thinking, without due care and attention. He would have sleepless nights where faces would appear to him, faces he had no memory of but knew in his heart they'd met their end on his sword. It had been so many years since he heard his name, since anyone who had known him could recognise or remember him. He'd sat in a room with Harpsong and heard the bard talk about him, tell stories of him as the 'Unknown Swordsman' and yet his old friend would look right through him, unable to see him or to even recognise him. No one ever did, the halfling, Akarash or even the mad wizard, none of them could see him as more than a random stranger even for a second. People he'd spent half his life with, fought with and bled with would look at him even if he stood in front of them telling them it was him grasping for a name he couldn't remember. They would look at him like he was a mad stranger, speaking nonsense at them.

He remembered that day in the aftermath of the great battle. The great war ended in a massive spanning clash between armies as they had invaded the Witch-Queens fortress. They had smashed the gates and with spell and sword, had broken the last defences of the Queen and her deathknights. Crushed the Takalan army and met on the battlefield at the foot of Deathmount where they clashed in one last huge crescendo. The Swordsman remembered to this day the look on his wife's face as Deathskull, the Witch-Queens half-demon son and leader of her deathknights crashed into her. He batted her sword aside without effort and ran her through. The Swordsman had seen red, charged forward swatting aside some soldiers on his way and clashed with the giant half-demon, the Tilak blade feeding on his rage and fuelling it at the same time. The huge, barbed sword of the over seven-foot half-demon came arcing round diagonally, a spray of Jaria's blood following with it as it swung wildly at The Swordsman. Side stepping, The Swordsman quickly slipped his blade against his shoulder and using the momentum of the blow he was blocking pirouetted around the giant half-demon, his blade following him in a dramatic sweep and taking a chunk of Deathskull's neck bone with it. With an inhuman roar the giant half-demon rolled back and pulled his sword up hilt first to block the blow he knew would be following up. Instead, the pirouetting Swordsman kept spinning round and with the magical sword in his right hand, sliced a gash in the half-demon's thigh. The still pirouetting Swordsman thrust the Tilak blade from behind piercing Deathskull's chest with the tip erupting from his breastplate. In disbelief the giant half-demon, The Witch-Queens son, Deathskull himself, fell to his knees, seemingly dead, falling forward with a thud as he planted in the earth. The Swordsman went to rush past when his foot yanked out from under him, Deathskull leaping to his feet, flinging The Swordsman half-way across the field of battle before charging after him. His sword lying nearly six feet away in the mud, The Swordsman tried to clear his head from the blow it had just taken against the rock underneath him as the giant half-demon roared its way across the battlefield at him. The giant, barbed blade whistled down at him and almost on instinct he rolled quickly out of the way. As he rolled past the giant form of Deathskull he kicked out at the half-demon's leg with the ball of his foot and with a crunch the half-demon faltered and fell to a knee. One more full roll in the dirt and he grabbed a discarded battle axe bringing it up to block the backswing he knew was coming. The giant, barbed, black steel blade hit the rock in the ground and split it with an almighty cracking noise. Dropping to a knee from the kick Deathskull grabbed his sword with both hands now and reversed the swing. Aiming straight where the puny

Swordsman was lying, cursing as at the last second the human pulled up a battle axe to block the blow. The non-magical axe shattered under the heavy, two-handed backswing but it bought the human essential seconds to leap out of the way and flip over with a spinning move. Like a dancer, covered in mud, blood and all the horror of the day, again the human faced off against the half-demon, as light as a ballet dancer, black tilak blade back in his hand, swinging gently as if ready to spar with an ally. If Deathskull didn't know the man's wife lay dying meters away he'd swear the human was enjoying this. The infuriating little human swung his sword a few times with a look on his face that brooked no doubt if there was any fear in him, it was not showing.

With a wide swinging motion Deathskull moved slowly, steadfastly forward deep whoom, whoom noises coming from the motion of his blade. Deathskull approached the little human, who's limbs seemed to be thinner than the giant blade that was rhythmically whirling towards him. Deathskull twisted his bone and night black skin into something approaching a grin as he prepared to unleash hell on this human. The Swordsman began to laugh, it was deep, guttural and primordial. This wasn't a laugh of humour, like he'd heard a joke from a great master bard. The humour, if there was any was mirthless and cruel. Suddenly Deathskull saw The Swordsman for what he was, a weapon wrapped in human skin, a creature that fought with more than training and skill but with a natural almost to his core instinct for combat. He realised in that moment The Swordsman's eyes were on the blade; he was humming along. Seeing what was coming Deathskull reversed the motion of the blade and reared it into a criss-cross pattern blocking the leap before it started. The Swordsman leapt anyway, humming as he did in rhythm with the swords motion, pirouetting through the sky as if he were dancing with Deathskull's blade. The half-demon tried to alter his motion but before he could the leaping Swordsman had spun, leaping past the half-demon's whirring, barbed blade and the black, legendary murderous Tilak blade had been plunged to its hilt in Deathskull's chest. The Swordsman dove past rolling back to his feet, unarmed again and light footed as if he hadn't moved, he flicked another discarded weapon (some dead deathknights barbed blade) with his foot and caught it as it flew into the air, ready almost at once for the next round. Deathskull looked down at the pommel of the Tilak blade, a green and blue painted world with two swords plunged through it, one the tilak blade, the other Deathskull had never seen before. He wondered in that moment seeing the symbol so close, what was that other blade? He looked up at the human who by now had realised Deathskull would not respond and whose expression had changed. The cocky, infuriating, insufferably smug Swordsman looked sad, almost empathetic towards him as he struggled. Deathskull dropped his sword which splashed heavily in the mud. The Swordsman realised in that moment the fighting had stopped around them as everyone had stopped to watch the two generals and a pallid silence had fallen over the battlefield at least in the vicinity of this fight. Deathskull fell to his knees, arms hanging limply by his side. The Swordsman walked up to him calmly, measuredly and placed one hand on his shoulder nodded solemnly at him and yanked the Tilak blade out of his chest. Deathskull's last sight before his eyes closed (so he thought) forever was his own black blood spurting out of his chest, coating the black Tilak blade which radiated with a feeling of endless lust for demon blood temporarily waned as it feasted on his. That moment would haunt the half-demon for the rest of his days because as history soon learned he did not die that day; not him.

No sooner had he pulled the ichor-coated blade from Deathskull as for the second time today the giant half-demon flopped over in the mud. Without even acknowledging the delight of the blade as it sated itself on demon blood The Swordsman spun on his heel and ran across the battlefield. His heart pounding in his chest, as much from the adrenaline of the fight as with the terror of the wound he saw Deathskull inflict on Jaria minutes ago. Weaving and ducking through the fighting he slid the last few feet through the mud, blood and rain on his knees, before scrambling over to where she lay prone. Cradling her in his arms as a small group of his friends and soldiers flanked around him, though with the fall of Deathskull the tide of the battle seemed to be beginning to turn. None of this mattered to The Swordsman however who had his Jaria in his arms and was softly calling her name. She looked up to him, the light in her eyes fading and grabbed a handful of his hair in a vice like grip and dragged his head down to her ear, "don't you dare wallow. This isn't about me and you, this is about the thousands who followed us into this. Get up. End this." In his mind's eye The Swordsman felt a flicker as she spoke, almost like there was a tiny gap in the memory in his head where she had said his name before her voice picked up again. "You finish this, you'll survive, because it's what you do and when it's over, don't you dare wither away. Live. Just live, you might not have earned it, but I damn sure did. Live for me my love." Her breath gurgling as she finished, Jaria sighed, in a way that ripped his heart asunder, her final breath was the exact breath she made when she was overwhelmed by love. He knew it should have brought him comfort, in this moment though it just brought him rage. He could remember every aspect of that moment beyond that one simple moment when she called his name. Her hand released its grip on him, and the light went out almost at the same time the entire sky went dark as clouds black, and grey lit up with blood red lightening. A hand on The Swordsmans shoulder spoke his name and the same blip in his memory happened where his name should have been. He looked up at the unnatural magical darkness highlighting the sky with blood red bolts of lightning, he looked from the sky to the battlefield, looking for the familiar sparks and explosions of magical combat. Seeing the gate to Deathmount and the flashes of light as the cloud of sorrow and fury parted from his mind and he recalled the small group led by Harpsong who snuck into the castle. Sneaking in under cover while The Swordsman led the armies with the Crown Prince Branthar and the old paladin Varan Arfiran. Gently he laid his beloved's head on the ground and looked around at his men, "you look after her." His tone would brook no disagreement or objection. He wiped the Tilak blade on his leg and turned on his heel and sped off at full pace towards Deathmount his friends and the Witch-Queen herself. His memory fogged and swirled; he heard the Witch-Queens final words in his head. The bard Harpsong and the paladin Arfiran seemingly unconscious or dead. The two most powerful wizards he had ever known, the mad wizard and Akarash Beliheim, bound in some kind of dark dimensional fog that looked part mist, part liquid oozing as it held them from a dark rift at her back. "You pitiful fool, you think you can march in here with your armies and your swords? I have mastered the realm of the damned! What makes you think you can even reach me with that blade? Godsblood steel or not, you'll die where you stand, and my kingdom will str..." And the halfling stabbed her in the back. The Witch-Queen's face froze in a look of incredulity as she struggled to process what had just happened. The halfling, Tatral Valenstorm who was an explorer and saw himself as a glorified cartographer with a nice dagger, had just killed the most powerful being on the planet. The halfling screamed, the Witch-Queen gasped and like a bad dream come to life she slowly melted into the same black liquid smoke that she had called forth from the rift and all of it, including the remains of the Witch-Queen were sucked back through the rift as it shrunk and disappeared with a light 'plop' noise that undercut the weight of the moment. The Swordsman fell to his knees as the darkness that had hung over a decade of his life, his friends' lives, his wife and nearly every single person he had known just ended with the most ridiculous of noises. Laying on the ground clutching his weapon arm, the dagger clutched in his fist in obvious pain the small halfling looked over at him and asked confused "is that it? Is she gone? Is it over?" Varan Arfiran and Hanalan Harpsong started to stir at the halfling's words and looked around confused at the scorch marks in the ground where the Witch-Queen had stood. Someone was laughing, The Swordsman realised it was him. The two great wizards slumped on the floor where they had fallen looked at him in puzzlement as the laugh turned to a roar as all the rage, frustration, fear and every blend of emotion that had been corked inside him for so long erupted in howling laughter that seemed to come from his very core. Valenstorm sniggered, the great wizards and Harpsong started too. Eventually even the paladin joined in the deep booming guffaws of the great, grim knight seemed in his mind's eye to shake the room and there they stood generals, Arch-mages and heroes. The leaders of this revolution and the men who had just ended the reign of the Witch-Queen Barvara were laughing, exhausted and not even sure why. He felt the tears on his cheek and the burning in his lungs as he laughed himself raw as the memory pulled back into the mists of time.

The Swordsman's mind tumbled through the years like he was trapped inside his own past without ever knowing really who he was, like a stranger looking over his own shoulder at everything he'd ever done. Inexplicable choices that he couldn't understand, barely remembering the man he'd been when he'd made them. He would land in memories of him when he was young, so much buried rage, such directionless chaos that he would rip like a wind through the lives of others sowing chaos like a tornado then strolling away. He had been so angry and never really known what at. The haze of drunkenness and combat, wine and blood mixed as intoxicants in his memory as in his sleep The Swordsman would flinch in embarrassment and shame at his younger self. In his sleep he mumbled audibly, "no brains, all heart." And a coughing fit followed, with a thud he woke up, having rolled off the small anonymous mattress onto the wooden floor. He blinked, coughed again and popped open an eye. He had no idea where he was or even when; the days had blended into one another again. Scraping his feet across the floor he pushed himself up against the wall into a seated position and sighed heavily, his right hand reaching out casually for the Tilak blade and feeling its presence as his fingers brushed it. He glanced over at the sword and back at the empty, tiny room he was sat slumped on the floor of. Everything was anonymous, unadorned with life or any personality, as his eyes scanned the room he scoffed. He recalled the aftermath of the battle, the emptiness he felt and the feeling that haunted him that he should have died in that battle. He felt cheated to have survived and the more everyone tried to celebrate him, the worse he felt. Like he was living someone else's life he felt so heavy, so burdened and he didn't see himself as a general, a hero or a soldier. He was a rogue, a sellsword and a wanderer who lived his life by whimsy. Now he was the most famous face on Karn, and he wished, how he wished he could disappear. If he only knew the levels to which Barvara had threatened not just the land but the heavens and the boon, he would be granted by the mysterious God known as The Hidden one maybe in hindsight he would simply ask that he could rest. That he had died in the battle, or one of the hundred times since that he'd felt a blade swing against him.

He sighed and looked at his shadowy reflection in the dark window "Who was he? This man I used to be, reckless adventurer or great hero? I don't see either of them in the mirror just a sad old drunk who can't seem to die." He eyeballed himself in the window with regret and a small ember of bitter rage. "Why won't you let me die?" He asked himself as the tears came and the hollow empty hole that seemed to be all that was left of him welled up inside him and threatened to consume him. He gripped the Tilak blade suddenly angry at the freshness of his memories of the life he lived before and the people he'd lost, and he felt the blade try to soothe him as the Witch-Queens words echoed in his mind, "Godsblood steel." The soothing waves of calm coming from the sword were lined with something else, something he could almost taste; The promise of a purpose.

CHAPTER 9

The edge of darkness

Three words Ander Halfsword would never forget. "Can you kill?" They were burned into his mind, not just a question, a mocking slur, a threat and a promise of vengeance. He was supposed to flinch, he was supposed to die in that moment, no more than seven years old in a gutter in Port Darkness. He was tiny even for a starving halfling, sewer rat in a city with thousands of starving, homeless children of all kinds. He struggled to remember what it was about. A chunk of mouldy bread or cheese he thought. He remembered the brute's face, that sneering tone at this tiny bag of skin and bones with a hawkish nose but like every single person before and most of them after, the giant brute had underestimated one thing; Ander's survival instinct. This was long before he'd adopted the surname Halfsword, when he was just a whelp, sired to starve and die under the grinding heel of the boot of the Takalan Empire. Dispassionately, he sliced the brute's throat and watched fascinated as the man's lifeblood had gurgled out there in the gutter and mingled with the sodden dirty street, diluting the gutter water as it did. Ander was fascinated, he was elated as he calmly lifted his mouldy prize from the corpses hand while prodding it with the dagger, he'd lifted from the brute's belt to cause the threat. "Can you kill?" The large man had asked, "yes," thought Ander, "what's more I enjoyed it." He had gone through the large man's pockets thinking on what to sell, the dagger was going nowhere though it had taught him for the first time in his life that he did have a talent. With years and training that talent would become a skill, killing was the only thing he had ever truly enjoyed. He didn't see it as wrong, he didn't even see it as murder, though he was not averse to it. Combat, swordsmanship, and killing? To Ander Halfsword they were an artform. He remembered the first time he ever picked up a sword, that tingle of excitement that shot up his arm like the first time touching a lover, there was nothing to describe it that matched that feeling in him. Like breathing fresh air for the first time. Absently he lifted his sword, its gleaming edge was sharper than any blade had right to be, his most prized possession and his dearest companion. He sighed and looked past the blade at the pale and sickly elf at the other side of the fire. "We had a job Aera. Keep to the job, what do I always say?" He scoffed at the elf, he was never sure if she was listening to him or the voices in her head. Her head never moved, she stopped as if in conversation with some unseen person and intoned in her whispered melodic voice, "keep to the job." A giggle escaped her lips but as with everything the elf did it was off, unnatural, and trilled like the death rattle of a songbird. "A black wave of darkness is coming Ander; we don't want to be in its way. However..." She left the rest unsaid, but the halfling understood. "However;" he repeated, "if we wait and we play the situation right we can swoop in during the confusion, kill the halfling and take the dagger." Ander stared again at his sword; he didn't like it, but he'd seen that face on Darkhorne before, it brooked no argument. Ander knew she tapped forces he didn't understand, had no desire to understand. As he looked from the blade to his forearm, his hairs standing on end as goosepimples ran up his arm he knew, though he couldn't explain why, but she was right. If there was any sign of some impending attack, of an army of shadow and death approaching he couldn't see it. Only the foolhardiest of soldiers would begin an attack at The Edge. The campsite at this tavern held hundreds of adventurers from the fresh faced to the battle scarred. Ander looked around at over a hundred supper fires as adventurers of all types from all over the heartlands and beyond. Some oozed magic both items and spells and others with shiny new backpacks and untested steel. Attacking one adventurer would be trouble attacking four or five hundred packed and ready to go out into the world would be ill advised. He turned back to the elven witch and nodded, "okay, so what do we do?"

Tatral sighed, his private office (outside of his private chambers) was the only room he could really be alone. He absently rubbed his weapon arm; it wasn't even really aching but after so many years it was as much for comfort as to ease any pain. He looked up so much he felt his neck creak with the strain. "For a human Akarash, you are far too tall. Tell me again, you need my dagger? Someone was asking about the dagger recently. I think? Akarash, would you sit down!" He shouted waving at the empty chairs in the room. The wizard sighed, "I told you Tatral, I'm not actually here, this is a projection. I'm on an entirely different plane of existence and it is far too early in the day for you to already be this drunk." The judgement in the wizard's tone was like a cudgel to Valenstorm's already swimming head. The Wizard's voice boomed on "and I did not say I needed your dagger, I said you might. I had a premonition; a great darkness is coming, and you are in danger. Find your dagger, find some of your old companions like the bard or the paladin. You are clearly no longer combat ready." The wizard stared with a pang of guilt at the halflings arm and softened. "I just mean to protect you Tatral, we all owe you a debt, I owe you a debt and what you did can never fully be repaid. Just be careful, keep safe and if all else fails, hide." Tatral looked up at the wizard and saw love and what might have been a tinge of fear in his eyes and sighed "That's just it Akarash, I don't have it. I lost it years ago when I killed the dragon." He pulled his eyes from the Wizard's gaze, feeling Akarash's ire raise again as the wizard spoke "you lost a Godsblood blade, fighting a dragon?" The exasperation in the wizard's voice was all too familiar. "You never cease to amaze me halfling, but that makes it all the more serious, it's the blade the darkness is after, there are only a handful of them in the world and the darkness has only the memories of the dead to find them." The wizard sighed again softly. Be careful my friend, my spell's time is at an end I will try to contact the bard, he can protect you. The image of the wizard faded and to the empty room Tatral Valenstorm said, "it fell in the river. I didn't realise the dragon was dead and by the time I did, well, it was gone." He looked around as if the empty room would answer him and sunk into his chair. He looked at his hand scarred and burned from that defining moment not just in his life but in the future course of the Heartlands of Karn and fear and sorrow draped over him again. His hand shook as he reached and clasped the heavy gold goblet. He tensed it for a moment till it stopped shaking and took a deep drink as he closed his eyes and tried hard not to think of the past or the future. Tatral burped and looked back into the huge goblet and decided just for fun, he'd include the present. Sometimes it's best just not to think too much at all. He lifted the goblet drinking deep and again closed his eyes.

Darkel Morefrow lingered at the edge of the campground, he had slipped away from the party after dinner. Talk of adventure, excitement and all the heroic deeds they would perform and dangers they would face turned his stomach and he felt himself going pale at the thought. He had no love of danger, no desire to rush headlong into the wilderness and seek out dark caverns or wake ancient evils like the fools he had befriended back in Vandarn city. Necessity had caused him to flee the Swordlands and adopt the name of Darkel. He'd known Darkel from his youth, well enough to know no one would ever question that he was or wasn't him. Darkel's was the first corpse he'd reanimated in his quest for what was considered in some circles forbidden knowledge. He had tried to explain to the village elders when they'd found out, tried to tell them that it was for their good he did this. That he was learning secrets of the flesh that would allow him to cheat death, elongate life and even raise the dead. He still heard the screams when he closed his eyes, the threats of death and fire from friends, neighbours and even some family members were laid upon him, blaming him for everything from bad crops to unsolved murders. He'd fled with just the clothes on his back, his lab was burned to the ground with everything inside including poor unfortunate Darkel, such as was left of him. When he presented himself to the Circle wizards for training, Falner was dead and his name was now Darkel Morefrow. Falner died in that fire and would never return. Then Darkel's sister came to the towers, to learn to be a mage and return to bring honour and the power of a circle wizard to their hometown. He had thought Darkel an orphan, no family was how he'd described himself, but a sister? He had built a whole life within the Circle as Darkel, leaving that behind would mean leaving everything he's built, everything he's accomplished, and he couldn't do it. When she'd heard a wizard, a necromancer no less going by her missing brothers name was a couple of years ahead of her in the training of a Circle wizard she'd become obsessed with finding and meeting this Darkel the Necromancer. He'd fled, first to the far corners of the Swordlands before relocating to Vandarn city, the best place outside of The Takalan Empire to disappear without a trace. There he'd met Urnalk and Gormin, two idiotically naive and heroic, wide eyed fools dreaming of magic and adventure. Darkel couldn't help himself, their confidence and joy for life was infectious and despite his trepidations and his dislike for discomfort and of course most of all his abject cowardice he befriended them and cut his teeth on adventuring with them in the lands around Vandarn city. It was there that they learned of an ancient mage's tomb, rumoured to be underneath a forest to the south near the Mad wizard's wood. He nearly laughed at them when they asked if he would travel to face this danger with them. Darkel had no intention of traipsing into the wilderness to face a dark and trap filled tomb. Until he heard a young brunette Enchanter had been asking around the Circle school in Vandarn city about him. She'd somehow tracked him down again; would the damnable girl never stop? He sighed and looked out over the rolling green fields as the wind blew in from the early evening darkness towards him with the smell of fresh grass, fragrant flowers and then, rotting flesh. More in confusion than in fear Darkel sniffed the air, he wasn't sure if the others knew he was a necromancer rather than just (as he had told them) a wizard. He knew they suspected he was hiding things from them, but they were so trusting they'd never even thought to query him. As a specialist practitioner in the Necromantic arts however this smell was not un-usual to him and certainly not unpleasant. He sniffed deeply and opened his mouth to breathe in the scent as it rolled around inside his nose and mouth, he could sense the darkness. No mere spell here this had the stink of the divine, the extraplanar and something else. Something he couldn't identify but that ran through the tingling magic in the air like a spine of iron holding all this together. Necro-mancy, death and the divine all mixed together with some manner of arcane will that seemed to dominate the others like a leash on an unruly beast of burden. Darkel looked around as a halfling stormed past with dark brown hair and unflinching eyes, two magical looking swords rhythmically swinging from his hips as he did so. Follow-ing behind him a sickly-looking, paler than seemed natural elf. As she followed Darkel noticed her long flowing hair hadn't so much lost its lustre as it had been matted with small bone fragments weaved through it. She seemed blissfully unaware of as she slipped along behind the halfling muttering to herself. As if warned of his observations by some unseen compatriot she turned oddly yellowing eyes his way and smiled at him. Darkel felt his skin crawl, as if something deeply infernal had just observed him from beyond some unpierceable veil. The elf stopped following her halfling friend for a second and in a sickly-sweet singsong voice turned to Darkel "such a shame, so much potential. I would have liked a keepsake if I had time." Then as if answering some unspoken question, "I know he's not dead yet, but a girl can dream and besides, the sands are running out, no? Good luck little wizard." Darkel was about to protest, to demand answers to defend himself with some minor magic. Before he could articulate anything, the sickly-looking elf had turned away. She swept away, following the now irritated halfling back towards Valenstorm proper, muttering to herself about lovely eyes in such a way that had Darkel thinking she would have plucked them from his skull if she only 'had time.' A cold, wet shiver ran the length of Darkel's spine. He could feel ice cold sweat running the length of him as a very real chill gripped him as much from the Sickly elf as from the dark magic in the air.

Darkel turned back to the small fence and stared out at the beautiful landscape, the lush, lively grass of the rolling hills of Valenstorm and tried desperately to make any kind of sense of the odd feeling of strange alien magic in the air. A voice in the darkness called to him. A cacophony of whispers and near silent screams coalescing into a single voice that echoed in the background voices around it, dripping with shadow and malice it was sharp, female and powerful as if it crackled with lightning. "Falner, long have I searched for one such as you. One with a link to the dead, to the damned." Darkel spun on his heel thinking someone stood behind him with a start as he faced nothing but a clear dark evening sky "Who's there?" he stuttered, feeling all the hairs on his body standing on end as shivers of ice ran up his skin. He lowered his eyes to the ground where a small pool of bubbling black tar that seemed part liquid, part black oily mist. Shadowy gas started welling up in the ground before him just on the other side of the fence he stood next to. The liquid was thick and viscous, almost like a living goo that bubbled and popped, each popping bubble though would change to excess mist that would rise and dissipate from the puddle. It felt in Darkel's mind almost hypnotic as it undulated and grew and before he could process what he was seeing it started to rise out of the puddle like an odd morphing shape of ooze and mist that reeked of putrid death. The aura of rotting flesh and sulphur all around the air tasted like rot and was thick with the tang of iron on the tongue. Darkel was only too familiar with the stench as the air filled with death and rot and instead of horror or trepidation as some may. He reacted with curiosity and professional interest as the putrid pile of rotten goo seemed to form into the shape of a tall slender woman of either tholan, human or elven descent. The exacting of it was hard to tell in a figure made entirely of black viscous goo that would bubble and trail black mist with every move. The detail though was exquisite, almost as if it was possessed by a figure with heavy lids which flitted and opened as the long, languid form unfurled with glopping, popping noises before him.

Eyelashes flitted in the dark, impossibly thin strands of black liquid of unsure shape or origin. The mouth moved yet nothing happened but inside his head Darkel heard a cacophony of background voices seeming to merge into one, powerful, commanding voice with the echoes of countless others woven through it. As the dread noise of the voice echoed through his head, he realised it was not the same voice but a different, far more ancient voice of something that had never been mortal. "It is not entirely unsuitable, hold its mind in place while we explore." The echoes of the voice rattled around in Darkel's head as he attempted to move, to turn, even to scream but nothing came. He felt the sheer, overwhelming power of the magic, which was echoing through his mind, crushing him like a giant iron vice clamping down on his consciousness as the ooze lunged at him silently while a maddening cacophonous screech echoed in his mind. Arms reached out and grabbed his head as the woman's face distorting and melting before him lurched at him in a rotting, black kiss that enveloped him as black ooze slid down his throat and nose, around his eyeballs and down his ear canals as he felt the rancid slimy goo scraping against his eyeballs and innards as it filled him. His body and his mind were suddenly drowned in a sea of souls as he realised the putrid corpses of a thousand dead had filled his airways. Overwhelmed him so that all that remained was a kind of rotten primordial goo and an immense presence commanding everything, even him inside his own body as it consumed his insides and left only rotting goo behind. Finally, he could see out of his eyes again as the last droplets of black goo dripped from his orifices and turned to a wispy black mist that was lost in the evening air. His body burped involuntarily, and more black mist escaped. He felt his body stiffen but not under his command as dark, malevolent presences lurked within and reached out with their consciousness and flexed his arms and legs and fingers and toes. He felt his body start to move, awkwardly at first before getting more and more comfortable as he watched mute and helpless as he walked right past his camp and his friends towards Valenstorm, in the direction of the pale elf and her halfling companion.

Something woke Tatral, though he couldn't say what. His eye opened a sliver as he looked at the hairs on his forearm rising in warning that something was wrong. Lifting his head, he gave it a shake and looked around the room for his goblet on the floor. Laying where it had rolled out of his hand when he nodded off. He turned to his reflection in the silver water jug at the side of the room. "Now that washn't verr shmart wash it?" Tatral realised he had drunk rather more than intended, maybe the old wizard was right. He usually was. Pulling himself up to his feet Tatral wobbled slightly then straightened himself, tugging at the bottom of his shirt as he did so. He let out a small chuckle at his own ridiculousness though it rang slightly hollow in his own ears. With a sudden annoyance he swooped down and scooped the errant goblet up from the floor holding it almost as a cudgel when he arose his face flushed with the effort. Tatral looked around him at the large empty chamber and as he did on the edge of his hearing he could hear a commotion, magic and fire, shouting and the all too familiar music of steel ringing out in anger. Before he could stop himself Tatral found his legs moving towards the door, almost instinctually to run and join the fray, find out what was happening. His curiosity had always been his defining trait, his most reliable response to any unknown. The years of war though, the trauma and of course the wound in his arm that held the slow burning pain, even now decades after the act, that would define his life from that moment on stayed his hand. He found himself stopping as inside his natural courage and curiosity, fought his fear and trauma for dominance. Which meant instead of action the halfling, the man many called hero found himself rooted to the spot, unable to run either to or from the fight. Be it the wizard Akarash's warning, or something unusual about the noise of the fighting. A noise that seemed to be getting closer and had an odd one-sided noise, familiar to Tatral who himself had been in combat over the years. Had fought with most things that walked, slithered or flew and had developed some kind of sense when things didn't sound right. He felt his hackles rise and a dread feeling turn in his gut.

The door swung open with such a bang that Tatral jumped, alarmed by the suddenness of the noise. Expecting to see his town guard he was surprised that instead, that it was a small stony-faced halfling lightly armoured and wielding two clearly magical blades, one of which was so sharp it almost whistled as it swung through the air. The halfling warrior scanned the room dispassionately and his eyes rested on Tatral like a hunter locking eyes with his prey. Still unmoving, giant golden goblet in hand like a huge, bejewelled cudgel Tatral stared at the other halfling, slightly smaller and much leaner in frame than himself. As their eyes locked the younger halfling marched at an even pace across the room till he was face to face with the First Citizen of Valenstorm. Neither halfling even seemed to notice the sickly elven witch Aera Darkhorne enter the room, she paid no heed to the two halflings staring at one another with burning intensity and instead floated ethereally around the room as if she was dancing to music in her head. "My companion here is looking for a dagger, a dagger he thinks you have, Mister Valenstrom." She trilled in a slightly off-key sing song voice, "unless you have it very well hidden though, I don't think you do have it do you." The silence hung in the air with all the weight of the unanswered question as the two halflings continued to stare at one another. The tension and the hush were shattered instantly as a tall slender human dressed in Circle wizard robes that Tatral could tell even from the corner of his eye were from the Necromancy school, came lumbering into the room. Something was not right about the human though, Tatral noted there was a kind of dark, black, viscous liquid seeping and rolling around the human's pores. Still trying to keep his eye on the dangerous looking halfling opposite him, he glanced out of the corner of his eye noticing the human's eyes weren't cast in shadow. They were full of this strange black ichor, a substance that cast Tatral Valenstorm back to that fateful day, the dark portal that the Witch-Queen Barvara had opened in the dying minutes of that final battle. The shadowy part mist, part liquid was the same substance that had enveloped the Mad wizard and Akarash Belieheim rolling out of the dark dimension opened by the Witch-Queens portal. Suddenly his eyes were transfixed on this strange necromancer with literal shadows for eyes and in this instant the younger halfling armed with the swords also turned to stare at this strange shambling necromancer, filled with rancid shadow goo. Instantly a flash of gold lit up the corner of Ander Halfsword's vision causing his warriors instincts to flash and before he even was conscious of it his left-hand sword had risen and mostly blocked the older halfling's goblet. With a soft scraping sound, the goblet slid along the blade before making an even softer thumping noise as it collided with the soft side head of the younger man. As white light and pain overwhelmed Ander, Tatral seeing his moment spun on his heel and with surprising speed for his age and girth the old halfling sped across the room away not just from the shadow-cloaked necromancer but the halfling warrior too. Leaping up he slid over his own table knocking ornaments and a candelabra over as he did. Like an acrobat Tatral flipped over and landed lightly, cat-like on the floor at the opposite side of the room and turned already running for the door that led to the outer chamber, hopefully thereafter the courtyard and escape. He chuckled to himself as the bard Hanalan Harpsong's words from years gone by echoed in his ears, "remember Valenstorm! Where you're running to often isn't as important as to what you're running from!" He could almost hear the bard's laughter in his ear as they ran from merchant guards, from deathknights, from monsters and dozens of other things they often left behind them in the dust. He glanced over his shoulder expecting the younger halfling to be in pursuit and instead saw the sickly-looking High elf in pale blue robes singing wistfully into her open palm. Three putrid skulls wreathed in green flame sprouted from a small black circle of shadow in her palm. She sang to the skulls in an ancient tongue and then cocked herself sideways at the fleeing halfling and spun launching the three screaming skulls with black and green trails of mystical flame roaring along behind them. Cursing himself for a nosy fool Tatral turned and ran for all he was worth but the screaming of the skulls, shimmering and translucent as they closed around him with uncanny accuracy. All three skulls smashed into his head, none had any physical impact but the screaming which reached a crescendo as the skulls impacted, tore through his skull like a horrific bell forcing his entire head to shake and buffet under the weight of their psychic attack. At the exact moment of impact, Tatral heard voices, a deathknight who's throat he'd slit breaking into a forward camp, a city guard from a Swordlands prison he'd killed during an escape attempt and a Goblin from a far-flung tribe he'd fought with while mapping a desert. All three screaming about the lives Valenstorm had stolen from them! This caused Tatral to lose his footing and stumble forward skidding face first into the far wall with the tortured screams of the damned echoing in his head.

Tatral shook his head clear of both the screaming and the impact with the wall and rolled over onto his back. He hoped against hope he still had time to turn and run before the halfling or even worse the shadow of the necromancer had caught up to him. In the distance he could see the shadowy necromancer floating over the table he had just slid behind. The sickly elf witch stared on in fascination and what Tatral could only describe as a kind of sick wonder at the shadow creature before them. Seeing something block his vision he turned to find the young halfling, the one he now recognised as the halfling who'd pressed him recently about the dagger. That damnable dagger. He looked into the cold merciless eyes of this contract killer, and he could see there was no quarter there, no negotiating, pleading or bargaining. This was not someone who could or would be reasonable, this was a man who was like his steel; cold, unbending and unyielding. A sharp-edged weapon with a simple, painfully straightforward purpose, to kill. Tatral shrugged at the younger man "sorry kid, I don't have it. Lost it years ago. Killed a dragon with it. I'm always losing things, I liked getting treasure, never had much use for keeping it." He laughed, nervously, quietly his eyes ever on the black shadow coated necromancer, whose shadow was filling the room and took a shape he recognised. A shape from Tatral's nightmares, the shape he saw when he woke up sweating in the wee dark hours of the night. His ultimate fear made life, as the shadow grew and undulated into the same shape as the shadow the Witch-Queen cast on that fateful day. His eyes drew back to the halfling who simply shrugged and replied coldly, "then we're done here." And with that Ander Halfsword plunged his sword through the old halflings heart with no more effort than a hot knife through chilled butter.

Halfsword shrugged as he looked down at the old halfling and over his shoulder said to Aera "It's a shame. I was a big fan as a kid." He wiped his razor-sharp sword on the halflings coat, accidentally cutting the jerkin as he did before he continued "they say you should never meet your heroes. Not sure why, he was hilarious." The lack of response from the elf, the feeling of being flanked from behind, whatever caused it the halfling warrior ducked to the side and pivoted on his feet to see the shadow enveloped necromancer they had passed earlier. Both he and Aera had heard the commotion though the witch had been far less surprised than he to see shadow corpses fall upon the edge and try to breach into Valenstorm proper. It would have been a massacre if not for the ill-advised vector of approach as the shadow army rose from the ground into the face of somewhere between four and six hundred adventurers and Valen-storm in general. The Edge was a well-known favourite not just of green novices but grizzled campaigners of all varieties and some of

the most powerful people on Karn could be found eating mush-
room soup on the edge of this vast campground. What should have
been a sudden and devastating assault by a shadowy undead force
found itself overmatched by grim scar-covered barbarians, wizards
dripping with magic and bards and rogues. Also, with what looked
like an army of servants of Vandarn from paladins to priests who
all rallied together. The adventurers had pooled their resources and
struck swiftly, brutally and innovatively to smash the spine of what
would have otherwise or at the other, eastern edge of Valenstorm
been a much deadlier assault. The necromancer's hand lashed out at
where Ander would have been and was batted away by his sword. A
couple of fingers were lopped off and as the severed digits tumbled
to the carpet, he saw the shadowy goo that covered them slip off and
turn to mist before they hit the ground.

The shadow of the necromancer stared at the dead Tatral Valenstorm before turning its distorted features to the other halfling. With
a voice like a thousand whispers each clamouring for purchase and
wracked with pain warped into a strong, commanding female voice.
One not used to asking permission or hearing dissent, snapped out
"Ander Halfsword. You have failed, you have no dagger and no
leads. What's worse you have denied us our vengeance, a few seconds
more and the soul of the one who damned us would have been ours
to torture for eternity. By murdering him you have saved him from
us!" From behind a sickly and unsettling sing song voice rang out
"Not quite no leads mistress, we know where the dagger fell." Aera
Darkhorne with something approaching reverence in her normally
mocking tone spat out. Ander knew the elf well enough to know
when to let her speak especially on matters of a mystical nature
and simply held his tongue and his breath. "Aera Darkhorne." A far
more inhuman voice intoned from the shadows "You are a perfect
vessel. A servant of the pit and one who's manipulation and control

over it is proficient enough not to be consumed." Another voice more cacophonous and rage driven responded, "At least not immediately." The head of the shadow-tinged necromancer turned slowly and completely wrenching backwards until Ander was looking at the back of its head while it turned as if on a swivel to stare at the sickly elf. "Yes." The powerful female voice intoned, "she is somewhat perfect isn't she." Without another word the shadow seemed to seep from the necromancer and slither across the floor to the waiting Aera who unfolded her arms and welcomed the shadow with a near tantalised glee. The shadow slid up, in and around her leaving behind the husk that was Darkel Morefrow or Falner depending on when you asked him, his jaw hung limp and his eye sockets were burned out with nothing but whisps of smoke. All that lingered was a strange, charred smell that reminded Ander of barbeque. Whatever had been possessing him was no mere shadow, it had been something powerful and clearly with more than one voice. Ander looked from the husk of the Necromancer, that appeared to have been used up and burned out with the effort of containing the power of the entities within for what must have been no more than half an hour. With trepidation Ander wondered as he turned his head from the charred remains before him to Aera, how much of her could survive any length of time with this immensely powerful force possessing her body. As she lowered back to the ground and opened her eyes though it was Aera's off-key singsong voice albeit with the cacophony of disparate whispers behind her that spoke. "We have other opportunities for the Godsblood weapons we need but we should dispatch forces to the dragon bridge, find the dagger in the river. The City of Valenstorm is of no use to us, no purpose in throwing souls at it. There is The Swordsman, the tholan wizard and of course the barbed, Demonsblood blade of our son. A Demonsblood blade would not open the portal, but it could return our son. They say his soul is with Dracor but that God killer will not deny us him if we have his blade." Aera's head tilted to one side as another voice within her head, that of one of the inhuman things within growled furiously "what of the halfling? His failure should not go unpunished?" For what felt like the longest second of Ander's life there was silence as some internal struggle played out inside Aera's head. Finally, Aera's singsong voice led the cacophonous chorus of torture with "he is valuable to us, we shall keep him alive. For now. Come Ander, we have work to do." With that the possessed figure of the witch spun away and swept out of the room with such a subtle change in gait that Ander could not help but notice the slouch was gone and instead was a proud and regal bearing, striding confidently. Ander looked down at the corpse of the First Citizen of Valenstorm and shrugged "Sorry old man, but it sounds like I saved you from an actual fate worse than death." And with that the younger halfling spun and followed Aera out of the room. As suddenly as the shadow army had fell upon Valenstorm it was gone, leaving corpses in its wake. For their part the adventurers and people of Valenstorm fared far better than the shadows by sheer weight of the power and number of adventurers on site this evening. A targeted attack had however punched through both the outer city wall and the central inner wall to pierce the grounds of the First Citizens estate. The main doors were smashed and the personal guards of Valenstorm lay dead in the wake. One of them having been ripped physically to pieces and the trail of destruction telling of the heroic last stand of those guards through the halls right to his private office which was in tatters. The burned corpse of the necromancer, kneeling with its neck broken and wisps of smoke coming off it still lurched over the curled corpse of the great hero, adventurer, explorer and halfling Tatral Valenstorm who lay dead, in a pool of his own blood.

Tiny twinkling blue lights shimmered in the air near where Ander Halfsword had stood just before, next to the charred and burned corpse of the necromancer. The sound of a thrumming harp undulated with the glow and ebb of the lights until out of the brightening lights formed the shape of a human. He was no more than his early thirties with short chopped blonde hair and shining smiling blue eyes. His armour as his weapons and small collection of musical instruments were all lightly adorned as he winked into existence, long sword already in his hand. Seeing the corpse of the halfling before him a tear rolled down his cheeks and he fell to his knees. Swiping the Necromancers charred corpse to one side to make room, he gently unfolded the halfling to lay him on his back and laid the halflings hands across his chest. Slipping his pack off his shoulder he reached in and muttering to himself, fished about for a short while before lifting out a large, flawless diamond. "You know old friend; I don't normally keep these just lying around. Akarash did say come prepared for anything though. It seems as usual the wise old one's guess was right. Now let's see, this will take a while. Preparing the area and the halfling, he placed the diamond in the corpse of the halflings clasped hands. For nearly an hour the bard fussed and fidgeted around the halfling before pulling a small harp from his side and finding just the right tune he smiled wistfully and sang "So we sing our friend to rest, we ask you stay for one last test. We would ask and call you to come back to home, you need not travel this journey alone." With the small song ended a large wind blew through the office curtains and tablecloths blowing and the diamond being blown out of the halflings hands as it crumbled to dust and blew away in the wind and the fingers in the halflings empty hands slowly began to twitch.

"Easy Tatral, rest easy. I have pulled you back, but it is not a spell I cast lightly." The young blonde bard smiled down at the older Valenstorm. "It was lucky Tatral that I was able to redirect myself so quickly, that I had the necessary tools to get here and bring you back." The old halfling opened his eyes and smiled "Hanalan Harp-song, bard of the realm you've spent so much of your life looking after me, yet you look less than half my age? Still you're sweeping in to save me from myself and my folly. Tell me bard? What did you wish for when the Gods came calling after what we did on that day?" Harpsong laughed "Ever the inquisitive eh halfling? Yes, my vanity won out and that's why you look at a man so young and you Tatral, what did you wish for little one?" He raised an eyebrow already knowing unspoken the answer the halfling would avoid. Looking up from beneath heavy lids the halfling smiled "I've always been lucky Harpsong, you know that. It's my impeccable..." The Old halfling stopped to cough loudly and prolongedly before continuing "timing." The two chuckled before the halfling rackingly coughed again as the bard slumped exhausted against the table from the exertions of using so powerful and dark a spell.

CHAPTER 10

City, Country, God

Vandarn City, capital of the kingdom of Vandarn, a state built upon the service of Vandarn, the God of justice, duty and skill. Built by tradition, by the ancient and hierarchal Church of Vandarn. Historically it had been a place and a society of tradition, Kings followed the word of the church, and the church followed the leadership of the Kings. Hand in hand the state worked with very little structural change and with Kings, royalty, nobles, merchants, workers and peasants through the generations, all knowing their place in the structure and build of society. Rarely with any fluctuation, other than the adventuring classes who would come from any walk of life and often would step out of the traditional hierarchy of Vandarnian society by means of power, combat prowess or mystical means. Historically, as a Church the Vandarnian religion was archaic, patriarchal and xenophobic in its traditions, in its power structure and in its influence over most parts of society in the great, expansive kingdom. Church knights, an ancient order and military branch not just of the church but traditionally also the kingdom were an important part of this structure. They were fierce, religious warriors who marched on orders of the church but equally under the banner of the King as the titular head of state and church. This meant any division of church and state would be hard to define. The lines of government so closely intertwined with religion for hundreds of years, until the Witch-Queen invaded, slew the old King and claimed dominion over the land. In those years of war and rebellion the Witch-Queen's occupying forces in the city of Vandarn were under constant siege and guerrilla assault by a once great mercenary warrior named Stee Jahns. A man whose force would, during those years of war and rebellion, work hand in hand with the church knights under the firm unflinching leadership of the mountainous paladin Varan Arfiran who was their leader at the time.

Disillusioned with both the paladin hood and the church in the aftermath of the great war, Arfiran resigned his place as head of the knights just as the church, knights and all found themselves in need of more political than military leadership. What had followed in the years after the war was intense wrangling between the church and the civic council. The council had been created by the New King to give voice to the common people of the kingdom, the merchant and noble class had always held influence over the city and kingdom's finances, and the powerful State Church of Vandarn. The church had for too long been both the largest political and military influence in the kingdom. With the new King, also a trained church knight, they saw a chance for a renaissance of church power in the kingdom in the wake of the Witch-Queen Barvara's devastation. What they got instead was a King who had spent his formative years traveling the road as a penniless adventurer surrounded at eye level by poverty, suffering and the poor who had been hardest crushed by the invasion. This was a king determined to redress the balance of the common folk of his kingdom, who had been ground under an ancient, theologist, patriarchal system for far too long. A reorganisation and a reshuffling that the King had found nigh impossible, encountering a sea of bureaucracy that rose against every change he tried to make. Older, wiser and more subtle than in his youth, King Branthar Vandarn had turned into something of a political animal, meeting cunning not with the sharp of his blade but his wits, and endless committee and council meetings were where he excelled in the modern City. "The secret," he had once told Arn with a wry smile that had more than a hint of the young man he had bled beside on a battlefield of death, in a storm of demonic clouds all those years ago, "is patience. Wait them out. It's the only way you can defeat your enemies in a council chamber."

The modern Vandarn was an alien place to Arn, having spent so many years on the road he realised every time he came back that he had become a stranger to the city, to his people and to the very principals he had once swore to defend. He had to return to Vandarn to give his report of what Joselyn and he had found on the Takalan border near the half-demon's old fortress. The reports of Deathskull's end had been accurate, there were no armies amassing within Takal and it had been safe to assume the claims of peace and promises of non-aggression were to be believed and had the ring of truth to them. Then they passed the Quotiy Swamp Forest, a place of legend where it was said the Godslayer Dracor had slain the God of death and disease. The God's murder, spilling the pestilent one's blood into the forest turning it into a putrid swamp of warped, magical horror where hideous mutations and monsters grew in the sick, dark swamp that the forest had become. As they passed as close as they dare, on guard for some of the horrors that could sneak out of the swamp if you wandered too close, they saw it. A slow-moving army of undead of all shapes and sizes, as if the corpses had risen out of the ground cloaked in an odd kind of shadow that seemed to morph and mutate between mist, fog and liquid as it oozed and twirled between states. With a shape and darkness that Joselyn had never seen before and a seemingly uniform but unusual intelligence, that army of shadow cloaked undead had turned towards Takal and only a small force on noticing them had hunted them back across the plains.

On the way into Takal when they had passed the wide empty plain that had been one of the largest battlegrounds of the final days of the war, Arn's already usually stony face had grown grim and dark with the memories of his previous visit here. Haunting memories of standing on the battlefield, clad head to toe in plate armour, shoulder to shoulder with armies of his countrymen. Shoulder to shoulder with his friends and people from all over Karn who having been backed into a corner and ground down under the boot heel of the sheer Takalan military might and had nowhere left to go but to fight back. Arn was the closest to a traditional military leader the combined amalgam of armies had mixed in with mages, adventurers and people from all walks of life. Hopelessly outnumbered by the giant faceless armies of the Takalan military machine, headed up by their Skull mask clad deathknights, their black blades and skull masks made in the image of their own leader. The half-demon son of the Witch-Queen herself, Vanyusa Deathskull. A beast of a humanoid standing over seven feet tall, his head, skull shaped and a sickly white colour with dark, shadow filled eyes and his giant Demonsblood steel blade, barbed and almost unwieldable by anyone without his unnatural strength and sheer demonic power.

The battle had raged for three days, spanning miles of arid and lifeless plains all the way to the river that sat at the foot of Death-mount where those dark final moments had played out. Where they had watched a hole ripped in the universe that would have summoned something world ending from the depths of some dark pit where Barvara had been drawing power. Like all who were there at the end, he would be haunted by the memories of what he saw in the days that preceded it, by the deaths of thousands on that battlefield both at his hand and by his side. Haunted by all that he saw in the final moments and the warped and sick darkness when he stared into the tear in the universe. He had been flattened by the power of the Witch-Queen and watched helplessly from the floor, alongside Harpsong the bard as the Unknown Swordsman had faced off against her. They had watched sluggishly from the floor as the halfling did what they could not, accomplished what the great and the good of the world could not and ended the life, the doom and the power that the Witch-Queen had wrought. With a dagger of Godsblood steel he'd proven himself in that moment the bravest and truest of them all. For all his greed, his foolishness and his apparent cowardice. It was not the great paladin, the master Swordsman or the almighty mage that ended the war but the little, chubby, doubt and fear laden thief who with one fell stroke had saved the world. Arfiran's shame, his guilt that washed over and through him in that moment would haunt him till the day he died and when the Gods themselves came to those who had brought forth this rebellion against the darkness and asked, what boon would you ask for saving not just the world but the heavens above? Arfiran had asked in that moment the only thing that possessed his thoughts. Wisdom, the wisdom to know what was right, to see the false for what it was, the vainglorious and the shallow. For the wisdom, the insight to know right from 'good' as boons go, it was as much curse as gift for he could see the short sightedness, the selfishness and the folly in others as much as in himself. He resigned his commission, left the church, the army and the service of the kingdom, though not his God he served humbly as a soldier. The greatest military leader in Vandarnian history, now under the pseudonym 'Arn' was a scout. Though they may have thought that a mountain of a man who looked more wall than soldier could not hide, that he did in the Vandarnian

Civilian army keeping the outskirts of the kingdom safe, far away from the politics and the strife.

Joselyn shivered, more from the memories of the last week than the rain, standing at the main gates to a city she'd sworn her life and fealty to protect. All her life she had dreamed of being a church knight, like heroes in her childhood stories, valorous and steadfast, bastions of faith and guardians of the realm of Vandarn against monsters, demons and evil. Her apprenticeship wasn't going how she had expected, politics and dogma, changing rules and a time of internal strife in the church. When the opportunity to be loaned out to the Vandarn civilian army and work in the scout core as an apprentice came up Joselyn leapt at it. The idea of being out in the frontiers and seeing the edge of civilisation had been a thrill she longed to experience, a fulfilment of her childhood dreams. Joselyn had felt at times in the chapter house where she had been training to be a church knight, that her progress had been stymied and she had been overlooked again and again, all of which made her think that maybe she could get out there and see a little of the world. She hoped that if she could find some adventure, she would then be able to return with pride to the Chapter house and be taken more seriously on her journey to become a great church knight like in the stories she was weaned on. When she moved to the civilian army commanded by the general Stec Jahns they had all called her a 'church' type, it was clearly some kind of slight from those who considered themselves 'crown' soldiers. Joselyn often wondered if that was why Arn took her under his wing, the giant paladin had been the unironic definition of both a church and a crown soldier. For all she had come here to serve City, Country & God Joselyn had to date only ever been inside the city of Vandarn once. The sheer size of the place was overwhelming, and she had barely scratched the surface in her only visit. All her life she'd heard great stories of the grandest city in the world, quite the contrast from her upbringing, coming from the quaint and idyllic farmland of Valenstorm and its provinces with a pest of a little sister and doting parents. All she had wanted was to join up and be part of something greater and here she was, having raced across wastelands and wilderness, chased by some unheard-of form of undead with a grizzled and experienced old man who had become not just a mentor but a kind of father figure to her. Joselyn had run the gamut of emotions with her superior in the beginning, never really knowing how to take the mountain of a man. Grim and gruff with very little patience or need for comfort. His steady measured approach never seemed to alter pace, but his kindness and his gentleness radiated from him with every interaction especially with those in need, or those who were hurting. For a greying man-mountain who had obviously seen more war than she could imagine, Joselyn found Arn often woefully naïve. As they grew closer though, it occurred to her that what she saw as naivety was in fact a deep wellspring of hope that people could be better than they are.

At that moment, Arn stormed through the main gate, his face foul and covered in fury, grumbling to himself as he approached. "Damn fools, years and politics may change but a fool is still a fool." Shaking his head as he approached Joselyn who handed him the reins to his horse without a word while the old man continued to rant quietly to himself. "The King is too busy with matters of state to concern himself with a band of undead on the borders of another kingdom, especially one going in the opposite direction." Arn growled. In Joselyn's mind the words "king" reverberated. She had thought Arn going to speak to some official, soldier or politician but the King himself? She side-eyed the old man, "you eh, you know the King well do you Arn?" A sly smile played on her lips as she unconsciously tapped her fingers against the symbol of Vandarn that was hidden beneath her shirt collar. Without reacting Arn marched on his horses' bridle gripped like steel in his fist, she imagined if the horse had fought him, the mountainous paladin would have dragged it all the way out of the city. His boots pounding the muddy road he continued to rant, he might as well have been talking to the horse as Joselyn for all the attention he paid to her. "The boy becomes more politician every time I come here; you'd think I was some errand boy bringing missives about tax reports! Surrounding himself with soft handed, soft-spoken snakes who are more about coffers than competence!" He stopped so suddenly that Joselyn nearly barrelled right into him, her own horse taking a moment to realise they were stopping and yanking on the bridle as it nearly walked past her before stopping. The face radiating off the old paladin was inscrutable. Joselyn waited for the next revelation to come from him and just as she finally opened her mouth about to say something he exclaimed "Akarash" with such suddenness that again Joselyn involuntarily jumped. She looked at her mentor as if he'd sprouted a second head before replying to him "Akarash?" He smiled broadly at her and nodded. "Akarash Beliheim, one of the greatest wizards that ever lived on Karn. He is almost definitely still alive, he used to advise the old King and if anyone can get through to the King that something serious is happening, it'd be Akarash. It's not a short ride, all the way across the Swordlands so we'd better pack well and get ready." Joselyn's incredulity hadn't shifted an inch. "The Swordlands? I know who Akarash Beliheim is Arn, every child in Vandarn does but aren't we overreacting? Rushing across the land to find a hero of legend to tell him some zombies are attacking another kingdom? Also, with all due respect, we're scouts. We're not generals or wizards or church knights, we scout, we report, and we move on. That's your words Arn, not mine. Now you want to travel the entire length of two kingdoms to find a wizard who might not even be there and tell him what? A strange dark force is invading the kingdom that he fought alongside you against?" Joselyn realised now they were shouting at each other in the middle of the main road out of Vandarn even their horses seemed caught in the awkwardness of the moment. Arn's face was incredulous as his frustration, rage and impatience fought for dominance on his face, "I... I know child. I just don't know what we do now." Arn sighed and seemed to deflate slightly. "I'm sorry Joselyn, I just feel so powerless. It's amazing how quickly our voice goes from a roar to a whisper. There was a time that my word would have been enough to raise armies and now? I can barely even get an audience with a boy I practically raised." The old paladin sighed heavily and patted his horse's neck. "I am lost as to what we do next." He looked over at her with a kind of weariness that aged him, like she was looking beneath the surface and what lay under was a tired old man. She smiled at him and shrugged. "Then let's go back." Arn looked at her with puzzled eyes, as Joselyn let out a small laugh. "Look what do we do, we scout and gather information. So, let's go back, monitor what happens when the undead forces hit Deathmount and then report back. At the very least we can be there in case they turn their eye toward Vandarn and it's a lot more useful than standing here shouting into the wind."

They stood in silence for a minute, understanding the danger and what it meant to ride back into Takal, the site of the great battle and an entire empire of people who hate the old paladin and for what? To track the movements of an army who seemed to be aiming at his most powerful foes. Joselyn climbed into her saddle and looked at Arn curiously, "so it's decided? We're going to ride into the heart of an empire you've spent your entire life fighting, to try and protect the very people who have sworn repeatedly to destroy you?" Arn chuckled along with the young woman and lifted himself into his saddle. "Well," the old paladin sighed, "no one ever accused me of being too smart" and with a wry grin he turned and aimed his warhorse north. Joselyn looked over her shoulder at the Capital city she swore her life to protect but had never really experienced and muttered "next time" to the old city, before turning her horse and following up the road north after her mentor and friend.

CHAPTER 11

Dead again

Leskat had lost track of how long he had stumbled in his half shambling march across the plains. He sometimes felt in control of what had once been his body and at other times being a passenger imprisoned in the flesh that had once belonged to him. Always though the dark shadows of other presences, something ancient and malevolent lurked ever at the back of his consciousness, a dark amalgam of thousands of whispering voices always there. Background noise that pervaded everything, like dark tendrils of distilled horror tickling the edges of his awareness, occasionally pulling at his senses and emotions almost in a kind of playful torture. With no seeming care it would pluck at something and Leskat would relive his worst moments or perhaps be overwhelmed with terror, rage and sorrow all at once. This endless nightmare had dragged so long that his own memories, his own consciousness seemed lost in this ocean of darkness. Sometimes he could hear the screams of the other corpses around him as they each lived their own nightmarish undeath trapped inside their former bodies. The dark force that seemed to move them all like pawns on a chessboard, drove them all mad with endless torture as it willed their corpses to act. Again, in Leskat's mind the midnight-black blade tore through his head and as his life seeped out of him, he could sense its hunger, its rage and its desire for combat. As passionless as The Swordsman had seemed, the sword had been the opposite, thrilling in the fight and the taste of death. That last, terrible memory working like a beacon, Leskat and the small shambling group turned again pushing towards a different direction, just southwest of the lands of Dern.

As they passed the outskirts of Dern Leskat's memory went straight to his youth. In his travels he had come to Dern looking for opportunity and instead found a place heavy in laws and light on mercy. Steeped in a harsh, strict tradition of law and punishment, intolerant of freedom and diversity, they seemed suspicious of any-one that didn't fit their view of normal. All of which meant that Leskat stood out more than he ever had in his home of Kuhvne, suspicion, fear and a particular kind of obedient, socially acceptable xenophobia pervaded like an unspoken slur everywhere he went in the kingdom. Leskat tried to push the memory to the back of his mind, but the dark tendrils of oozing black sliding through his corpse and his brain saw the memory and prodded at it mentally unravelling the memory and forcing Leskat to relive it. They had been in Dern for a month, a group of six, to call them adventurers would be too generous and thieves too mean, graverobbers and tomb raiders would probably have been more accurate. A map to an ancient elven burial site, the entrance to which was said to be near the western borders of the lands of Dern near the border of the elvenwood. They had tracked it and though they had to dig to find it, they uncovered the tomb and gained access, though one of their number, a human named Orat had fallen to a trap at the entrance. Leskat had never seen an acid trap before and had watched transfixed as Orat's face and hands melted from him like hideous gut-churning butter, leaving hideous malformed remains that haunted his dreams for months after. When they entered the tomb, they had unknowingly broken a seal which meant undead guardians raised from their rest to wreak revenge on those who would loot this sacred gravesite. Essalth, a Lizardfolk Cleric from the Mountain Marsh, stood firm in the face of the undead, his faith in Necirate the Goddess of Beauty and Nature resolute and steadfast right up until they ran him through. Essalth died incredulous, burdened by his failure and doubting the strength of his resolve in the face of ancient elven evil, the Lizardfolk's innards spilling across the tomb floor. The other four survived, Leskat being able to slip in and out of the tomb in the confusion with enough speed and subtlety to fill his backpack full of treasures, leaving with gold and gems enough that the endeavour wasn't wasted and the deaths of his companions didn't feel like a folly. As Essalth lay screaming into the darkness facing his end, Leskat rushed out of the rear room, urging his friends with obvious alacrity to flee the tomb before the undead guardians could catch up with them. The four made it out of the tomb with inches to spare. The guardians, unable to cross the threshold stood pacing back and forth agitated like dogs pulled back on a chain, constantly straining to chase the interlopers who whooped and laughed with fear, relief and greed at their survival and the bag full of goods that had been retrieved. If only they knew the horror that awaited them as they made their way back to Dern.

Proximity to the Tilak blade shook Leskat from his memory, from the return to Dern, the accusations of tomb raiding, the words "lesser races" being pointed at those of his group not wholly human or elf. The last memory that played across his senses was the grinding, stretching, creaking noise as the noose had stretched his neck. His disbelief as he woke among the pile of corpses discarded for dead. The fact he had survived the hanging (however barely) had either been missed or considered unimportant by his captors. Those days were the darkest of Leskat's life, the torture, the hanging and the slow, fingernail crawl through the rotting corpses of his friends and the things he did to survive in those moments were the most awful, soul and stomach turning of his life. None of which matched up to his death, rotting and trapped inside his own corpse as the plaything of some unspeakable evil which delighted in toying with him as some kind of undead slave. As one, the group of shadow laden undead turned directly south, approaching the main road leading into Vandarn from Takal. In the distance was the elvenwood, Leskat noted the very tomb he had looted in his youth in the hills between there and here. Facing right towards the forest that was the border of the elven kingdom, without warning his eyes and head pivoted to the right, where a solitary horse had turned from the road out of Dern and south towards Vandarn proper. Instinctively Leskat could sense the Tilak blade and assumed the slumped form in the horse's saddle must be the drunken Swordsman that wielded it.

The sounds of military precision in movement were at odds with the slow, shambling shuffling of rotting zombie bodies. Seemingly conflicting noises lifted The Swordsman's head, hungover as it was from his saddle, a miserable reverie broken by the odd noise. The Swordsman glanced around at the road, but the only other travellers were two horses in the distance to the south. He looked casually over his shoulder to see something in the region of forty shambling corpses, moving rigidly and uniformly down the road towards him. Even in its rotted state he recognised the half-orc he had slain in Kuvhne those months (or was it weeks) ago. Limping forward with a small unit of undead at its back, focused and uniform even in their shambling. The Swordsman couldn't tell why but he knew instinctively they were here for him. Maybe it was the Tilak blade sensing something he didn't, maybe it was the tingling danger sense of a seasoned warrior alerting him of the fight to come. Either way he simply shrugged and looked around, slipping off his horse and taking his pack from where he'd tied it to the stolen horse's saddle. He dropped his pack casually on the ground and slapped the horse's rump, which immediately caused the beast to trot off back in the direction of Dern and probably from where it had been stolen. Any witness would have sworn that it was with casual disinterest that the ageing Swordsman stepped away from his pack to the middle of the road. The Swordsman set himself, drawing the Tilak blade which tingled his fingers and arm with anticipation of bloodshed and a thirst for the black shadowed ooze that he hadn't felt from the blade in years. The ageing Swordsman, with a flick of his head to clear his greying, black braid from his face, almost light-heartedly drew a line in the road with the tip of the Tilak blade, a foot in front of him and gently started to sway, like a dancer limbering up for a performance. Dispassionate as The Swordsman had seemed through all this from within his corpse prison Leskat noticed The Swordsman smile, he had seen the smile before; dispassionate and mirthless. It reeked of hollow emptiness and in Leskat's memory The Swordsmans own words reverberated: "I kind of wish you had got me." Leskat could feel his own realisation that The Swordsman longed for death seep into the black oozing shadow that were his strings, puppet master, jailor and saviour all on one. He could feel the ancient amalgam consciousness pivot inside him as thousands of whispering voices spoke as one, "so the little Swordsman wants to die? Let us grant his wish and take the blade." With which the shambling corpses sped up. Propelled by a power their limbs did not have, at speed to clash into the waiting, grinning face of the lone, ageing warrior swaying and grinning, now from ear to ear with a kind of horrific glee at the force about to clash with him.

The last few days had been strange for The Swordsman. Since the deathknight guard captain had come for him, he had spent his days with a strange sensation coming from the Tilak blade. It was exuding pointed feelings of purpose and danger and the sense that something was coming. His nights had been spent dreaming of days gone by, of the dead and the living and all of those he hadn't seen in years and more pointedly those who could not see him. In the days after the death of the guard captain, The Swordsman had moved on from one end of Dern to the other. Eventually making off as the sun rose, with a pack full of supplies and a horse that had been left unmanaged. The itch for the road coupled with that strange feeling from the sword. He rode groggily in the early morning sunrise heading for the link up with the large north/south road linking Vandarn to Takal which is where his next choice would hit. South and Vandarn where the man he used to be had many friends and foes or north to the dark and brutal kingdom of Takal, with its seemingly endless dark corners where he could hide, drink and hopefully disappear into a hole. As he sat astride the horse, he felt a thrumming excitement from the sword on his hip. Tearing his attention away from the two horses in the distance riding in his direction and turned his head north. Feeling the urge from the sword as he faced down a crowd of what looked at first like zombies until he squinted and saw a black, oozing shadow dripping from them. A shadow that was familiar and that gnawed at his memory from those years facing the Witch-Queen and her armies. He cast his eye down at his sword. "This is what you're so excited for? I know, I recognise it." Nodding to himself he slid off the horse, grabbing his pack as he did. Slapping the horse roughly on the rump, sending it back to Dern and probably its rightful owner, he dropped his pack by the side of the road. As he gripped the Tilak blade and slipped it from its sheath he felt its anticipation, excitement and something unusual from the blade, fear. The Swordsman's head swirled with a thousand thoughts and feelings at once. Realising that he was in real danger here he felt his fingers tingle as he started to sway and limber himself, something he hadn't felt in years; a sensation like waking from a long slumber as something stirred in his stomach. He felt alive, he felt awake and like his blade he felt fear pour through him like an old friend. He realised he was smiling and not the mirthless, joyless smile he'd grown accustomed to. In that moment he realised he was really looking forward to this, in a moment that could be something he'd at times longed for, an end worth living for.

As the blood flowed through him, he drew a line in the dirt road with his blade and started to sway and dance. Energised by the swinging blade which infected by his verve started to thrum with longing for the battle ahead. The ancient artifact forged in legend and the last of the three parts of its set. Forged and imbued with ancient powerful magic to be the dark edge of a balanced and powerful set with a core purpose, it's twin lost, the amulet that was the key to its powers thought to be destroyed. The Tilak blade was the last surviving artefact designed to defend the lands of men from demons and the divine alike. Trying to find purpose in a world where it was alone and directionless. It found itself not for the first time infected, guided and influenced by this human. This simple human with all his doubts and self-loathing and fear, more of what was inside than what was out. Facing insurmountable odds from a darkness erupted from the deepest hole in the realms of the dead and The Swordsman was happy. For the first time in years, he was excited, he was grinning. The Tilak blade let itself be carried along on the wave of passion and hoped this wasn't the end of its journey with this human.

The Swordsman glanced down at the Tilak blade, his grin wide as could be, and he thought, "this. This will do, come on you beauties." And the first of the zombies crossed the line. As they did, he slashed mostly through one's waistline. The blade arced up and sliced under the armpit up into the neck of another, slicing through and decapitating it. Quickly dropping down to one knee, pulling the blade through its hamstrings cutting both legs off at the knee. He leapt back to his feet with a little jump, landing into a swaying dance as he swayed back and forth waiting for the next of the undead to approach. From inside his flesh prison Leskat watched as something he'd never seen before unfurled. The human danced and spun and wove his way through eight of the undead, like a dancer who knew the moves in his bones. More importantly with every slice of the black blade on his fellows Leskat heard not just their screams. He heard the screams of the thousand voices inside, of the ancient evil that had been holding their strings like a puppeteer, the very contact of the blade burned through them like mage-fire. This seemingly unstoppable oozing shadow, burned and recoiled at the black blades touch. Whenever it touched the shadow he could hear its glee, the blade was doing what it was made for, and it thrilled in the act. By the time Leskat neared the fray less than thirty of them were left and not one had landed so much as a blow on the ageing human. His black and grey hair whirled in the wind, braids and all as he spun and danced his way like an ageing belly dancer through the throng. From inside his flesh prison Leskat could hear the human laughing, full heartfelt laughter of genuine joy. The sword, Leskat realised was not the only one here doing what it was made for. Then with the unseen eye of ancient evil swivelling on the situation Leskat heard a voice different to the one that had guided him. Something less ancient and inhuman, something very mortal turned the entire force and eight of the undead rushed at the human like a wall. The hatred this new presence had for the human was so palpable that Leskat could taste it in his soul. A throng of rotting, shadow filled bodies crashed into the human and overwhelmed him, the Tilak blade spinning from his grasp. Leskat could hear the human talking, cheerfully complimenting the undead on their efforts as he grabbed collars, skulls, whatever he could and smashed them together. Without even pausing The Swordsman thrust his thumb into shadow and puss filled eyes to grasp the skull of the undead and physically beat them together before wriggling his way out. Battered and bleeding with his clothes ripped and torn, The Swordsman retreated as the over two dozen remaining undead started to circle him, cutting him off from that magical blade as Leskat made his way round the outside. His objective clear and simple, obtain the blade while his men tore the human to pieces. The human's Swordlands accent grew thicker with tiredness and injury, but his joy was still as incessant and insane as it had been in the start. Goading the undead throng, willing them to take him if they dared. He seemed fearless, Leskat quickly corrected himself, not fearless, relieved. The human wanted this, Leskat understood, in his life he had wasted so many years making mistakes, choosing wrong things. His greed, his fear, his anger and his cowardice so often shouting down the better voices till they grew silent and the beast he'd let himself become was all that remained. Leskat thought of his youth, of the hidden one and the God of secrets tenet that the truth of our being was hidden beneath years of regret. He wished in that moment that he'd made different choices, that he could be free to learn from all he'd seen and heard since he died. His mother would have laughed, "how like you little piggy. You learn your lesson an hour after class is finished." He'd have loved the chance to prove her wrong. He saw the black blade that had slew him in the dirt and the powerful, evil woman's voice, elven and Takalan and domineering in a way he could not resist. In concert with the cacophonous chorus behind it, she screamed at him "TAKE IT!" Without hesitation even if he could offer it, Leskat reached over and grabbed the sword. He felt it burn his hand, he felt the female voice scream, and, in a moment, he was no longer in Dern. He was south of Vandarn at the head of a strange undead army lurching in the darkness, but he felt a heartbeat from himself, his voice elven and female. The attack they planned relied on killing the weak and turning them, Leskat could see it unravelling in his mind's eye before he snapped back to his own flesh prison. The black Tilak blade before his eyes as his hand raised it up to the sky in triumph. When without notice from behind a greatsword of impossible sharpness sliced through his arm, his chest and hip and clove him asunder. The Tilak blade flew from his grasp into the dirt and Leskat saw his rib cage and below tumble into the dirt beneath him.

The Swordsman felt the wave of undead flesh and bone hit him and he punched, clawed, grasped and kicked. He pulled himself up to try and see above the throng around him and just as he started to go numb, he went limp. "Finally." He sighed and let the wave start to pass over him when something grasped his wrist. A hand pulled and ripped him from the throng, yanking him over her horse's rump a young woman, clad in armour and wielding a sword with the other hand peeled away from the throng before screaming, "Arn! I got him, go!" The Swordsman cursed as he realised they were going to run from the undead, until he heard a voice, one he thought he would never hear again. A voice that wouldn't run, not when fighting was an option. Varan Arfiran, paladin, general, soldier hove into view. His razor sharp greatsword swinging from horseback he cut through the throng of undead slicing chunks of them apart. He slid off his horse and faced off against the others as they surged at him, he hacked them like ranger would a tree. Bits of shadow-soaked bodies tried to reform until Arfiran spoke some words that coated his blade in a shining white light which burned at the shadow when it struck and in minutes the throng was still. Fighting his way out of the young woman's grasp The Swordsman landed on his feet, still dizzy from the blows. "Arfiran!" The old paladin turned on him, "you're okay sir. They're gone. They're dead, you're safe." The Swordsman snorted, so like the old paladin to save someone who didn't want it, he'd rescue a fish from drowning the arrogant old fool. Sighing he looked around, "my sword, where's my sword." He saw Arfiran look at him with that same puzzled blank look everyone who knew him had, like something inside their brain was itching and his heart sunk. He realised the paladin had no idea who he was, as little idea as he had himself as to his name. To the paladin he was just a stranger in peril. Turning from Arn he looked over at the chest, arm and head of the half-orc he'd slain in Kuvhne. The remains of the half-orc were still moving, still infected by the black shadow pulling itself through the dirt towards the Tilak blade. He walked over and kneeled between Leskat and the blade. "Sorry old friend, I can't let you have that. You must have some story, if only you could tell it. To The Swordsman's alarm the disembodied corpse spoke, hurriedly shouting in the same rasping voice it had in life. "They want the blade, the Godsblood. It hurts them but they think it can free them." One pleading, rotted eye looked up at him as a shadow image of the one he'd ripped out when he stabbed the creature in the brain to kill it. Leskat, what remained of him continued, "army, south of Vandarn. Coming from Valenstorm. Please, save them. Warn them." The Swordsman cupped the rotting skull in his hand and looked with a deep sunken sorrow that was filling his gut at the torture this thing must have suffered since it died at his callous hand. "Please." What was left of the half-orc pleaded, "Kill. Me." The Swordsman felt his cheeks damp with tears for this poor thing and he gently slid the blade of the Tilak sword into the head of Leskat for the second time. The shadows melted and all that was left was the dead, very rotted skull of a one-time thief, braggart and villain. The Swords-man recoiled at the joy the Tilak blade attempted to impart to him as it slid through the rotting black shadow remains of the creature, The Swordsman, what was left of him wept for the man he'd killed twice now.

Leskat tried to open his eyes before he realised, he didn't have any. Terror took over him as he realised the sleep of oblivion hadn't taken him and he was still trapped in the dark of the afterlife. Aeons of suffering in the darkness at the hands of the ancient evils that had held him in the pit flashed through his consciousness before a voice, that was not unlike the darkness spoke to him. It was simultaneously youthful and ancient, melodic and brusque, trilling and deep but it inspired no fear, no trepidation. "You summoned me Leskat, you intoned my name before you did something unheard of in life. You sacrificed yourself and you performed one heroic act that could well have saved the world." Leskat, panic rising thought what dark force held him now but as he did, he realised it was the Hidden one. He tried to reach out but felt the power of the inscrutable God all around him. "One deed performed after death isn't enough to redeem you Leskat. I am not here to judge you though, I'm here to give you what you've earned. A chance, just that."

And with that, what had once been Leskat was gone.

CHAPTER 12

It's not the sword that kills you

The quiet, unassuming, simplicity of the cottage wouldn't have been so glaring if it wasn't for the location. At the edge of the Sword-lands, within a mile of the Dragon-Sir River and standing in sight of the dragon bridge while also being perilously close to the cursed ruins of Hven, a city razed to the ground many years before. A city that now seemed to be the ruinous home to any number of monstrous and unnatural things. Things that ambled, crawled, oozed and flew around but seemed to avoid this idyllic little cottage which stood somehow separate. This beautiful little thatched cottage with its tiny harvest ornaments in the window and its quaint vegetable garden, cabbages, carrots and potatoes all lined with a small wicker fence. As if it were somehow unseen by the chaotic landscape around it. At the edge of the cottage's small farm was a chicken run and a sizable bird house that would seem to the common pigeon more of a mansion. If Urnath hadn't met the man who lived here he would have been stunned to finally see this place, though he'd heard tell of it many times. Knowing Akarash Beliheim stood at about six and a half feet tall Urnath's first thought was how didn't the wizard constantly bang his head on the door? A door which seemed better suited to a retired peasant farmer than a worryingly tall arch-mage who, it was rumoured, travelled the planes between not just Karn but dozens of worlds and had done for hundreds of years more than most humans even lived. As Hrasse trotted up the winding path to the simple cottage it was as if the old horse knew the journey well though Urnath himself had never been there. The sound of chopping pulled the old tholan sage from his reverie as it occurred to him the wizard must be home. The rough hooves of the horse clipping up the path distracted whoever was chopping wood as with a thunk the sound stopped. Then around the corner, shirt open at the chest and sleeves rolled to his elbows stood a handsome human in what must have been his early thirties. A shock of chopped blonde hair and sparkling blue eyes that looked like water reflected in diamonds, stared up at him from above a smile that was disarming as it was distracting. Urnath felt fifty again to look at the vibrant beauty on the young man's face. Urnath gave his head a little shake and smiled back. "Hanalan Harpsong, eyes take me, but you don't look a day older than when I last saw you and that must have been twenty years ago if it was a day." The bard laughed as he wiped his brow with the back of his arm and waved his other arm as if by explanation, "Urnath you mad old tholan goat, how are you! I'm afraid if you're looking for our host, he isn't home. Many years ago, we used to work on the old man's farm between adventures. It is I'm afraid a long story and if I come here and he's not home I will generally just get to work. I came here to check up after he sent me on another errand, after all these years he still treats me like an assistant!" The broad, beautiful grin and flashing eyes of the bard were full of joy and hypnotic charm as they always had been. Urnath realised he too was smiling, and he could almost swear even Hrasse was happy to see Harpsong.

Harpsong moved over to some wicker chairs and pulled a large wineskin from a bag slung next to it before fishing back in for two small wooden cups and plopping himself into one of the chairs. "Come Urnath, sit, drink and tell me what brings you to the old man's door." A look of sorrow or seriousness must have found Urnath's face as the bard looked suddenly grave and filled the tholan's cup to its brim. Pulling himself down awkwardly from the large tholan horse, Urnath shambled over to the table grabbing at his books and packs as he stumbled into the seat across from Harpsong. Taking a huge gulp from the wooden cup, he took a deep breath before looking studiously at the bard, who seemed not to have aged a day in the decades that had lapsed since he'd seen him last. "I'm sorry Harpsong, these last weeks have been heavy on both my body and my heart." Urnath found his voice cracking just thinking about what came next, "High King Crothan, my liege has died." He reached into his robes and pulled the Godsblood axe from its folds as if offering it as proof. He felt the sorrow wave over him as he held it aloft, seemingly coming from the axe that had been with the High King for over two hundred years and the old King used to talk to like it was an old friend. The bard sipped his wine and smiled warmly at the old tholan nodding as he said, "I met him once you know? It wasn't long after we first met. The Swordsman and I were seeking aid and somewhere to hide from the Takalans during the war. We were chased all the way to the mountains and the old King hid us. We drank so much that night I thought I might expire there and then, war be damned." The bard poured them both another cup and he and the old tholan wizard talked of the High King, the war, Akarash and old times. They talked of their friendship when the bard was the age he still looked and of the bard's wife Annia, a subject which seemed to tinge the bard with the same sorrow Urnath held for the death of his beloved King.

Urnath arched an eyebrow at the bard when he mentioned Annia, "your wife..." He left the question unfinished though the bard shook his head and waved his hand. "No, no she's alive. Or she was the last time I heard, like all things my vanity was my downfall. Those of us who fought at the end, at the rip between dimensions Barvara had caused were granted a boon by the Gods themselves. In my vanity I wished based on my fears and I was granted absence from my fate. I will not age and if I avoid misadventure I will not die. That's why I look the way you remember me. I haven't aged since that day." The bard's laughter was gentle, and sorrow-filled like a brook running dry. Urnath could feel the air thicken though he wasn't sure if it was the wine or their shared sorrow and regrets mingling with the wine thick air. "Do you regret it? The boon?" He almost didn't want to ask but from under heavy lids the bard's sparkling diamond blue eyes were thick and wet with unshed tears. Harpsong stared almost hypnotically at the old tholan and sighed. "She couldn't stand it, watching me stuck in a moment of time while she aged, she said it was the most selfish thing I'd ever done and I'm ashamed to say she was right. I have a family, I never even thought of them when I uttered my wish." Harpsong paused to drain his cup before continuing. "I had chosen myself, to indulge my fear of ageing, of getting older and dying, over everyone who loved me, who I'd ever loved. I've spent years losing things, losing people. I can't remember my best friend's name because of what I feel must have been his boon. My wife could barely stand to look at me and I lost her, I lost my daughters. In the years since, I claw like a falling man to the cliff edge trying to hold onto those who still care. Going to wild and ludicrous extremes to keep the few others who still live. That's why I keep coming back here and tending to an empty cottage. I know the old man will come back eventually and before long he will be the only person who remembers the famous bard, Hanalan Harpsong. I'm a fool Urnath, a stupid, selfish fool who wished for something I should have never had. What's worse, do I regret it? Of course, I miss my friends, my wife, my daughters and I feel at times like my body is a prison for my soul. Youth should be left to the young, my friend. To my shame though, I'd choose it again because I'm still afraid. I'm a callow and vainglorious fool. It's not Necirate I should be singing for, it should be Dracor the vain." He sighed, looking down into his empty cup before refilling it, he offered the wineskin to the tholan who waved him away with a faint grin. "Crothan used to say," Urnath cleared his throat before continuing as much to block his cracking voice as to calm himself, "he used to say that the Gods can't grant wishes because they can't understand us. He used to call them foolish children with massive toys. Power, omniscience but no wisdom, not mortal wisdom at least. He hated them, all of them, I even feel sometimes he hated Thol himself. I often wondered why. At the end as he rode up that endless icy path to a place of legend to face a God, I started to realise that the man I'd stood beside my entire life had lived countless lifetimes of adventure before I was even born. He asked me to find a life, it was his final wish but all I seem able to do is mourn him."

Harpsong smiled at the tholan before refilling his cup and laughed, "it's not the sword that kills you." He intoned gravely, before raising his cup at Urnath, "to Crothan." Urnath raised his cup in kind. "Crothan" he simply repeated, his voice welling with sadness. Harpsong continued, "that's what he told us, that night in his tent, halfway up a frozen mountain drunk on ridiculous amounts of cheap Swordsland rum. He asked why we fought the Witch-Queen, a drunken thief and a shallow bard, facing down the greatest army the mortal world had ever seen. He said he just wanted to know what made us think we could achieve anything. The Swordsman, my best friend who I travelled with almost my entire adult life. The man who is like an itchy memory in my brain that I can't seem to recall, he laughed at the High King like he would a tavern clown and told him he had always thought he'd die in an alley, drunk with a dagger in his belly. It might as well have been a Witch-Queens' dagger. He'd never wanted anything, believed or expected anything from life and a meaningful death was even beyond his hope. Dying on a sword was how he always saw himself going out and he might as well have saved some lives and avenged some evil. I was so drunk I bellowed with laughter, these two grizzled warriors talking of death and doom, and I laughed. I told them both I didn't want to die by the sword. I didn't want to die at all, I wanted to be young and beautiful and drink and dance and love and laugh all the way into eternity." Harpsong stopped for a moment to take a deep breath and a long drink of wine. "I'd seen paintings of Crothan in his youth, huge and muscular even for one of your people. Long flowing raven coloured hair of most of the Crolloran, a sharp smile and bright eyes, not too dissimilar to how I remember The Swordsman in my mind's eye, if considerably larger. By this time, he was old, older than even your people live, wizened and withered but still in that giant way he had. His hands were withered and bony but still huge, akin to shaved bear paws. That's when he told me, pointing one of those huge bony fingers at me and stared at me in that moment with a look that could stop avalanches, but I'm sure I don't need to tell you about the withering stare of your King and closest friend. He said to me. It isn't the sword that kills you. It isn't the danger or the impossible odds. It's the quiet, the thousand nights of calm. Death on the sword is a mercy. The thing they don't tell you about facing down monsters is the only thing worse is learning to live without it. When you've faced down pure evil, everyday life is just a thousand quiet deaths, and the real prison is knowing tomorrow will be the same as today. I've heard your High King's voice every day since I was granted my greatest wish by the Hidden one. No Urnath, it isn't the sword that kills you. It's knowing you'll never feel that intensely again."

The old tholan had clearly been travelling long and hard and before his third cup was empty and was drooping from his hand and Urnath was snoring. Hanalan Harpsong looked at the man who in human years didn't look a day over fifty, though Harpsong knew tholans aged at a wildly different pace than humans and to nearly twice the lifespan. Lifting the cup from his hand Harpsong gently dropped a blanket over Urnath and returned to his chair emptying the tholan's cup into his own. "I'm sure you won't mind old friend if I finish the wine, eh?" Smiling at the sleeping man he tipped his cup to the watching horse and drank deep and before long ended up slipping off himself. Safe in the comfort of knowing that despite their location nothing would endanger them in the borders of the Archmage's small cottage. Harpsong's dreams were an amalgam of the years gone by, of the people they'd lost and the moments that had defined them. In his dreams he remembered feeling like a hero, that moment between saving the world and facing reality and the realisation that the rest of their lives, all their lives, would be about a moment now behind them. The biggest thing that would ever happen to any of them had already happened. Even asleep he wondered if that was why he clung to the Archmage Akarash, the wizard had been offered no boon nor had he asked. The Gods, Harpsong felt, were afraid of Akarash. A wizard beyond normal mortal power who travelled the planes as simply as one walked through a door and dared challenge the Gods was understandably terrifying to them. Harpsong knew he had clung to him because to Akarash, this was not the greatest or largest moment in the wizard's life. Harpsong knew Akarash had come from a legacy of wizards, a father who was ancient and terrible, a brother who was about as powerful as him. Akarash had told him stories though, stories which to hear, his brother was with a temper unbecoming one with such power at his fingertips. Valenstorm's eyes shone at him in the dark, scared and wounded the halfling had seemed almost sad that he had been saved. Trauma and fear of the Witch-Queen would haunt the little halfling all his days and if Harpsong was honest they would haunt him too. He had seen himself reflected in his stout little friend and that face of mortality had shaken the ageless bard to his very core. He saw patterns in it all, so soon after Akarash summoned him to aid the halfling; to find himself sharing a cup of wine with the right hand of the High King, whose words were like a portent of how Harpsong had spent the years since that fateful day. Harbouring a feeling like everything was bubbling below the surface. As if the great evil, the great war and everything before and after had been woven together like some vast tapestry of intrigue not yet completed, all of which mingled in his mind like a thick broth of memory and imagination together in an unsettling, wine drunk sleep.

CHAPTER 13

Fall of night

Lucia lay in the darkness, covered in mud and exhausted. She couldn't remember when she had last slept, beyond a few fitful hours of exhaustion when she would pass out only to be woken by the endless shuffling of the army of walking corpses nearby. She tried to cry but no tears came. She'd shaken and cried and wrung herself over the last few days, until there was so little left that she felt numb from more than just the cold and wet. Fear from more than the terror of feeling stalked by an army of shuffling, shadow filled corpses and the days and nights of exhausted, nerve-shredding terror that seemed to be the key component of her every waking minute of her existence. Every time she closed her eyes, she was back in her parents' home. Surrounded by their corpses with Arlo lying in his own blood, a strange, slow, glopping noise as his blood pooled on the floor, the only sound between her sobs as she buried her head in her knees weeping. She had never felt so utterly alone in the universe as in that moment, and she relived the feeling every time. She was back there, wishing the earth would open and swallow her whole, as her mind worked itself through the devastation at Mar-thatch. She and Arlo had watched the entire marketplace either rounded up or slaughtered by these strange undead. The harrowing escape in the direction of her parents' orchard and the horrific events that had left her sobbing in a ball on the floor as her closest loved ones lay dead, mere feet away. She recalled the feeling when the odd glopping noise stopped, and she lifted her eyes to see Arlo, his head turned towards her staring at her almost in admiration it seemed, silently mouthing her name. For that moment she had felt elation like a crescendo of a wave, before her heart plummeted back down into her gut as she saw his eyes were black and glossy, as if they were made of oil. Her eyes widened in horror as she took in the sight of his neck, still having been torn out but now filled with the same black, oozing, liquid mist she'd seen everywhere recently. For a few precious moments Arlo continued calling out to her in silent desperation, until the oozing black mist seemed to somehow assert itself. His shining black eyes snapped wide open, and Lucia could sense something else, something alien staring at her through her lover's eyes. Like a droplet of ice-cold water an almost primal fear slid quickly down the length of her spine. Lucia and the thing that was holding Arlo's corpse in thrall had stared at each other in almost suspended animation, until she leapt to her feet with surprising agility and spun on her heel and fled. She didn't look back, she didn't stop, and she didn't think of anything beyond the urgent, overwhelming need to flee, to run and to survive. She knew this land like she knew her own hand, running straight across the field and barely slowing at the trees and bushes of the orchard. She slid through one bush where she knew it was sparse, down a slick embankment into the river and let the current take her for a while before stopping by yanking on a branch in an identical way she had done maybe a thousand times before in her young life. Pulling herself up onto the opposite embankment, she had allowed herself a moment to gulp down a lungful of air noisily before she realised how loud she was being. Realised that the shadow drenched corpse of Arlo was probably stalking her even now, as their friends and loved ones had stalked each other in the village and her parents had so ruthlessly attacked them mere moments ago.

Lucia shook her head though she did not open her eyes, not wanting to relive the moment again. Every moment from that one onward had been a combination of running, hiding and feeling stalked by the ever-growing force of shadow filled corpses all around. She made her way in the direction of the village of Arnstop by the river that divides southern Vandarn from the main road to the capital City. Lucia had been thinking that next to Valenstorm the best stop would be the giant bridge that spans the river and the large public building beside it known as the Anstorm's cross adventurer's rest. A large building built by the foresting community in the aftermath of the great war, to thank the ragged group of thieves, vagabonds and adventurers who had banded together to form the men of the sword. A group which had been an underground movement, who before the war had been a small band committed to fighting slavery in the Swordlands. Who grew in the darkest of times to a force that defied the Witch-Queen herself, until they formed the core of the resistance against the invasion. Like the Edge in Valenstorm, the adventurer's rest was known for hosting large numbers of adventurers at any given time. Lucia figured between that and its proximity to the main road to Vandarn city she would find escape, help or a path to safety somewhere on this road. For days though, everywhere she turned more of the shadow filled undead appeared, gathering into groups and then uniting into a small army. When they turned north Lucia realised she had cut herself off from Valenstorm, Mar-thatch and even from turning back. With no choice but to carry on she kept her distance and found herself following their movements as a way of keeping enough distance from them, to not be detected. A couple of times she had spotted Arlo, the huge gouge in his throat filled by the same black oozing shadow as the rest of the corpses around him. Her immediate panic rising every time she saw him, as if their bond as lovers and lifelong friends would have somehow alerted the thing using his body to detect her. She felt also (she was sure only in desperation) that somehow part of Arlo was in there. A few times she saw two actual living beings, though one didn't look too far off a corpse, a sickly looking, pale, high elf in midnight blue and black robes side by side with a lean and hawklike halfling. Silently they moved through the host, though the halfling looked horrified with every step. Unlike most halflings Lucia had known, this one was hard faced with an expression akin to a mountainside that had been blasted into a scowl by centuries of harsh winds. In his eyes though, even from a distance she could see disbelief and horror and constant glances at the sickly elf by his side. Other horrors and nightmare visions from the last few days flashed before her eyes in such quick succession she ended up opening her eyes. As if the rest of her senses were sparked to life with her eyes, the smell of the rotting flesh, excrement and a myriad of other putrid and horrific odours assaulted her nose.

Lucia felt her stomach churn, she'd barely eaten and only dared drink fresh rainwater with these things trampling through every stream or river she had passed. The tiredness, the hunger, the fear and the despair held her in place and she felt the cold, wet mud pulling her down almost as if it was telling her just to lie down, give up and take an easy death. Easier than Arlo, than her parents. She sighed and felt weary as heavy lids started to collapse over her eyes, until a voice in her head that sounded like her sister barked at her, "get up mouse!" Her eyes snapped open, and she sighed again, pulled herself out of the mud and climbed the crest of the hill on her belly to observe the army again. "Joselyn," she muttered to herself, "you wouldn't be afraid, would you? You wouldn't stand for it. Probably give the fear into trouble for having the temerity to stand against you." She smiled as she thought of her older sister and felt her strength returning to her.

As little girls they had worked the orchard, fought and played and dreamed of the lives ahead of them. Joselyn had always been the good sister, Lucia had always known the shadow her sister cast would be long, would get longer the older she got. Joselyn was fearless, steadfast and honourable. Even as a child, she was stronger than most of the boys and the most natural leader Lucia had ever seen. Ever the family hero, their mother would call her 'our little church knight'. It was small wonder Joselyn had grown up to be a squire, no one was shocked when she left for the city and the chapter house of the church knights of Vandarn. Joselyn was a hero, Lucia always knew that and at times resented her for being so perfect, so flawless their parents would boast that they thought her heart was carved of oak so stout and strong she was. She had laughed at that, "who would want to be a dusty old tree?" She had giggled at her father when she heard it. Though she had recoiled when he turned his scowl on her, his arm pulled back only for Joselyn to stand between them, like she always had, jaw set and ready to take the hit for her sister. Their father's hand had wavered, and he seemed to shrink in the face of her stoic defiance. He spat at the ground "Lucia, you're no oak, you're like a field mouse, a little pest that nibbles and picks at the food then runs and hides, quick and scampering, never wanted and never of use!" Lucia had watched as Joselyn's hand balled into a fist and realised she had meant to strike their father. Lucia had screamed, in rage, in frustration and a myriad of other emotions she couldn't really understand or unravel yet. "I hate you!" She had screamed, right in her sister's face. She had no idea why, but she was beyond furious at Joselyn while all her sister had ever done was protect her and she hated and resented her for it. That was the last time she'd seen her, she had turned and ran, all the way over the hill to Arlo's where she'd hid the rest of the day. Only sneaking back after dark, her mother hadn't even waited up, they hadn't even come to look for her. Joselyn had gone to the church that night to become a squire, the years that followed hadn't been easy. Lucia had clung to the thought that one day she would be old enough to go and start her own adventure. Run away, become an adventurer, she was fast, she was razor sharp and had grown so slippery and sneaky from years of hiding from everyone that she had indeed become like the field mouse her father had called her. In her sister's letters she had always called her mouse and Lucia was okay with it, she saw in Joselyn's letters what her sister had seen. What her parents had seen as her flaws were in fact her greatest strengths.

The host of undead had stopped, the strange sickly elf standing eyes shut apparently arguing with herself. Turning to look at the halfling at her side the sickly elf said something, looked around at the army and in what seemed to be a small cloud of darkness the elf and the halfling disappeared. The army paused for a moment, unsure of what to do next before lurching forward as if some unspoken instruction had driven them on without the sickly elf to lead them. Lucia saw her chance and slipped back down the hill, finding energy she hadn't thought was within her she made for the river. Realising that if she could make the other bank before darkness, she could go straight past Anstorm and head for the city, for safety. Her legs were on fire as she ran and slid and more than once tumbled and fell down the hill. The ice-cold water that hit her as she fell the last part into the river overwhelmed her so much that she nearly let the current, strong as it was, yank her away downstream. At the last moment she grabbed one of the struts holding the bridge and held herself tight to it. Gasping for air, gurgling and coughing when water would lap over into her mouth. She cursed herself for a fool for thinking she could survive; she would drown, or she would fall into the river and hit a rock and then drown and if she survived then what? Arrive at the other side of the bridge in time to see thousands of undead bearing down on her with nothing but roads and trees for miles. It might be easier, she thought, to let the cold and the tired win. Even as she thought it Lucia knew she wouldn't, Joselyn would be furious if she just gave up and died. Slowly she tried to massage her cold and aching muscles into life. She pulled and clawed as she climbed across the outside edges of the bridge, until after what felt like an age with every fibre of her body screaming at her. By sheer force of will Lucia landed with a ridiculous 'plop' noise in the wet, muddy embankment at the other side of the great river. As she lay there gasping with a loud wheezing noise which took her a few seconds to realise was coming from her. In her head Lucia heard her sister's voice, "it's okay mouse, you're okay. You're safe." Instinctively Lucia looked up into her sister's shining eyes and smiling face. Older, travel worn, and battle hardened but she was there, crouched over her, arm held out smiling warmly "come on mouse, get up."

Joselyn reached out and pulled her exhausted sister out of the mud. Lucia looked around wildly, confused and nigh delirious with exhaustion, hunger and fear. Joselyn pulled her up and hugged her tight, if she had any doubt this was real in that moment. She knew the feel of her sisters embrace, so tight it hurt, and she could feel Joselyn's tears falling onto her cheek so tight was the embrace. An odd middle-aged man sat on a horse by the road. Unremarkable and shabby, long black hair, streaked liberally with grey and a shabby unshaven grey stubble, only his eyes shone bright and hypnotic blue like two small clear pools on a summer's day. She looked back to her sister as Joselyn's tears flowed freely and unashamedly as she held Lucia in her arms pulling back and staring deep into her bedraggled little sisters face. Her smile fading when she saw the despair in her face, "mouse? What are you doing here?" Lucia felt the tears come, what little she had left, she looked her sister deep in the eye and simply said "all of them. They're all..." Her voice trailed off into silence as her energy sapped. She nodded over at the shabby traveller and back to Joselyn. "Arn?" she said quizzically, by way of trying to avoid talking about the last few days, lest what remained of her willpower collapse again. Joselyn laughed quietly, "no mouse, just a traveller, somehow connected to all this. Arn is on his way, hopefully." With that she took her sister arm in arm and pulled her back up towards the horses where the stranger had dismounted and was pulling a blanket to wrap around the exhausted Lucia.

The stranger had refused to allow them to light a fire, but they sat by the roadside next to the two horses, blanket wrapped around Lucia as she rested. They hadn't spoken a word since they collapsed, though they ate some dried meat and cheese. Lucia drank heartily the water and then the stranger's wine. After she'd sated herself and sat in silence a while she looked down at the wineskin in her hand and relayed the last few days, ending with her last, desperate run to the bridge. For what felt like the thousandth time in the last few days, tears flowed. She looked up and stared at her sister, "so you see there are hundreds, if not thousands of them just over that hill and if we don't get out of here before they set off again? All of that running will have been for nothing." The stranger who had introduced himself as just a Swordsman, looked over the hill and placed his hand on the hilt of his sword. The sword giving off an odd, unsettling aura of magic that Lucia could almost hear. He looked back to Joselyn and smiled. "If the old man doesn't get the answer he's looking for, we might not have time to wait for him. I said coming here was a bad idea." Joselyn scowled at him and turned back to Lucia, "Arn will be here, he'll make them listen. He's the most stubborn man I know." Lucia smiled at this, marvelling at the woman her sister had become as much as the irony of her sister calling anyone stubborn. The thrumming noise from the sword became insistent enough that Lucia could now just about hear it.

The Swordsman noticed her staring and nodded, "you hear it too? Good ears lass. Excuse me a second." The man stood, stretching stiff joints that creaked as he did, he waved away Joselyn as she reached for her sword "there's only two or three of them. Scouts probably." And with that he walked down towards the river's edge, limbering and stretching as he did like a dancer preparing to perform. He was still smiling broadly and swinging the pitch-black bladed sword in his arm as he walked. Lucia marvelled at how casually he approached the river even when three skeletons, drenched in black oozing mist as much as water, emerged from the river marching uniformly towards him. Still limbering and now gently swaying and almost dancing his way down towards them, he waited for the first to lunge, its short, bladed sword thrusting directly at him. Still, he waited till it was nearly past his defence and then flipped his sword sideways and he pirouetted around the side of the lunging skeleton. Snapping his sword back towards himself he yanked the blade and with a crack it fiercely pulled through the skeletons neck bone and its head rolled aside as the skeleton collapsed in a heap. The black mist dissipated from it as had happened to Lucia's parents in the farmhouse. Still twirling, The Swordsman clicked his heel off the ground and spun in the opposite direction, bringing his night black blade down over his shoulder to prevent a blow that the second skeleton was either too slow or too simple to attempt. Seeing the skeleton hadn't taken the bait, he laughed melodically and with pure joy as he clasped his second hand on the sword and swung it straight up through the skeletons jaw and skull. The magical blade burned the black oozing mist and caused the skull to shatter as it split under the razor-sharp blades blow. With a small, elegant leap The Swordsman took to the air and again pivoted the blade, this time straight down where he landed. Twisting his body to one side to avoid the clumsy lunge of the third skeletons short blade he drove his blade downwards through the top of the third skeletons skull. The final skeleton collapsed in a pile of bones as the black oozing mist slid off the skeleton and dissipated. Still swaying, still dancing back and forth on the riverbank The Swordsman hummed to himself happily as he swung back and forth in an oddly hypnotic and elegant dance of death. Turning back to the still seated sisters he smiled happily at them before turning back to a noise at the other side of the river. Suddenly stationary as a statue he froze, turned back all joviality gone and a face that was grim and suddenly looked as old as it had when Lucia had first seen him on horseback. "Time to go," he intoned gravely. Walking briskly back to them, he sheathed his sword with no more playfulness but a blinding speed and efficiency. He stalked past the girls and swung himself straight back up onto his horse, urging it a few steps further down the road as if to stand it between the bridge and the now rising sisters. Joselyn did not hesitate, the last two years on the road with Arn as a scout in service to Vandarn had honed and sharpened her military church knight training. Sharpened it in a way that she hadn't realised in the early days, because she was under the command of the greatest military leader the church of Vandarn had ever known. Gathering her own belongings, she did not even look to Lucia till she had swung up onto her horse but as she was settled, she held her arm out to her younger sister, pulling her up onto the horse behind her with ease, aided by her sisters not inconsiderable agility. The Swordsman's wineskin still in her other hand Lucia held on tight, as Joselyn nodded to The Swordsman and spun her horse northwards and bade the beast to ride. Lucia glanced backwards at The Swordsman as they started to move and saw conflict in his face. She could almost sense that he wanted to stay, to ride south and face the horde of undead head on but he saw Lucia staring at him as he glanced back, and he winked at her. His hand reached instinctively to the sword hilt on his belt, and he patted it. He gave a wistful glance back at the bridge and what must obviously have been the approaching horde on the other side and muttered apparently to the sword on his hip, "not yet." Turning back north he reluctantly followed along behind Joselyn and Lucia, away from the approaching army and the prospect of near certain death.

CHAPTER 14

The shield of man

Arn had left Joselyn and the strangely familiar Swordsman at the signpost, turning left towards Vandarn city while they turned right. She was going to do what he and Joselyn had done for these last few years, scout ahead. She would ride into danger and assess the threat. Arn mused as he rode ahead of them that he'd never normally abandon his charge to a stranger, especially not one who was so obviously a thief and a drunk. There was something about the strange shabby man though, Arn felt he trusted him, believed him and felt something like an itch in his brain, like the presence of his God, Vandarn inside his head the presence of The Swordsman felt similar, uncomfortable but welcome. He rode towards the signpost, a strange cultural oddity on the road to Vandarn, where the north-south road turned east and west that this small strange wooden sign that seemed like it would collapse in a strong wind had been destroyed thousands of times. During the occupation the deathknights would make a show of destroying it, nightly. Just for the first ray of the morning sun to bring it back from shadow. From time immemorial the sign sat there but gave no directions. Every day with the light of the sun it would have a different message, sometimes nonsense, sometimes portentous and sometimes even personal messages to some person or other. Worshippers of the mysterious God, the hidden one, would often claim it was a sign of his power and influence over Vandarn's own capital city in defiance of Vandarn himself, although it was said to predate the city by thousands of years. As Arn passed he barely slowed, simply pulling his great horse around with near inhuman strength and control as both rider and horse were as one. He saw out of the corner of his eye the carving on the simple sign today, "your aim is true; your will is the bow." He nodded grimly to himself before uttering a short silent prayer of thanks to Vandarn and then with an internal nod to the Hidden one too. "They will listen" he said to no one except maybe his horse. "They will listen, or I will make them listen." Arn set his massive jaw and urged his horse on, the rhythmic thundering of its hooves was the only noise to distract him from his righteous fury. When he had first got his steed, he was already in Karn, still a young man and a little lost, missing home. He had immediately decided to name it 'Thirel' after his twin brother. Even though they had never been close. Thirel had loved nature and the provincial woodlands where they had been born and grew up while Varan had always had a love of duty, military precision and had been born with an urge to serve. Both brothers had always had a strong sense of right and wrong though they wildly differed on what that meant. They argued endlessly about his brother's obsession with the natural world and the crimes perpetrated on it by the march of civilisation, which Thirel saw as the more civilised societies taking land from nature and the natural world. Arn in contrast had always valued things like family loyalty, duty to your King, state and country. He had always thought of himself as a shield for those who could not shield themselves. Thirel would argue that none are more in need of a shield than nature against man and so they would begin the whole argument again. Every time the circular nature of their endless debates had irked a young Arn so stubborn his brother was and now, now he missed him. He would sometimes hear his brother's voice in his head and could see more clearly that they had made the same arguments in the same way about the same things. Much like their look other than his long black hair and his brothers short curly, blonde hair they were almost identical, people had always commented that their eyes were the place you could really see it. Probing, wise and bright, both brothers' eyes were like having a bright torch shone on your darkest corners where you felt there was nowhere to hide. Arn could only imagine what his brother would say to an army of undead rising from the ground and its assault on the world. Probably something akin to what he was about to demand the King listen to.

The guards at the gate swept people aside when they saw the giant paladin coming. They recognised not just the livery of the scouts but the unique warhorse and giant paladin atop it. Few people cut such a figure as he thundered, pace unaltered through the gate and up the main road, towards the towering castle in the south of the giant city. Children were pulled out of the street, wagons hurried to pull back as shouts of warning and fury raced ahead of the thunderous hoofbeats of the horse's charging pace. Arn prepared to pull up on Thirel's reigns as they approached the palace's outer gates, reinforced after the defeat of the Witch-Queen so that the castle and its outer grounds could be used as a fortress ready for a siege should something like that ever happen again. Impressive as the giant gates were, veined with steel bonds and magical wards, both divine and arcane in nature. Arn's attention was more drawn to the royal guard captain who judging by his face had rushed to the gate to warn the guards not to impede the old paladin as he even now pulled the guards aside to make a path for the paladin, saluting as Arn passed him. The first person to do so in so long that it felt alien to the old man, like he was a ghost from another life. Another life that haunted him, salutes made Arn think of the war, the chaos and the death that even now he could smell on himself like the shadow of past mistakes that haunt and echo in the quiet moments. He nodded at the gesture as he thundered past atop his horse and hoped he'd managed to keep the distaste for the gesture from his face. Fighting the sudden flash of memory of a different life where he had stood in front of armies, when he had made decisions that had sent thousands, tens of thousands to their deaths. Varan Arfiran, paladin, church knight, general, soldier and at least to his own mind mass murderer. Remembering all the times he had done this before the giant warhorse pulled to a stop in the main courtyard, right outside castle Vandarn's great entry hall. This was where dignitaries, nobles and other great leaders would traditionally be greeted by a full diplomatic retinue. No such frippery was waiting for Arn at the top of the opulent staircase. Instead stood a giant of a man in chainmail. Not many men could stand eye to eye with Arn never mind tower over him, not many humans at least. At about seven feet tall Stee Jahns was one of the only who ever could. A fleeting thought passed through Arn's mind questioning, as so many must have before if there were giant blood somewhere in Jahn's ancestry. The Steward of the King, bodyguard and probably knowing King Branthar, his closest advisor. The giant man held his hands upright palms out, seeming to want nothing more than to calm the older man. "Lord Arfiran, the King asked me to greet you. He will be with us momentarily, after your unannounced visit the other day news got back to him of how you were, let's call it mishandled?" Arn looked up at the giant steward and thought he saw a flash of nervousness pass the large man's face. He worried at how angry he must look. Had he known how his grim visage unsettled people and maybe if he could sense how this huge warrior, renowned for his skill was supressing awe, fear and panic as he stood in the path of a living legend. A hero who had literally saved this world, a man who had faced down the armies of death and darkness and led the united armies of the free lands to victory in one of the bloodiest, longest and most hard-fought battles in recorded history. Had he known, Arn would probably have blushed and given his own feelings about his 'heroics' he would probably have felt no small amount of shame.

"Arn," the old paladin growled suddenly, Stee Jahns had stood at the right-hand side of the King for years. He had faced down giants and monsters both on the battlefield and in more personal settings, he once had commanded the greatest mercenary company in the land of Karn. This old man standing in front of him though, even without the reputation of who he was and what he had accomplished, seemed to be made of granite bound in steel. So cold and so unbending it seemed that walls would wilt in the face of him. "Excuse me lord Arfiran?" The old paladin looked up and into the eyes of the giant steward, "my name. Is Arn. No one calls me Lord anything anymore, least of all the steward of the King. One side lad, I need to speak to the boy, and I don't have time for delicacy or nonsense." Stee nodded and patted the air with his hands to placate the grim paladin before taking a step to the side and gesturing the paladin continue, before falling wordlessly into step beside him. Stee felt the steel gaze of the paladin upon him before the old man spoke like granite slabs sliding against one another "at least you didn't bloody salute." Stee allowed himself a smile. "The King warned me not to, I think he was worried you'd knock me on my rump if I had." The old paladin looked up at the younger man who was now grinning broadly and Arn winked at him. They walked the rest of the way in silence, just the clinking of their swords and armour for company as they walked in the comfortable silence, the unspoken bond of those that had bled together on the battlefield.

Branthar Vandarn, King of the city, state and kingdom of Vandarn. Head of state, titular head of the church. Paladin of Vandarn and one time adventurer and rebel living rough and fighting through squalor for years, to free his kingdom and those neighbouring from a Witch-Queen who had swept across the heartlands of Karn like an ill wind flattening everything in her path. Those days were long gone now and the only time he ever got to wear his plate armour was in ceremony and his sword was an affectation these days. He longed for those days sometimes, even the nights where he went to sleep in the mud with an empty belly gnawing at him with hunger. They were hard days, but he was free, and he had a clear and visible enemy, goal and quest. He swept down the hall barely listening to the small gaggle of 'advisors' around him. Church leaders, city leaders and military men all vying to advise him the course of patience. As if they hadn't just seen what he had seen, an army of undead marching from the south and rural Vandarn towards the city. He saw some of the castle staff moving a tapestry as him and his wake of advisors and 'important' political figures snapped to a halt before barrelling into the unassuming work folk. One of them looked up at him and seeing the King blanched and looked away. "Sorry lads!" The king bellowed and with a wave of his hand and a spin of his heel, spun himself to the side away from the workers and like a cresting wave the gaggle of officials spun after him. An unassuming wood elf near the back, one of the King's own staff, simply there to keep everyone on track, nodded in a friendly way to the men as he glanced at their handy-work. Like a flowing robe of self-importance, the council of advisors rushed to keep up with the King who barrelled along like a force of nature, his moustache flowing, such a pace had he picked up in his excitement. "Orinth!" The King bellowed at the aforementioned elf, who had been lurking at the back like a shepherd of important men. "Do we know who it was who denied general Arfiran, hero of the war, access to the castle the other day?" The King's tone was playful but those who knew him knew well enough not to laugh or even to mistake the query as jovial. "No, my liege," Orinth intoned with an uncharacteristically flat tone. The King sighed exaggeratedly, "it will no doubt go down as one of the great mysteries of our age then! Like halfling sorcerers!" The King stopped for a second almost causing a crash as the whole entourage came to a halt behind him. "Was that insensitive Orinth? I heard it when I said it and it felt a little um..." He raised an eyebrow turning his head towards the elf. Orinth nodded faintly at the King, "it could be construed my liege, as a touch condescending to the little folk. And you know sorcerers, something of a sensitive folk given the nature of their profession." He finished with the faintest of an eyebrow waggle at the King. King Branthar laughed, clearly enjoying himself and turned to face the throng of advisors and councillors, "I think I can manage from here gentlemen, knight Armont? Don't go too far I suspect we'll be sending some orders your way very soon." With that the King waved a hand at the throng of men ushering them away. "Come on Orinth, let's go meet a hero." And the King swept slightly more dramatically than necessary out of the room.

As soon as Branthar and Orinth moved through the doorway to the next room the King's playful countenance disappeared like a mask falling and the King turned grim. His jaw suddenly reset itself in front of grinding teeth, and he began to mutter angrily under his breath, all semblance of the jovial persona he had been cloaked in simply seconds before gone as if blown away in the wind. Orinth watched his King thoughtfully, even given the gulf in ageing between elves and humans Orinth was much richer in years than the King but the shorter-lived man had seen things Orinth could only imagine. As his right hand and the King's squire, he had been with Branthar since the coronation and the two had shared many a fire-side chat into the wee hours. It was not a well-kept secret that years of adventuring had given the King a great thirst for wine, especially for the stronger Takalan reds. The two had spent many an evening talking over cups about the King's adventuring days, hiding from the Witch-Queens armies, travelling from one side of the Heartlands to the other. While Orinth had come from far to the south of Vandarn he had, like many who came to the kingdom, pledged his allegiance to the Kindgom, the city and its King. Despite all his years and journeys Orinth often felt like a child in the presence of the human King. Even having lived more than three times as long as Branthar, not just because of the differing maturity of humans and elves but he'd not seen half as much as the younger man in all his times. He had not lived through the same horrors or been on the battlefield of some of the largest most bloody conflicts the heartlands had ever seen. The haunted looks that sometimes fell across the King's face would in themselves give the elven attendant nightmares. There was barely a single person alive that wasn't aware of the archmage Akarash Beleheim, the strange and indescribably powerful wizard who had been at the heart of the then crown Prince of Vandarn's escape and eventual key involvement in the revolt and rebellion against the Witch-Queen and her armies. He heard the King tell the stories of him and his friends clawing and scraping across the landscape for years. Of following in the footsteps of heroes like Arfiran, Harpsong, Valenstorm and even the Unknown Swordsman himself. To hear the way the King, the most powerful political figure in the entire heartlands would speak of these people in hushed and reverent tones would leave the elven man speechless time and again. To see the grim countenance upon his King was not unusual when they were out of the view of prying political eyes but now, knowing the paladin he revered almost idol-like, the man who had once commanded the entire armies of Vandarn onto the battlefield against a near unbeatable foe? Orinth saw something different in his King's eyes, not just the grim horror of the past, of the injury, of the trauma, the memories of those days wrought upon his features but a kind of hopeful worry like a child hoping for the approval and return of an absent parent. It was unusual to see such doubt in the usually unflappable King. Orinth had never met the legendary knight and paladin though all in Vandarn heard stories of his courage and honour, but to make the King wilt like this with just the thought of his presence then perhaps the legends were true to a word.

The King and Orinth stepped into the large, empty audience chamber, King Branthar sweeping into the room as he always did, nothing in his countenance now betraying his wonder of the older man he came to meet. No sooner had they crossed the threshold than a voice made of granite sliding on granite called out "Branther!" Only to be chided by another voice, "King..." Orinth looked over to the table at the foot of the steps leading to the throne and there standing next to the gigantic bodyguard of the King Stee Jahns was the man they referred to as 'Arn'. Though not as tall as Jahns, the old paladin seemed somehow to loom imposingly next to him. Broad shoulders and built like a war machine in shining black, scale armour. Once jet-black hair now fighting a losing battle with steel grey but somehow statelier and commanding in lieu of youthful. Blue eyes shone out of a grizzled and chiselled face like piercing diamonds, although the paladin never looked directly at him, Orinth felt himself squirm under the gaze as if being judged by a scornful God. Orinth had heard tales of men who stood in front of dragons and standing here in the presence of this legendary figure with eyes of ice blue fire, he felt the wonder and terror that he'd read of in those stories. The King's giant bodyguard seemed also to be uncharacteristically uneasy and nervous in the face of the older paladin, who stood unmoving like a statue as the King and Orinth crossed the giant hall towards them. Stee Jahns having remonstrated the older paladin now glanced at him nervously, if the older man had heard him, he hadn't given any hint of it. Instead, the old paladin general and hero-turned-scout stared at the King. Both men, eyes locked in unspeaking communication as the King and Orinth neared the table, a strange tension filled the air causing Orinth to glance nervously over at Stee Jahns. The giant bodyguard looked back at the elf with a similar look of nonplussed confusion and just as the two men silently communicated their concern the two paladins, King and scout roared so suddenly with laughter that the other two men jumped at the sudden noise. Embracing heartily and noisily the two men laughed and cried squeezing each other and slapping each other's backs with such a deep and authentic explosion of emotion that Orinth felt somewhat like he was privy to something private and seeing some unspoken bond laid out before him. When the two men pulled apart Orinth could see Arn with tears streaming unabashedly down his face as he drank in the sight of his King. Arn spoke in that deep granite-like voice which trembled slightly with emotion "Branthar, my boy. You look old... And soft. All this kinging is clearly civilising you; can you even lift that magical toothpick of yours anymore?" The King's laugh started deep in his belly this time and roared out of him like an eruption, both men were laughing hard while Orinth and Jahns stood awkwardly to the side. As quickly as their brevity started, it died almost instantly. Both men took on grim countenance as the King looked down at the table in front of them where Orinth had unrolled a map scroll he had been carrying showing the area south of the city. Pointing at the map near the village of Anstorm the King looked up at the older paladin and began, "I'm guessing you're here about this? The undead gathering south of the river?" Varan Arfiran nodded solemnly, "yes King Branthar, these are no ordinary undead though. Something foul and dark is at the heart of it. A strange oozing mist that we have both seen before; both faced before." The King nodded, the rare sight familiar to those few who ever fought the Witch-Queen Barvara and her minions personally, the strange oozing mist that erupted from the dark source of the Witch-Queens powers. Looking over to his giant bodyguard Stee Jahns the King nodded. "Go fetch knight Armont Stee, I told him to not wander far and tell him we need a retinue of his best. I'll go put on my armour." The King turned to leave, clearly excited until he met Orinths face. The King's attendant was still entirely passive but now standing directly in front of the King, staring right at him with a very deliberate lack of expression on his face. Branthar nodded curtly, clearly annoyed and turned back towards Arn. "I am reminded that as King I cannot rush out on horseback swinging a sword into the midday sun. General Arfiran? Would you do me the honour of leading a squad of church knights against the foul undead army amassing?"

CHAPTER 15

The Demonsblood blade

Under the infamously named Deathmount, a giant mountain near the southern border of Takal, lay a series of dark and maze-like caves and caverns. In the time of the Witch-Queen Barvara, the edifice of the mount was carved into a horned and fanged skull, in honour of her half-demon son Deathskull, and so the eponymous heart of darkness finally lived up to its name. The mountain's name predated the skull though, beneath the mountains were endless caverns and subterranean lairs that Barvara and later Deathskull himself would lurk within, overseeing terrible experiments in the name of Lazarus or Dracor. Deathmount was in fact named for the dark obsidian like rock which was veined with a glimmering black ore that seemed to have seeped into the stone, the land and the earth around it. Legend said it had been the blood of a dead God that had poisoned the land. Everything was a dark, midnight shade so much so that historians of ancient Takal used to suppose that it was either the cause of the drow or the cradle of their civilisation. It was a little-known fact that in their legends the drow would speak of their ancient ones who, fleeing the betrayal of their surface cousins, settled in a land of darkest night. That they were adopted by it as they were by the darkness of the underlands. When they settled there and found safety and succour in this land it had taken them in and changed them as they had bonded with and changed it. A symbiotic relationship that had given the drow their weapons, their magic and their connection to the other planes. A connection that had been the seed and the source of their power in their eventual domination of the dark underlands of Karn. There were those who would speak of the drow as evil. To suggest they were somehow poisoned by the darkness that had become a part of their physiological make up after generations of the drow had birthed their civilsation and their number from this cradle. The previous identity and the history of the surface-dwelling drow having been lost over the generations, popular mythology said that like the original children of the Gods the elven siblings had fought to break their own identity from one another in the eyes of Gods. The drow had always been freedom loving and expansive, always looking to change and develop and grow. Their surface cousins called them evil, though in truth the drow had more in common with many of the younger races that followed the elves than their stuffy surface cousins. The judgement of their surface cousins was reductive in the extreme and indicative of the unchanging arrogance of their nature. Over the centuries though the drow had lost touch with the cradle of their civilisation, until that is the Witch-Queen had claimed the abandoned mountain as her own and extended her kingdom here. She had Turned it from a forgotten relic of drow history into a dark place of mystical experimentation and inter-planer dabbling. Inter-planer dabbling that had as rumour and legend referred, after a brief affair with an arch demon resulted in what the Witch-Queen saw as one of her greatest weapons in her thirst to conquest the lands of Karn and beyond. She had named her son Deathskull and from the moment her half-demon offspring ripped itself from her womb she treated it with the care of a precious magical artifact, nurturing its growing power and strength. Deathskull was half-demon, half-drow and had a close connection with the magic of the land and of Death-mount itself. He grew up within the dark caverns, its magic seeped into him growing his power as well as his strength. She crafted her son as one crafts a weapon of great power with the care of a master craftswoman and every stroke of her forging hammer was measured and deliberate. Born back when the pact of the Nine, the elder Gods, was intact and kept the divine or the infernal from touching foot on Karn, Deathskull was an aberration, a thing that should not be able to step foot on the world and yet he was born, lived and grew here. Even the most powerful sages and wizards could not and to this day never have discerned how the Witch-Queen had bypassed divine law in a way that allowed her infernal offspring to live and grow on the world of Karn. By all rights, he should have been banished upon birth by the weave of the pact. Deathskull spent his entire life on Karn, something that should have been forbidden. The half-demon never recovered from his mother's death though and spent his remaining years afterwards scouring the planes for some way, some deal, some pact to bring the Witch-Queen back. Her power however had become such as to worry powers across the planes including the Gods themselves and all it seemed had been fruitless in his search. Until he died Deathskull remained sequestered in Deathmount. He had practically given up rule of the Takalan empire to generals and civilians who squabbled over the scraps of the once mighty empire that had conquered the heartlands. Even after his death Deathmount has remained a dark place that even the lords of Takal left to its own machinations. Rumours spread across Karn that it still was running the same sick experiments and warped dimensional scrying that Barvara and later Deathskull had overseen in their time as masters of this dark place.

Physically Deathskull had every inch of his Demonic heritage, his elven skin was a luminescent black. It was similar to his drow heritage but patchy and did not rise above his neck, wrists or ankles and similarly in patches across his chest the skin stretched and broke and where there was no skin a hard bone covered everything. He was lit from within by a black, shadowy darkness that seemed to move behind his eyes, nostrils and mouth. Razor-sharp fangs that seemed to be part of his skull rather than traditional elven teeth and jagged horns naturally protruded from his skull and chin giving him an altogether terrifying appearance. As soon as he started growing horns at puberty though, the Witch-Queen had them filed down, both from the skull and chin and the skull polished to look as mortal as possible. The result of the filed, polished skull was as if someone had pulled the skin and flesh from a skull, polished it and filled it with shadows. It had as people surmised the desired effect the Witch-Queen was looking for; her son was inhuman but terrifyingly close to the familiar. Scholars noted that he continued filing and polishing his skull long after his mother's death. He was a terrifying knight and a powerful warrior, whose might in battle was matched by the fear that he induced in even his closest allies. He was seen as an inhuman monster with a fanatical devotion to his mother who he related to as if she were his deity. A kind of God-Queen that he all but worshipped. The giant barbed blade hung in honour, facing the throne that was once so obsessively its former masters. The throne was every inch the very spirit of Deathmount, carved from stone so infused with Godsblood that it was black and reflective. It moved so you could see your face in it, warped by the curves and angles and the many spiked edges that protruded from it. More than reflective though it was near hypnotic, the black seemed to move under the surface as if it were a living thing, swimming just beneath the surface of the stone. Like most surfaces in Deathmount, when you stared at the throne of the half-demon it stared back at you.

Arvaran Demisi had often tried the throne out. As the leader of the remaining loyal deathknights and one of the leading candidates for the new Emperor of Takal, he had often sat on the throne but every time he did, he suffered terrible visions and nightmares that haunted him for days afterwards. He was one of the first infernal blooded beings to step on Karn outside of Deathskull himself. This was taken as a sign of the breach of the pact preventing divine or infernal creatures from setting foot on the lands of Karn. Standing staring at the throne had become something of a habit for the ageing infernal blooded Warlock. As a warlock of the pit of the lost and damned, many within the castle thought he was communing with his patron or even Baravara or Deathskull themselves. The truth though was the throne made him uncomfortable and he would stare into it as he mulled tough decisions. The other leaders of the nation had been meeting over a council of leadership. Where each member would get a vote on the political future and leadership of the council and though he had not been named he knew they were thinking of him as the chair or leader of this council. It was not emperor, but Arvaran could see the possibilities, he would oversee all Takal and be the actual and titular leader of the nation going forward. He could start to enact his plans without too much oversight or worry. As the darkness beneath the stone's surface shifted under his gaze, he felt his skin crawl and shiver. He recalled the last time he sat upon the chair and his skin burst, ripped, and seemed to reshape itself into thousands of tiny spiders, crawling all over his now skinless body. They slid over and through, into his eyes and mouth and every orifice they could find, gnawing on the sinews and crawling through impossibly tiny spaces inside and around him. Overwhelming his senses with the feeling of their tiny legs upon his eyeballs as they explored their new home. He had screamed so loud that it reverberated around the rough carved throne room for minutes, echoing back at him from dark corners. He clawed at his own skin and face for a moment before the vision faded and he realised he was simply clawing at his own skin and had risked nearly pulling out an eyeball in a confused fit of fear. He had never sat in the throne again, though the failure irked him, and he would stand here and stare at it. His pride had told him not to bow and agree to the council and instead to fight. A civil war though would set them back years and open the entire kingdom to attack from their neighbours; Or worse from within. He thought of Deathskull, his once master an unforgiving and inhuman thing barely capable of love and yet being devoted to his mother more than Arvaran could fathom. He had worshipped his mother as some kind of deity, beyond failure, beyond death and beyond anything. He had spent every day from her death onwards in a search to somehow resurrect her. It had consumed the rest of his life and atrophied one of the greatest armies the world had ever seen until it was an unrecognisable smattering of smaller armies, each hiding in their forts waiting for the desertions to come. In the years that followed they did come. More and more over time the once proud army of the deathknights became adventurers and mercenaries until the very name deathknight had become a kind of Oath sworn order of soldiers no longer even officially allied with the armies of Takal. Who themselves were now fractured and infighting like children arguing over their slice of their parents' estate. If what it would take to unite the armies, the sense of purpose and the move towards the future would be a council of leaders, with him at the head? Arvaran would acquiesce and lead Takal, at the head of a council rather than from a throne. A throne that gave him nightmares and tore at his mind and his sanity so that he could neither look at or away from it, and trapped him often in that dichotomy.

Arvaran was torn from his reverie by shouting, the faint tingle of magic in the air and the most unusual sight, a sickly elven woman in black and shimmering, midnight blue robes that themselves looked almost sick and worn out. At her side a halfling with the look of a seasoned killer, Arvaran had met enough killers in his time to know just from a glance that this halfling was deadly and unforgiving. The guards were shouting as the elf and her companion who had just appeared out of thin air and strolled casually into the large carved out cave that served as Deathmounts throne room. Arvaran had so many questions, chief amongst them was why the wards hadn't prevented this, the magic protections hadn't immolated this elf and her guard immediately and why magical alarms weren't screaming. He took a single step forward, beginning to think through spells in his head to teach these interlopers a lesson. The sickly-looking elf turned her head at an impossible angle and stared straight at him. Something in the way the elf looked at him sent a cold shiver right up his spine. The elf regarded him almost quizzically, "you would be Arvaran yes? We never met you, but our son speaks so highly of you. Have them bring us the sword." She pointed as she spoke, at the giant barbed sword made of black demonsblood steel on the wall. As she spoke the elf stared at him with eyes that at first looked black but then as Arvaran looked closer he realised it was shadow that seemed to move and seep beneath her eyelids. So mesmerised was he by her eyes he almost failed to notice that as she spoke it was like a chorus of voices were coming from her mouth all at once. Some of them ancient and inhuman which rumbled below the others akin to some great and terrible beast. When the dark rumbling voices at the base hit his ears, he was reminded of K'laakarri. The Shadow dragon that ruled the once military fortress of Vaastraak in Northern Takal with that same slithering and silky tones. The voice that held him though was not that or the crying of pained and pleading voices that made up the chorus, but the voice layered on top, the voice that reeked of power. A voice that brooked no argument and that was used to command. Arvaran caught out of the corner of his eye a look of horror, almost fear on the face of the hard faced and ruthless looking halfling. The halfling and Arvaran shared a look of meaning and just as Arvaran realised the halfling was not scared of him or his men but of the thing shaped like an elf that was with him. Misreading the situation one of the guards, a large burly half-orc Arvaran had heard the others call Surm charged at the elven woman his barbed sword swinging. Almost blindingly fast the halfling had slid between the half-orc in barbed plate mail and the elf, a short sword slipping out from under his cloak its tip pointed so that it pierced the half-orcs leg just under the kneecap. Using the guard's momentum against him and with a deft flick of his wrist and a horrendous cracking and tearing sound the sword slipped up inside the kneecap and tore the leg apart. The entire knee buckling the guard who Arvaran was now sure was called Sarn, dropped his heavy barbed sword and reached out to grasp anything for purchase, his mind blanking with the blinding pain from his knee. A pain so overwhelming he never noticed the halfling step subtly to one side. As he did his other hand producing a small, thin dagger that faced upward from the back of his hand just as Sarn or Surm collapsed, and the beginnings of the half orc guards scream were silenced as the fragile looking dagger buried itself up to its hilt in his neck. With an imperceptible flick of his wrist the halfling had removed the dagger and sword and both were again hidden beneath his cloak, all while the visible, almost too sharp sword at his hip never moved. Arvaran almost nodded, terrified, still deadly and in that moment the halfling reminded him of an animal, lashing out anything to came too close. It was more than that though the halfling was clearly protecting the elf, or whatever was possessing the elf.

Arvaran raised a hand to the other guards, motioning for them to stay back as the entire hall bristled with how quickly and dispassionately the halfling had sliced apart a man more than two times his size without so much as a raised eyebrow. Arvaran tore his eyes from the halfling whose hands were unseen beneath this cloak and whose sharp eyes scanned the room cautiously waiting for the next attack. Turning to the sickly-looking elf who still stared at him with impossible eyes Arvaran smiled "excuse me lady, as you say we have not met, despite which you stand amidst my throne room as if it were your own." The sickly elf looked around as if she saw the room for the first time. "Your throne room? This is our throne room, was our throne room. Bring me our sons' sword, you so usefully recovered." Without paying Arvaran a single moment's more notice she strode across the throne room and settled upon the throne without even pausing or hesitating. Arvaran opened and closed his mouth without saying anything and instead stared blankly at the halfling as the small warrior nodded on his way past to stand aside the throne as if a leather clad bodyguard in a room full of plate mail.

Arvaran waved to his men to bring the sword over, two of whom laid the giant barbed blade at the foot of the throne. Doing mental gymnastics in his head Arvaran followed the two men keeping his eyes on the sickly elf. "It is not an elf I address right now, I guess? Why the Godsblood blade? None but my departed lord Deathskull could really wield it, certainly not your bodyguard who its blade alone outstrips in size." At Arvarans words the sickly elf glanced over at the halfling as if only just realising now that he was still here. "We are in fact elven or were, and it is not in fact, Godsblood that is, the blade is Demonsblood crafted in the image of the Godsblood blades, steel unfortunately so rare and impossible to forge we never had enough. Our son's blade will not fulfil our purpose, we cannot crack the veil between realms with a mere Demonsblood weapon. What we can do with this is summon the demon whose blood crafted the blade. Now step aside Arvaran of Deathmount as we return your master to you and our son to us." Shadows seemed to seep from the throne, from the elf or whatever was using the elf as a host. Arvaran thought of the chance that some part of the Witch-Queen was inside this elf as a terrifying but exciting prospect. The shadow seeping from the throne, seemed to surround the giant Godsblood (or rather Demonsblood as he had just learned) blade. A strange Formless shadow seemed to lift and surround the blade until what looked like the shadow of a large, clawed hand seemed to wrap around the blade and grip it. Arvaran could swear he saw the blade move as if the shadow were hefting it in its hand to feel the weight. Before his eyes the shadow formed and solidified as suddenly, he realised the elf was chanting under voice in a low melodic sing-song that seemed slightly off, which Arvaran quickly realised was a summoning. It was in fact the kind of summoning they specialised in here extraplanar summoning. He started preparing spells, wards and importantly touching his thumb on his ring of teleporting in case he needed to flee to safety.

Atrun, the captain of his personal guard sidled up next to him warily "My lord?" Was all the question Atrun dared utter and that was barely above a whisper behind the skull mask of his blackened helm. Without looking at him or even turning his head Arvaran carefully whispered "I feel, Atrun that we are facing history come to life. I've been around long enough to know when I'm being swept up in something huge and in times like those?" Arvaran paused at the question he asked himself and glanced over at the halfling whose fear and fury were mingling with no small amount of confusion. He clearly wasn't even sure what he was doing here. Arvaran sighed gently and answered himself "we must try simply not to get stepped on by history." As if in response to the warlocks comment an almighty Eldritch storm erupted in the roof of the cave and black lightening shot all over striking walls and furniture and one unfortunate guard who was melted in his armour, filling the air with the stench of cooked meat, burning leather and melting steel. The cacophony of voices that were erupting from the sickly elf grew in number and volume as thick black shadowy smoke poured from her mouth. It started to fill the room as it seemed to shift between mist and liquid, bubbling and spreading around the room before being pulled into the shadow forming around the giant Demonsblood blade where it started to form and solidify. Arvaran saw a huge hulking outline with giant horns and rippling muscles, over seven feet tall and filling him with an almost preternatural dread. A dread that was so familiar that in a strange and twisted way also filled him with joy as he realised finally what was happening. It started at the shadow hand that clutched the giant, barbed, shining, black blade as it solidified and seemed to drain in colour till it was hard ivory coloured and like a hand with the skin pulled back. Sinew and patches of black skin covered the joints and knuckles of the hand as the shadow retreated and morphed up the arm. Stretched, almost translucent blue-black skin formed with patches of exposed skeletal armour plating in patches where the skin was stretched too thin. Slowly the mist receded all over to reveal a thing that was part drow elf but mostly demon skin stretched over a skeletal plating. The bone armoured clawed hands and feet ending in razor sharp bone talons and at the chest and clavicle the dark drow skin retreated to armour plated bone up to a skull that had two giant horned ends jutting out from the chin. A row of razor-sharp ridges jutted along the jaw leading up to two giant razor-sharp horns erupting from the skull. An almost impossible mouth of bone with tiny patches of drow skin covering in small bits and a mouth entirely full of razor-sharp fanged teeth and finally the eyes. Two giant empty skull sockets where the remaining shadows seemed to be sucked in through and when it opened its mouth to join in the scream of the sickly elf a dark well of shadows was revealed to be within. The sickly elf and the freshly reborn half-demon screamed in unison until the cacophony of voices seemed to reverberate around the room. Like a sliding scale, the source of their screams seemed to somehow shift from the sickly-looking elf to the giant half-demon that now stood before them. The half-demon, casually wielding a six-foot black barbed, Demonsblood blade in his right hand as if it were nothing and staring around the room with eye sockets filled with moving, undulating dark shadows. Arvaran stood motionless, stunned into silence as seven feet of half-demon stood naked before him raw, unfiltered and very much alive. His lord Deathskull, Emperor of Takal stood before him once again. He had never seen his master's skull so wild and unkempt, and it gave him an even more inhuman and demonic style. He could feel Atrun next to him shaking with fear, either from the demonic aura of fear that Deathskull exuded or simply from the sight of this monstrous warlord reborn. Arvaran gently laid a hand on the guard captains' forearm and patted him imperceptibly to try to calm him. This would not be the time to run, scream or otherwise draw the attention of the demon so recently summoned from the underworld.

So obsessed was every pair of the eyes in the room other than Ander Halfswords on the giant demon that seemed to have somehow erupted from Aera Darkhorne's mouth, summoned by the giant black blade that was taller than the halfling himself. No one else seemed to even notice the sickly high elf lose consciousness as the last of the demonic, black shadow left her body. Limp and unheeded it slipped from the black throne into a heap on the floor. Ander moved, slowly, silently and swiftly to the fallen Aera's side without a sound he slipped his arms under her, and half carried half dragged her behind the throne. Quickly taking her out of the line of sight of the throng of deathknights, wizards and warlocks who now seemed almost as one to be kneeling in fealty to the giant half-demon standing before them. Ander had one thought that took up his entire universe right now, how could he possibly get himself and Aera out of here and when she awoke, if she even did would she even be her? He looked down at her sickly face and saw on her unconscious form that familiar half sneer that she seemed to have permanently plastered to her face and even in this awful place. Lost in the darkness of Gods, demons and death he allowed himself a smile and a promise, she would be the same sick weirdo she had always been, if only he could get them both out of here alive.

CHAPTER 16

A wizard's worth

Akarash Beliheim, at last count he thought that he was four, maybe five hundred years old. His brother would know, Arran was always better at remembering these things. The old fool had still been floating around on that boat, from realm to realm, world to world chasing artefacts and powerful magics to contain, destroy or utilise when he'd been trapped by a dark God in a far realm. Other than being wizards, brothers and sons of a powerful, multidimensional archmage they couldn't have been more different. Arran had blonde hair and blue eyes, fastidious, cold and calculative but with a terrible temper. A product of his birthplace and his mother (also a powerful wizard and politician) he was raised in magic, in a highly magical land and practically grew up in universities and libraries, steeped in magic and lore. Akarash was nearly half a foot taller than his brother, with the brown eyes, thick black hair and darker skin of his mother's people. Akarash took great care in his appearance, his robes, staff and turban were as much a part of him as his magic. He was more reckless than his brother, having been raised in a small farming community his path to learning was more languid but no less studious. His mother did everything to ensure the potential of his blood came through and come through it did. He didn't have his brother's temper though and his was very slow to burn. When raised though his temper was just as terrible, he found out in later years that was probably genetic. The brothers were opposites in other ways too, Arran would scowl his way through a day, shouting at everyone with a thinking that if he was confused or unsure, he would spread it around to make sure everyone knew it was a problem. Akarash, unlike his brother would smile his way through the day and his wife Desolonora would often comment that Akarash would be reading and unconsciously grinning as he did, so in love was the man with books and learning that his joy would spread across his face as he did.

Over the years Akarash had seen so many things mad Kings, Witch-Queens, men and monsters of all shapes and varieties. While he wasn't naïve as his brother had often accused him of being he still, after all this time and all these years of walking worlds and planes believed in justice, kindness and looking out for one another. He still believed after all this time that most people were basically good and that it was the duty of the powerful to protect society and those within it. Across dozens of worlds and hundreds of years he had seen kingdoms rise and fall and saw the inevitable cycle of the more power you clutch at the more emphatically your empire would crumble. So Akarash Beliheim didn't have a great and glorious wizards tower, no giant arched parapet crackling with blue and purple lightning and magical flame. He lived in a cottage, with pumpkins and cabbages and a doorway too small for his giant frame. If not for his turban he would probably have a permanent bruise on his forehead due to the disparity in doorway versus wizard dimensions. Of course, there were wards, dimensional portals and magics built into the construction of the farm but the appearance, the atmosphere were all throwbacks to his childhood farm life and very real, with the smell of baking bread, early morning yard work and all the regular background activity and buzz of rustic living. Deslonora, his wife had been destined to be a hedge wizard when Akarash's brother had chosen her as his apprentice, quite simply because she had been expelled for a magical duel with the circle's at the time evoker wizard. This had tickled the elder Beleheim brother and Arran had taken her on as his student. As Arran and Akarash were children of a thousands of years old interdimensional archmage. It was a funny quirk to begin with that Desolonora and Akarash were of similar ages, temperament and power. Desolonora was more scribe and librarian than Akarash, spending most of her time as the senior librarian in a huge library on a distant world she often referred to Akarash as 'just a wizard' it was a wife's joke and a good one. She would playfully mock his single-minded pursuit of knowledge of the fundamental powers of the universe as a vanity project and assuring him he'd be much happier in charge of a good library. He had saved multiple worlds from endless disasters over the years, disasters his wife's divination magic had warned him of. With protections her abjuration magic had been enacted to protect him. It tickled Akarash to think that all the worlds, the cities the powerful governments and heroes who thanked him for his part, his wisdom and his influence who didn't realise how much of that was the woman with low slung glasses who was reading things straight into his ear from her great library. He would tell adventuring heroes that no one saves the world alone and he would smirk like his brother because they wouldn't realise the was talking about the unseen voice in his ear, Deslornora. The one time he met the elf Hal Greyback, the elf had flippantly called him fearless. According to Deslornora's records Greyback was three thousand years old, probably the most powerful elf still living in any realm. Master of an interdimensional network of adventurers and spies. Akarash had laughed in his face. He cringed a little when he thought of it, "My brother is fearless. I am simply well informed." He wasn't exaggerating or bragging, he was stating simple fact. There was no force in this world as indefatigable as someone with a four-hundred-year-old, archmage, librarian at their back. Akarash, along with perilously few others, his brother Arran, his daughter Amberlie, his nephew Joinville maybe understood that he lived and died on the knowledge of one of the wisest women he knew. It wasn't his rambling journeys through dimensions that had warned him of what was to come on Karn, it wasn't his brother the all-powerful archmage or some deep and dark knowledge from a forbidden source. It was a book. A book his wife had found while searching for their daughter who had embarked on her own mage career and journeyed beyond their abilities to scry. Deslonora had stumbled upon the darkness that was rising and Akarash had, as ever leapt into action at her guidance.

He had warned the halfling, he had alerted the bard when the halfling fell. Akarash had so many paths to walk and he had no choice but to chase his missing brother trapped he believed in a dream realm for the artefact that lived upon his ship. This artefact was one of the few known in existence that could destroy any magic item regardless of power. Akarash and Deslonora's daughter had been his latest apprentice, when they had lost the ability to scry her. They feared the worst and had been pouring not inconsiderable power into finding out what happened. So Akarash had not the time to spare to find what Godsblood weapon would be the one to end the Witch-Queens final plot twenty years after her death, but he would lend them what power he could. Which is why he had held off, allowed Harpsong to live at his Karn home. The immortal bard who spent his time with Akarash because his own lack of mortality scared and embarrassed the bard. The bard had feared his own mortality and when the Gods of Karn had offered him any-thing he'd asked to be exempted from death, from ageing, from the burdens and as the bard would never learn the benefits of growing old. Akarash and Deslonora may have lived beyond the normal span of most humans, but they aged and grew old regardless, two wizards, so bookish people ageing, as slow as any powerful wizard would but ageing, nonetheless. The bard had no idea of the cost of eternal youth, though attachment to the wizard helped him deal with the loneliness of never growing old. In the back of his mind the wizard had sensed the bard Harpsong and the ageing tholan and their time at his farmhouse. Though even he could not see the name of the Unknown Swordsman. The God known as the hidden one whose power he surmised outweighed the rest of the Nine ruling Gods of Karn seemingly had erased it from the cosmos. Akarash knew where the warrior was, though a simple human with a strong love for ale and wine, though a human weapon with an uncanny natural ability with a blade in his hand, Akarash knew as few did that the Unknown Swordsman was a lynchpin. Not because of his skill with a blade, not because of his charming personality if it could be called that. Not because of some blood or birthright, this was no great inheritor of legend. His mother worked a tavern, and his father was a mercenary, no one was foretelling the coming of this man and yet the world would hang on the balance of his choices like a reflection on the sun. Oblivious as he was, the Unknown Swordsman had been a fulcrum upon which the world spun. Even when he had nothing left to live for his will to survive seemed somehow to be larger even than him, his survival was like an inability to lie down and die. Like most innocuous adventurers who seemingly never lived up to their potential, The Swordsman had been marked for a greater fate than he imagined and a stricter path than he had hoped. Forces in the universe stronger and more primal than the hidden one had intentions for the poor, sad old drunk who had no more distinguishing mark than his excellence with a sword and inability to forgive himself for surviving the past. Akarash had followed them all, the band of heroes who had saved the world, tried to protect and guide them without influencing their lives. The Swordsman, the bard, the halfling, the Princess and the paladin. He'd hoped they would move on, live their lives but none of them ever could. They'd taken their Gods boon and as people usually do, ruined their lives with it. Akarash had taken note, he didn't want to challenge the Gods of Karn but if he did it wouldn't hurt to have the knowledge how. He and Deslonora had done the research and the now Gods Ramlar and Dracor weren't far off his or his brother Arrans power level when they destroyed two Gods. Akarash knew why the Gods feared him and frankly he understood. If his brother was at his side they could sweep the Gods resistance aside, what worried Akarash was the temptation and what it would cost them in their humanity and in their soul.

Akarash was sat in the dimensional portal that linked his cottage to Desolnora's library at the desk he generally used. He was hunched over a crystal ball but with a large tome written in a long forgotten ancient language in front of him, glancing between the two, indulging his inability to do a single task at any given time. Scrying far away realms for any sign or trace of his brother or the usual detritus his brother's friends usually left in their wake. Whilst in between reading this ancient tome for hints of dark and lost artefacts that may have been used to lure his brother. His mind though wouldn't stop wandering back to Karn. He glanced over to the back of the study where a large carved and polished oaken wood staff delicately carved and lacquered with gold through the grain. Flowing and joining at the head of the staff into a smooth finned dragon skull with two pointed horns at the top and sliding over into the long regal snout of a gold dragon, with eyes that managed both to be pure gold and yet seem to flick around the room looking at everything. Occasionally little puffs of smoke would emit from the nostrils like a smoking pipe in action. The staff seemed to him to be staring at him, he cast it a dubious glance "shut up." He told it for good measure and tried to return to his studies, "I can't," he continued as if answering some unspoken retort, "I need to study if I am to find and invade the dream realm. Finding my brother is the only path to finding my daughter, so I don't have time for Witch-Queens and dead Gods!" The staff impassively released another small puff of smoke from its nostrils. Akarash sighed deeply and faced the staff again. "Do something like what? I already sent the bard to save Valenstorm didn't I?" His voice rising the ancient wizard slammed his hands on the desk and shouted at his staff, "I DON'T HAVE TIME!" Just as a tall slender woman whose hair had almost completely lost the battle from bright orange to steel grey and whose face wore the wrinkled lines of years spent laughing and smiling. "Akarash, love? You can scream at it all you want; it's never going to answer you. It's just a staff." She smiled affectionately at the frustrated mage who was now glowering at the gold dragon Staff of the Arch Magi, gifted to him by a powerful gold dragon who was also a not inconsiderable archmage in its own right. If he heard his wife's admonishing tone, he didn't acknowledge it, simply straightened his turban which had tipped slightly askew in his ranting and stalked over to the golden dragon's head staff. Grasping it with a suddenness unbecoming and lifted it to stare eye to eye with the golden dragon head that topped it. Without turning around, he finally responded to his wife, "Do you know Deslonora, I've had this stupid staff for over a hundred years, and I don't think I've ever really used it." She laughed gently, "so it is just taking up space you say?" She laughed softly as she spoke. Akarash turned his suddenly devilish eyes on his wife. The Gods of Karn told me not to interfere in their world, I know. But I wouldn't be helping, just throwing out an old piece of junk that's been cluttering up my study, right?" Deslonora waved him away dismissively "The archmage's staff of the dragonlords? We have too much junk in this place altogether anyway." Then she turned with sudden seriousness and slammed her hand on a pile of books that came up to her midriff. "Touch these books and you'll be reading with frog eyes for a hundred years though, you old miser!" To which Akarash smiled broadly and smoothed his beard. Smiling past the staff at her, "I suppose I should get rid of this thing then." He said playfully and then turned and with a faint humming noise, walked through the portal back to his cottage on Karn.

Urnath had awoken to the sound of someone digging, the sound felt like a knife in his skull. The problem with spending time with bards he remembered was the hangovers. He slowly arose, fighting his own body and inability to balance and lumbered outside to find Harpsong turning over soil happily. This man had saved the world and here he was smiling happily, doing manual labour on a vegetable patch. Urnath chuckled to himself which made his eyeballs feel as if they were about to roll out of his skull. He clutched his head and dunked it under the water tap pulling on the handle to let ice cold water pour over the back of his head, soaking it. When he straightened up the bard had stopped his work and was leaning on his hoe, "Urnath! Good day friend!" Waving his hand around at the blue sky as if to offer evidence to his claim. Urnath raised his hand half in greeting, half in hope Harpsong would stop talking, or at least lower the volume. Harpsong continued, "I received word from our host this morning, he asked that we wait here for him. He's bringing something to aid us and information. Finally, we might get a clear picture of what's going on!" Urnath dropped himself into the chair he'd passed out in, the first night here and sighed. It occurred to him Beliheim better hurry, or Harpsong might poison Urnath with more of that damned wine. The sudden darkness of a shadow loomed over him giving him a start, almost as if the universe had heard him. Urnath looked up into the sight of an exceedingly tall human, almost taller than him he noted which was impressive for a human to match heights with a Tholan, even one as short as Urnath. Dark purple and blue robes with a large cloak which seemed to oddly glint in places, like stars shining and an understated purple turban, tucked neatly and highlighted with a small sapphire which was relatively plain for the opulence of the wizard it was attached to. Looking up and down the old wizard who Urnath assumed could only be Akarash Beleheim his eyes rested on the staff in the wizard's hand. Vibrating sheer, barely contained mystical power, the staff was made of mahogany lacquered with gold and topped in the shape of a sneering gold dragon. The power radiating off the staff was unlike anything Urnath had felt outside of standing four feet from a God a few nights ago. Urnath could feel the human wizard's eyes on him and coughed politely as he tore his eyes away from the staff to the wizard who similarly radiated magical energy the likes of which urnath had only sensed when he met the God Ramlar. "Master Be-liheim, I am Urnath Spellbinder of the Rath'kalt I was court wizard to the tholan High King Crothan thronebreaker of the crollaran. He was not just my King; he was my closest friend. He bade me go and find a life for myself before he…" The tholan paused to collect himself before he continued; "Before he died. I was confronted by the God of chaos and war as I entered The Swordlands. He bade me take the axe and close some portal that was never fully closed. I thought, well I remembered Crothan talking of you and thought to seek your guidance, your counsel?" Urnath looked expectantly at the tall human, finding his eyes drawn to the large blue gem in the human wizard's turban.

Akarash lowered himself and as he did a small bench of stone sprouted from the ground and rose to meet him. He settled down upon it with a weary sigh and his palms rested on his knees. He smiled as a schoolteacher might smile at a student who struggled, a smile of patience, kindness and warmth. He nodded to Urnath as he started, "you see Urnath, thousands of years ago back in the beginning of the recorded history of the heartlands of Karn there were as there are still, many portals dotted around the land. It is said that in those days, so many minor Gods and Demi-Gods wandered the lands that they wore the fabric of realms down, poisoning the land with their excessive magic. It was a destructive and unruly time with the Nine, who sit as the most powerful in Gods being lenient and indulgent of their children as they played and fought and and schemed across the land. Then one fateful day, two wizards appeared from an ancient and distant land Ramlar the black and Dracor the vain. They were powerful beyond measure, as powerful as a mortal could be without divine power flowing through their bloods. They were also evil, unruly and chaotic. They brought their chaos to Karn, and they carved a kingdom for themselves. They slew a few of the Demi-Gods and minor God-kings who were dotted throughout the land and ruled large swathes of land for over a hundred years rising to minor Godhood themselves. Ramlar God of dragons and Dracor God of disease. As their power grew the two Gods who originally held the offices of Chaos and Death grew fearful of the power of the two mortals and levied the Nine to banish them. The Nine voted against them and the two Gods decided to deal with the issue themselves, and entreated Ecaur, the Goddess of greed to pretend to side with the mortals only to betray them. When they attacked though they found Ecaur had betrayed them in favour of Ramlar and Dracor, the fight that followed was immense, it left scars upon the land that are seen even now. The great rift was the result of the God of chaos and war's sword sweeping down on Ramlar. The Quoity Swamp forest near Takal was a result of the God of death and disease's demise. Dracor had ripped his heart out with his bare hands and as his blood fell upon the earth it befouled and warped the land. As the two Gods died, as their blood seeped into the land and where it fell it soaked the earth around it, changed it." Urnath, listening rapt to the human wizard found himself involuntarily blurting out "Godsblood!" And the old Human wizard smiled. "Exactly my friend. The blood of the Gods seeped for thousands of years under the land. However, the Nine were so shocked that two of their own could be murdered that the names of the two dead Gods were stricken by the hidden one, never to be uttered again. Ramlar and Dracor who assumed the mantles of their vanquished foes were admitted to the Nine but banished to their tower of ice far in northern Thol. The Nine decreed that nothing divine or infernal would ever step foot on the land of Karn ever again and for thousands of years nothing did."

Akarash, lifted a delicate teacup from a tray Urnath had been too rapt to notice Harpsong lay down before them and nodded his thanks to the young-looking bard. He sipped the tea slowly, refreshing himself before returning his attention to Urnath. "You see when the two dead Gods were slain, no one quite knew what to do with what was left of them. What is remembered, endures. And nothing so endures like an idea and the two dead Gods, even with banished names were an idea that would fester, endure and who knows what would happen if left unchecked. So, to close the lid on it the Nine bid Lazarus to cast the remains into a dark pit where they could never escape. A pit that would become the pit of the lost and damned souls. Witches and warlocks would make pacts with the pit; 'Give me power and I will release souls from the pit to freedom.' A great deal for both witch and lost souls but it started to weave a path, a link from the pit of the lost and damned to the real world. Deep within this pit something dark started to take shape, from the corpses of two dead Gods. A deep dark and hideous power that knew not quite what it was but knew only two things, hunger for souls and rage. Thousands of years passed without incident, something awful and formless gestating and growing at the base of the pit of the lost and damned until about two hundred odd years ago. A wizard, a necromancer of the drow named Vidar of the spiderwood, first broke the barrier and found a way to directly harness the dark, poisoned souls from the deeper well of the pit. He used it to warp and reshape the spiderwood from a drow surface outpost to twisted, undead and evil place filled with warped and hideous mockeries of life. Vidar would have opened a clear gate to the pit of the lost and damned if not for the heroic actions of a young Barbarian, wielding a Godsblood axe. That Godsblood axe in your very hands. The thing known only as the Formless arose from the pit of the lost and damned to be unleashed on an unsuspecting world by this drow necromancer, only to be subdued by the young Crothan. His axe could not however close the portal, even 'apparently' killing the drow necromancer could not close the portal. The folly of the Gods was about to wreak vengeance on the entire world, so Ramlar feeling responsible appeared to Crothan and offered him a deal, breaking the pact of the Nine to not touch the mortal world, the God of Chaos lent Crothan the power to absorb the rift, to close it. In exhange for keeping it for two hundred and fifty years, Ramlar offered the barbarian he would live to see his three hundredth year. Upon Crothan's three hundredth birthday, Ramlar would be prepared to take the rift and close it. Crothan saved the world, was granted a long life in return and no one knew how close they came to utter destruction, hundreds of years ago." Akarash again paused, sipped his tea and urged Urnath to do the same. The tholan had forgotten about the cup in his hand and stared at it as if it were alien to him before gingerly taking a sip. It was thistle tea, the taste of it sharpened him and he stared back at Akarash asking "The rift, when Ramlar took it from Crothan? It did something didn't it?" The old human wizards smile dropped. His face grew somber, and pale and he nodded solemnly, "yes. You see when Crothan faced the Formless, it was an entity without direction, consciousness and was a primal beast of divine power driven mad into something eldritch and awful. It flowed where it could without reason, consciousness or form. Something changed, twenty years ago. I was there when it happened, I was witness to the men of the sword, to when a halfling saved the world. I had thought I was so clever, I had played chess with the Witch-Queen, and I was sure I had won, by ensuring there were multiple Godsblood weapons I had an ace in the hole, what I hadn't realised was so did she.

Vidar of the Spiderwood, apart from not actually dying at the hands of Crothan had a sister. A twin sister, named Barvara. She had learned of the pit of the lost and damned from her brother and had investigated the dark corners of reality for ways to mould and manipulate the pit to her own ends. What had been thought to be a pact or affair that had somehow allowed her half-demon son to walk upon the land of Karn had been something much worse. The thing that she gestated inside herself was no child borne of a demon from the underworld. Deathskull was made from her dark rituals, directly from the pit of the lost and damned souls itself. A child of the damned, not only a form of pure evil but a link to the pit of the lost and damned, the source of her power and a gateway between the two realms. We had thought Deathskull dead, but he had disincorporated, not really complete without the life force of his mother. He lived on for nearly two decades before dissolving into a pool of Formless like a simulacrum losing its shape. When Ramlar took the rift from Crothan, in that split second the piece of the Formless that had once been Vanyusa Deathskull sensed it and latched onto that rift and so it was that a link, tear, a hole in the barrier was created. Barvara had always known she might fail; she had prepared for it. When the halfling killed her and the portal closed Barvara was sucked in, into the pit of the lost and damned. Much like Ramlar and Dracor thousands of years before, she had been ready, and she had amalgamated herself into the thing that was once two dead Gods. Joining her consciousness to theirs along with thousands of other damned souls she had made pacts with to create a Formless guided by her massive intellect and personality, with the influence of others and able to control the lost and the damned of the pit and now with a link, a rift that they could use to return. That very link had created a breach in the pact to prevent the divine and infernal from walking on Karn, which is why things like infernal and divine blooded beings started to appear after the war. I have felt the rift she formed in the moments when Crothan died. Like putting a foot in a closing door. She has resurrected and possessed her son, Deathskull is alive, and he is housing the spirit of the Formless. Led by what is left of the Witch-Queen, so yes, the Godsblood weapons are important again, they are essential to kill Deathskull before he and Barvara complete Vidars plan finally and unleash the unspeakable thing that is the Formless on the world. So, you must go, you and Harpsong, take this, the archmage's staff of the dragonlords. It is the perfect weapon should things become desperate it is one of the most unique and powerful artefacts I could hand you, I will send you to Takal, take the axe, take the staff and find a way, other allies are also already on the way. Find them and help Harpsong do what he was born to do. Save the world, again."

Urnath looked at the human wizard in awe as the robed and turbaned man handed him the powerful feeling staff. He felt the dragon eyes at the head of the staff peer into his soul and then looked beyond it at the empty stone bench the wizard had been sitting on moments ago. It slowly sunk into the earth, Akarash Beleheim was gone, all that was left was Hanalan Harpsong, outfitted for adventure and combat and with a large smile on his face, looking happier than Urnath could imagine, and the bard said in his sing song voice "Well? Let's go save the world!"

CHAPTER 17

From the mouth of evil

Alerted by the sound of mailed boots double-timing down an adjacent corridor Ander was startled from his slumber. Refusing to open his eyes just yet as his brain tried to remind him, he wasn't in fact in his tent in the camping ground of the Edge tavern in Valenstorm and that in fact none of the subsequent time was a dream. He felt the warmth and heat of Aera's thigh beneath his head and realised he had passed out with the elf for a pillow. Slowly a throbbing in his side called for his attention as he recalled his attempt to drag Aera Darkhorne's prone body from the throne room while all eyes were focused on the reformed body of Vanyusa Deathskull. Ander had never even seen Deathskull before yesterday, though the half-demon enjoyed legendary status while he was still alive. Seeing the black, amorphous liquid like mist erupting from Aera's mouth and eyes and take shape into the giant warrior was one of the most horrific things Ander had ever seen. When Deathskull had formed and all the knights and others around him immediately dropped to their knees to see their master reformed and alive in front of them, Ander had seen his moment and half dragged the unconscious form of Aera from the room. The last thing he saw was Deathskull cursing that his blade, the giant barbed sword that others could barely lift was in fact Demonsblood, his blood, borne of the pit of the lost and damned and not in fact pure Godsblood. All of which meant his own sword would not be sufficient to break the seal on the dimensions. Not sufficient to open the portal that Deathskull, now with his mother's voice echoing through his mouth claimed would allow "us" and something called "the Formless" through into this world. Ander was a swordsman, a mercenary and a killer. He didn't know really what any of this meant and the only one who could answer those questions for him had been unconscious in his arms. What Ander did know was that he didn't want to be around for its arrival. As the half-demon possessed by some kind of gestalt entity that had summoned him forth from whatever hell he had been residing in, cast his sword aside and looked around he realised the sickly elf that had been its vessel was gone. He turned with horned face and bellowed, "Find the elf! We are not done with her!"

Ander had gotten halfway out the room before stumbling over guards. He'd been gravely injured in the ensuing fight but had used his speed, his surprising strength and deadly skill, he was a warrior true, but Ander had not learned to fight at the foot of some great master, knight or soldier. Ander Halfsword had learned to fight in the foulest gutters, where people would murder over stale bread and three feet of dry alleyway. Ander even now, all those years removed from the gutters of Port Darkness Ander still fought with the desperation of a starving gutter rat and his willingness to do anything to survive. His injury having happened when he had in short order taken down two guards turning his back on the third. Ducking under the remaining guards predictable swing, Ander had spun only to see the guard had raised his shield and set himself thinking he had gotten the drop on the halfling, the halfling lacking his size and surely his strength. Ander had assessed it and nodded, "it's a price

I'll pay." The halfling had said as much to himself as to the readied guard and leapt into the air with such suddenness that the guard had barely time to raise his barbed sword. Twisting to the side Ander was not impaled on the barbed blade but instead slid down the side of the blade. Accepting Its wicked barbs tearing at his armour, clothes and flesh as he slid agonisingly inside the guard's sword. His impossibly sharp sword sliding effortlessly through the guard's eye and into his brain. As the now dead guard had fallen, his body taking a second to catch up to his impaled brain. Ander had cleaned his sword on the guard's black cloak nodding to himself in satisfaction even as he felt his side begin to burn where he'd raked himself.

The next few hours had been a case of finding a dark corner in the caves and hiding there. He'd bound his wound and sat down, Aera still unconscious and breathing shallowly, even for her. Another commotion had obviously started elsewhere in Deathmount and he could hear the noise even here in the lower caves where he had hidden himself and Aera from the searching guards, deathknights and whatever else lurked down here. Ander tried to rise and immediately winced at the tear in his side, typical deathknights, the guard had poisoned his blade. Ander craned his head to look at Aera, deathly pale and breathing light, a dimming light. His wound would prove fatal without help and he was unsure if Aera's already fragile constitution could withhold the trauma of what her body had just been put through; "well Aera, I promised I'd stick by you. I stayed by your side and now look at us. You're a husk and I'm going to die, poisoned, in a cupboard floor, in the basement of the worst of monsters' lair, in the same damn country I spent my life trying to escape. Ander laughed and it quickly turned into a cough, a sickly wet cough that made him think of Daern B'Narre, the Drow poisoner Aera and he had worked with in the early days, "You'd call this a death rattler I suppose Daern? At least you'll never have to worry about me finding you and cutting your head off like I promised, eh?" Ander chuckled to himself and realised he was already feeling lightheaded. He tried to focus, to stay awake almost as if he realised if he passed out neither him nor Aera would ever wake again. Blinking Ander was suddenly aware of a soft golden light shining through the cracks in the door, he started to curse his carelessness in not assuming poison on the barbed blade. Shaking himself awake, trying to force himself to lucidity at the sound of the door opening. Ander watched in horror as a tall slender deathknight entered the room, a soft golden glow emitting from one hand and seemingly guiding the deathknight to them, in the other a dangerous looking magical flanged mace. Seemingly to herself the deathknight said "I've found them. Yes, definitely the ones they're looking for. Both are half dead though the halfling looks almost conscious. I'll deal with them you just scout the base and see if you can find the portal; And Kerwin, don't get caught." The tall slender deathknight turned her skull masked face to Ander and nodded, raising the mask to what must have been a look of surprise on the halflings face. Beneath was no hardened warrior but the gentle, regal features of nobility, lined with wisdom a woman in her mid-fifties who had the easy air of command. This was someone who was used to being listened to, used to having her orders followed. Ander had followed a few of them in his time. "You must be Ander Halfsword?" the human woman smiled as she knelt to reach out to him, Ander tried to level his sword but by this point he could barely lift it. Her black mailed hand rested gently on his cheek, and she muttered some words he couldn't quite understand, somewhere in there he thought he heard her say something about Necirate, the Goddess of beauty, nature and peace. A slow flowing warmth spread through Ander and inch by inch like an oncoming calm he felt the poison and the pain recede and his strength return.

Touching something on her belt the black deathknight armour fizzled away and left was the sky-blue plate tinged with white. As the deathknight helmet disappeared to be replaced by a thin band of gold barely containing black hair lined with grey and white as she smiled down at the halfling her hand moving to the sickly elf beside him. "Annia." She said softly, still smiling, "My name is Annia and if my spies are to be believed you are Ander Halfsword and this is Aera Darkhorne? Your friend is sick because she is still tainted from the possession, something ancient and evil that was once a God possessed her recently, only her previous connection to the pit of the lost and damned stopped it consuming her completely. I can help her, I can save her, but it won't be easy. Right now, all I can do is keep her alive, but I'll need your help to get us out of here." Ander was stunned to suddenly hear Aera's voice, even more stunned at the relief and happiness he felt to hear it. "I can teleport us out of here?" The elf croaked, barely having the strength to speak but still retaining her oddly off key creepy singsong voice. Annia, who Ander was quickly deducing was 'the' Annia, Princess of Hven and the leader of the men of the sword was shaking her head at the sickly elf, sadly with a wan smile. "I'm afraid not Aera, it's the Godsblood seeped into the stone. Unless you're attuned to it, you'll find the results unpredictable, we'd be as likely to end up buried in a stone wall. In a minute Ander will be back to his fighting best and we'll have to get you out of here the old fashioned way, Necirate forgive me." At this last bit she looked down at the symbol on her chest an intimately private moment between her and her God that she played out unashamedly in front of the two mercenaries laying before her. Ander, his strength returning pulled himself to his feet, Aera smiled at him, in what he thought was supposed to be affectionate, it instead had the aura of a feral cat regarding a mouse it was about to gut. Ander, before he could stop himself found he had taken the sick elf's hand. "I made myself a promise when you were unconscious Aera, we're going to get out of here. I'm not fucking dying in Takal." He turned his head towards Annia, "Thank you. Princess?" The last word was a question, in response Annia raised her eyebrows then nodded briefly to confirm to the halfling that she was indeed who he thought she was. The halfling smiled, it was his turn for his face to take on a predatory demeanour, a look that Annia regarded sadly. She knew violence would be necessary but the look she'd seen on the halflings face she'd seen before, on the face of the Unknown Swordsman countless times. Ander Halfsword if what she'd heard was good, very good and he was about to enjoy the bloody vengeance he would carve out of Deathmounts denizens on their way out.

Whispers flowed like wine between the men and women around Arvaran, every time he turned to see who spoke though the whispers would stop. He was on the verge of becoming emperor of Takal, finally at least in a manner and now? Deathskull was back, with what sounded like all the spirits of the pit of the lost and damned along with him. He martialled his small force as they headed to the main balcony overlooking the valley below, ten deathknights and 3 wizards. Some of the best men still loyal to the throne. He knew what his master had asked was a long shot but with a clear platform away from the Godsblood's influence on magic he could use the pit of the lost and damned to fulfil his masters' orders. They reached the balcony, and he called forth one of the wizards. "You are in luck Talara, you will be the vessel to bring glory to the empire, to Deathskull and to the world." And with that he conjured a shard of pure black which oozed black mist and plunged it deep into Talara's breast. The wizard looked on in mute horror as unseen a spirit of some dark and twisted thing deep within the pit of the lost and damned rose up and filled the wizard's body. Some strange popping and cracking noises accompanied the transformation and the eyes filled black and shining. "You ssssummoned me?" A voice that was not Talara's but instead used it as a vessel to carry its own voice. Arvaran, didn't even look up. "You know your mission spirit?" The thing that was recently Talara nodded and immediately just stepped off the balcony.

Arvaran turned to see, wreathed in ghostly flames the disembodied head of his younger brother, the first person he'd ever killed, screaming its way towards him. He knew the spell, everyone who made a pact with the lost and damned did. That didn't lessen the psychic trauma as the skull tore through him, its screams coming from inside his head. Shaken he looked around as his men, horror on their faces saw the halfling, the human and the sickly pale elf, a twisted grin on her face mumbling under her breath to the decapitated heads of one of Deathmounts many guards. Too late Aravaran recognised the next spell the sickly elf whispered to what was clearly the focus of her spellcasting. All around him and his men suddenly an awful darkness started to lick at their legs, arms, hands and tentacles grasped up at them and one by one pulled them down. Every one of his men around him fell held in place by slithering, viscous dark shadow coiled hands and tentacles. His men screamed as the life was literally sucked from them by the pit. Arvaran focused his power on escape, it took all his concentration and no small portion of his power, but he walked safely out of the darkness slithering around him, singed but not held or truly burned by it. Patting down black shadow flame from his robes he looked over at the sickly elf, being held up by a tall blue armoured human woman and smiled at the two women. "Nice try elf, my turn." And he raised his hands quickly calling one of his most powerful magics to mind and as he uttered the words quickly calling on the power of the pit, he suddenly felt a blinding pain in his right hamstring and tumbled screaming to his knee. A quiet voice at his right ear, so close the breath was hot on his neck whispered, "hush now." And he felt something so sharp it almost didn't hurt slicing at his throat, he tried to scream but it came in an almost inaudible gurgle, and he felt excitement, almost glee from the halfling at his side as his eyes rolled over into darkness.

As the large pool of shadow receded and left in its wake a pile of desiccated husks, and an aura of screaming as several spirits were dragged deep into the pit of the lost and damned Ander rushed across, conscious of the strange crunching, sucking noise the receding shadow made as his boots passed through the remnants of it. He leaned over the edge of the balcony shouting back to Annia "No sign of it, whatever he did to that wizard she's long gone." Annia nodded, "We can't worry about it Ander. This is the moment of truth; I need reach out and hope at least some of my old companions will answer the call." Ander turned back and helped Aera to sit on the stone floor fetching a bottle of glowing red liquid Annia had given him. Letting Aera take some more sips from it, hoping to give her enough relief to survive this before turning back to the Princess, "Whatever, we're not leaving till this is done. After what they did to Aera, we're with you until these bastards have paid." His face a grim mask of vengeful fury.

CHAPTER 18

A wave of darkness

The first thing Joselyn heard was the rumble, a rumble like she'd never heard before. She had heard tales, mostly from Arn but she'd never heard anything like it, it was punctuated by gasps and the occasional cry from the small band of locals fleeing the undead her small group had gathered on their journey north from the bridge. Next came the banners, she counted ten as they appeared over the hills crest, all Church knight banners, she tried to identify some of the units. Most were from Vandarn city, a place she'd still never been. Finally, they came, three horses at first, clearly King Branthar at the front flanked by two giant steeds each carrying a man of about seven feet in height or more. A grey roan larger than you'd think one could grow and another large black coated horse she knew like her own. No one could mistake the giant, powerful steed of Arn. Varan Arfiran, even at this distance the sheer aura of strength and righteousness that radiated from him was like a beacon in a dark night. Behind them a hundred Church Knights, in formation, in Unison. The thundering noise stopped as the force came to a halt. Joselyn heard Lucia gasp, some of the gathered people who had followed them north cheered, somewhere in the throng a child cried. Branthar and Arn separating from Stee Jahns and the men, trotted over to where Joselyn, Lucia and The Swordsman waited. Watching behind them a small smattering of refugees, fleeing their home after being roused by the sound of marching dead and with no other plan following the armed trio as they rode purposefully north. Joselyn smiled as broadly as Arn, both mentor and student delighted to be together again. Arn nodded at her and ignored the custom of no one speaking before the King, spoke first, "Joselyn! You're well child, what do we know?" He glanced at the younger sister, almost no word was needed to see the resemblance, like a wild animal version of the older sibling one arm around Joselyn's waist, the other clutching at a near empty wineskin. It occurred to Arn the young woman who was clearly Joselyn's sister was drunk. Tearing his eye away from the sisters to The Swordsman who looked grim and grey, he shared a silent nod with the weary looking Swordsman, and it might have been his imagination, but he felt almost a glimmer of affection and camaraderie in the other man's eyes. King Branthar trotted and turned his head smartly to Arn, "well General? Did we just ride a hundred of Vandarns finest out into the wilderness on a wild goose chase or is there a fight ahead?" As if to answer the King, Lucia gasped a second time from behind her sister's shoulder. As one, the others turned to see what she had gasped at, the horizon on the south suddenly swarming with a small but expanding sea of shadow dripped, walking corpses. Arn ground his teeth in consternation. "There's too many sire. If you send a hundred men down there, you'll be a hundred men short to defend the city." As if assessing the situation like an experienced general himself, The Swordsman piped up, his Swordslands accent thicker than it was before, "there's no more bridges to hold them back. If you're going to hide behind your walls, you'll need time to get the people between here and there gathered up, to say nothing of these people here." He waved behind him at the small but huddled masses before looking over at the swarming dead, "Someone needs to slow them down." The words hung heavy in the air, Arn nodding along with what this stranger was saying. Arn smiled broadly at the King, "give me the Dragonscales. We'll hold them off."

Branthar nodding at Arn turned back to give his instruction to the men, the Dragonscales. When Varan Afiran had been the commander of Vandarn's forces in the war, the Dragonscales were his men. Named for the black Dragonhide Arfiran issued to every knight. Probably one of the most elite units in Karn. There were ten of them here, ten of the best. Some advisor, probably Orinth, had told King Branthar why they were being stationed in the castle but as usual, he hadn't been listening. Turning to the civilians Branthar smiled, suddenly all diplomacy and charm, the King turned it on like a switch, "People, I think it's probably best if you get behind the wall of knights, eh?" With the broad confident smile of a man who'd come to save them. Stopping briefly to clasp arms with Arn, the two men silently sharing a moment of long held brotherhood and an unspoken bond between knights finally he simply said "City, Country and God." Arn nodded and returned the familiar Church knight greeting "City, Country and God; My King." Branthar turned and trotted his horse back over to Stee Jahns with a train of suddenly adoring refugees in his wake. From their sullen group together Joselyn and the others saw the larger man protest and then slump in his saddle and agree as scared people weaved through the wall of knights and slipped behind them. Some of the younger less trained knights holding out hands as they passed offering comfort. The Dragonscales however, did not flinch, didn't even look at the refugees in their midst. Joselyn observed the military precision with which ten knights peeled out of the group and marched a few hundred yards down the road only to come to a perfect, uniform halt and await further command. Joselyn started to speak but Arn held his hand up, as the sound of a womans voice drifted in the air. Arn looked over at The Swordsman and saw him hearing the same thing. On some level Arn knew, he understood what that meant, who was slouching, greying in the saddle across from him. Arn allowed a smile to play across his lips as he shared a look with The Swordsman, the same message playing across both their minds. "Deathskull is back, possessed by the spirit of Barvara or something formed from it. Help needed please get to Deathmount, holding an ingress point at the high balcony. They're close to finding a Gods-blood weapon and if they do, we're all damned. Arn, Han, if either of you get this. Please, hurry." Arn noticed The Swordsman patting his black bladed sword as he nodded along to the message. Taking in the message Arn turned to The Swordsman and the sisters, "Sorry Joselyn, this is a one-way trip, and we know it. I think I've trained you enough and besides, you must take our friend here to Takal, to Deathmount. The only way we end this, is by ending an old foe and closing a rift we thought sealed twenty years ago, and this time we do it properly." Joselyn looked at Arn like he had gone mad, "Arn! You..." Her throat closed and she coughed, struggling to get the words out, "you are more than a mentor Arn, more than a friend, more than a teacher. I don't have words." She urged her horse closer and reached out to Arn, who clasped her hand in his giant one. "I know Joselyn, for all I have done, training you, spending these last few years with you have been some of the happiest of my life. I couldn't imagine being prouder of anyone, student, friend or daughter. Thank you, Joselyn. For everything." The old paladin's voice grew gruffer with every word, eventually he stopped before his emotions bubbled up. Joselyn looked over at him with pleading, sorrow and guilt and reached out to hug her mentor and hold him tight, her sister sitting awkwardly behind her having to hold onto the saddle not to be toppled. Joselyn leaned over and whispered something in Arn's ear just too quiet for Lucia to hear with the paladin nodding along to what she was saying. Then she released him from her embrace and sat back in her horse, tears streaming openly in her eyes. Arn and Joselyn shared a long silent moment staring straight at each other and then both nodded and the large paladin gently turned his horse around. Without looking back, he rode off to his group of ten knights and spoke quietly to them as the others looked on. At the crest of the hill the King saluted smartly with his sword towards the small group and then the remaining men following the King did the same. With that Branthar, Stee Jahns and the ninety remaining men, leading the refugees turned and headed back to Vandarn to help evacuate the people along the way with the time Arn was about to buy them.

Joselyn sat rooted on her horse, Lucia clutching her sister's hand slightly tighter than was maybe necessary and could only vaguely hear The Swordsman saying something about leaving. No force on Karn could have moved her from in that moment. She watched as Arn after talking to his men turned south and started off at a slow trot, picking up pace as they went, before long they were at a full gallop. The sea of the undead was held mostly in place by the trees and the hills around the edges of the road, a great black wall of shadow and rotting flesh. A wall that shattered when the group of faithful paladins, church knights, soldiers of Vandarn city, country and God smashed into them, divine magic radiating from their weapons and their very auras. In those first few minutes full swathes of undead fell below their swords and their shining bright divine magic, that flowed from every Dragonscale unit paladin. A pile of corpses collapsed under their hooves as seemingly unending waves of undead swarmed again and again and again. Every time, each man slew five or ten or even twenty of the undead men, beasts or monsters another wave poured over the horizon. Joselyn wished she could see how deep the reserves of undead were. Having travelled near them for so long, Lucia alone knew in full truth just how many there were. The answer to their numbers lay in her tears, her sobbing and her inability to look. She kept her eyes buried in her sister's hair as the only hints of her fear. The Swordsman sat with a grim impassive stare, tallying the totals but equally bracing a heart that had seen this scene hundreds if not thousands of times, who had himself ridden into impossible odds and expected to meet a similar fate. As the waves grew and the time to clear and destroy them grew longer and slower the moment that seemed to be frozen and endless also seemed to be hastening, horrifyingly to an inevitable conclusion. One of the knights lost his horse, for a brief time, actually rallying the men with the loss and burning back the dead with the light of his divine aura and magic. When his compatriot's horse went down and the two waded in, back-to-back it raised a small cheer from the other eight soldiers. Arn remained silent on his horse, his giant sword waving through swathes of undead like butter, the shining glow of his faithfulness to Vandarn adding a glowing burn that seemed to burn out the darkness in every moving corpse it hit. The others soldier's cheers quickly died down as another wave of undead approached. A few of the men glanced warily at Arn, looking to him for orders, seeing at this point that he was the only one of his men still on horseback, Arn rode to the back of his men and dismounted. Whispering to his horse and touching his forehead to its nose, Arn gently kissed the horse on the nose and patted it gently with a nod. He turned his back on the horse and marched back among his men, parting them with a hand on one's shoulders. Even from here the sisters and The Swordsman could almost see jovial aura to the giant paladin Lucia even lifted her head when she heard The Swordsman chuckle, "he's enjoying this. "

Arn gently kissed his horse's long nose as he said goodbye to the companion that had been with him for so long, a paladin's gift from

Vandarn, a loyal steed that would be with him till the end. Arn knew this was the end, he had no fear, and he did not want Thirel, his brother's namesake, to end with him. In his mind if the horse lived beyond him, he could imagine that somewhere out there his beloved brother could also have survived, thrived and lived a full, happy life. Arn gripped his greatsword in one hand, hearing it whistle comfortingly through the air as he turned back to his men, placing his hand on one of their shoulders he moved to the front of their angled line. He could feel the grin on his face, he had cheated death so many times, survived so many moments of certain doom. The men were all younger than him, though some of them looked scared, nervous or even a little resigned he saw no doubt. These men would not break, he looked around them his grin falling to a serious scowl, "it is my honour to die beside you today. We are the shield of men, for City, Country and God. For Vandarn!" Arn screamed the last and the paladins charged the undead. They hit the ocean of undead like cannonball hitting tissue paper, the enemy line collapsed under their assault as they tore through the lines again and again like an axe on kindling. Slowly, a relentless press of shambling corpses started to close rank around the Shining beacons of paladinhood. Backs to one another the paladins formed a tight circle and again and again waves of undead on every side fell to them. Eventually a small zombie, laden in dripping viscous shadow, that must either have been a child or a halfling plunged its bony hand through the armour of one of the men. The tiny skeletal, shadow covered hand plunging deep into the man's stomach and tearing out his guts, the man being pulled out of the circle and to the ground. Then there were nine. After what felt like an age another fell and then quickly another. Seven men and Arn, back-to-back in a deepening hold surrounded by the undead, as wave after wave of shadow laden corpses smashed against them. Before long there were four of them left. Three soldiers and Arn, and the first of their fallen brothers, rose and turned on them.

In that moment the corpses of their fallen suddenly among them the remaining soldiers fell. Alone now Arn swung with great fury, his sharper than possible greatsword slicing through all the risen corpses of his men. Creating a small hill of corpses that the old paladin climbed on top of, a moment of respite as he saw forty or fifty deep undead on all sides. In the distance, Arn saw the tiny figures of Joselyn and the others, rooted still watching, unable to tear themselves away and felt a pang of relief when he saw that his horse, Thirel had joined them and was milling next to them. He smiled peacefully, and raised his sword in salute to his companions, not even sure if they would see the salute from all the way up there. He turned and readied himself as the undead closed from all sides. A powerful mailed gauntlet clutched Arns ankle from the pile of bodies underneath him and yanked him from his crested hill, he slid down and was again on the ground. He swept his greatsword and bought some space until the dragonhide wearing corpse of a woman he knew rose up in front of him, inside the reach of his blade. In that instant Arn thought of the woman's name, Shellae, he had knighted her, given her this armour he had crafted himself out of dragonhide. Finally, all at once the shadow filled back wave of living corpses flowed over Varan Arfiran.

Joselyn stared, still rooted to the spot with tears in her eyes as Arn raised his sword in salute back at them and then like an ocean, a wave of shadow and darkness swept over her mentor and friend. She waited, still staring with Lucia tugging at her arm and Thirel, Arn's horse nuzzling at her hand but Joselyn was counting, waiting to see if Arn would rise, undead like the other paladins. Still long after the gap of time that had been between the others falling and rising again, she waited but still there was no sign, maybe he'd risen but she couldn't find him. Stubbornly she stared, fully believing she would have seen his distinctive height, bulk and the greatsword that had always been practically part of him. She hadn't even realised her sister had slid off the horse and was now yanking at the reins, leading both her horse and Arn's horse Thirel. As she was turned away from the mass of undead, she finally awoke, looking down at her sister and then over at the paladin's warhorse who radiated a similar kind of sorrow to her own. "No. Lucia, you take this horse, I'll ride with Thirel." Was all she said, no mention of her nigh paralysed staring at the massacre below. Silently and sullenly, Joselyn slid down from her own horse and hefted herself into Thirel's saddle. Without waiting for her sister Joselyn moved Thirel around and both rider and horse sullenly started to ride north. The Swordsman turned and followed without a word; his head bowed in a silent, internal reverie as he mourned one of his oldest friends. Mourned a man who barely recognised all the evidence in front of him, that one of his closest friends and comrades stood beside him. Varan Arfiran and The Swordsman had stood shoulder to shoulder in battle after battle, in the war to save the entire world. They had been the only two along with Annia to understand the burden of leading armies against those impossible odds with the fate of the world in the balance. Annia, the only other person he'd ever known to lead armies against an evil this powerful the only other person who could share their burden, their knowledge and the weight it lays upon your soul for ever more had been the one to send the message both he and Arn had just heard. He hoped Arn was at rest, just thinking about it made him curse the fact the sun kept rising on him every day. The Swordsman again resigned himself to the fact he was going to keep going regardless of how he might feel. So, he turned his horse and followed the sullen young woman north.

CHAPTER 19

Dreams of a King

Gartan Emand had made the journey from his native Haartiff in the Swordlands to the tholan settlement of the tribe of the snow cat several times a year, always at the same time. The snow cats, though primarily nomadic in nature, were the most reliant of tholans on outside trade. Staying closer to the edge of the great glacier than most of their brethren; seen in the tholan realm as a kind of link between the tholans and the outer world. In the olden days they had been mainly raiders, coming down off the glaciar to raid settlements as far as the Swordlands. As High King Crothan had revolutionised not just tholan life to be less nomadic, encouraged advancements, civilisation and commerce, the tribe of the snow cat he had helped evolve too in the last two hundred and fifty years. Trading frequently with the Snow Elves and the Drow of nearby settlements, Gartan had inherited the route and the job from his father, his family had been trading this route for two hundred years. Coming back with gold, precious gems, Drow and snow elf magic to say nothing of other, rarer elven and tholan trinkets to be forged as crests and attachments to weapons and armour in Haartiff, the heart of the best human made weapons in the Swordlands. His predecessors had often travelled the route heavily laden with expensive guards, sometimes even tholans or elves especially in wartimes or times of great political upheaval. Gartan had relied on a few alternative security measures, first and foremost, reputation. His primary trading partners were Snow elves, Drow and tholans, not even the most precocious of bandits would want to make an enemy of those three groups. Gartan was also quite handy with both sword and spell and not entirely unfamiliar with poisons. In the twenty years since the war when he took over this route, he'd been robbed less than a dozen times and had not lost so much as a copper in the process and gained a few items albeit with a few scars alongside. He kept other things as surprises too, black powder bombs, hidden compartments, retractable spikes on the wagon, the wagon itself reinforced and last but by no means least a few hidden spots along the route where he could stash the wagon in a pinch from pursuing eyes. Gartan had seen some things over the years, dragons flying overhead, armies, merchants and monsters. With guile, bribery and understanding of the swift changing nature of politics in the Swordlands his father had managed to keep his business going after a fashion for the entire of the Witch-Queen's invasion. Not one to risk upsetting anyone though his father had secretly donated weapons and armour to the men of the sword, "things fall off wagons, what can you do." His father would say to him when they dumped parcels of equipment in the forest for the rebel group to find. The truth of it all had been burned into Gartan's soul, we are merchants, traders and smiths. We run our forges and trade our goods and no, we can't afford politics and such things as taking sides. Gartan had taken over the business after the war, he'd never had to make any kind of decision about Witch-Queens and wizards, heroes and villains. He'd met the bard once, Hanalan Harpsong walking the road near the Dragon-sir River as casual as you like; singing a song about a Princess. The bard had nodded to him and walked alongside the wagon for a while, chatting and singing songs. Gartan had asked him about the Princess Annia, the bard had mumbled something and changed the subject and when Gartan had asked where he was going, he said he had been going to visit an old friend.

Gartan's reverie was broken by a horrifying slithering, shuffling noise which made him look up and his horses stutter to a stop. The familiar clicking and creaking of hooves and wheels rolling over dragon bone and wood of the dragon bridge. Even at times like this, midday with the sun overhead was always an eerie almost heavy aura to the entire space around the bridge but especially on it. At times it was as if you stood in a moment of history. It was not, as Gartan immediately thought where you wanted to hear such an inhuman sound. He soothed the horses as he raised his head and looked all around the bridge and the skies, Gartan wasn't a man given to panic, he dropped his reins and slipped down off the wagon, patting the horses on his way past to calm them. Walking to the edge of the giant dragon's ribcage that made up the bridge Gartan looked out over the river to see if he could locate the noise. As he did, the river split with a giant splash and a thing cloaked in in shadow with large leathery batlike wings that were dripping not just water but also a kind of liquid shadow that turned to mist as it dripped off the wings, long spindly arms and legs with huge claws at the end and a long curling devils tail. Inside the mist and shadow demon, holding it together seemed to be what looked like a female human wizard, either dead or in some manner of doomed torpor unaware of the thing that had hijacked and was growing from her corpse. The thing looked at Gartan with dead womans eyes as if it were examining him, assessing him for a threat that his short sword seemed woefully ill equipped to provide. Gartan and the shadow creature faced off for what felt like an age to the smithing trader before the thing cocked its head as if listening to unheard alarm and spun and flew away into the night.

Gartan noted as it did that in its hand was a long, slender and curved dagger. Way more expensive than anything he'd ever seen or forged, with a blade of pure obsidian or some other kind of black shining metal that glinted and sang to him of power and danger so much that he desired the blade, even in the face of this shadowy demonic abomination. As it disappeared into the midday sky Gartan realised his entire body was covered in a cold sweat and as he looked down, he saw his hand was shaking with a fear that had started in the small of his spine and shaken him to his core. He gripped the bridge for support and took a few deep breaths, leaning forward to feel the sun on his face for just a second before leaning back and taking a deep breath. Gartan looked around him incredulously, shaking his head and muttering to himself, "This bridge, this place." He sighed to himself and walked back to the wagon, patting the horses as much to comfort himself as the beasts, "every time. Every single time we come here something ridiculous happens. I swear this bridge will be the death of me." Climbing back up on his wagon he clicked his tongue and the horses started rolling their way over the dragon bridge, as he lowered off the other side he sighed. The relief of being past the bridge as evident in his breath as in his eyes, "not this time though eh lads? Not this time." With which Gartan Emand rode away from the dragon bridge shaking his head at the latest fantastical, horrifying thing in an ever-lengthening list that had happened to him on, near or around this cursed bridge.

Just outside the borders of Vandarn, north of the lands of Dern and south of Takal's southern border lay a kind of scrub land. A dry brush land, a kind of no mans land, south of the Takalan city of Kes, the ancient and pestilent Quoity swamp forest to the north east. To the West the hills and the dense forests of the old elven kingdom where it was dangerous to wander unbidden. Many a wanderer has stumbled unknowing into elven territory only to disappear never to be seen again. This little patch of neutral territory wedged at the edge of the cold unforgiving Vandarnian principality of Dern, the far edges of the elvenwood and the swamp forest that marked the borders of Takal, had in the past been used as a kind of no man's land for peace talks and diplomacy. Camping here while waiting for other factions seen often as a sign of peace and a request for talks. It wasn't accident or opportunity that Hanalan Harpsong had chosen here to wait for the paladin Varan Arfiran. Arn had never really taken to Harpsong, he'd shared a bond of war with The Swordsman, he'd understood the weight of responsibility and dedication to a higher purpose of Annia, he'd even enjoyed the gentle and good humour of the halfling, despite his tendency to exaggeration and excitable nature. Something about Harpsong had always rubbed the paladin the wrong way, Harpsong had always believed it had been how similar they were in unforeseen ways. Both were arrogant, unshakeably confident in their abilities and as much as the paladin denied it over the years, they were both not above using their powerful personalities to influence others to get the job done. The way Harpsong had seen it though, the only difference was that he was honest about what he did and how he used his charm to sway people. Harpsong had made a small camp with a combination of supplies and some mild magical effects, the bard had done it with such casual ease, almost as if he was on autopilot. Urnath had found watching Harpsong's casual automatic manner oddly soothing. The bard must have crafted so many camps this way over the year that it was an unconscious series of actions that he rhythmically strolled through. Tending the horses, Hrasse not taking to Harpsong had refused a feedbag and the bard had ended up dumping the tholan horse's feed on the ground in front of her. Until that final moment when he sat down with a sigh and poked the fire with hot tea boiling over top. The smell of the woodsmoke and the tea was enough to cast the tholan wizard back to thousands of camps with the great High King Crothan, Urnath had never taken to travel or camping but his King had loved it. He would sleep on the ground with not so much as a second thought and took any excuse to travel the long way to faraway lands on one trip or another. Even as an old man nothing could keep the High King in his seat. Pulling his mind back to the present Urnath took a seat on a small stool of wood and leathers Harpsong had set up for him, oddly comfortable and Urnath could smell the hint of magic in the crafting of it. He smiled at the bard who was happily humming to himself and stirring the tea impatiently, "so Harpsong, what happens now? Are we waiting for your friends?" The bard smiled coyly at Urnath's question. He paused as if searching for the words, "friends? I doubt very much Valenstorm is coming, given how he was when I left him, I very much feel he'll be hiding, regrettably at the bottom of a bottle, not that I blame him after what he's been through. As for the paladin? I'm not sure I'd ever have called him a friend. That man has disapproved of my very existence for so long it's hard to imagine him saying my name without spitting. Clash of personalities let's call it, but he's an ally, or at least he was twenty years ago. He'll be here. That's why we're sitting right here, the most neutral territory on Karn a no man's land between two kingdoms that have been at war on and off for centuries. To him a peace offering and to me, a kind of private joke at his old fashioned and uptight manner." The bard chuckled to himself, thoroughly amused by his mocking little act of childish defiance in the face of Varan Arfiran's stiff propriety.

Urnath looked around him. He was in the High Hall in Crothan's throne room. The long hall with the table of chiefs, twenty unique thrones for the Kings of the tholan tribes who would come to sit with the High King and discuss the matters of state. The room was empty, cold and draughty in a way that could chill a man from bone to heart. Crothan never complained, he complained about everything else in life, relentlessly wishing he was on the open road, wandering and carefree like in his younger days. Complaining about his throne being uncomfortable and the pains he got sitting on it, never the cold though and never the draughts. Urnath would wear his full court robes of ceremony every time they were in here. Most thought it was him being a stickler for tradition, a man who minded the rules and traditions that marked and honoured tholan culture. A very close few, the King himself and the few people Urnath had ever shared his bedchamber with all knew, it was simply because he couldn't stand the room. The draughts of cold air that caught you like nothing else in life. He realised the King was on the throne staring at him in that odd way he had, "Urnath! I said I thought I gave you an order?" Urnath startled at the King's familiar barking voice turned. "Sorry my King, I..." Urnath stopped, suddenly unsure of where he was, what he was saying. "I, I didn't know my King, I didn't know what to do and then, I mean then Ramlar appeared, he told me it was important and I..." Urnaths rambling, mumbling discourse stopped in the middle as he looked around him lost, confused. "You were lost." Crothan said matter of factly. "My father told me a fable when I was a boy of the first snow cat tamed by our tholan ancestors, its mother had died and a hunter had found the litter, frozen and close to death. He nursed them, tried to save them but one by one they all died, except the runt. See being the runt of the litter, the weakest of the group he had always had to fight harder to get milk, to keep warm or to be fed at all. Everything was harder for him you see, because he was so small, so weak. He fell more often so he had to be better at picking himself up off the ground. His legs would tremble and sometimes he would fall again, but that little runt wouldn't stop trying, he'd lift those trembling legs up again and again and again until they learned to hold him up. The hunter weaned him, fed him and cared for him till he was strong. Till his weak muscles turned lean and powerful, till he grew and skinny became lithe and resilience became cunning, and the runt had become like the hunter. The hunter and the runt would run together, chase game together, eat together and when one slept the other sat guard. One day the hunter took the runt into the forest and unbuckled his collar, told him to leave and threw rocks when he wouldn't. He told the runt to be free. The runt wandered, lost in the forest not knowing where to go. Three weeks later he turned up back at the hunter's cabin, his lost collar in his mouth; looking for his friend. Just in time for the hunter's funeral. They say that he sat, dutiful by the hunter's funeral pyre. Refused to leave, to abandon his companion's side, because the snow cat was loyal to his kin and that small tribe of nomads, this cat by their side saw the spirit of Thol in the snow cat and to honour him became the tribe of the snow cat. One of the totem tribes, born of the loyalty and dedication this one runt had to his family, when he had become strong and the other weak, he went from protected to protector. That's what family is Urnath, loyalty. What always bothered me about that story Urnath, is that stupid old cat, standing by a grave rather than living his life, hunting hares and fucking other snow cats! I didn't tell you to go get yourself killed on some damned fool quest I told you to go get a life!" Urnath had been listening rapt, he had missed his crazy, absent minded cranky old King so much. He felt the tears pour down his face openly, unashamedly and with a bittersweet beauty he had missed his beloved friend so much, "That's not strictly true my King, you told me to go find the kind of life I wanted. This is what I want to do, I've lived, I've loved, and I've lost. Losing you though my King, that left a wound even handsome young bards wouldn't be able to fill, so I'll charge into certain death and if I can, I'll have a hand in saving the world. I'm too old to start again and I am far too old and too stubborn to go serve some other King or find some handsome young lover, so I'll take the wizard Akarash's staff, I'll charge into Deathmount and if I die there, it'll be a good death.

Good enough." Urnath saw the old King smile, weeping openly also as tears rolled unchecked down his leathered old face. The King looked at him with a look of such beatific calm and whispered, "goodbye my son. I'm so proud of you." And Urnath awoke, his cheeks wet as he stirred groggily under his blanket to see the bard Harpsong, still at the fire which now was barely embers, tea swirling in a rough clay cup in his hand. Without looking over at Urnath, Harpsong spoke, "They're here."

Empty battlefields

Lucia had imagined she had felt the worst of it when she had been limping, running and fleeing. Alone in the dark, in pools of mud and dirt running from her home trying to avoid a shuffling army of barely sentient undead as it ambled north idly. This last week or so had been worse, even with her sister who had become unrecognisable in the years they had been apart, she was not the arrogant, strong young women Lucia had known. This Joselyn was scarred, and battle tested, wounds you both could and couldn't see, scarred her body and her soul. She was quiet and reflective and seemed to be fighting an internal battle ever since she had seen her mentor sacrifice his life for a handful of refugees he'd never met, without flinching or even a second's pause. Joselyn had barely spoken a word in that week, though they had barely rested, barely been able to with the shuffling sounds of shadow covered, undead beasts pursuing them the whole way. A few days ago, a handful of what had once been dogs or jackals or both had leapt from the woods, having finally caught up with them. Joselyn hadn't even turned around and The Swordsman, the sad, tired unshaven old drunk had slid from his horse and much like the bridge before when she had first met him, had suddenly come to life his black blade weaving hypnotically as he started to sway from side to side. All as if he were preparing for a great dance and as the undead canines leapt, he wove his sword like a wizard or a sorcerer casting a spell. Drawing unseen patterns in the air before him that seemed to slice and chop and swat away the animals as if they were nothing. All of which resulted in an acrid burning smell and inhuman screams when the sword bit through their shadow cloaked corpses. Nothing even came near him as he spun and leapt and pirouetted through the air, casually weaving his way from left to right and back again his sword like a wild conductor's wand as he waved his way through a symphony of death that these devil dogs even knew their part in. When it was over, he spun on his heel back to the girls and bowed, smiled a crooked, mischievous smile and had that strange youthful glint in his eye again. When he saw no real reaction from either sister, Lucia still horrified and trying to process the undead dogs and things that had attacked and Joselyn, had simply pulled up Thirel and her and the horse had watched impassively, she never even reached for her sword. Lucia was worried, The Swordsman simply sheathed his black bladed sword which seemed to thrum causing The Swordsman to pat it and mutter to it "well, at least your happy." and slowly remount his horse before turning the quiet, exhausted little party north again.

The Swordsman had tried to convince the two sisters to go with the knights, to turn off and head to Vandarn, to Dern and even to the Elvenwood, he had promised to teach them the phrases for safe passage in elven, but they would not be deterred. The elder one could at least fight, so like Arfiran in her combat style that almost immediately when he saw her with the blade in hand, knew the old paladin had trained her. The younger sister though had a look on her face like she was in the middle of some nightmare she expected to wake up from back home in her bed. He knew the look well; he had felt it before every battle he'd ever fought. Standing with an army of men, looking down on another army of numbers beyond counting waiting on the cusp of a nightmare of death and fear. He loved swordplay, he loved combat and though it shamed him to admit it, he loved his bloodthirsty side, temper it though he tried with compassion it was a dark monster inside him that he had succumbed to many times in his life. War though, thousands on either side in an inescapable moment which always felt too big, too horrific and too expensive had always filled him with terror. As mercenary, as foot soldier and especially as general. The Swordsman even now had sleepless nights where the images of young men and women under his command had been sundered upon the battlefield and died in the dark and the mud, bleeding and crying his name. Every one of them his fault, his responsibility. It was a weight that hung on him heavier than all the men he'd killed by his hand combined, and that weight was heavy enough. In his youth he had been callow enough to imagine himself some kind of swashbuckling hero, merely using his relentless skills to ambush slavers, robber barons and monsters. Never once stopping to admit the awful and dark truth to himself, he enjoyed it. Harpsong had imagined them heroes, he'd spun tales of The Swordsman's skill, his reckless heroics and his easy charm but the bard had never been able to see past it to the truth. For all he dressed it up The Swordsman was a killer, as cold as the coldest assassin. Annia could see it, sometimes when they would be resting or hiding from the Witch-Queen's army, he would catch her looking at him with distaste, worry and something akin to pity. She would never admit it and though the bond of friendship and affection was strong, he knew in her heart she would always see him for what he was, one bad day away from being a cold-hearted killer. Harpsong was so in love with the story, the magic of it all and the 'legend' of the men of the sword. He was never a hero, he could see that clearer than ever as he rode here and now, north with two young women, riding into the heart of darkness and near certain death. One stricken with grief, the other overwhelmed with fear and him a sad old man whose heart, like everything inside him was worn, empty and almost done.

Lucia saw the fires first, the younger sisters exceptional vision making out the glint of fire before the others had even looked up, "There's a camp ahead." She said, half hopeful, half in fear as the other two raised their heads in the dark and peered ahead looking for the faint glimmer of the campfire. Joselyn trotted Thirel out in front. The large warhorse's heavy hooves pounding the scrub brush with intent. As the party approached the campfire, they could make out two men, one under a camping blanket still awakening and the other casually sat by the fire but positioned so the light and smoke of the fire obscured his face. "Varan Arfiran, you old con man. What could possibly bring you riding north to the border of Takal?" Joselyn startled at the mention of her mentor's name, stopped in her tracks. The Swordsman however lit up upon hearing a voice that he knew like his own, that of his brother in arms, his best friend and the man who had saved his life literally and figuratively countless times over the years. He started to ride forward and then remembered, Harpsong wouldn't be able to recognise him, to see him and even the presence of the Tilak blade wouldn't be logic enough to prove to even the bard that his best friend stood before him. His hope crushed as soon as it had started to rise, he settled in his saddle and turned to look at Joselyn, coughing to shake her from her shock. Joselyn looked over at The Swordsman and then back to the bard, "I'm afraid friend I am not Arn, my name is Joselyn, his squire, his student." She had barely spoken to The Swordsman or Lucia for the past nine days, now her first words were of Arn. Her voice choked, and she fought back tears, even now her grief was so palpable, even now it was like a presence amongst them. The bard bounced to his feet with a broad grin, "Joselyn it's me! Hanalan Harpsong, surely you remember me child! Where is the old fool? Swanning about being all knightly at court with King Branthar? Too good to come save the world himself?" Joselyn nearly startled at the bard's playful words almost screamed, but as she turned to speak The Swordsman slipped from his horse and stepped forward, "I'm sorry friend. Arfiran is gone, he sacrificed himself. Saving people from this shadow, this thing." His somber tone bringing the bard down with a crash, Harpsong looked over The Swordsman's shoulder at the young woman, "oh Joselyn, I'm so sorry. I am a callow fool. Why are you here? Surely you don't mean to come into the demon's den with us?" The young woman nodded, still unable to speak. The third horse gently rode up beside her and her younger sister reached out to take her hand and comfort her as The Swordsman laid a hand on Harpsong's shoulder. "Han, she is grief stricken still. It will take her some time, come let's have some of that tea." The bard looked at The Swordsman for a second as if something in his brain was struggling, something like an itch at the back of his head and then he smiled at the broken and greying man before him. "Of course, friend, is that the Tilak blade you have there? I guess that's why you three are here. Two Gosdblood weapons is more than enough I think to end the threat. We can close the portal with either one of them, I think." Nodding to the rising tholan wizard and the black bladed axe at his hip Harpsong continued "Crothan's axe. One of the most legendary artifacts on Karn. And here you come with another? By Necirate, Annia might even be pleased to see me at this rate." And the bard turned away from The Swordsman and started to make more tea, not even waiting for the young women to dismount their horses.

Morning rose over the camp with a nervousness that felt as if it was wary to what it would find there. The Swordsman was awake, he hadn't had a drink in about three weeks, he had slept little and what sleep he'd found was fitful and filled with unpleasant dreams. He sat by the dead fire running a whetstone over the tilak blade. The blade was magical, an artefact forged in a time before measure, of unmatchable power, it needed no sharpening. The sword had tried to impart this to The Swordsman many times over the decades they had been bonded but still, he went through the motions. Like a ritual of weapon care as much a part of the man as the heavy burden of guilt, however well-earned, that he took everywhere with him. He glanced over at the bard, sleeping happily in the morning light. His best friend in the entire world, his closest companion and the man who had introduced him to Jaria, his beloved wife. He had simply looked past him, talked around him and barely noticed him. "Is that the Tilak blade?" He had asked without any recognition, simply dismissing what his brain was telling him, moving swiftly on. All evening as they had talked, told their disparate stories, the girls of the escape from the army of shadows and dead and Harpsong of the death and resurrection of Valenstorm, the shadow thing they chased and of Akarash Beliheim's warnings and instructions. All of them looked in worried awe at the dragon's head staff the tholan wizard held as the bard told and embellished the story as bards are want to do. Every time The Swordsman had spoken, mentioned Akarash, Valenstorm or Annia, the bard had nodded and responded but in the same detached way as if he hadn't really registered who had spoken while still answering the question. As he sharpened the blade, he thought back almost in meditation of the years of adventuring just the two of them wandering the Swordlands getting into trouble. Then when Annia joined them and they started fighting slavers, formed the men of the sword and the years together fighting the war. A tiny band of rogues and thieves who grew in number and weight until they stood at the cusp of the mountain they now were headed to at the head of an army. To kill the Witch-Queen, smash her army and stop her opening a portal to some dark pit that

The Swordsman hadn't really understood. Unspeakable evil, doom for all races on Karn was all he knew, all he needed to know. He'd leave the details to the others, and he led the army to war. Shoulder to shoulder with Arfiran. Even without recognising him the paladin had realised that sense of camaraderie, it had been almost like the old days just to see the old paladin again. This though, if any one man should and could see him, recognise him standing in front of him it should have been Hanalan Harpsong. The two men had travelled together most of their adult lives and here they were travelling into death and darkness once again for the thousandth time and the bard couldn't even tell. It would be a story the bard would have loved, if only he could see it enough to tell it.

The sun now fully rose and the others began to wake, The Swordsman put away his blade and started to make tea and gather supplies for breakfast for his waking companions. The conversation that morning was terse, nervous and impatient. No one it seemed was in the mood for camaraderie, friendship or waiting, as if the weight of what lay ahead pushed them all to rush forward. The impact of Princess Annia's message like a spell, drawing them with all alacrity to Deathmount and what lay ahead. After eating in relative silence, they rode north. The tholan wizard using his magic to summon two strange beasts for him and the bard to ride and keep pace with the others. As they crossed the border into the Northern kingdom of Takal, turning west before going north if only to avoid the Quoity swamp forest and whatever twisted evils might crawl or slither out of there. The small party had ridden for days in relative silence, occasionally Harpsong would engage the sisters, looking to learn more about them but the dark sullen weight over everyone kept silencing him. In time they rode through the miles of battleground where twenty years ago, they had fought the largest battle in the history of the heartlands. The Swordsman who was quiet for most of the journey withdrew even further as they crossed the plains where the battle had been, his thoughts stuck in the past with the events of that day. Of Jaria dying in his arms, of the promise he made her and had failed to live up to every day since. Her silken voice in his mind's eye, her accent curling around the hard consonants as she made him swear, "You finish this, you'll survive, because it's what you do and when it's over, don't you dare wither away. Live. Just live, you might not have earned it but I damn sure did. Live for me my love." The others, at least he hoped, hadn't seen his face as they rode but tears had been streaming down his face as he spent half the journey across the once battlefield reliving not just that moment but every year with his wife. They had never known peace together though Jaria had spoken of it often. All the times of separation through the war as they fought on different fronts or different missions her wisdom, her kindness, her skill with a blade and her sharp and at times cold humour. She was everything The Swordsman wasn't. Strong, not just physically but mentally and in a way that allowed her to deal with the weight of responsibility and life without being crushed by it. Her final moments replaying again and again in his mind. As they neared Deathmount he stopped suddenly and wordlessly slid off his horse. The others stopped and stared at him, Harpsong again looked that same quizzical way he had in the camp as if something was itching the back of his head. Dropping to his knees The Swordsman touched the ground where she had died, looking up at the waiting companions he simply said "Sorry. I had to stop. I had to, to have a moment." He turned away from them to the empty ground and could almost see Jaria, lying in his arms the light slowly fading again and allowed the tears to come, "I'm sorry love. I just, I just couldn't. I'll fix this if I can though and then, well hopefully then we can be together. I love you." And he rose, looked over at the party who were looking at him in a mixture of confusion and embarrassment. All except the bard, who had a look on him like a man with a puzzle he couldn't quite work and instead stared at it till his eyes went blurry. The Swordsman climbed back up onto his horse and looked around. "Well? We're not going to save the world sitting down here, are we?"

CHAPTER 21

On the cusp of twilight

Annia, Ander and Aera had retreated from the platform nearly two weeks ago, reconnected with Annia's small band of men of the sword and resupplied. Annia had explained to the two mercenaries that without a Godsblood weapon they couldn't prevent the portal from being opened. However, without a Godsblood weapon at least Deathskull, or whatever that was possessing him could not open the portal. Even with the crack that Barvara or the entity that had once been her, had managed to force when the Barbarian High King died. Ander had asked how they knew anyone was coming, especially with Godsblood weapons. Annia had just smiled, "I know my husband. He'll find a way, probably something to do with that damned arch-mage Beliheim. But he'll find a way." As obsessed with vengeance or saving the world as Ander was, even he himself wasn't sure what had motivated him to demand to stay, he had always been so cold and calculating in the past. Something that had been at his core, his desire to survive above all else but here he was camping with slave-freeing folk, waiting for an opportunity to sacrifice himself to stop something inhuman rising out of the pit of the lost and damned. A pit Aera had made a pact with before they met and was the source of her inhuman powers and he thought, probably her madness. At the thought of Aera he glanced over at her, asleep again. The closest she had been to being lucid since the thing inside her had erupted from her to form the half-demon Deathskull had been when she used her magic to annihilate the group of Takalan knights and wizards on the balcony of the tower. She had been either asleep or stuck in some fitful waking nightmare, as if she was half stuck in the pit of the lost and damned and half in the waking world. Occasionally she would become lucid and stare into Ander's eyes alternatively asking him to save her or kill her, or both. Ander had never before been in a situation he couldn't murder his way out of. It did cross his mind to put her out of her misery, but something always stayed his hand. Not the very least of which was the large human cleric of Necirate who no doubt would disapprove of what she would see in her simple way as an act of murder rather than mercy. It was more than that which stayed his hand though. Aera Darkhorne had been his companion, his friend and what else? More? He wasn't ready to face that possibility quite yet, regardless of the fact they had been together for so long now it felt like he had become part of her, and her part of him. He rose from his conversation with Annia without speaking and tended to Aera, he could see her starting to wake and tried to get her to drink some water, she grabbed it from his hands greedily and gulped down the entire jug abnormally fast. Staring wildly into his eyes she mumbled as she often had, "they're coming, they have the sword with them. We can't let the sword come here! IT WILL KILL US!" She screamed again and started to babble nonsensically but exhausted quickly and collapsed into a pile and unconsciousness yet again. Annia turned to Ander and smiled "At least she had some water, I swear she's getting better. Her strength returns with every day."

A human dressed in green slipped into the tent and nodded at Annia, "it looks like they're coming. Definitely Harpsong at least." Annia nodded and smiled at Ander, "well maybe you should leave Aera here, but it looks like it might be time go. I'm not sure she's fit for what is to come." As soon as Annia mentioned her the sickly elf witch awoke leaping to her feet. "We... I mean I am ready and fit to travel, the waking nightmares will not stop until the portal is closed. Properly closed so trust me, you need me, at least as a barometer of success." Her voice was singsong, off key and oddly melodic, something it had lacked recently and the sound of its off key and unsettling tone made the halfling smile too. She was getting back to her creepy and mildly disturbing self, though even looking at her Ander could tell she was hiding pain; how much he couldn't tell but it was there. He nodded at her and turned back to Annia "you heard the lady, lead on. Her connection to the pit will be handy before the end I promise." Ander went over to Aera to give his shoulder for her to lean her hand upon and with his help the pair followed Annia out into the night at their small camp. The camp had been hidden by elven magic at the foot of the giant Deathmount and outside, down the hill, riding casually towards the giant mountain shaped like a demon skull, was the oddest group Ander had seen in some time. A shabby looking warrior with no armour and a single black bladed sword, a strangely thin old tholan carrying a large powerful battle axe on his hip and a large powerful looking dragon's head staff and two young women, one armed and armoured exactly like a member of Vandarn's scout force and the other, ragged, unarmed and completely out of place. The two young women were so similar that Ander immediately saw they were sisters. Finally at the front of the group a bard dressed in casual blue and yellow as if he were enroute to some ball, clearly his idea of travelling clothes, his short choppy blonde hair, blue eyes and broad charming smile, a simple sword at his side and a small harp on his back. Even had he not been a keen observer Ander would have known Hanalan Harpsong anywhere. There were paintings of Harpsong all over Karn and his smarmy, cocky smile was as unmistakable as the inexplicable rage the bard engendered in Ander who against all reason wanted nothing more than to stab the smug look off his handsome face.

Annia took a deep breath as she looked down at the approaching party, curious that Varan wasn't here, the paladin wouldn't miss this, then she saw the young woman he worked with riding his horse and her heart sank. The old man hadn't made it had he. She held her sorrow in check, she had work to do and there would be plenty of tears to be shed in the days to come. She turned her eyes back on her errant husband and tried to suppress her frustration and anger. Annia was in her mid-fifties, she felt she was holding up rather admirably all things considered. Her hair had more than a little grey in it and her body a few more lines and maybe some of the edges didn't fall quite the way they did in her youth, but she was pleased with it. That silly old fool looked as he had during the war, he'd cut his hair again in that awful choppy way she hated, and he hadn't aged a day. He hadn't aged a day since the war, since the Gods had seen fit to reward the heroes of the war for their part in preventing what they had called the end of the land and the heavens above. Annia felt her hands balling into fists and realised she was going to have to ask Necirate for some patience in the next two minutes. She forced a smile which unfortunately for her ended up coming out like that of a dragon about to bite its victims head off. She approached her dismounting husband and held out her arms, "Han. You're here." She looked around the odd band of companions, "and you brought friends? Joselyn, it is good to see you again child. You look well." Joselyn approached Annia and bowed slightly, "My lady. I pledge my sword to you, to freedom and to all the men of the sword in the days ahead." Her voice was measured, stiff and cold. It reminded Annia of the old paladin so much she almost sniffed to miss Varan Arfiran's presence. Urnath and Annia had met a couple of times over the years and knew each other vaguely enough, the old tholan wizard hung back but nodded curtly with a slight smile to the Princess which she returned with a smile and a slight nod of her own. Still on his horse at the back of the group the shabby swordsman was smirking in a crooked way that was vaguely familiar and brought strange feelings of annoyance and affection in equal measure. Quickly as she looked over, Annia's view was drawn to the younger woman, dressed in ragged, near ruined clothes and with a look of utter bewilderment. The similarity to Joselyn was unmistakable but this girl was younger and had a softer and less grizzled look than her sister, though right now she resembled a half-drowned kobold with mud for makeup. "Who do we have here? Joselyn's sister for sure but who beyond that? I am Princess Annia Harpsong, leader of the men of the sword and the owner of a bathtub and spare armour." Annia smiled at the overwhelmed looking young woman who smiled sheepishly, "I'm Lucia, I'm from umm, Mar-Thatch. Umm and daggers." Lucia said flatly "I'd like daggers." Now a little of her sister's steel crept into her voice along with a good portion of her own rage, exhaustion and sadness. "These bastards killed my Arlo; I want some fucking revenge." Tears were now streaming down the young woman's dirt-stained face. Annia rested an oddly gentle mailed hand on her shoulder and looked down at her like a saddened mother would a hungry orphan. "Kerwin, let's get her cleaned up and kitted out and Kerwin? Don't forget the daggers." Annia turned her attention back to Harpsong, "Han. What a broken little band of curios you've brought to me my love. Despite everything I'm glad you're here, I wasn't sure you'd come." Harpsong smiled and fought to keep the sadness and regret from washing the smile away as he embraced his wife, "Annia, love, I'm sorry. I wish, well I wish I could change things but right now I've got what we need so let's get prepared and get up there before

Barvara and whatever else is up there opens a pit and summons something called the Formless."

Lucia lay in the still warm water and cleaned herself up for what felt like the first time in forever and every muscle in her body as it unwound had ached and screamed at her in pain. Nowv as she found her brain quietened, she let her arms and legs flop, and her head fall against the back of the metal tub. Her mind drifted, bringing her images of shadow filled undead, dying knights and the screaming of horses, Arlo's face, his rotting shadow filled corpse and her parents. Her parents dead, Arlo dead and now what? Following into Joselyn's world surrounded by huge, important people, powerful people and here was little Lucia the apple girl. She should stay here; she should have stayed with the refugees and returned to Vandarn but her stubbornness, her fury and her need to be strong in front of her sister just wouldn't let her. Besides, Joselyn was holding on by the thinnest of threads and only Lucia could really see it. Her sister needed her and little Lucia the apple girl wouldn't let her down, not now. Lucia lifted her hand from the tub and stared at it, wrinkled by the water it trembled before her, not from cold or even fully from fear, she was too numb for something as simple as fear. Lucia had watched everyone she loved die, everyone she had known and lived around day to day for years torn to pieces in front of her eyes. Then fled for days and ridden for so much more that she couldn't keep track, surrounded by strangers and a sister who was transformed from the girl she knew into a hardened warrior, a knight in all but name. Joselyn was not only not out of place with these great and powerful heroes, but she was also clearly one of them. Lucia looked over at the torn rags of her dress, she'd worn it specially to market to excite and tease Arlo, instead it had witnessed the end of her world. A world she had longed to get away from and instead had seen ripped, torn and burned to the ground in front of her. She had no home to go back to, Joselyn was the only thing in the world she had left and if Joselyn was going to go into the foulest place in the existence and die trying to save the world then little Lucia the apple girl was damned sure she was going with her. Lucia clenched her fist and stared it down with sudden unbridled fury, the fist stopped shaking and she smiled, rage and determination fixed themselves on her face. To no one in particular, Lucia simply said, "Good."

The Swordsman entered the large tent slipping in at the back as the conversation was already underway. Annia and Harpsong arguing even though they were agreeing was something he'd been listening to all his life. The tholan wizard Urnath trying to be the calming voice of reason. The unsettling sickly elven woman in pale blue robes urging them to move, saying time was getting short, but in between moments of lucidity odd bouts of madness and nonsense sprouting from her. Joselyn, still somber and in and odd mourning state while her younger sister had returned. Lucia stood at her sister's side, hair now tied back in a ponytail but still wild with it, she had chosen black leather armour that looked sturdy but designed to let her move with both speed and agility and seemed to have more daggers dotted about it every time he looked. Lucia said nothing and never strayed from her sister's side, but the young woman had an all too familiar mixture of determination and fear on her face. Then there was the halfling, sitting at the back taking no interest in the discussion, leaning against a pillar slicing an apple with a dagger as he occasionally darted an eye at the sickly elf. There had been a time when The Swordsman would have been over there in amongst it, he'd be the voice of reason and the arbiter, usually he'd have ended up making the decision about the approach and the plan. That was another him, a man with a name and friends and a whole lot of other things that only existed now because he remembered them. He glanced over again as voices started to raise again and then over at one of the tables Annia's people had set up for the meeting. The nearby table had been set with fruits, meat and small plates of pastry, water and fruit juices and even a couple of bottles of East Takalan red had been set up. The Swordsman looked around before grabbing one of the bottles and slipping outside.

Night in Takal fell so swiftly that in the winter months it could come in no more than two dozen steps. Walking one minute in daylight and the next in such darkness you could struggle to see your hand in front of your face. The Swordsman could almost smell the fall of night though there was no twilight to hint at the impending darkness. Memories of years gone by danced like elf children in his mind, planning battles, running from the law, from armies who had been hunting them for weeks or months. Sleeping in mud or in the crawlspace of some farmhouse or tavern. They had been cold and tired and worn out, but it had been where The Swordsman had shone, he wouldn't have been afraid to admit it had been the happiest years of his life. From the early days when it was just him, Harpsong and Annia, to the height of the war when the men of the sword had become a link between the war effort and the people of the Swordlands, Vandarn, Shoui and even Takal who were being ground down by the machine of the Takalan occupational forces. By the time the war was coming to an end the men of the sword had gone from an outlaw gang who fought slavers to an entire army of misfits, rogues and rejects. The entire war effort had sprung up around them and before they knew how, The Swordsman, the bard and the Princess had the whole world looking to them, expecting them to do something. Jaria used to mock him that finally his callow charm had some real-world applications, and it was up to him to make use of it beyond free drinks and pretty girls. He had been a cheap drunk with a nice sword before the war, and suddenly, there he stood the fulcrum upon which the world spun armies at his back and armies across the field. One of the greatest military minds in history at his shoulder looking to him for guidance. It had been so much, too much for him, he'd never wanted any of that. He had escaped alcohol with a purpose, the men of the sword, fighting for a just cause and running from the law. An underground base in some old ruins in the southwest Swordlands, Harpsong and Annia, the mad wizard, the halfling, Fist and his daughter and then more and more as they grew. That purpose had then put him face to face with a Witch-Queen and yes, they saved the world and all it cost was lives, Jaria. Where did he end up? He'd asked to be forgotten when the hidden one granted him a divine boon and forgotten he was. Just an old nameless fool with a nice sword and as inevitable as time or the setting sun, the bottle found him again.

He shrugged and pulled out the cork with his teeth, spitting it out and watching it roll carefree down the hill he'd sat on. So lost in his own memories he hadn't noticed the halfling watching him till now, a slight swagger and a particular gait. The Swordsman had seen hundreds if not thousands of the like and at his height many men, women and others like the halfling had challenged him to duels and less civilised versions of the same. He could see it in the halfling's, walk, his smirk and his eyes. Probably lived a similar life to The Swordsman, raised in a gutter, learned to kill before he learned to fight, had probably stolen more in his life than he'd paid for but had paid in other ways, harder ways than money. The halflings eyes were cold, inured to the harsh realities of life as a survival mechanism. The Swordsman had caught the way the halfling and the sickly elf looked at each other, he wasn't even sure they realised it yet, but something was there. The Swordsman took a swig from the bottle and let it sit on his tongue for a few seconds before slowly swallowing, letting every drop have a conscious moment of its own on the way down. He turned to the halfling who was walking casually toward him, eyeing him with wary intrigue and winked with a kind of half smile. Ander nodded casually at the smiling Swordsman and took the bottle that was offered, "not interested in the planning? Or are you not coming in with us stranger?" He took a swift swig and handed the bottle back to the ageing Swordsman. The Swordsman's smile turned into a broad grin, and he chuckled ironically to himself, "no friend, my days of planning and organising these kinds of things are long gone. Not that anyone would care about what I have to say. I'm just a guy with a sword." He patted the black bladed Tilak sword absently and winked again at the halfling conspiratorially, "just a killer with a blade." He eyed the clearly magical, razor-sharp blade and less obvious one on the halflings other hip and then back up at the halfling with a look of understanding, camaraderie and a look that bore into Ander, a look that said to the halfling *I know you.* Ander for a second was unsettled, this human was in his mid-fifties if he was a day, he was clearly a drunk and despite being at the very heart of everything no one paid him the slightest bit of attention. As The Swordsman took another deep draw of the bottle Ander took a seat nearby and sighed, "I'm not even sure what I'm doing here. Every instinct in me says to get the hell out, run and go find some well-paying low risk job where my blades have the answer to any question that might be asked. Aera and I have been travelling together for nearly eight years though. I just, I feel like I shouldn't abandon her now." The Swordsman smiled an easy, comforting smile and nodded knowingly, "it's not always easy to walk away from the people you love. Even if they look right through you." He sighed and continued, "I hate this place. Takal, I always have it took my freedom, my life path and decades from me. It took my wife from me over there." He pointed back across the plains to the site of the great battle, "it took my hope and my future up there." Again, he pointed this time up at Deathmount, "and it took everything else, about fifty yards over there. I hate this fucking place. Apologies, I know you're Takalan;

but you see here I am and I'm not even a hundred percent sure why. Sometimes we must go where the river takes us, follow our gut or the ones we love, even into darkness." Ander bristled slightly at the word, love. It was a complicated word for him and not one he'd ever truly understood. Loyalty, duty and the price of both he got, love was a different situation entirely. "At least it sounds like you know what this is all about!" Ander suddenly snapped, "all I know is one minute we were on an ordinary job and the next I'm supposed to pick sides on the fate of the world. As for love? I'm not even sure I know what that is. I never thought I'd be somewhere like this, it's just..." Ander paused as if considering how honest he should be with his next words. The Swordsman finished for him, "you always thought you'd be the bad guy?" Ander nodded silently as The Swordsman reached out and gave his shoulder a gentle squeeze, "and the good knights wear white and gold and the villains all wear black. Life is never black and white friend. Look at me, a washed up drunk the world forgot but this thing they're trying to unleash, this Formless? It's a creation of the pit of the lost and damned." He leaned back and took a deep breath just thinking of it, "I saw it the last time, something so dark and awful and beyond understanding, it was like looking at raw undiluted hate and rage. This isn't about good and evil, right and wrong or some petty squabble between the Gods of chaos and order. This about survival, for all of us. The old wizard told me about it once, not the tholan the big guy, Akarash Beliheim. I think he has the same distaste for the Gods as I do for Takal. He told me we all have things inside us, parts of ourselves that we bury or try to smother deep inside ourselves. Parts of us that we hate and don't want to live with, so we bury them, with drink, with detachment, with purpose or whatever poison works for us. Just so we don't have to think about those awful, weak or evil things that live inside us. Akarash told me, the Gods are the same, but no God is going to grab a bottle of cheap whisky and get black out drunk;

so, they created a dark place down deep in the darkest corner of their realm and gave it a fancy name for forbidden things, the pit of the lost and damned. They buried their mistakes, their darkest acts and the souls they had used and abandoned, the things they had no use for. Then they acted surprised when it mutated and melded into something terrible. That was the key he said. They buried it in the dark and forgot about it, left all their worst mistakes alone to die in the dark." The Swordsman turned to the halfling his face as grave as the halfling had seen it, "That's what happened he said, nothing dies in darkness."

The tent flaps swung open and Harpsong strode out, the others hot on his heel, he turned to The Swordsman and Ander with a huge grin, "Okay!" he half shouted cheerfully, "Let's go save the world!" And in a much flatter, tired tone "Again."

CHAPTER 22

The Formless

Annia looked around her as they creeped through the halls, unlike the others she was no stranger to this place. Over the years her men of the sword had kept a steady watch on the place and often she or one of her lieutenants would sneak in using powerful or non-magical forms of disguise. She knew the paths and myriad tunnels of dark Godsblood stone so well as she had thrown herself into the work of the men of the sword after the war. Combatting slavery and trying to improve things for the people of Takal and leaving another arm of the men of the sword in their traditional Swordlands home. She didn't want to go home again not after Harpsong's boon from the Gods. As young teenagers they'd fallen in love, despite his flighty and unreliable manner he was for the most part a good partner, a great husband, a good father to their daughters and a fun travelling companion, they had been happy. Before the war, during the war and even when times were hard, they relied on one another. They had talked over so many of the long dark nights about after the war. They had dreamed and planned of a little farm, of growing old together and working the land. No more adventuring or being chased halfway across the world. They would grow old together, hand over the reins of the men of the sword to Kerwin Forrester or one of the others and live for themselves. Then for his boon from the Gods of Karn Harpsong had chosen to never grow old, never age and be frozen in that moment forever. They'd barely spoken after that day without screaming at each other. He hadn't had a clue what he'd done, why she'd felt so betrayed. It didn't enter his mind for a second to speak to her, to not choose something so divisive, he never even thought of her until he saw her, and it occurred to him, she might not have asked for the same thing. So, Annia had done what she knew, returned to the men of the sword and started a new fight, making life better for the people of Takal and continuing the guerrilla life against men of power and influence. Only this time and for the first time she was alone. No Swordsman, no Harpsong. She couldn't even look at him after that and for years they barely spoke. She still loved him but even all this time later she wasn't sure she could ever forgive him. She looked over at Harpsong and found him deep in thought, feeling her gaze on him he returned it, looking exactly as he did on the day of the battle all those years ago. His hair was shorter but other than that, not a moment different. Immediately she thought of her own ageing, the lines on her face and the grey in her hair and had to look away. She glanced over the sisters, serious and scared they were an anomaly here. Stumbled into situation that they should never have been in and next to them the tholan wizard Urnath, who seemed just as scared, unsure and out of place, even with the powerful arch mage's staff in his hand. The sickly elf witch Aera and her ever loyal companion Ander who watched over her constantly, his face a blend of worry and irritation. Occasionally the halfling would glance over at the greying Swordsman who brought up the rear as if for reassurance. The Swordsman would smile or nod at the halfling every time a strange bond of warriors or of the private conversation they had shared clearly marking the men. Which made Annia look at The Swordsman, something about him made her brain itch like she was trying to remember something from a half-forgotten dream, familiar and yet completely alien. His hair had (like hers) started to grey at the temples and he had the tired look of a man who had seen too much and drank too much and all of it had settled on his features, he looked tired and sad and alone. Annia made a mental note to ask him his name when the opportune moment occurred. Her observations and thoughts came abruptly to an end as in front of her Kerwin Forrester, the human ranger who had come on as her second in command during the war waved for them to stop and then beckoned Annia up to his spot. "Princess, it looks like they're preparing for something, I don't know if we should act now or wait for Deathskull." Annia looked around at the motely little band and nodded, "We wait for Deathskull, or whatever thing is using his form. I can guess what and I'm sure Barvara is behind it, or what of her remains inside the Formless. We wait, but not you Kerwin. Someone needs to hold an escape route for whoever of us survive this. You aren't to die here, you're our way out. You understand?" Kerwin nodded, knowing better after all these years than to argue with his orders.

Annia settled on the ledge, the others slightly behind her down a few steps. Urnath and Harpsong slowly climbed up next to her, the old tholan looking for all the world like he felt he'd made a terrible mistake. Harpsong was grinning from ear to ear, the stupid fool was having the time of his life. "What are you grinning at you fool?" She scowled at him though against all her judgement she felt herself having to fight to stop herself returning his smile. Harpsong beamed at her, "you're so cute when you're angry. I missed that and I missed this!" He whispered loud enough to startle and worry Urnath. "Don't worry wizard, I know these halls the sound won't carry well and there's enough whispers of the dead in this place that you'd never know which is which." He smiled patting the tholan's shoulder before returning to Annia, "come on, tell me you don't miss this? You and me against the world and facing down some terrible evil like back when we were kids!" His infectious smile was both infuriating and delighting Annia and she struggled to stop the smile from infecting her face. "You still are a child, not even an over-grown one! A man of your age with the face of a stupid little boy!" Harpsong was chastened for a second until he looked around and saw her face had softened and the very traces of a smile was teasing the corners of her mouth. Harpsong reached out and squeezed her hand gently. Annia squared her shoulders and attempted to harden herself, but his touch had eaten into her resolve instead she gently shook her head and rolled her eyes, "idiot." She whispered smiling at him. Harpsong felt his heart leap into his mouth, here at the edge of death and at the worst possible moment he finally felt like he might be able atone for the worst mistake he'd ever made. Letting down Annia wasn't unusual for him, he'd always been shallow and self-obsessed; but he did love her, with all his heart. "And all I had to do was march into the jaws of death, I wish I'd thought of it sooner." Chuckling to himself he smiled over at Annia and seeing her face had frozen in a mask of horror he followed her gaze before hearing Urnath Gasp.

Something that looked like Deathskull had entered the room, his giant black plate mail armour, lined with jagged spikes and skull motifs. His huge barbed black blade which it turned out was Demonsblood rather than the necessary Godsblood they required. His skull was the same polished white it had always been, but his once smooth human shaped skull had not been filed or buffed and jagged horns protruded from his skull in a kind of crown and from his jaw like a jagged bone beard. He oozed not just terror as he always had but the same strange black oozing mist that seemed to be everywhere these days. He marched up the aisle made by the massed forces inside the room. He was followed by a strange, winged creature that seemed to float along made almost entirely of a kind of shadow cloaked, oozing black liquid that when it dripped turned to black mist and dissipated. Inside its shadow form the corpse of a human dressed in Takalan wizard robes seemed to be at its core, as if the creature of shadow and ooze was created from the corpse and sprouting from it. There was a hush in the great hall as hundreds of deathknights and wizards within held their breath with an audible air of expectation at what might be about to transpire. The thing that looked like Deathskull stopped by the throne, a throne full of whispers, spirits and rumoured to contain part of the pit of the lost and damned within it. He turned to the massed crowds and with a voice that sounded like a chorus of hundreds. All tied together with three main voices, two of them dark and inhuman, reverberating throughout the hall but led by one main, louder and stronger voice that of the long dead Witch-Queen herself, Barvara. "Long have we waited, long have we been robbed and with irony, the very blade that killed us, that ended our reign shall be the catalyst for a new reign, THE FINAL REIGN!" And the large half-demon pulled Tatral Valenstorm's dagger from inside it's cloak and plunged it deep into the seat of the throne muttering in a dark arcane language some manner of dark spell. The throne cracked, slowly at first but then as if it was straining to hold back a flowing river the throne exploded, sending shards of smoothed black, Godsblood stone in every direction. Some were injured a few were killed by flying debris but the entire hall stood transfixed as something oozed out of the throne.

The first thing that came was the smell, like rotting meat and rusty iron, coupled with darkness and the stench of death. A large Formless thing made of oozing black liquid and mist that at its centre was grainy like churned oil slicked meat and bone ground and rotted for thousands of years. It flowed and pulsed and rose up above the shattered throne like a giant oozing Formless blob of shadow and death. Everyone on the ledge stepped forward, staring in horror at something only a handful of people including only The Swordsman among them had even glimpsed before. Already twice the size of the throne and only at its beginning of oozing through the black portal that had opened where the throne had been a black, oozing tendril of grainy goo shot out and grabbed at a nearby deathknight. It pulled him in with an audible and horrible 'plop' noise which added his voice to the disembodied screaming coming from every inch of this pulsing, growing Formless thing that seemed to be oozing into our dimension. Every flash of light from a lantern or candle caused it to recoil slightly before realising the light could not harm it as it moved in every direction at once as if it were made up of a myriad of consciousness rather than just the one. Annia, Harpsong and the sisters were discussing what to do, at least a couple of hundred deathknights, mages and clerics stood before them to say nothing of the half-demon, Deathskull and the winged shadow creature at his side. No one noticed that Urnath had muttered a few words of magic to himself and levitated himself quietly to the floor of the hall. Taking a deep breath, the tholan wizard looked down at the arch mages staff he had been given and nodded at it, "I'd have very much liked getting to know you staff, to have explored your power and what we could do together." He said as much to himself as to the staff, he looked up at the hall before him and gulped down some fear. "The others are right, this is too much, too dangerous and here Akarash Beliheim has given me one tool with which I can end it all without any of my friends back there suffering." Without even blinking the old tholan wizard moved through the crowd. Most were staring agog at the giant Formless thing growing overhead as Urnath strode up the aisle to stand in front of Deathskull and the winged shadow demon next to the portal where the throne had been. "In the name of Crothan Thronebreaker, High King of the tholan people, I bring a gift." He smiled at the confused crowd, turned towards the Formless and the winged shadow creature who started to fly towards him as Deathskull started to move back and a part of the Formless slithered between him and the wizard like a shield. Urnath held the Oak and lacquered gold dragon's head staff above his head and the staff gave out a defiant puff of smoke from its golden nostrils as if it were trying to breathe fire on all the darkness around it. Then after a long, silent second Urnath broke the staff over his knee.

Harpsong had seen a mages staff of power broken before, a retributive strike the circle mages had called it. The Mages of the Circle Wizards found advancement in a variety of ways, past a certain point though it was only achievable through Dead man's shoes. In a tradition that held that carefully observed rules must be met and that to hold the highest standard of tradition, cheating in a Circle duel was to court a sentence of death even if you won the duel. Often the duels would be to a yield but frequently given the ego of wizards they would result in death or worse. More than one catastrophe has been borne of an over eager wizard duel. So, it was the last time he saw a wizards' duel, when one of the wizards, Taelia Sparrowflame who in fury at being on the cusp of losing the duel cracked her staff over her knee causing such a retributive strike. The explosion could be seen for miles and when it was gone? An area the size of a small building was wiped out, the charred remains of Taelia's opponent lay in the crater that had been created in the blast. Taelia and the two halves of her staff though must have been obliterated, disintegrated completely as not a single trace of them remained. Harpsong regarded Urnath, in the centre of the cave staff held aloft, he instantly knew what the wizard was thinking. This staff though was no ordinary magic item, a living staff of the arch mage, imbued by Akarash Beliheim with the soul of a gold dragon was unique and vastly more powerful than most magic Harpsong had seen in his life. As the wizard began to break the staff over his knee, Harpsong grabbed Annia and yelled "Down!" to the group pulling Annia down behind the ledge in time to shield them all from the blast as heat radiated over the ledge and some of the Godsblood stone melted under the blast from the exploding staff. Every member of the group was ducked behind the ledge and didn't see the blast, that is of course except for Aera Darkhorne, fascinated by the scene before her, hypnotised by the sight of the Formless. Unlike most witches or warlocks who made pacts with the pit of the lost and damned it wasn't the lost souls of the pit Aera's connection was with but some unspeakable horror deep within the pit that had driven her mad when she was just a girl. Some of the voices inside the cacophony of voices coming from the large Formless thing in the centre of the room, were eerily familiar to the sickly elf some of them she was sure she'd put there herself. This thing was at least part of the entities within the pit her pact was tied to, and she was mesmerised by its presence. Watching the old tholan wizard confront the half-demon was but a mere distraction, glancing her eyes over at him and seeing the myriads of shadow figures inside the demon that people without a link to the pit of the lost and damned would not see. Strange inhuman figures that haven't seen daylight for thousands of years, but she could not keep her gaze from the Formless, barely even realising that her hand was reaching out as if she could touch it. Out of the corner of her eye she noticed what the old wizard was doing with the staff and quickly conjured a magical shell to protect her from the ensuing blast to continue her gaze upon this vast and terrible shapeless thing before her. Watching from behind her shield Aera was transfixed as a silent flash of white engulfed the centre of the room before a giant fireball in the shape of a huge gold dragon roared up into the air and expanded before exploding over the entire room with a flash of flame. Screams crossed over screams with crackling, burning and popping noise as flesh seared, blistered and charred in the ensuing flame that seemed to last longer than it realistically should have until eventually the screams died down and the only screams were coming from the Formless. A thousand hungry mouths opened inside the mass of swirling shadow and rotting black goo. Black smoke arose from hundreds of corpses, the only things still standing were the Formless and the half-demon Deathskull. Deathskull's cloak had a few licks of flame sticking to it but otherwise he and the Formless were unharmed. In mere seconds Aera realised the mist rising from the corpses wasn't smoke or shadow, it was the souls of the dead. Though some were devoted worshippers of other Gods, Ramlar and Dracor largely, it seemed the Formless didn't care. Its mass of hungry mouths sucked in the souls of the dead as if their mere proximity and the inhuman things hunger made any other option untenable. Aera was fascinated and overwhelmed, she looked at where the tholan wizard had been to find an epicentre, a burned circle around where he had been but at its heart nothing. The site blasted clear with no remains as if the tholan wizard and the two halves of the staff had been blasted into oblivion with the sheer heat of what had clearly been a living staff of incomparable power. Aera looked down at the others, still cowering behind the ledge and in her off-key singsong voice said, "It didn't work, she's angry now." At this her companions rose one by one to see the devastation the wizard had wrought. An ocean of death, the wizard had apparently disintegrated himself and his staff and in the process killed every living thing in the cavern and even the winged shadow demon at Deathskull's side. The entire party stood in horrified awe for a just a minute except Ander Halfsword, who took a step away quietly in this moment.

Ander looked around and when he could be sure no one was watching dropped silently to his knees. "Ramlar. I've never asked you for much, I've never given much, but I've seen you and I feel like you've seen me. I'm no worshipper but we have an understanding, right? I'd like to get Aera out of this, but I see it; it's maybe not possible. I've spent every minute of my life trying to make sure there was one more minute of my life." The halfling opened his eyes and glanced over at the elf. Despite being preoccupied with what was happening before her, feeling his eyes on her she glanced over at him, her face suddenly solemn and almost empathic, at least for her. He darted his eyes back to the front and closed them, "I get it Ramlar, we don't get to choose the length of the battle, just how we fight it. If this is it? If I'm coming down to you then I'm going to claw and bite and stab and fight every second of it. I'm not here to beg for my life, I don't owe you anything and I never promised you shit. I just want you to know, mortal to God, all I want, the only thing I want; right now? Is for the next few minutes to make myself and maybe even you proud." What passed in his mind for a prayer given Ander moved slowly to his feet and turned around to face the horror before him. He glanced around to check no one had seen a moment of weakness in the unshakeable little man, Aera was staring at him and something horrifying was happening, it took him a minute, but he realised she was, in her own way smiling at him. He let a little of The Swordsman sink into him and winked at her, drew his sword and moved forward beside The Swordsman who looked down at him and nodded with a casual camaraderie that belied the seriousness and the weight of the moment.

CHAPTER 23

Without pause

Aera Darkhorne stood, still transfixed by the Formless as it consumed the souls of the dead deathknights and Takalans from the cavern. Seeing each soul causing the thing to pulse and grow even as it still pushed through the portal that had opened when Deathskull had performed the rite and thrust the Godsblood dagger into the throne. As her companions made their way down to the cavern floor, Aera didn't move, she barely glanced at Ander, the halfling she'd been travelling with now for years. He had pulled her from the throne room when the shadows of Gods and Witch-Queens had left her body to reform the half-demon Deathskull. Possible by way of his link to his Demonsblood sword, which had been crafted from his essence. The emptiness of the space inside, where the entities possessing her had taken up was like a gulf and had Aera's grasp on reality not already been somewhat tenuous this might have broken her. Instead, she felt free, like the removal of the other presences inside her, had freed up space in her mind and her soul that she had not had access to before. For the first time in years, into that space poured thoughts and feelings and drives that she had buried or thought destroyed in the rolling, horror-filled nightmare that was her life. She had felt the halfling's eyes on her when he appeared to be praying though she knew of no man nor God that the halfling would swear fealty to. She attempted to bring him comfort but it had been so long since she had known joy or comfort, had expressed genuine feeling for someone who was alive other than hatred or revenge that her smile even as she attempted it had been twisted and wrong. So instead, she was now focused on this thing, this great and terrible thing she knew from the voices in her head this was the formless, an ancient amalgam being that dwelt at the bottom of the pit of the lost and damned. The spirit of it was what had possessed her in Valenstorm, with the puppet strings being held by a part of it that was formed from the Witch-Queen herself. Barvara, Empress of Takal, mistress of the deathknight legions. A witch and sorceress of demonic power. Aera could still taste the lingering shadow of the Witch-Queen in her mind and was using every ounce of her will to deny that shadow power over her. She held back for fear that if she should join the fight; she could not tell what side she would be on. Instead, she followed the group with her eyes as they headed down to the edge of the chamber, the two young sisters, Harpsong, Annia, Ander and The Swordsman as they entered the cave with Annia and Harpsong at the front striding forward to confront the half-demon.

The Swordsman walked at the back of the group, gone was the man twenty years ago who would have charged in at the head of the group, who would have rushed in and taken down the half-demon without doubt or fear. That man was long gone and so he walked at the back, almost unsure if he should be here. He saw in front of him the sisters, Joselyn so strident and fearless while Lucia was struggling to make herself move forward so petrified she was of this monstrous place. Annia stepped forward as it became apparent, she had been preparing to summon the power of Necirate she tried to use her magic to banish the thing coming through the portal. Deathskull's head spun to face her and the hand that was free flicked up, a bolt of pure black energy blasted out straight at her, only to hit the diving Harpsong square in the chest, he'd flung himself in front of his wife and taken the full blast of the dark energy. Harpsong hit the floor with a thud as Annia turned her attention from the portal to the half-demon before her. Harpsong crawled back trying to shake off the damage but struggling to get back to his feet. Black tentacle like tendrils peeled off from the Formless and whipped themselves at the bard. Ander Halfsword rushed forward and sliced a few of them off with his razor-sharp sword. The bits that he sliced off seemed to collapse into shadowy mist before him. Still, it was all the halfling could do to hold off the lurching, snapping limbs that flew at him from the Formless. Lucia, seeing the halfling getting overrun while he provided cover for the retreating bard, forgot in an instant her terror and rushed forward with a dagger in either hand. Joining Ander in fighting off the encroaching tentacles while her sister lurched forward sword in hand. Joselyn ran past Annia as the Princess squared up to Deathskull unafraid and almost indignant; Joselyn leapt into the air and in an overhead chop that angled it-self into a diagonal swing her blade met Deathskull at the point where the neck met the shoulder. Her blade shattered, she fell back, shaking with vibrations and staring at the handle and hilt she still held as if trying to fathom the missing blade. Joselyn looked up just in time to see the huge black, barbed steel greatsword swinging towards her at speed. She started to turn herself and only because of her speed it glanced at her, sending her skidding across the floor and into a pile of charred corpses. Blood was pouring from her head and face where the barbs had torn at her and again, down holes in her armour as she skidded to a halt in a heap behind her sister and Ander. Annia's mace loosened in her hand, a white light glowing from it with the presence of Necirate, she twisted the handle, and the head of the mace came loose to show a chain hidden in the head and handle. Annia swung the now loosened flail upwards in a swing straight at Deathskull's jaw, he reeled back as the magical flail struck him, divine flames burning at his skull and chest as the flail lashed off him. He staggered back several steps before whirling his giant, barbed sword over his head with an almost musical whistle of air as it whooshed between the wicked barbs protruding from the giant blade. Deathskull brought the full weight of it down upon Annia, who reacted with her shield breathlessly, hammered down to one knee with the power and weight of the blow. Her shield, like her resolve held, for now.

Harpsong dragged himself along the floor, his chest was burning as black fire raged across his chest. Pulling himself towards Joselyn's prone body with one hand, the other patting out the black burning fire on his chest. He laughed grimly as he saw the young paladin's squire staring at him in confusion and fear, gashes and rends up and down her body in her armour, skin and clothes from the giant barbed blade of the half-demon. He smiled at her as he approached, now half crawling and in obvious pain "that's the thing about bards." He said through gritted teeth, "we pick up things from everywhere." He reached out with his hand and placed it on the groaning young woman's shoulder with his grin widening, "I picked this up from my wife." At which he started to mutter in a singsong voice and Joselyn felt a strange glow flow through her and she swore she could hear a harp playing somewhere. As the magic flowed through Joselyn the younger woman started flexing her arm and looking around, she could see Annia face to face with Deathskull, overwhelmed but holding her own. Lucia and the halfling Ander were fighting increasing numbers of tentacles from the giant formless thing in the middle of the room which was still pouring itself through the portal. Joselyn looked over at The Swordsman who had seemed to be in some kind of trance but seeing Annia one on one with the half-demon had started to run across the room, so light on his feet he was practically bouncing with every step. Joselyn, suddenly feeling much better from the bard's magic looked down at him, grimacing at the wound on his chest he held out his hand. There offered to her was the battle axe of the High King of the tholans, a large double headed axe of gleaming black steel that seemed to draw your gaze into it. Intricate carvings and tholan runes edged the battle axe and it hummed with powerful and ancient magic. The bard nodded at her, "the formless, not Deathskull, we need to use the Godsblood steel on the form-less." With that he pulled himself over into a seated position, still clutching at his wounded chest. Joselyn nodded mutely at the bard, he'd pulled her back from the brink and handed her one of the most powerful magic weapons she'd ever seen. As soon as she held the axe, she felt the weight of history on it, the weight of legend and she felt its fury. This axe had been carved by Dwarven Kings of old, an ancient symbol of brotherhood between the Dwarven Kings and the tholans of that era. A weapon of terrible power for a great King of old. The axe had been through wars, adventures and campaigns and been lost to legend for thousands of years before it was plucked from the darkness by a Barbarian, wanderer and exiled tholan named Crothan. This was no King, no Thronebreaker or legend it had been a young man looking to make his name in the world. Delving into the dark places in the lands looking for ancient secrets and dark evils to destroy. The axe had been overjoyed to be in the hand of one of its own, a man of such reckless fury that he was almost born to wield this axe. They had been together for over two hundred and fifty years and the axe had spent much of the time since his death in mourning. As Joselyn gripped the axe from the hands of the injured bard, she felt the axe's fury and frustration amplifying her own as she thought of her mentor and his sacrifice in the name of Vandarn. She hadn't realised as she started moving towards Lucia and Ander, but she had been swinging the axe in her hand. She thought of home, of Arn, of her now dead parents and all her sister had suffered because of this thing and the half-demon at its side. She realised she was growling. "City. Country. God." she growled quietly to herself, and she didn't run. She moved calmly, measuredly as she strode across the hall, swinging the High King's axe in a sweeping arc that sliced off seven reaching tentacles from the front of Lucia and Ander as she passed them. With a steady pace she headed straight towards the main mass of the formless as it poured through the portal before them. Joselyn slowed to a halt right in front of the throbbing, pulsing mass of shadow and ooze, gripped the axe in both hands and in an overhead swing planted the axe deep in the mass of ooze which recoiled and screamed from a thousand mouths as it shrunk in agony under the blow of the Godsblood axe. The power of the axe though, while damaging to the Formless seemed to lack the necessary power to slay the thing immediately.

Hearing the Formless scream, Deathskull's giant demon head spun from where it had been focused on trying to end Annia and started to storm over to where Joselyn stood only for a blur of movement to flash past him and a searing pain in his arm causing him to drop his giant Barbed sword. The huge figure of Deathskull turned to see a sad, old drunk wielding the Tilak blade. The laugh that emanated from Deathskull had Barvara's voice. As The Swordsman strained, he could hear Deathskull his old nemesis in there as well as a few more inhuman sounding voices reverberating at the back but all of it unified under the raw undeniable command of the Witch-Queen herself. "You? You could not defeat our son twenty years ago in your prime. Now with all the damned behind his sword arm what chance does an old drunk like you have in this moment." As she spoke Barvara's voice from within Deathskulls head she heard Annia behind her speaking in divine tongues and divine magic with the smell and taste of Necirate wracked through her and she felt the withering touch of divine harm burn Deathskull's muscles and very being. Deathskull dropped to one knee and The Swordsman used that knee as a launching platform, leaping up into the air and flipping over started to bring his sword down fast upon the shoulder and neck of the kneeling half-demon. With blinding speed, Deathskull rolled over to his back, barbed sword once again gripped and the barbed and pointed blade pointed upwards at the sky and the diving Swordsman. Seeing the danger, The Swordsman adjusted what he could in mid-air and aimed the Tilak blade directly at Deathskulls giant barbed sword. The two blades met the tip of the Tilak blade hitting the side edge of the larger, barbed blade and as the two powerful artifacts clashed, sheer magical power won out and the far more ancient and steeped in mythology Tilak blade snapped the larger blade like a dry branch. With a loud crack, the top half of the Barbed, Demonsblood sword skidded across the ground and the leverage given The Swordsman by the blow allowed him to roll backwards on the floor and bounce up to his feet next to Annia. The Princess of Hven, Annia turned and stared at The Swordmsan she'd barely noticed up till now and looked at him with a confused but familiar look, something in her brain itching as she did. Focused again she turned back to the rising Deathskull and unleashing a bolt of pure divine light right at the half-demon which burned on his chest and caused Barvara to lead a cacophony of screams from within. The giant broken, barbed sword swung again with sheer power right at The Swordsman and Annia in a wide arcing swing. The Swordsman raised the Tilak blade to parry but the sheer power of the blow sent him flying as it then flew into Annia's shield finally smashing the now shattered steel shield in two and knocking the Princess similarly back to the floor. Without another thought of the two who were on the floor instead focusing on another scream from the formless as the Godsblood battle axe buried itself again into its giant oozing mass. Deathskull swung the giant broken blade at Joselyn who almost without looking swung the axe in a block that reverberated the giant, broken, barbed blade back. She turned from the Formless and grinned a mirthless executioners grin as she faced up to Deathskull, swinging the axe in diagonal arcs as she approached him. Deathskull, backtracking defensively as a couple of swings hit his shoulders and arms deflecting them with the broken, barbed blade as he stepped back and slowly started to lower. Seeing her moment Joselyn lifted the High King's Axe above her head and then yanked back as black tendrils from the Formless held her in place. The black axe fell to the ground as tentacles from the formless turned on her and held her in place, burning her as they grappled her. Almost as if at Deathskull's command other tentacles reached for Annia and The Swordsman. Flipping up to his feet The Swordsman rushed, swinging the Tilak blade at the tentacles. As soon as the blade hit the tentacles the entire formless shuddered, Deathskull also shuddered. The Tilak blade sung and screamed with joy as it tasted the infernal and divine blood of the Formless. It burned the very consciousness that it was forged in the times before time to hunt, that of dark and evil divinity. The shock of it caused The Swordsman to stumble and pause, staring at his blade as he realised the sheer terror and damage it had caused the Formless simply with a cut. All thoughts of Deathskull gone from his mind and almost as if he were listening to the blade as it sung out to him in hunger for more of the blood of the Formless. The Swordsman nodded at his blade and simply said, "okay then." In that instant he turned and saw Harpsong, across the room propped up against a wall and breathing heavily, trying to focus to cast a spell. The Swordsman grinned at him with a cheeky, crooked grin that he'd used on his best friend a million times over their youth. Realising the bard would probably not even recognise him he nodded once more, turned and without pause spun on his heel, light as a feather as he ran full speed across the room. Flying up into the air The Swordsman brought the Tilak blade down hard, right into the centre mass of the Formless. The blade was buried up to its hilt in the foul-smelling thing and then the formless, the Tilak blade and The Swordsman all seemed to deflate and shrink back towards the portal. The formless rolled around The Swordsman it screamed a horrific, scream of its death throes as it melted back into the portal, taking the tilak blade and The Swordsman with it. The portal shrunk as the last of the formless poured back through it and with a gentle plop the portal, The Swordsman, the tilak blade and the Formless were all gone.

It was a moment of silence as everyone in the room stared in dumbfound horror as the portal swallowed the Formless and The Swordsman before disappearing with an ill-fitting plop noise. Joselyn had fallen to her knees where the formless had dropped her, axe behind her and out of reach. Ander Halfsword was on both knees, his swords above him where he had been fending off the tentacles of the formless that so suddenly shrank back at the touch of the Tilak blade of The Swordsman. Annia and Harpsong at opposite sides of the room on the ground injured, dazed and struggling to focus and Aera Darkhorne screaming in psychic agony as the death throes of the Formless echoed endlessly inside her skull. The only other noise was a scream of pure fury Barvara's screaming voice tore through the room with her unbridled rage at her plan being thwarted. Raging at the loss of contact with the part of them that existed inside the formless, burning, withering and dying deep within the pit of the lost and damned in the deepest of hells. Now cut off from all but her half-demon sons' body where she was trapped along with the few voices of dominated souls stuck in here with her, including her son. Inside Deathskull's head her voice reverberated out "KILL THEM ALL!!" and her son taking command of his body for the first time drew up his will to obey. The broken, great, Demonsblood, barbed blade rose up and begun to swing down on the young woman on her knees before him, "Yes Mother." He intoned gravely as he brought the blade down.

Suddenly crying out "NO!" Aera instinctively disappeared in a cloud of black smoke and reappeared between the half-demon and Joselyn, summoning up a protective field of black opaque magic which the black barbed blade shattered on its way down. The blade, slightly deflected by the shield and raked right down the front of the sickly elf whose screams turned to agony from the blow. Ander, leaping to his feet ran full speed at the half-demon both swords out, Aera collapsed in a pool of blood into Joselyn's arms. The half-demon took a step back and reared to strike again, both the sickly elf and the human whose arms she lay in dying, the sword started to come down. Ander rushing across the room knew instinctively he would be seconds too late to prevent the second blow. A curve of pointed black Godsblood blade pierced Deathskulls breastplate below his chin and a dagger tip appeared covered in his thick black demon's blood. Deathskull stood in silence, incredulous. Inside Deathskull's head Barvara and the remnant souls from the pit screamed in fury, terror and shame. Joselyn pulled herself and Aera out of the way as the suddenly paralysed, dead, giant half-demon toppled forward and landed with a reverberating thud on the ground. A curved, ornate Godsblood dagger protruding from its back as behind it with a face of grim determination stood Lucia, staring at the dagger she had pulled from the throne. She looked down at the corpse of the half-demon and gasped breathlessly, "I might just be little Lucia the apple girl, but you can't have my sister demon." And reached over and pulled the Godsblood dagger from the demon's corpse.

CHAPTER 24

Vandarn

Annia pulled herself up, cradling a broken arm where Deathskull had shattered her shield. She rushed as quickly as she could on unsteady feet, supported by the now overwhelmed Lucia as she headed over to apply some clerical magic and save the life of the dying Aera Darkhorne who lay now cradled between Joselyn and Ander. She knelt between them and reached out, half expecting Aera to already be dead but instead finding her breathing and stable, she glanced over at Joselyn who smiled shyly, "I, I never intended to take my oath but damn if Arn hasn't rubbed off on me." Annia smiled back at her, "Thank you, paladin." Annia pulled herself up to her feet to find Harpsong limping towards her, still clutching the wound in his chest as they half collapsed into each other's arms. She smiled at him, "oh Han. You idiot. Are you okay?" Harpsong looked at her with mischief in his eye, "i'm gravely wounded my dear. I think I'll need someone to nurse me back to health you know?" Annia laughed at him and wrapped her arms around him, "do you think that was him? Now that he's gone, I can almost see it. The name and the face I still can't remember but I'm sure that was him." Harpsong's breath caught in his throat and in his mind's eye he saw that cheeky, crooked grin, it burned into his soul and then the way the man had spun on his heel and without thought, without pause had leapt into the mouth of evil. "It was him." He felt his voice crack as he spoke, "I don't know how I know, but I know. It was him." Harpsong felt tears roll down his cheek, "I haven't seen him in twenty years, I still can't pull his name onto my lips, but I know he's gone, I know that was him." Annia leaned in as the two held each other and mourned, she whispered in his ear, "Let's go home Han. Let's go home to our girls." She had used a basic spell to mend her arm and though it was still hurting she let Harpsong lean on it and the two slowly moved back the way they came, Harpsong called back to the others, "wake Aera up or carry her. We need to get out of here before the entire mountain comes calling." Suddenly realising the weight of the bards' words Joselyn leapt to her feet and turned to carry the unconscious elf, stopping, and turning back for just a moment to grab the High King's, Godsblood axe and loop it through her belt. Turning she nodded to Ander and easily lifted Aera's unconscious form, "You go first Ander, I can carry her." The halfling nodded and turned to follow Harpsong and Annia. Joselyn, Aera now in her arms looked around the cavern one last time, wishing she had time to process everything that had gone on here today. This moment, this crucible of her life would be something she would live with and examine for years, if not for the rest of her life. She realised something in that moment and turned to smile at her baby sister, still looking shell shocked and staring at the beautiful, Godsblood dagger in her hand. Joselyn nodded at Lucia, "thank you by the way mouse, for you know, saving my life." She paused and looked around the room "oh, and the world too." The sisters laughed and followed the others out of the room.

The Shadow filled dead around the lands had lost their shadow when Lucia had plucked the dagger from the Godsblood throne and though they did not immediately fall back into death. They were now nothing more than an army of normal undead. The Vandarnian Army outside Vandarn had swept the undead aside with unit after unit of church knights led by a few small bands of heroes who had travelled from Valenstorm and other places to heed the call for aid. Harpsong had checked in on Tatral Valenstorm and found the old halfing an even paler shadow of himself than he had been before, the bard wondered if he'd done the right thing in bringing him back. Akarash had often told him that sometimes even the kindest deed, done for the wrong reasons can come to ill. Seeing the old halfling live in fear and with the trauma of his past had made the bard wonder if he'd saved the halfling for his own selfish reasons rather than Valenstorms good. Annia had handed the men of the sword over to her right-hand man, the Ranger Kerwin Forrester and the men of the sword had left Takal to return to their native Swordlands. Annia and Harpsong once they had rested and healed and gathered their children, had travelled to Akarash Beliheim's farm looking to take the wizard up on a previous offer of travelling beyond the borders of the lands of Karn or even this plane of existence. Whatever came next, they agreed that they would face it together, they had wasted enough time.

The horse's hooves were slow and rhythmic and more than once had almost lulled Joselyn to sleep. They had been on a far more leisurely pace than the ride north. Joselyn sat astride Thirel, the horse had chastised her when they had returned for her absence in a way that reminded her of Arn. It gave her great comfort to have the older paladin's horse with her as she realised, she was now starting out on her own paladin's journey. She glanced over at her sister Lucia, dressed in black leather and a heavy travelling cloak, her face grim even now and her free hand still clutching the Godsblood dagger at her hip. She was amused by the sight of her slight framed, tiny sister upon the giant tholan horse that had belonged to Urnath and they recalled being named Hrasse. The giant horse had decided that only Lucia would ride her and was equally determined Lucia would ride no horse but her, biting any horse she tried to sit on. Behind them she could hear Aera muttering to herself, she had thrown herself between Joselyn and the half-demon's blade back in Deathmount. Now Joselyn was determined they would find someone who could help rebuild her mind. The psychic trauma she had experienced being touched by the Formless and all the things that existed within it had sent her into a spiral drowning in madness from which she rarely surfaced. Ander was no doubt riding alongside Aera at the back, staring worriedly, protectively at the sickly elf as she lurched in the saddle, muttering to herself. Joselyn hoped they could beg favour of King Branthar, she had to report to the King what had happened regardless. In truth though she suspected Princess Annia would have already spoken to the King using her magic given what the Princess had said when they parted. Days after climbing down from Deathmount, the human Ranger Kerwin Forrester had been ready, and they had abandoned camp and relocated to another camp that had already been prepared to rest up and heal any who survived and were wounded. The moment of crucible had clearly bonded Annia and Harpsong, the loss of the tholan wizard or maybe the drunk Swordsman had touched them, and both had leaned on each other both physically and emotionally since the events in the throne room of Deathmount. Their own arguments forgotten or burned away in the fires of danger and near certain death and all that had been left was an enduring love affair. An affair that if the legends and the stories were true had started when they were teenagers and survived adventure, peril and even years of war and being on the run, survived saving the world only to be strained to breaking by the reward for such. Annia and Harpsong had lost something in that room which Joselyn would never truly understand but it had strengthened a weakened bond, and the couple could barely stand to be separated. Annia had confided in Joselyn that she had decided they were going to leave the men of the sword to Kerwin. Maybe they would adventure, maybe they would find a small farm and retire. Harpsong had apparently been talking about asking Akarash Beliheim about starting him ageing again or stopping Annia's, but Annia had little interest in immortality, though travelling the planes together under the archmage's guidance had put a little twinkle in the Princesses eye. Whatever they decided there was something Joselyn found comforting in the fact they had found one another again after spending so long estranged over something they could not change. Joselyn thought over the times she had travelled this road in recent months, retreating from Takal being chased by a shadow filled undead dragon, coming across The Swordsman surrounded and running out of options. It was the last time Arn and her were on this road was the last time they were together; she had felt the voice of Vandarn in Deathmount's throne room. It had been Joselyn's connection to Vandarn that had saved Aera's life, she had seconds left when Joselyn had finally used a connection to Vandarn to heal the dying, elf witch. She now could feel and sense Vandarn's presence and felt imbued with his divine power, it also made her feel as if Arn was still in some small way present.

Lucia could feel the entire journey back, Joselyn constantly eyeing her and hovering near her, searching for any kind of reaction. She wanted to tell her sister she was numb; she was overwhelmed about everything. Not too long ago she had been a girl who sold apples in the Mar-Thatch market, and here she was, every one of her friends, family and the man she loved dead. She had fled and seen an army of seemingly impossible to kill undead made up of the people from her life marching across her country. She wielded a dagger whose history was tied into the mythology and legends of the world. She'd strode into one of the darkest, most evil places in the heartlands, surrounded by people who seemed not to notice she was just a girl who sold apples. She wanted to scream, she wanted to cry and shout to the heavens that this wasn't supposed to happen to her, she wasn't ready for this. Instead, she sat upon a King's horse with a dagger that she could sense and feel, almost like a living thing with opinions and feelings. She had killed one of the most feared and terrible beings the heartlands of Karn had ever known. She barely remembered doing it. She had seen Joselyn's sword shatter on the half-demon, she'd seen the High King's axe damage the Formless, the axe which now lived on her sister's back. She'd seen the screams and agony and the immediate death of the giant Formless thing as the Tilak blade had pierced it. In all that chaos Lucia saw Deathskull attempt to slay her sister, feeling helpless and weak in the face of it. Lucia felt it was too big, too much to process as she watched her sister die, and then Aera had teleported in front of her, she'd taken the blow meant to slay her sister and paid the price. In that moment all Lucia could feel was rage, glancing over and seeing the Godsblood dagger said to have belonged once to Tatral Valenstorm. Its hilt deep in the throne, without thinking Lucia had grabbed it. She had felt its excitement at bonding with her and spun on her heel to rush at the half-demon's back as he raised his sword to throw a killing blow down on Joselyn and Aera, huddled together beneath him. Lucia had thrust with everything she had left; tears streaming down her face, she'd plunged the dagger through Deathskull's back. She replayed it again and again in her mind, had she really killed a being, a collection of beings that were among the most powerful the land had ever seen, torn down by the girl who sells apples in the market at Mar-Thatch. All the people who died back there, were gravely injured and would spend time recovering and here were the two sisters, riding powerful horses, wielding magical artifacts and riding back to civilisation to report to the powerful, the acts of the brave. Lucia looked over at

Joselyn who smiled, they had ridden with heroes, fought and bled with legends and what lay ahead was a new life, a new world created from the ashes of the old. Lucia sidled Hrasse over next to Thirel, reached out and took her sister's hand. Joselyn looked over at her with a gentle smile and Lucia squeezed her hand three times quickly before releasing and looked up at her sister, she wasn't quite ready to smile. To show her sister that she was or that she would be okay, but she rode next to her. A camaraderie of not just sisterhood but of combat, of the hard ridden road together and so followed closely by their new companions. A stone-cold killer with two swords and a sickly-looking elf witch whose sanity was at best tenuous. The two sisters the paladin and the girl who sold apples at the market in Mar-Thatch, rode over the hill and saw the highest towers, the shining flags as Vandarn hove into view and with it the future they had earned.

Hope

Cold winter air hung over a devastated battlefield. Sparse dried grassland under a sprinkling of hoar frost which spread over everything on the ground. As buzzards and carrion eaters soaring above bore witness to the devastation and nothing stirred as the mass of birds in the sky contemplated their meals. An overturned wagon had been used as a barricade with arrows, bolts and javelins protruding from its side and the ground below it, puddles of melting snow, mud and stale blood among other more unpleasant things. Part of the ground nearby was scorched where magic fire had struck. A dead orc lay next to the scorched patch of earth. Half his face burned clean off and leaving him in a manic death grin with exposed bone and dried green orcish blood splayed like paint across his remaining face. A crow pecked at his back, at a gap in his armour where a simple longsword was buried halfway up its blade. As this orc lay dying his face on fire someone had run him through, stabbed him in the back. Three bodies in a pile beside the orc moved, startling the crow, who immediately flew into the sky to safety, still loitering though in hopes of returning to his meal. The pile moved again before a single grasping hand, coated in blood and mud reached out and grabbing the topmost corpse for purchase, pulled itself out from under the pile, clothes and armour ripped and covered in blood, dirt and worse. Out he crawled, lifting himself to his feet realising he'd lost his boots in the mud he stood, the only thing moving in a sea of winter morning corpses. Feeling the back of his head, he caressed the lump and the dried blood that had poured freely and caked into his hair. He caught a glimpse of himself in one of the corpses shields, long raven black hair with braids at the temples and the back, mildly stubbled face, shining blue eyes and even under the mud and bloody stains and bruises an easy, charming handsomeness. About twenty-three years old, a lifetime ago. He reached out for the sword and yanked it from the orcs back, sizing it up as a decent enough weapon. He gave it a couple of casual swings as he looked around, slowly walking through the remnants of the battlefield till he found what he was looking for. Dropping himself down to the frosty ground he yanked at the new corpse's feet until he had both boots and then took his time pulling them on. They'd fit well enough and were more expensive than any boots he'd ever owned himself. Patting the corpse on the rump in thanks he stood up and moved on. In his mind's eye he recalled this day, he'd signed up when drunk, aimlessly looking to alleviate the boredom. Had waded into a muddy valley on a cold morning in the Winter month of Ramla. In a fight about two brothers who couldn't decide which one would be King or baron or whatever title this tiny Swordlands kingdom had. The Swordsman hadn't cared, he'd been young, drunk and bored. He vaguely remembered being passionately in love with someone though in the misty fogs of memory he could remember nothing of the person, not even their smile. He had fallen in love often at that age and with as much depth as a street performers wooden puppet. As a result, in a fit of self-destructive boredom he'd signed up as a mercenary with one of the armies, even at the time he hadn't known which. He'd been showing off, dancing through the battlefield, slicing his way through his opponents without care, barely noticing or checking if his blows had been fatal and then he hit the orc. He'd pirouetted into a stabbing motion, buried an inch or two of steel in the Orcs gut and spun to leap away. He'd never underestimate the strength or passion of an orcish warrior again after that, the huge green skinned soldier had hit him, hard on the back of the head with the flat of his hammer. The Swordsman had wobbled, thrown up, pissed himself and passed out. Heading back across the battlefield on his way out he realised the corpse he'd pulled the sword from was his old friend the orc. He patted the dead orc's shoulder, "thanks for the lesson, friend." he'd muttered groggily as he passed. Miles from anywhere, freezing and wounded. He vaguely remembered he'd found a fur cloak on one of the dead officers, and a horse blanket that had covered him enough to get back to town.

The memory faded and The Swordsman found himself in darkness, he had no idea where he was, or how long he'd been here. He remembered lunging into the Formless oozing thing, Tilak blade leading the way and he thought that would be it. Death, rest or whatever you wanted to call it. He tried to open his eyes but found he couldn't, he tried again, and he was in Kaz, the small town where they'd named the tavern after the sword, he'd bought a hiding place with. Sat in the Warrior's sword tavern, he was at a table at the back of the room, he lifted his feet and felt that sticky sensation the tavern always had, through his boots. He looked up at the sword and was suddenly confused, he'd never been back to Kaz after he donated that sword. He'd never seen it hung over the bar, never been in the tavern after it was renamed to the Warrior's sword. He looked around suddenly as all the patrons ignored him, "this isn't a memory." He said matter-of-factly to no one in particular. A tall lithely, muscled man in plain brown leather approached from the bar, two tankards in hand. He looked familiar, similar even, long straight raven black hair, if slightly straighter and shorter than his, piercing blue eyes and that same impish smile, though his nose was different and his features slightly thinner, longer somehow and more serious. "No son." The familiar man said, "it's no memory." The man smiled an all too familiar smile, slightly crooked and a unique blend of mischief, warmth and indulgent glee. The Swordsman unsettled stared at him "who are you?" he finally managed. The taller man smiled and placed the two tankards down in front of him. "We've never met. I was a mercenary, a soldier. I wasn't as good with a sword as you, but I was better with so many other weapons and no, I didn't quite have your way with people, but my strategy was impeccable. My name was Manragon, but you probably guessed that by now. I've watched all your life, as you made mistakes and bad choices and sometimes seemed to delight in failure and self-destruction. Despite yourself though, you found your way to do the right thing, sometimes only as a last resort. No one would ever call you a hero son, but with a blade in your hand my boy? You were an artist, an incomparable master of the form and so stubborn, you get that from me. Regardless, you saved the world; twice. I know, you want to rest, and you've wanted it for some time, wished for it, even prayed for it to any God that'd listen, you kept going though, getting up, going through the motions and wishing for someone to end it all for you. Good thing you didn't though, eh? Woosh! You didn't even hesitate just threw yourself at it, soon as you thought it'd work. I never wore this; I never got the calling though I learned after I passed it was close. I'm proud to say it's chosen you." The lean, hawkish man slid something across the table to The Swordsman. Looking down at the hand and back up at the man claiming to be his father he raised an eyebrow quizzically. Manragon smiled at him warmly, "I know, you thought this was it. Dead and buried and rest. You've been called son, the amulet is ancient and powerful and sentient, and it doesn't get owned, it chooses its bearer. Just trust that wherever it takes you, is where you need to be." Manragon lifted his hand and there, on the table before The Swordsman was a long chain, holding an amulet he knew like his own hand. Exactly like the hilt of the Tilak blade, like the symbol he'd chosen for the men of the sword. It was a planet, two swords, one the tilak blade the other a light bladed mirror of it thrust diagonally through the world. He reached out for it and as soon as his hand touched it, he sensed it. Like the Tilak blade but without the thirst, the hunger for violence. The amulet was more benevolent and had a kindness about it. He knew instantly that it had a plan for him. He looked up at his father, for the first time in his life he looked upon his face, so similar and yet so different. He imagined this must have been what Manragon had looked like in his prime, as he pondered that he started to realise the room was going dark. In seconds he was in darkness again.

His very first sensation was his eye trying to open, crusted with gunk he had always called sleep making it hard, next was the small puddle of drool under his mouth. Forcing his eye open and without rising from where he lay, he pulled his arm across his face to wipe at the drool and slowly waited as his consciousness pooled together and reformed into shape. He'd been dead, or he'd been dreaming. Nothing that wasn't real had this much drool and cold, clammy sweat he decided. A cold shiver told him he was outside. His bed had been a thick patch of Lucious grass, his pillow had been his own arm against the foot of a tree. Slowly and with aching joints he pulled himself off the ground and looked over to the disapproving glares of a woman steering a wagon down a large highway. Smiling The Swordsman took a deep bow with an exaggerated smile and when the woman scowled, he winked at her. Laughing softly to himself he stretched and patted himself down, his hand immediately reaching for the tilak blade. Finding his scabbard empty for the first time in decades, he was separated from the blade. He felt slightly freed by its absence. He'd never been interested in money or magic and felt somehow lightened by the freedom of not having ownership of such a powerful artifact; Until he felt the cold steel of the amulet around his neck. "You did this?" He accused the necklace to an obvious lack of response. He stretched again feeling fluidity and motion flow back into his limbs, he wondered how long he'd been asleep as he felt spryer and lighter than he had in years, he hopped gently from limb to limb with a kind of limbering sway that spoke of the mischief in him and the lightness he felt, body mind and soul. He realised he was smiling and nodding, to himself or the amulet though he wasn't sure which. The Swordsman strolled down to the road and started in the direction the wagon had gone. He passed a puddle of rainwater and bounced down onto his knees to splash water in his face, smooth his hair back and as the water settled and he blinked it out of his eyes he saw something that made him gasp. His hair, the silver was gone, the wrinkles and the wear and tear from the years of alcohol and hard travelling had been smoothed. If he could have guessed he was thirty something again, the age he was at the very height of the war with Barvara, the best he had been. But with many more years of experience, wisdom and learning. He laughed again and smiled, a smile without pain. By the hidden one how he'd missed that smile. "I guess this was you too, eh?" He asked the amulet. "You couldn't have made me twenty-five, no?" He muttered amusedly. Laughing to himself he jumped up and resumed his journey. He walked for a while before the road crested the hill and there, below the horizon was the largest city The Swordman had ever seen. Towers and giant statues, on and on it sprawled built in the shadow of a mountain with large, busy docks on the south and smaller camps and farms all around it seemed even from here as if it teemed with life. Innumerable tiny lights shining and dimming from within it like a container stuffed with fireflies and life. Larger buildings closer to him at the north and it seemed the further south the city went the smaller, more squalid the buildings got apart from the giant castle at the foot and around the mountain. The Swordsman found the smile on his face turn into a grin as he stared at this massive sprawling metropolis, and he realised that he was nowhere near home, he was somewhere completely alien to anywhere he'd ever been. He looked down on the city before him like fresh fallen snow and The Swordsman was about to put his first footprint on it.

He stopped right at the crest of the hill and looked behind him at the spot he'd woken up, Harpsong, Jaria, Annia, Arn, Tatral, the Swordlands, the war and yes even Barvara and Deathskull. He'd be leaving them all behind, it felt oddly like he was betraying his past and his stomach churned to think of how everyone had suffered and died and here he was beginning a new adventure as if none of it had happened. The years of darkness and shame, in the shadow of the war. He'd wasted years after the war trying to drink himself to death or fall on another's sword. Here he was skipping along the road as if he was some fool who'd never struggled, suffered or betrayed people. The Swordsman took a deep breath and sighed. "Fine, you want me to go out there and what? Change the world, make a difference? Every good thing I ever did was by accident. I never met a bottle I couldn't let down so how do you expect to give me youth and strength and suddenly I'm not a self-indulgent old drunk who gets lucky while everyone else suffers for my mistakes?" He felt the tears come and a weight in his gut as his heart sank realising, he couldn't just shake off the years like he was washing his hair and then he heard it, in his mind's eye, Jaria's voice "and when it's over, don't you dare wither away. Live. Just live, you might not have earned it but I damn sure did. Live for me my love." The tears flowed but he smiled, a soft, gentle and wistful smile and he nodded. "Okay, okay. One more adventure but then I get to go home and see my wife, okay?"

And he wiped away the tears on his sleeve and started down the hill with an unfamiliar feeling stirring in the pit of his stomach, a feeling of hope.

The end.

The Heartlands of Karn

The Heartlands of the world of Karn are varied in size and content. One constant however remains. The struggle for survival, power or freedom continues in myriad ways across the land as in the overcrowded heavens above. Below are a brief description of each of the disparate places that form the heartlands.

Vandarn

The oldest of all the human kingdoms, Vandarn, is at the heart of Karn, a land of civilisation and peace. Under the land however ancient creatures and a whole other world lie in wait. Within its borders ancient civilisations ages older than the world of men lurk, from the giant forest of the Elves to the abandoned ancestral home of the Dwarves of the Heartlands.

The Shoui Kingdom

The people of Shoui are a people whose roots lie in honour and a great history, they came here a little under a hundred years ago from the east, a small band of settlers seeking a new life. However, they suffered badly in the crushing grip of Barvara's rule in the brief time she dominated the land. The focus towards rebuilding the military in the years since Barvara's reign, resulted in a strong militarised presence as their leadership is determined not to be invaded again.

The Takalan Empire

Once home to the Witch-Queen Barvara and then by her half-demon son Deathskull, this kingdom is now deeply divided.

With the death of Deathskull and the various political, military, and mercantile factions vying for power the dark kingdom. Takal is currently embroiled in an ongoing civil war. What has always been a dangerous place has become even more deadly in recent years.

The Swordlands

Home to most of the legendary heroes of Karn. Densely populated and overcrowded. A kingdom comprised of small city-states, everyone fighting for more land and power over their neighbour. Petty kings and foolish barons dominate this land. Most forget about the common people, who cannot lift arms to defend themselves. The history of the Swordlands is long. However, the legend of the men of the sword and the Unnamed Swordsman has given the commoners hope of a future where all can stand up for themselves, this has led in recent years to several civil uprisings and some small but significant changes in the makeup of some of the independent states.

The Frozen Kingdom of Thol

A cold and frozen wasteland named for the Tribal Ice god Thol. The tholan mountains were once a broken land ruled by cruel Frost giants. For the last two centuries though, under the uniting banner of the great tholan High King Crothan, the clans of the children of Thol have carved a kingdom out of these frozen lands. The dragon Sir River marks her borders.

MAP - THE HEARTLANDS OF KARN - 273
Blackvia Woods
Bal
Ve'as
Kaster
Vaastrak
Stalvar
Deathmount
Kes
Port Darkness
Fallius
Ten Fort
The Quotiy Swamp
Luxiya
Chun-Yi
Ki-le
Vun-tai
Sundhi
V'asta
Frozen Forest
Tower
Tholla
Faerkeama
Shi-Kara
Kahn Forest
the Tholan Peaks
Tribe of the Sn
The Ice Forest
Garr'ua
Mistra
Elvenwood
Fort Greyback
Ela'th
Asr're
L'Carr
Elveness
Vassa Ph
Es'eth
Callare
Tasele
Z'as
Es'vae
Varn
Dern
Thern
Skarn
Teris
Hangedman's Cross
Vaske
The Bandit Wastes
Kushne (Bandit Home)
The Sicklewood
The Spiderwood
Kai-vath
Ast
Kavind
Caves of Vidar
The Tower of
The Circle
Astarvan
Akarash Belikeim's Hut
Durkil
Ruins of Hven
F'seth'ha
The Drow Fo
The Druids Grove
Terlin
The Signpost
Riverdale
Riverwood
Vandarn
The Mountain Marsh
The Forest of the Art
Forest of Daravan
Kal's Tower
Daravan
Gre'ass
Davin
Vultures Cross
Draalk
Keill
Men of the
Anstorm's Cross Adventurers Rest
Anstorm
Terlath
The Reuilian Wood
Viass
Kalos
Akeln
Kaz
Dusta
Asralt
Deristal
Tri-City Area
Trueton
Stum's Place
Haartif
Brax's Keep
Dwarf Keep
Kus't
Arni
Kau
Necirate Falls
The Hi Kingo
e Dragon Mountains
The Great Stone
Valenstorm
Mar-Thatch
Pilgrame'e
Hold of Varan
Dwarven Ruins
The Great Rift
Zandur's Keep
Hell Keep
The Mad Wizards Wood
Istarn Isle
Lover's Lake
Island of the Red Tower
The Valenstorm Desert
Darnstop

<u>Nine of nine even in time.</u>

In its earliest form the Vandarnian Calendar was developed by the Circle of Wizards its nine months named after the greatest Wizard from each of the nine schools, the days of each week were subsequently named for the first official head of each of the nine schools that make up the circle Wizards. The formats and spellings have morphed and changed over the centuries and in many cases bear little resemblance to the original format. Most of the great names are lost to history as records have perished in one disaster or another but there are still one or two that pique the odd historians and lend themselves to vigorous debate among the interested parties.

There are 9 days in a Vandarnian week
There are 5 weeks in a Vandarnian Month
There are 9 Months in the Vandarnian Calendar
In a Vandarnian year there are 405 days, 81 weeks and 9 months.
There are 45 days in each month

Months:

Baelos (Bay-Loss) - Winter - The beginning of the year is when it is coldest, Baelos is when people prepare themselves for the year ahead. Baelos is the time of Winter when people look forward to the year ahead and back at the year gone by.

Necire (Ness-Eer) - Spring - The beginning of Spring is when the world breaks free of winter and the year begins in earnest. Celebrated widely as when the year really begins a time of beauty and life and fresh starts.

Nartfen (Naart-ven) - Spring - Over the course of Nartfen things begin to grow and new plans get formed and the world opens. Danger, excitement and life start to sprout. New adventures and new plans are enacted in the heart of Nartfen.

Drac'r (Drak-Eer) - Summer - Quite often in the heartlands when summer comes it is with a searing wave of heat. Like an insipid, slow burn summer comes on and before people know it they are cooking in their chainmail.

Freldine (Frel-Deen) - Summer -In many parts of the heartlands Freldine is where the heat overtakes. In the Swordlands where the sun is strongest the grass dries out. Even in the lands of Thol the height of Summer is when the ice and snow roll back, and grass shows and the tholans and even the Highland tholans find patches of grass and softer earth showing. As the pinnacle of summer hits from the Swordlands to the Tholan mountains everything changes and for the month of Freldine the summer heat can get to be too much for many people across the heartlands

Kendath (Ken-Daath) -Summer -As Kendath passes the air becomes cooler and more airy late summer winds cool even the hottest parts of the heartlands find relief in the cool Kendath winds.

Egine (Ae-Gene) - Autumn - The time of year when the world starts to cool, the harvests start to come in and the work of the harvest season begins, often considered the time of year when the work of the year really begins. Many in Karn consider Egine the time of year to get things done and complete their long term and short-term goals, "I hope to have it done by Egine-time)

Yulen (Yoo-Len) - Autumn - During Yulen is when the people of the lands prepare for winter, they store up their food and fuel and start to seal and repair their homes in preparation for the coldest and darkest of months.

Ramla (Rah-Mlah) - Winter - The Darkest of months Winter falls on Karn like a heavy blanket, the days suddenly shrink. The world becomes dark and dangerous, many try to stay indoors or avoid the wilderness as strange and evil things lurk in the dark.

Days:

Kedan (Keh Dan) - Birth of the week, the word originates in meaning to steel yourself for what is to come, "you must Kedanise yourself for the week ahead.

Mada (Mah-Dah) - Simply translates as "the next day."

Vustar (Voo-Star) - Thought to be a day of religious work, those who observe the 9 gods refer to this as the day of the gods, where we toil in their favour.

Belgan (Bell-Gan) - Belgan is believed to have been the most evil of the circle at the time of the calendars inception, the word has since come to be one of traditional ill omen, "Don't Belgan this" and "if we can just get to the other end of Belgan" are common phrases throughout the lands.

Visx (Vis-ks) - In ancient Vandarnian Visx is said to have meant "the crest of the hill." As the mid-point in the Vandarnian week it is seen as a day for celebration, for being grateful for the goals reached and a spur for those yet to come. For many this is a day of rest to reflect on the days that have passed and ponder on the days yet to come.

Ninti (Nin-Tee) - Ninti, the story goes was the first powerful Halfling wizard, an Evoker so the legend goes of furious temper, whose legend talks of her phoenix like rebirth after nearly losing a mage-war with a rival who thought her defeated she was said to have exploded so ferociously as to have accidentally disintegrated some spectators including no less than three Kings. "Ninti's wrath" is a common phrase throughout the lands.

Tusxk (Tus-ksk) - Outside of the established races in days of old those considered to be the lesser, more monstrous races have been denigrated within the circle, from the elven wizards of old down through the older races those of a more unusual fashion were been referred to as 'Tusxk' after the first great Orcish Wizard to sit in the circle. Tusxk was a Diviner according to the old tomes, the cleverest of beings and the most devilish and mischievous ever to hold the post of Diviner. Thus, the meaning behind the word changed in the lexicon of the circle and leterally the lands. To this day Tusxk is synonymous with wit, deviousness and manipulation. "He has the

Tusxk in him that one." And "He has a Tusxkian way about him, be careful around him." Are common phrases related to this day.

Hster (Hiss-Ter) - Named after the master of enchantment at the time of the calendar's inception, he was known to be quite mad and considerably evil. Rumour is he fell to the charms of a fae creature and left the lands to travel far abroad. Often referred to as "Almost there." Both for his disappearance and to signify that week is nearly at an end.

Yarid (Yar-Eed) - The only real traditional day of rest in the Vandarnian Calendar, most people take this day to reflect, spend time with loved ones and reflect on all that has come before. No major battle or encounter has taken place on this day for hundreds of years, the founders of the men of the sword are the only historical figures irreverent enough to have broken this bond and infiltrated the Witch-Queens lair on this day as a precursor to the great battle of Vandarn in 1063.

The Vandarnian Calendar timeline (also known as The Circle Calendar)

0 TCC: The first settlement that will be Vandarn City is founded, The Southflow, which will one day be renamed the Dragonsir river thaws for the first time.

100 TCC: The City of Vandarn grows exponentially, other re-corded, modern civilisations start to pop up over the heartlands.

202 TCC: The Circle Calendar is adapted to fit the modern world and renamed the Vandarnian Calendar. The days and months of the year are renamed to what will be used going forward in the Vandarnian Timeline.

302 TCC: Recorded, human settlements begin to populate the arid grassland that will one day be known as the 'Swordlands'

614 TCC: As Vandarn Castle is built and The Knights of Vandarn officially founded the first of the new 'kingdoms' in the Swordlands find their feet and the territory of the Swordlands is settled as much as it ever will be.

726 TCC: The first rumours from the Northeastern Mountains of the Heartlands come down of the Takalan Empire, a great emperor Takal has risen, and his Kingdom is spreading.

1000 TCC: Pilgrims banished from the east after a great war in their ancient Kingdom settle in the wastelands North of the Swordlands, founding the Shoui Lan Empire quickly fortifying the region as their own with vast armies and advanced agricultural practices they quickly turn the land to their home.

1019 TCC: Renowned Halfling explorer Tatral Valenstorm is born.

1029 TCC: The unnamed Swordsman who founded the men of the Sword is born in an alley in the Swordlands. (Hanalan Harpsong references this in his memoirs.) Princess Annia of Hven is also born to King Troom-Djerc.

1030 TCC: Hanalan Harpsong born in Hven to a noble family.

1050 TCC: The Witch Queen-Barvara rises to power in the Takalan Empire with her half-demon son known only as Deathskull at her side. DeathKnight's are formed as the Takalan Empire bristles.

1055 TCC: The Witch Queens army begins to spread across the heartlands.

1056 TCC: Barvara invades and takes over the heartlands, Shoui, Swordlands and Vandarn City fall. Takalan Banners are raised in all the heartlands south of Thol. The Vandarnian royal line is pruned with the Death of Kalen Vandarn IV

1061 TCC: Branthar Vandarn, the son of Kalen and the heir to the throne of Vandarn reappears in the Black Empire with companions and wrests the crown of Vandarn from Deathskull, lending hope to the rebel faction known only as 'the men of the sword' that the Witch Queen can be defeated.

1063 TCC: The men of the Sword, a resistance group led by the Unknown Swordsman, Hanalan Harpsong and Princess Annia of Hven rise and defeat the Witch Queen, killing her and apparently killing Deathskull. Unbeknownst to the heroes her half-demon son survives and returns to his sanctuary in Deathmount.

1064 TCC: With freedom and order restored to the Heartlands of Karn the heroes go their separate ways, the Unknown Swordsman disappears into the Swordlands, returning to his life of wandering. Princess Annia takes over the men of the sword and continues their original work combatting slavery in the heartlands. Harpsong begins his great chronicling and Branthar Vandarn is crowned officially the twenty third direct line, King of the City and Kindgom of Vandarn.

The war is declared officially over, and some sense of freedom and normalcy are restored across the heartlands and to the kingdoms beyond. The Kanefall Empire send its first ambassador to Vandarn in a decade.

1065 TCC: The first beings with demonic or divine blood appear on Karn, the magical source that runs through the world change subtly. The nature of magic changes as the laws that have governed the world of Karn for over a thousand years begin to take a different shape. Scholars, wizards and priests struggle to explain the change.

1084 TCC: Present day.

THE GODS OF KARN

THE BEGINNING

In the time before time, before measure, Karn was the playground for the nine gods who inhabited the young world. These nine gods each bore nine children, who each bore nine children; until the world was overrun with gods and the children of gods. As the aeons passed the gods each began to differ in many ways until each of the nine true gods had borne the gods who had borne the children of the gods. Children, who overran the virgin world, these younger races from the oldest of the magnificent elves to the youngest of the young goblins. All of them are the children of the gods. Gods who had been banished to the heavens by their masters, the nine elder gods. Since long before the beginning of the age of Vandarn a thousand years ago no god, no celestial nor devil nor demon other than the son of Barvara known as Deathskull had ever set foot on the lands of Karn. Twenty years ago, this changed. The death of the Witch-Queen herself shattering the ancient bond that held the infernal and divine separate from the mortal world.

THE GODS NINE

The younger gods are too many to mention in the space provided here, Karn has become something of a nexus for the divine and their heavens open to any. Divine or infernal who can touch this realm can hold some power over the lives of the mortals of Karn but none to the extent of the nine gods who preside as the ultimate arbiters of Divinity of Karn.

VANDARN - Justice, honour, duty and skill

The law of the heavens Vandarn is the judge and jury, and his priests tend to be of the same kind his symbol is that of a long shining blade tip pointed upwards with the upper half of the blade in front of the sun. Appears as a tall paladin in full plate with two eyes of glowing blue and a two-handed sword of pure light (lord of honour and knights, Master of Justice)

OSRRASS - Obedience, knowledge and enlightenment

The embodiment of scholarly knowledge osrrass remembers every single detail of everything she has ever seen or heard. Often the bookkeeper of the rough gods she follows her office to the letter. The very embodiment of the power she contains. Appears often as a small bespectacled grey elf with grey robes and many books stuffed under each arm (keeper of knowledge and master of words)

LAZARUS - Power of darkness, betrayal, slavery and the undead

Obsessed with power this god is the cruellest and most calculating. His every move and vote amongst the gods goes with whichever favours the cruel god most. His mastery over darkness and the undead is obvious to any who view the evil lord. Lazarus merely uses these offices as pawns in his games of power. Appears as a long flowing black cloak with fangs and nothing but shadows (Duke of Betrayal lord of lies, master of darkness)

NECIRATE - Beauty, nature, elegance, simplicity, peace and leisure

This goddess is the one aspect who does not follow her office to the letter she is a carefree god who enjoys nature and beauty in all its myriad forms of skin, soul and spirit.

She often appears in green leaves woven into a smock with a mighty bow, which fires shafts of light. She tires never to harm anything as she can see beauty in all living things and her clergy also abhor violence and many of her followers are themselves pacifist in nature.

(Lady of leisure, mother maiden, queen of life)

AVORUS - Balance, decisions, cycle and changes

This god is the one invoked by people when decisions and changes are afoot. She is the true mediator of all disputes and the true mistress of order and chaos. Avorus is in herself a contradiction that appears as a shimmering image that changes face as you watch, morphing between all races, faces and types. Her very appearance shifts as you look at her. (entrusted of all, bringer of change)

ECAUR- Wealth, safety, prosperity, selfishness and fear

As much to be feared as worshipped, Ecaur is a god of avarice and its cost. There is no deal with her without cost. The price often is a twisted cost of the deal, she might bring the rains but salt the land her worshippers are criminals, thieves and merchants, always looking for a better deal and to profit from the work of others. Appears as a wealthy merchant who wears a cloak of silver on the outside and black on the inside, she wields a short sword of dark red colour and hue.

THE HIDDEN ONE - Love, mystery, freedom, equality and secrets

Possibly the most widely spread religion in Karn, considered by many to be both the leader and most powerful of the nine. The hidden is a mysterious god whose appearance is rare, but their priests are everywhere, in all walks of life they spread the word of love, freedom and equality but can never resist the lure of mystery. Also, secrets are this god's portent and as such their appearance changes with every sighting. From the lowliest of butterflies to the mightiest of dragons only one thing is sure the hidden watches us all (synonyms are too numerous to mention they also masquerades as some of the younger gods)

RAMLAR - Chaos, war, fire, dragons
DRACOR - Death, murder, disease and the dead

Early in the life of Karn, two mortal wizards of great power from a faraway land, evil and cunning Ramlar the black and dracor the vain rose in such power as mortals often did in those early days to minor godhood. Ramlar of dragons and Dracor of murder, the two gods who originally held the offices of chaos and death were frightened by the idea that mortals could challenge the Nine. They decided to make an example of the vicious Ramlar and his friend but found themselves deceived by the evil duo and in a mighty battle which even now leaves its scars on the world of Karn the usurpers slew the old gods and assumed their offices. This was after a hundred year reign of terror that the two mages wrought upon Karn in their mortal lifetimes. The only true gods allowed to make their home in the world of Karn they live on the Ice Ridge which runs north of the known lands in their mortal tower of ice which reaches to the sky This tower also serves a kind of prison for the two who are not allowed to roam on Karn beyond this tower. Ramlar appears as a tall thinly built human with long straggly black hair in long black robes with twin Hammers that crackle lightening hanging from his hips. Dracor has short neat blonde hair and perfectly sparkling blue eyes and dresses entirely in ornate red robes inlaid with gold and carries a sword which oozes green deathly venom, though he does not need such a weapon as his touch means death. (Lord of chaos, king of wyrms, Dracor the diseased, lord of death, master of murder)

The age of Legend

Tens of thousands of years ago, the gods still lived and walked upon the lands of Karn. The heartlands were at the core of this, with the nine overlooking the land like aloof parents of unruly children. The greatest of the gods outside of the nine was Thol, a huge, wild Ice god who would hunt and feast and revel in combat and chaos like an embodiment of his brothers and sisters. The younger gods would coral the younger races then like the Elven and gnomish races, the earliest of whom legend said were sprung from the first flowers and plants, the roots of these plants said to be the first of the goblin and orcish races making these races long distant cousins and inexorably linking their fortunes and fates. Other legends say that the first God of Chaos in war with Vandarn Struck an enormous mountain and when the mountain split at the hammer strike it bled the first Dwarves and giant races. These legends, like most legends, have some truth in them. Though none can attest to the truth, the only thing ancient historians do know is that during the first age of Kingdoms of Men most were ruled by two evil tyrants who came here from another world it first tore the fabric of the world. Something every generation of Karn has lived with since, portals started to open which have never closed, even to this day travellers find themselves appearing on Karn or disappearing from Karn by stepping through portals, dotted in the dark corners of the land.

Powerful and cruel Ramlar the black and Dracor the vain appeared like a blight on the land while living God kings held a thousand kingdoms around them. In those early days of the world, the younger races were as pawns and slaves in the endless wars for power, glory, and artefacts integral to the very fabric of the world itself. These two mortals, powerful wizards, and warriors beyond the understanding of mortals today enacted a reign of terror across the lands. It was said, they challenged God kings and crushed empire after empire under their boots. As they grew in power and influence across the land, they started to shake the confidence of even the nine.

The Original members of the nine who held the offices of Chaos and War and Death and the Dead aligned with Ecaur. Together the three are said to have challenged Ramlar (who at this point had risen to a minor godhood venerated by Dragons who had once universally despised him) and Dracor (whose vanity had cause him to be cursed as the lord and god of disease) to war, attempting to destroy the two upstarts. The war raged across the heavens and left its scars on the land. At one point every god of the nine and subsequently those below raged in war crushing the younger races underfoot. Vandarn's Great sword striking the ground and becoming the great stone. The great rift in the earth caused by Ramlar defeated the God of War and Chaos. The great Quoity Swamp Forest that was borne of the blood of the god of death and the dead. The war had shaken the heavens and Ecaur betrayed her fellows of the nine to side with the upstarts who took their place. The war had spread through all the gods, young and old as gods and siblings slew each other. The nine met and decided that the gods would never again set foot on the world of Karn. Ramlar and Dracor who made a home in the land were not allowed to leave their tower which became like a prison. An ice tower that fell into legend, as no mortal could ever find it and if any has, they have not passed that information along beyond rumour and ill-fitting legend.

The age of myth

With the gods banished from the land, the younger races carved out the spaces for themselves. Tens of thousands of years ago as Elves of legend will tell you of kingdoms of Dragon kings and great sorcerers, sprawling elven kingdoms dominated the land with great Elven art and architecture, magic, and literature. Wars between the elder and younger of the races, civil wars among the elves and even the Dwarves and factions of Elves and Dwarves and other races erupting into a full civil war across the land of Karn, the races losing forswearing their heritages and fleeing underground. The ones remaining on the surface would say, those races fell to evil, worshipping evil gods in secret. Or for their telling retreating to the underground to worship them in secret or being forced from their homes and forced underground merely to survive as the general topological and gathered structure of the Heartlands of Karn formed the general shape they are today.

Towards the end of the Age of Myth, many things that are still recorded happened. The Dragons who had been supplanted by Dwarves, Elves and other younger races came in force and took The Dragon Mountains forcing the Dwarves to flee and the great exodus of the Dwarves which lives in history for the few surviving ancient and venerable Dwarves as the day their royal line Clan Linchen was nearly erased and they wandered desperate and dying until they found a new home in the heartlands. Cursed by the gods for their arrogance the heirs to the throne of the Dwarven and Elven kingdoms in the heartlands of Karn disappeared, thrown through portals, and thought to be never seen again. Hal Greyback the heir to the Heartlands elven kingdom disappeared and less than a hundred years later the same fate befell Cal Linchen the heir to the throne of the dwarves. Legend attributes these disappearances to the work of Lazarus, but no one ever knew for sure. The curse brought about by these began the downfall of the Glorious Elven and Dwarven Kingdoms and led to an end of the age of myth.

The Age of Men

Nearly two thousand years ago, from the ruins of the first kingdoms of men, the elder races, the Elves, Dwarves, Gnomes, Halflings, Lizardfolk, Dragonborn were joined by the second age and empires of the Humans as men joined the Circle wizards originally formed by the Elves and adapted to fit other races as humans do they grew and expanded and human kingdoms spread and popped up all over the lands. Where great elven kingdoms once stood suddenly stood kingdoms of men. As Humans became integral to the workings of the Circle Wizards, the council of Nine adapted the historical 'TCC' The Circle Calendar to incorporate 9 months, each made of 45 days divided into 5 weeks of 9 days each. This set to the settled turning of seasons brought the modern 'Vandarnian' Calander used today into existence, as a throwback to the old days of the Circle Calendar, the Vandarnian calendar still uses TCC for marking the current year, at least it still does as of this writing in 1084 TCC.

So it was, the Vandarnian Calendar became ratified, pinned from the moment the great City and Kingdom of Vandarn was founded. Now known by the new calendar as 0 TCC. The heartlands at this point began to shape into the kingdoms and places it is today. The Great Southflow at about the same time began to thaw and become a mighty river. Within a hundred years of the calendar's inception, human settlements would pop up all over the heartlands and over time, the lines of the different kingdoms formed as they exist now. The Kingdom of Takal formed and then as the the Vandarnian Calendar neared its first thousand years a mass exodus of pilgrims fleeing a great war/disaster in their ancestral homeland arrived and settled the plains north of the Kingdoms known collectively as 'The Swordlands' with the founding of the Shoui Kingdom, the nations of the Heartlands were complete and the age of men was officially marked.

The last hundred years

The settling of the Shoui in the Eastern parts of the Bandit Wastes and the beginning of the new Kingdom that was quickly established there. With the pilgrims bringing thousands of years of culture with them, this led to a period of growth in the heartlands as the last hundred years began.

Fifty years of prosperity and growth for the great Kingdoms of the Heartlands followed. Vandarns influence and prosperity saw many of the wilder parts of Vandarn mapped start to be settled, and the various warring factions in the Sword Lands rose and fell as powers, Kingdoms and fiefdoms rose and fell like the waves, the Shoui lands flourished and swelled to a great farming and economic force in the region bringing advancements that swelled the region and the entire heartlands standards of living. In 1050 TCC, almost as a perfunctory notice the Witch-Queen Barvara rose to the pinnacle of the political structure in Takal naming herself Empress with her half-demon son only known as 'DeathSkull' at her side. The deathknights were formed and the Takalan military machine started to churn.

Less than a decade after rising to power, having waited, and politicked the other Nations, luring them into a false sense of peace, the half-century of growth and peace in the lands was shattered with a mailed fist. The Takalan Empire came down out of the mountains like a plate mail clad wave of evil. It swept through the entirely peaceful Shoui lands almost unchallenged, the story goes that the Unnamed Swordsman was here at the time learning their ways. Though for the entire war Vun-Tai was never breached, despite a siege that lasted the seven years of the Takalan invasion of the Heartlands, Vun-Tai held. As the war began though the Unnamed Swordsman urged Yung Shoui the fifth (father of the current leader) to allow him to leave to return to the Swordlands to help them fight the invasion, Lord Shoui finally relented and as thanks the Swordsman gave him the magical sword he had been wielding as he arrived in the Shoui lands. To this day, it is still not known how the Shoui Lord got the swordsman out, perhaps with the same smuggling or magic that allowed them to survive the siege for seven long years.

The Witch-Queens army swept next down into the Sword Lands, the Unnamed Swordsman having fled Vun-Tai had tried to warn the kings and Dukes that formed the various leadership of the lands who were each too concerned with their petty border wars. The Circle Wizards simply closed their borders saying, "we do not get involved in politics." The Unnamed Swordsman was stonewalled and ignored by every kingdom's leadership, in fact, the only person who listened was the Noble, Bard and his one-time best friend Hanalan Harpsong. the two heroes joined up with Harpsong's wife, Princess Annia (formerly of Hven) to reform 'the men of the sword' their one time adventuring company formed to fight slavery in the

Swordlands and headed to an old keep on the edge of the heartlands where they plotted, prepared and returned to their old friends and allies of their youth to build a resistance against the oncoming wave of deathknights, witches and priests of the Witch Queen.

With no organisation and no unification, many of the Swordlands kindgoms fell without resistance and before a season had changed Barvara's army with Deathskull at its head had swept through the Shoui lands and the Sword Lands conquering and garrisoning everything in sight. Half a century of prosperity and growth had been wiped out, stockpiled, and taken to the vast coffers beneath Deathmount and for once not just the underfoot denizens of the Swordlands were starving, struggling and in chains either real or metaphorical. The streets of every village, town and city in the Heartlands bowed under the heavy mailed boots of deathknights. Annia, Harpsong and the Swordsman raced to the little-known wilderness home of the great wizard Akarash Beliheim, retired and rarely even on this plane of existence the great wizard never bothered himself anymore with earthly pursuits only maintaining his small home to manage his vegetable garden and grow his pumpkins. After much convincing he agreed to warn Vandarn of a plot by the Witch Queen to assassinate king Vandarn, too late they arrived in time for the Kings death, Harpsong and the swordsman rushing to defend the castle from the timely assault of Deathknights whilst Annia and Akarash rescued the kings only son Branthar, his best friend a circle wizard and an unsuspecting thief (who had been arrested that morning and was in the wrong place at the wrong time) and whisk the three to safety in the Swordlands, as safe as anywhere could be in this day. Vandarn, its city and castle fell. Deathknights trod the battlements of Vandarn Castle, Deathskull sat upon the throne in triumph. In under a year the army of the Witch Queen had taken the ultimate prize, the crown of Vandarn sat in her hand as the entire Heartlands of Karn bowed before her endless roll of deathknights. Annia, Harpsong and the Swordsman surrounded by the deathknights saw the battle was lost and decided wise discretion over foolish valour was called for this day snuck out of the castle and city in a wagon of dead, piled under corpses. Not before they managed to save the mortally wounded Head Church Knight. The near seven-foot, three-hundred-pound Varan Arfiran, near death and unconscious they pulled him from the fray. All four, dumped casually at hanged man's cross with the rest of the corpses. The heroes delivered the paladin to allies of his before meeting and enlisting the great explorer Tatral Valenstorm to the men of the sword, the famous Halfling swearing he would give his life to end the invasion of his beloved Vandarn.

Years of war, combat, failure, and loss ensued for the men of the sword. Mothers, Fathers, husbands, wives, and children all lost to the grinding war machine of the Witch-Queen and her army. A great battle at the gates of Deathmount finally ended the war, Akarash Beleheim and the mad wizard combined to combat the Witch Queen with magic to a standstill as the swordsman fought and defeated Deathskull and finally stood face to face with the Witch Queen, having downed Beleheim and the mad wizard, she turned to face the swordsman armed with his now famous Tilak blade as she prepared to smite him, Tatral Valenstorm stabbed her in the back with a dagger of mystical black steel. The unassuming halfling explorer with a single strike had saved the heartlands from a decade of oppression and war.

In the following years, the men of the sword went their separate ways, haunted by all he had seen Hanalan Harpsong could not return to noble life, nor could he sanctify or ignore the suffering of others. He walked from the battlefield and never stopped. He became like a ghost, popping up in odd places all over Karn as a kind of unofficial biographer of the Heartlands. Even now years after the war ended Harpsong looks not a day older rumoured to have made some bargain with his Goddess the great Nericate. He still pops up from place to place, occasionally, lending a hand or helping where he can. Armed with a flagon of wine and a song, or one of his now legendary stories. Tatral Valenstorm, explorer, adventurer and hero did not stop, he immediately set out to explore a few more places before settling down in a small house in the grasslands south of his beloved Vandarn, someone built a home near him, then another and another. In the years that followed Valenstorm has become a thriving and fast-growing city, south of Vandarn and a perfect rest stop and starting point for adventurers, heroes and would-be legends. As for the Unnamed Swordsman, his war was over, his wife having died at the hands of Deathskull in that final battle he had nothing left to give. It is rumoured he entreated the Hidden One for the one thing left he wanted. To be left alone, the mysterious god took the hero at his word and erased his name from the history books, from the memories of those who had known him but not his deeds. Even Annia and Harpsong his closest allies could describe him to you down to the glint in his eye and his crooked smile, but to this day could never tell you, his name.

And so the land recovered, some places reverted to type, the Swordlands going immediately back to the same old petty squabbles and wars, Branthar was Crowned King of Vandarn (having reclaimed his crown nearing the end of the war and having led the armies of Vandarn standing next to his two friends and the great paladin Varan Arfiran in the war) immediately changing things in the great kingdom to iron out some of the inherent intolerance of other races, banning any kind of slavery and the outdated class system that had kept poorer sections of the kingdom from thriving before the war.

Worn and jaded from years of war and having had his polished view of his beloved Vandarn burnished by reality, Varan Arfiran like so many veterans of the Great War put down his sword and his tabard and left the city. Within a year after the war, something changed. A demon-blood was seen on the streets of Ast in the Sword Lands, something thought to be impossible as no one of divine or infernal blood should be able to set foot on Karn due to the magic pact the gods had placed on the world in the Time of Legend. slowly but surely, something was changing, gods were free once again to walk the land, though the nine kept them in line even though they seemed not to know what was causing this change. Over time as with all things in the heartlands, they adapted and evolved, while unusual and worrying to see demonic and divinely touched beings walk the lands. They are still so rare; the lands have adapted, though even now the great priests and even the circle wizards cannot explain the changes as we head forward into the high freldine summer of the 1084th year of the Vandarnian calendar and all that is yet to come.

<u>Jay Graham</u>

Jay Graham is an actor, film-maker and award winning screenwriter from Glasgow in Scotland, where he lives with his partner Marieke and cat Bub. Nothing Dies in Darkness is his first full length novel. Jay has been a lover of Fantasy adventure for over three decades and has written countless adventures, short stories and tall tales about the land of Karn over that time. Jay's journey into fantasy began with such titles as King Solomon's Mines and Ursula Le Guin's Earthsea Novels. At the age of ten Jay and his Brother found Marvel Superheroes Roleplaying Game which they immediately rejigged to use in a fantasy setting which ended up being the nascent precursor to Karn. Not long after Jay found a four page review of Mayfair Games City State of the Invincible Overlord. A Tabletop Role playing Game setting. This very swiftly led to Dungeons and Dragons, Role master and hundreds of other RPG systems which became both brothers primary hobby through their teenage years. Jay credits Role Playing Games as being where his love of acting, writing and the creative arts originated. Over the Covid Pandemic, Jay had the time and space to perfect his first movie script which became his first movie as a Producer, Writer and Director, this also won Jay his first award in film making. A Best Screenplay award for his movie script 'Morning Jim' Dungeon Mastering D&D, Vampire & others became almost like a full time job for Jay during the Pandemic and led to him finally finding the time to pen his first novel. This one.